WESTERN BLUE

By the Author

Shadow Series

Moon Shadow

Shadows of Steel

Shadow Dancers

Enigma

Western Blue

Visit us at www.boldstrokesbooks.com

WESTERN BLUE

by

Suzie Clarke

2023

WESTERN BLUE

ISBN 13: 978-1-63679-095-4

THIS TRADE PAPERBACK ORIGINAL IS PUBLISHED BY
BOLD STROKES BOOKS, INC.
P.O. BOX 249
VALLEY FALLS, NY 12185

FIRST EDITION: OCTOBER 2023

CREDITS
EDITOR: SHELLEY THRASHER
PRODUCTION DESIGN: STACIA SEAMAN
COVER DESIGN BY JEANINE HENNING

Acknowledgments

Some stories authors write seem to tug more strongly at their heartstrings. *Western Blue* was one of them for me. Perhaps because the grit and tenacity of the women who helped settle the West were something to be admired, and a true inspiration for this story.

Thank you to my fellow writers Alaina, Jaycie, and Jeannie for their support and encouragement. They eased the heavy load and lightened my days.

And many thanks to my editor, Shelley Thrasher, whose silver-bullet expertise was as strong as the mountains and as sure as the setting sun.

For all the cowgirls at heart who sit tall in the saddle
as they ride into the unknown.

CHAPTER ONE

Late spring, 1868
Northern Nevada

Caroline Bluebonnet Hutchings—Blue—rubbed her rawhide-gloved hand over the worn, bent wood of the wagon wheel, then kicked it with the toe of her boot. She sucked in a breath and stepped back. "Now what?" Two spokes were barely attached to the hub, and the felloe was split. "Another damned problem. I swear. It's one mile forward and two miles back. This might do it for us."

The two-bow-top wagon cover had been patched three times. The back half had ripped again, and parts of it were so thin you could almost see clouds through it.

Martha, positioned on a nearby boulder, brushed strands of her long chestnut-colored hair away from her face. She tucked them under her bonnet. Although almost ten years older than Blue, she was a trusted friend and had been since Blue's youth.

She leaned on her elbows and surveyed the wagon, as if she had nothing better to do in the searing Nevada sun. "We've got less than a hundred miles to go. We've come all this way from Texas. You going to give up when we're almost there?"

Bone-weary from travel, Blue had no patience for a frivolous conversation. She waved her hand, dismissing Martha's question, but then thought better of it. The air draped over them so hot she almost lost her breath before she could get any words out. "Yes. I'm going to turn this beat-up wagon 'round and head back to Texas. Lord knows, it will endure." She wanted to smile, but that took too much effort. She removed her sun-bleached, faded brown hat and wiped the sweat from her forehead. "It's been a long trip, but I'm not about to quit. I suppose we'll figure something out." She kicked the wheel one last time, giving it a warning glare, then force-stepped to Martha and sat beside her.

She slipped her hat on and pulled it low in the front, then took off her gloves and slapped them against her dungarees. The dusk swirled in the air like campfire smoke. After months of travel, her stiff, coarse blue pants had finally formed to her body and fit comfortably.

"If we can reinforce the spokes, I think it'll make do until we can get a proper repair." Blue scanned the brush and gullies. The distant rims of mountains and the lush green of the pine and juniper were a welcome sight after endless travel. Faint shadows of the approaching evening were slipping over the mountain crest. "This journey has near kilt us. Are you still glad you made the trip?"

Martha chuckled, then hiked her long, full skirt to her knees, letting the air waft in around them. "It's killed, not *kilt*. You were taught the English language. Use it." She opened the canteen and drank, then wiped her mouth. "By God, Blue. I wouldn't change my mind for all the china teapots in Europe. There's nothing in Texas for me. Not anymore. My future is there." She pointed north, toward the mountains.

Blue licked her parched, sunburned lips. The salt from her sweat seeped into the cracks and stung like sin. "All I know is I've got six thousand, four hundred acres with some type of frame house. I can make a go of it. Still, it galls me that Nate got Papa's ranch and everything I was supposed to. He and his mother schemed from the day she got her hooks in Papa, and now they have it all. The ten-thousand-acre ranch, cattle, and all the money. Everything. He shouldn't have done it, Martha. It was wrong of him to cheat me out of my inheritance and force me from the only home I knew."

Each time she thought of it her heart sank, weighing her down like she'd dragged a burlap sack of rocks all the way from Texas. The dark brooding and anger swelled. She didn't like that it was there, but for now she wouldn't fight it.

Martha patted Blue's thigh, the years of her own torment and pain etched in her face. "It was wrong, and someday he'll get what he deserves."

"What he *deserves*? He took my property. My home. Papa wanted me to have it, not that poor excuse for a stepson, whose only ambition has ever been to get the property. And in the end, he did. Damned Nate Rawlings." She forced back bitter tears, determined not to give in. Besides, she couldn't afford to lose the moisture.

She slapped her gloves against her leg once more, harder this time, trying to beat out the anger in her heart. "If Papa's friend at the bank, Mr. Hathaway, hadn't hidden the deed to the property in Nevada, I'd have nothing."

"No matter how much it hurts or how wrong it is, you can't change it," Martha said.

She was right. No point thinking about it. "I telegraphed ahead to the Carson City surveyor's office to let them know I'll be claiming my property. I don't want any more trouble."

"It's probably best you did that," Martha said.

"I don't know anything about the land, except what's in the letter. Uncle Silas homesteaded it for only three years before he died. It's been abandoned for four."

She unbuttoned her shirt and pulled out the documents she always kept with her. She opened the limp, black leather flap and retrieved the deed, unfolded it with care, and reviewed the words out loud. "Six thousand and four hundred acres, with water and good timber." She tapped the paper. "This saved me."

"Read me the letter to your father again," Martha said.

Blue retrieved the tattered page from the pouch and began to read aloud.

July 23, 1857

To Rutherford M. Hutchings

Dear Ruthe,
Enclosed is the six-thousand-four-hundred-acre deed. It has a small lake and a running water source, which is part of the Carson River. It is about eighteen miles from Lake Bonpland, and the northwest boundary is abundant with trees.

Blue paused. "Then it gives the longitude and latitude." She continued to read.

The land was surveyed by me personally. I received your payment and look forward to our meeting once again when the opportunity presents itself.
Your friend,
Captain John C. Fremont

Blue carefully refolded the letter and deed and returned them to the leather protection, then pulled out the document from her father and read it silently.

January 6, 1861
To: Caroline Bluebonnet Hutchings
Daughter of Rutherford M. Hutchings and Rebecca Anne
    Bluebonnet-Hutchings

My Darling Caroline,

You are the light of my life. Be strong and have courage. No man could have a finer daughter than you. Upon my death, I bequeath to you and only you my acres of property and land located in the Nevada Territory. Enclosed are the details and deed. No matter what happens, know you are loved and cherished.

Your adoring father,
Rutherford M. Hutchings

She slid the letter into its place and then tucked the holder inside her shirt, looking northwest as she buttoned her top. A flash of movement near a group of junipers about a quarter of a mile away caught her attention. "Now what?" She repositioned, straining to see.

Martha stood and shaded her eyes, looking in the same direction. "I don't see anything."

"There." Blue pointed to a patch of dark brown just beyond the edge of trees. "I think it's a horse." It shifted, and a flash from something on its back caught her eye.

"There's lots of wild horses," Martha said, shaking the dust from her skirt.

"No. This one has a saddle. I'm going to go check. If you hear a gunshot, come a runnin'."

"You be careful. It could be a trap."

"I doubt someone's waiting that far away to lure me there to do me harm." Blue walked to her sorrel gelding tied to the wagon beside her prized black stud and grabbed the reins. Then, as an afterthought, she checked her handgun. She swung into the saddle and adjusted her seating. "Head toward it. But ease on over." She reined Traveler and took off, leaving Martha standing there, still shading her eyes, looking concerned.

She slowed as she neared the junipers. Whatever breed the horse, it had perfect form. Sleek. Well fed. It shifted nervously. It wasn't a mustang, or any other kind of horse she'd seen recently. Then it dawned on her. It was Mexican. A criollo. Rich brown with black legs, mane, and tail. It was a sight to behold. The saddle had a larger horn, and the seat wasn't as wide as a western saddle, confirming what she suspected. She stopped about twenty yards away and dismounted, taking Traveler's reins and walking carefully toward the animal. A mare.

She put her hand out. "Easy. Steady, girl." She stopped midstep.

A man lay on his side, just in front of the horse, his face pale, and his hair black as a Texas night. He appeared to be Mexican, but his skin was lighter so she wasn't sure. His hat lay near his head. She immediately saw the blood on his forehead and the small gash. Had he fallen? Was he attacked? Thrown? If he'd been robbed, why hadn't they taken the horse?

The animal remained close by, its reins dragging the ground. It whinnied and pawed the dirt, clearly agitated and uneasy.

Blue tied Traveler to a nearby branch and moved in.

The criollo sidestepped, as if to let her get closer to the man. She patted the mare's neck. "Thar now. Good job." She knelt and inspected the stranger more closely, placing her hand on his slim shoulder. He was lean and long limbed. He struggled to breathe. The blood in the wound on his forehead had dried around the edges. His lips were chafed and cracked. He'd been there for some time. Should she move him? Turn him over?

She couldn't see any other injuries or evidence of blood. What had happened? She'd started to drag him closer to the shade of the junipers when he moaned, then coughed. She spied the canteen on the mare's saddle, slipped it from around the horn, and offered it, holding the man's head for support. His hand, graceful with long fingers, clasped her arm as she encouraged him to drink.

He swallowed several times. "Thank you."

His voice startled Blue. It was soft, melodic, like the sound of the wind over water and sunshine. She inspected the slender figure more closely, the delicate facial features and long, dark eyelashes. This man who lay before her was no man—but a woman!

Blue momentarily startled at the discovery, then offered more water.

The woman held the canteen and drank with vigor.

When Blue thought her thirst was quenched, she corked the canteen and laid it beside her, then eased her to a sitting position.

The stranger moaned and touched her forehead. "Adelita?" she called.

The horse came forward and snorted, then nudged the woman's shoulder. She stroked its nose. "I'm all right," she whispered, her eyes fixed on Blue. They were the color of liquid gold mixed with copper, and they took Blue's breath away, stunned her, like she'd unexpectedly come upon a pool of clear water in the middle of a desert.

"Thank you," the woman repeated, but this time her voice sounded deeper, more pronounced. Was she trying to disguise it? She was dressed in men's clothing and was alone. Had she ridden with others? Did she get separated from them? Why was she trying to pose as a man?

It wasn't uncommon. Women weren't safe alone, not in this wild country. She and Martha had discussed if Blue should dress as a man for their travels but had decided it didn't matter. They both were fair shots, and if any man bothered them, they wouldn't hesitate to defend themselves. But this woman was alone.

"Can you stand?"

The woman nodded and reached for her hat, groaning when she tried to put it on.

"Here. Let me hold that." Blue grasped it and helped her to her feet.

The woman bent over and moaned, then staggered and went to her knees.

Blue guided her the rest of the way to the ground. "You may have gotten knocked senseless. Lie here. My friend will be along in a few minutes. She's good at doctoring and such."

The woman held her side. "He kicked me." If she was Mexican she had no accent. "I think my ribs are broken."

"Let me see," Blue said.

The woman shook her head. "No. I'll be fine."

"You aren't fine. Something's wrong or you wouldn't be on the ground. Don't fuss. Let me take a look."

The woman became more addled. "No!"

Blue grew frustrated. Why wouldn't she let her help her? Blue had already discovered she was a woman. To her it was clear. No need to hide it. Should she tell her she knew or let her pretend? She didn't know, but Martha would. She always knew the wherefores and how-tos when it came to people and the proper way of doing things.

Blue patted the woman's arm. "It's all right. Just lie here. Help's coming in the form of Martha Newberry. And Lord save you if you fight it."

The wagon's wheels creaked as it inched closer.

"If the wagon doesn't give out before she gets here, she'll fix you up."

"I don't need *fixed up*. I'm fine."

"Oh, sure you are, lying here in the dirt, blood all over your face. I can see how *fine* you are." Blue didn't need this aggravation, not after everything else she'd had to endure these last few months. She'd keep the woman's secret for now, if that's what she wanted. Martha would find out soon enough.

The woman lay back, mumbling into the earth. "I don't need help."

Martha eased to a stop. She grabbed her poke and clambered down from the seat. "What do we have here?"

Blue stood. "He's hurt his head and can't stand. The bleeding's mostly stopped." She pursed her lips and narrowed her eyes, presenting Martha with her most concerned expression.

"What?"

Blue shook her head. Would Martha guess right away? What if she wanted to unbutton the woman's shirt to see how badly she'd been hurt?

Martha dropped beside the figure, inspecting the injury, then reached into the cloth bag and pulled out some items. "You're going to need stitches, mister. I'll do the best I can." She handed Blue a clean rag. "Get me some fresh water from the barrel."

Blue hurried to the container and wet the cloth, wrung it out, and brought it back. What would the woman do when Martha started to touch her?

Martha wiped the blood from the wound, her hand brushing the woman's skin. She stopped abruptly. "Oh!"

That didn't take long!

"You aren't fooling me," Martha said. "Anyone with a good eye can see you're a woman. No sense pretending."

The woman moaned again. "Sí. Yes. My name is Isabel."

It'd gone better than Blue imagined. All that worry for nothing. Was it the presence of both of them, or did the woman have no fight left in her? Either way, it was over now. Blue knelt beside Martha. *Isabel.* A beautiful name. It danced on the air, like her voice.

"Let's move her and prop her up against the wagon," Martha said. "She thinks some ribs are broken."

"I better look." Martha began to unbutton Isabel's shirt once they got her situated.

Isabel lifted her hand and stopped her. "Don't judge too harshly. I was trying to get through the territory to my uncle's ranch in California."

Martha patted her arm. "Don't you worry about that. I don't judge a woman the way I do a man. Lord knows we have to do what we can to survive. You rest now and let me get to fixing you. Blue, help me."

Blue knelt on the other side of Isabel and assisted Martha as she removed her shirt, the extra clothing, and the binding around her breasts. Her laced undergarment was worn and frayed.

Martha lifted it and gasped at the dark purple and red where she'd been kicked. And from the appearance of it, it'd been more than once or twice.

"Most likely you do have some broken ribs," Martha said. "The extra clothes and binding probably saved your life. I'm going to wash you up and apply some ointment, then wrap your ribs to ease the pain. Once I get you stitched, we'll help you into the wagon. You're coming with us. We'll not leave you out here alone to fend for yourself, especially in your condition."

Isabel reached for Martha's hand. "I can manage."

Martha gently patted Isabel's shoulder. "I'll hear none of it."

So now they'd care for a stranger. More weight in a wagon already falling apart. More chores. Blue chastened herself. What if it was her? What if she was the one who needed help? Why did she have such selfish thoughts? Why couldn't she be more like Martha? Eager to help. Kindly in her ways. Sometimes the anger and misery of loneliness filled Blue's heart so full there wasn't room for anything else.

Martha continued to dress Isabel's wounds. "You may as well get used to the idea. No use in fighting a done deal."

Isabel nodded and brought her right knee up. "I hurt too badly to argue about it."

When Martha finished her doctoring, they helped Isabel into the wagon and made her as comfortable as they could. Martha gave her two fingers of whiskey for the pain, and Isabel went to sleep.

Now only a sliver of the top of the sun was visible on the horizon. "We may as well camp here for the night," Blue said. "There isn't enough daylight left to bother about. I'll unhitch the horses and get them settled."

Martha nodded. "It'll only take a little while to fix supper once the fire's going. Leftover stew and biscuits tonight."

"I love your cooking, Martha. You have a fine skill, among all your many talents. I'm blessed you came with me. I could have ended up like Isabel."

"We don't know yet what got her in her predicament. I'm sure you would have managed without me."

Blue continued to unhitch the two-horse team, chiding herself as she worked. She should be more charitable, more caring for others. Sometimes her own concerns swelled inside her so fully, she had no room to think of others. But she did have feelings toward them. She just didn't say it out loud.

Martha expressed herself so well. "It's not good to keep things inside all the time," she'd told her. "Sometimes you need to let it out, so your soul can breathe."

Blue needed to do better, even though it was hard. Best to start now. She walked toward Martha. "I wouldn't have been able to do this without you. I don't think you know how important you are to me. After your husband Charlie was killed in that poker game, and you found out he'd gambled the dry goods store away and lost everything, I thought you were as bad off as me." Was it proper to say that, or was it too personal? "But you can do anything you set your mind to. You're good with people. You have your business skills, and you're clever. All I have are my horses and my dreams." There, Blue had told her how she felt. Good, bad, or indifferent. She took in a steadying breath.

Martha stopped making the fire, went to Blue, and wrapped her arms around her. "Darlin' Blue. I've known you since you were a little thing. I watched you grow to womanhood. When your mama died I saw your heart break in two, and when your papa passed, I saw it shatter into pieces. Don't let disappointment and heartache break your spirit. Keep your dreams close and bright. You're building a new life here in Nevada. You're *clever* and smart, and determined. And those things are more powerful than dressmaking and meal-cooking could ever be. You're your own woman. I admire you so for that."

Blue returned her hug. "Martha, you're a wonder. Thank you."

Martha smiled. "Go on now and finish your chores, or we won't eat till midnight."

Blue made the tie-line and tethered the team, separated her four breeding mares and the stud, then secured Isabel's horse. She fed and watered them all. When she came to Isabel's mare, she stroked her neck, admiring her sleek coat. "You're a pretty thing, aren't you." Blue regarded her lines and confirmation more closely. Broad in the hips, good legs, and muscled up to go long distances. "You're built for work, that's for sure." She checked her mouth and teeth and determined she was no more than five years old. "Adelita?" The horse dipped its head and blew, then nudged Blue's shoulder. "I know enough Spanish to make out that your name means noble and kind. It fits you." She stroked the horse's neck once more, then made her way to the campfire and dished out a plate of stew. Sitting on a horse blanket and leaning back on her saddle, she started to eat a spoonful of the food but stopped. "Martha, how long do you suppose Isabel needs to stay with us?"

"I imagine she'll be with us a few days."

"I'm worried about the wagon."

"She won't be much weight. I'm sure it'll be fine."

"Do you think she'll want to stay a spell?" Blue slurped the stew.

"Mind your manners."

"Sorry." Blue wiped her mouth with the back of her hand, then continued to eat. "I don't know what kind of woman she is, but she seems gentle enough. She acted like she wanted to be on her way. We could use the extra help with the horses and such. I imagine she's a decent person."

"How can you say that? You don't know anything about her," Martha said.

"I see her horse. How someone tends to their animals tells a lot about them. And that animal is well trained and properly cared for."

"Well, she'll need at least a few days to recover." Martha sopped a biscuit in the remainder of her stew.

"She's most likely a good person." Blue finished her meal, laid her empty plate beside her, and picked up a pebble, rolling it around in the palm of her hand. Isabel's eyes flashed in front of her. The look she'd given her penetrated her thoughts. She'd felt it go into her, like a shot of whiskey on a summer night. She breathed deeply. Isabel was on her way to her uncle's ranch. Maybe she wouldn't want to stay? But then again, maybe she would.

The wariness seeped into Blue's bones and then doubt crept in. Could she make a go of the ranch? If not, what would happen to Martha? To her? Where would she end up? Going back to Texas was out of the question, after what she'd been through.

CHAPTER TWO

The haze of sleep lifted in the darkness of the wagon as a burning ache ripped through Isabel's side. At first the three cowboys had seemed friendly enough, but their demeanor changed when they approached. She should have been more cautious, more alert.

She remembered the kicks of his boot, the rifle butt against her forehead, the metallic smell of blood, and then everything went silent.

How long had she been lying in the wagon? She slid her hand to her side for the gun in the holster. Empty. She felt for the leather purse with the seventy dollars in gold coins in her left pocket. Gone. Had the men robbed her? Or the two women? What about her husband's rifle? Did they take that also? She tried to get up, but pain overtook her. Should she look for something she could use as a weapon to protect herself? She moved her hand along the surface beside her, touching a long, metal rod. She ran her hand up the shaft, finding more shaped metal at the end. What was it? Then she realized it was a branding iron of some sort. She could use that if she needed to. But these women weren't a threat. They hadn't robbed her. They'd attended to her with soothing hands and concern.

Blue's piercing green eyes held only care and kindness. Her hair, the color of straw when the sun kissed it, was tied back behind her long, elegant neck with a piece of rawhide. A contrast, to be sure. It should have been fastened with a silk ribbon, not leather. Her face was fair, yet it portrayed inner strength. She had a confidence about her, a declaration that she wasn't anyone to be trifled with. Isabel liked the weight of her hand as it rested on her hip. It comforted and calmed. She'd wanted to touch Blue's face, feel its warmth and softness, but it'd been a fleeting thought and vanished as quickly as it'd formed. Was it a response to her immediate need of Blue's care? If not, she'd have to guard herself. To be too open to her feelings would only bring pain.

The loneliness for a woman's touch lingered, sinking into her, filling her with a deep emptiness. Would she always feel this way? Would she never be satisfied like other women? Maybe if she had tried harder she could have been content with her husband. Was it her fault? Maybe if she'd done more it would have been different.

She didn't want to remember, but the images swept over her. When she tried to conjure other thoughts, all that came were the rememberings of the raid at the ranch—the images of her husband and both of the ranch hands' lifeless bodies lying in the dirt. It sickened her. She'd been in the bedroom, crying, feeling sorry for herself. If she'd been outside, she could have joined her husband and fought back. But they were killed before she could get off more than one rifle shot, and then she took a bullet in the arm. When the raiders came into the house, she escaped through the window and rode Adelita to the caves in the mountains above the ranch. A coward? She'd hid there until the wound was manageable, then returned to their home, gathered what meager belongings remained, and sold what she could. She couldn't go back. The raiders had taken the livestock and pilfered anything of real value. So she burned their home and rode away, determined to go to her Uncle Juan's in California, the only family she had left.

Now, she hoped her disguise as a man would work a little while longer. At least until she could get hired somewhere as a ranch hand and earn enough money to go on to California. Her deception hadn't been good enough to fool these women, but no one had gotten that close to her before now. She kept her face dirty when in public to add to the ruse of being a man. A binder around her breasts and material on her waist hid her curves, and she'd padded her shoulders to appear broader. She positioned her hat low to keep her appearance hidden. All in all, it was a convincing disguise and had served her well.

Martha was correct. If she hadn't worn the extra materials, she could have been killed this time. Certainly the attack and the man's repeated kicks might have done more damage than it had.

She'd been able to work her way as a charro on some of the biggest ranches along the route she'd taken. She came from a long line of horsemen. She had no sisters, but her two older brothers had taught her to ride, rope, and shoot. She was skilled in all these things. After her brothers died of cholera, she'd convinced herself she preferred to be alone. But her strong feelings of wanting to be with a woman haunted her. It'd been too long to remember since she'd had any kind of feminine touch, but when she'd looked into Blue's eyes, she'd felt the stirrings.

She was drawn to her, like flowers to sunlight. But she didn't want the thoughts or the longings. And especially not the gossip. No matter how hard she tried to hide her feelings, talk always eventually erupted. So she pushed the desires away when they were the strongest. Tried to ignore them. Yet they felt like a raging tempest when she looked into Blue's eyes.

She attempted to get up, but the deep, biting pain gnawed into her. She rolled cautiously to her side, holding her ribs as she coughed. She peeked through the opening in the canvas, spying the faint light from the remaining embers of the campfire. She tried to hold the spasm of cough again but couldn't. She curled her knees to ease the piercing stabs as they radiated up her ribs. The canvas flap opened.

"Are you ailing?"

Blue. She climbed into the wagon.

What an odd name. Was it a term of endearment, or did someone actually name her that?

"May I have a little water?" Isa asked.

"Yes. I brought you some." Blue handed her the canteen and supported her while she drank.

The water tasted sweet and pure, and Isabel drank freely. She returned the container to Blue when her thirst was quenched. "I'm sorry to be a bother."

The light from a full moon shone through the tattered canvas, revealing Blue's slight smile. "You're no bother." She spoke in a hushed voice. "Lie down now, and try to rest. It won't be long before daylight." Blue covered her with the blanket and touched her arm. "I'll leave the canteen here beside you in case you need it again. Would you like another drink of whiskey?"

"No. I couldn't trouble you anymore."

Blue laughed. "No kind of fuss. It's right here in my pocket. I snitched it from Martha's stores."

Isabel heard the cork pop from the bottle and smelled the strong scent of alcohol as Blue lowered it in front of her.

"Take a couple of sips." Blue helped her to a sitting position once more as Isa reached for the whiskey. Her hands trembled from a spasm of pain.

Blue frowned. "They hurt you bad. Did you get a good look at who did it to you?"

Isa nodded. "There were three of them. The one who kicked me, a big man, had a small nick in his right ear. I'll never forget the ugliness in his face. Hatred is the only way I can describe it. They laughed while they did it." The ache in her ribs raged as the vivid images played over and over in her mind.

"Most men like that have scars in one form or another, Isabel."

"Would you be offended if I asked you to call me Isa? My full name is Isabel Juliana Segura Aguilar."

"Lord aw mighty, that's a mouthful of name. Isa is fine with me."

Isa tried not to laugh. "Why do they call you Blue? Is that your given name?"

"My name is Caroline Bluebonnet Hutchings. Bluebonnet was my mother's family name."

"Was?"

Blue lowered her head. "She died when I was just a sprout."

Isa felt her pain. "I see."

"My papa called me Blue, and it stuck. Caroline is much too formal. It doesn't suit me like Blue does."

"I think Caroline suits you perfectly, but if you wish, I shall call you Blue."

Blue remained silent in the filtered moonlight. Only the sound of her breathing and her scent lingered, a mixture of horse, bread, and campfire. The combination was comforting and brought a sense of safety.

"What about you, Isa? Where do you hail from?"

"I come from just across the Rio Grande."

"How did you end up here?"

"I traveled across the Rio Grande into Texas to get ranch work and earn enough money to go to my uncle's place in upper Northern California. I went through the New Mexico and Arizona Territories. Then I headed toward northern California but ran out of money and changed direction toward Carson City when I heard of work. That's when I was attacked."

"You've traveled even farther than we have. And alone. You've got mettle. I'll give you that."

Isa took another sip of the whiskey, then handed it to Blue. "Where are you headed?"

Blue corked the bottle and stuffed it into her back pocket. "We've got about a hundred more miles to go." She hesitated, as if she wanted to say more but didn't. "I better let you rest. Try to sleep a couple of hours. And don't worry about your horse. She's settled in nicely with the others, and I watered and fed her. I'll put your gear in the wagon when we pack up to go. You won't be riding for a few days at least." Blue stroked her arm.

Isa reached for her hand. "Thank you for all you've done. You and Martha are very kind."

Blue nodded. "I don't know what I would have done without her. She was an unexpected companion on this trip."

"Whoever she is, she has a very gentle touch. And so do you."

A hint of a blush appeared on Blue's cheeks.

Her shyness intrigued Isa.

"Well, you're welcome," Blue said. "See you in a few hours." She left the wagon.

Isa settled into her makeshift bed and tried to get comfortable.

What would her prospects be now? No money for resupplies. A weapon? Hopefully, the rifle would be in the scabbard in her tack. But that was doubtful. They'd taken everything of value, which would include the rifle. She'd know for certain later. She had no clear path now and needed to sleep. She could sort things out after more rest.

"Caroline." She breathed the word out in a hushed whisper. The sound and feel of the name momentarily caressed her lips. The heat of the whiskey warmed her stomach. The memory of Blue's touch lingered, then drifted away like a leaf on the current of a stream as she eased into sleep.

CHAPTER THREE

Blue fastened the collar and harnesses to the horses, then buckled the traces. She placed the breeching, then checked to make sure it was even. She could have done it blindfolded. Martha stored all the truck in the back. Blue eavesdropped as Martha spoke to Isa about her comfort.

"I can sit with you in the front," Isa said.

"No," Martha said. "It's best you lie still for the day. We'll see how you fare this evening."

"Is there any mending or repairs I can do to pass the time?"

"Oh, aren't you a dear."

The smile in Martha's voice floated in the air as Blue took the worn leather scabbard attached to her saddle, walked to the rear of the wagon, and peered in. She withdrew the rife from its position in the tattered pouch. "This could use some restitching with leather, if you can manage it." She offered it to Isa.

Isa reached for the rifle holder and nodded as she inspected it. "It's pretty beat-up. Do you have leather lacings, or do I need to cut some?"

Blue handed her the tied bundle of stripping from inside the back of the wagon. "Use what you need."

"And the needles and hooks?" Isa asked.

Martha, who had climbed up into the front of the wagon, handed her a beaded pouch. "Everything's in here."

Isa took it with a graceful motion of her hand. Everything she did fascinated Blue, even the way she'd eaten her breakfast when it'd been brought to her. She'd spooned the beans with care, placing the biscuit near the pile on her plate. Blue had been careful to make sure the coffee and biscuits were hot, and that she had a generous portion of honey. Isa had eaten with an appetite and then thanked her. Twice.

Isa smiled at Blue when their eyes met.

They were a deeper brown today, almost liquid, and seemed to beckon Blue.

She felt the beat of her own heart. Heard it in her ears. Sensed the rhythm of her breathing. She gazed deeper into Isa's eyes, grasping the wagon to steady herself. Did she look too deeply? Had she violated some code of conduct? She wanted to apologize, but she didn't quite know what for. Heat crept up her neck and pooled in her cheeks.

"I'll have it done for you later today," Isa said.

Blue nodded. At least she thought she did. She wanted to linger with her, but she couldn't think of anything to say. Besides, they needed to leave. The sun had been up for almost an hour. "Thank you." It was all she could croak. Disappointment in her social inadequacy rattled in her chest and joined the heat in her face. She wished she'd paid more attention to the proper way to behave when her father had tried to teach her. But she'd refused. She wanted to be out among the horses— riding, ranging, herding with the men. Her best friend growing up had been Samuel Andrews, the banker's son. They did everything together. Then he went away to college. And when he returned after four years, he was different, but she was the same. Now, at twenty-five, she felt uneducated and inadequate in every way. She was able to say good-bye to him before she left Texas. She knew he had thoughts of marriage, but in her mind, they were nothing more than dear friends.

He had told her, "Friends marry and can be happy together. It's long past the time we both should wed."

But Blue had no interest then. Yet now a need for a soft and gentle caress pulled at her.

Should she talk for a few minutes? That's what Martha had done, and she should as well. But the words wouldn't come. Frustrated, she loaded the rifle into the wagon, then risked another glimpse. Now an evident sadness appeared in Isa's eyes, and her expression had changed, like a cloud suddenly blocking the sun. "What's wrong?"

Isa looked away. "Nothing. It's nothing."

"Yes. It's something. Tell me?" Why didn't she tell her? She'd asked. Isa should answer.

Isa hesitated, then held her side as she spoke. "They robbed me after they beat me, and I fear they took my husband's rifle. Now it's confirmed because I don't see it among my things."

She lowered her head.

Blue's instinct to comfort emerged. Should she climb into the wagon and sit beside her? What should she say? A heaviness filled her chest. What if Isa didn't need comforting? Unsure of what to do, she held on to the wagon board that separated them. Isa was married, but why was she alone? What had happened? Should she ask? She took the risk. "Your *husband's* rifle?"

"Yes. The only thing I had of his when he was killed."

Now Blue'd gone and done it. She'd opened a wound, and they didn't have time to talk about it. No time to find out the rest of the story or help Isa with her pain. All she'd heard was that Isa's husband was dead. But she couldn't leave things like this.

A piercing sadness lingered on Isa's face.

"I'm sorry for your trouble," Blue said.

"It's all right."

A soft hitch in her voice heightened Blue's attention.

Martha leaned into the opening. "I 'spect we have lots of time for such talk later, you two." She shooed Blue away from the wagon.

Blue hesitated, then tethered the broodmares together and tied Adelita and the stud to the back of the wagon.

They stopped for a rest just after the sun reached mid-sky.

Blue eased Traveler beside the wagon and wiped her face with a checkered handkerchief she'd tucked inside her hat.

"Lord, it's hot, Blue." Martha removed her bonnet and fanned herself.

"If it's this hot in May, what's it going to be like in full summer?" Blue asked. "I hope it eases as we get closer to the ranch. Let's go over yonder and rest in the shade of those boulders. I think we'd fare better if we sat out this heat for a few hours, then went on."

Martha scanned the area and nodded. "I 'spect so. We'll need water soon. No sense in getting heated if we can travel later."

They made their way to the shade and unhitched the wagon. Blue separated the stud, then secured the rest of the horses. She watered them and returned to the campsite. Martha had helped Isa to a blanket. She sat against one of the boulders, Blue's scabbard in her hands and the rifle beside her. She glanced at Blue and smiled again.

The comfort of it slid through Blue like honey on a hot biscuit. She spied the leather braiding now running along the seam of the rifle holder. "You're done already? Did you see this, Martha?"

Martha stopped what she was doing in the wagon and came over to them. She bent and inspected Isa's work. "That's fine stitching."

"It's not quite done, but almost," Isa said. "I need to finish the bottom and reinforce the trigger side. That's where it gets the most use. I'll measure it again before I stitch the rest."

Blue's excitement spilled out. "It's better than when it was new. Papa bought it for me years ago. That's fine work, really fine work."

Blue went to the wagon and inspected the wheel. "I think the reinforcement on these spokes is gonna hold."

Suddenly Adelita reared, then bucked, breaking loose from her tie-down.

Blue startled.

Two of the mares backed up and broke free from the rope, then galloped away before Blue could reach them. The stud reared but couldn't break free from where he was tied.

"What in the hell?" She ran to the other horses and grabbed their halter ropes to try to settle them. It was then she heard the sound. "Rattlers!" She released the horses, including the stud, and let them run. "There must be a nest. Damn! I should've checked better." She froze. A few feet in front of her, a rattlesnake coiled and readied to strike. Before she could draw her gun from the holster, she heard repeated rifle shots. The snake hurdled through the air and landed near her boot, its head no longer attached to its body. Two more snakes lay near the rocks, also dead. She turned to see Isa with the rifle held to her shoulder, still aiming.

Blue couldn't move. She tried to speak, but words wouldn't come. She'd been an instant away from being killed. The snake that had started to strike was at least four feet long. She stood unmoving, her heart racing. Everything else faded from view but Isa.

With the gun still pointed toward the rocks, Isa maneuvered toward her. "Don't move. I'm not sure I got them all. Are you all right? You weren't bitten?"

"No." That was all Blue could get out of her mouth. Her heartbeat pounded in her throat. What had just happened? Isa had saved her. Not only that, but she'd shot three snakes in just as many seconds. And hadn't missed once.

"I'm going to check closer." Isa tracked toward the boulders.

Blue finally came to her senses. "Wait. I'll go with you." She drew her pistol and walked in step with her.

They found no other signs of more snakes. When they were sure the area was free of danger, they returned to the wagon.

Martha wrapped her arms around them. "Almighty mercies, that was close. I've never seen anyone shoot like that. The Good Lord above must have sent you to us."

Blue nodded.

Martha held Blue's face in her hands. "Darlin', are you all right?"

Blue patted Martha's shoulder. "It's okay. Isa saved me."

"She surely did."

"You did the same for me," Isa said. She lowered the rifle, held on to her side, and peered in the direction the horses had gone. She walked a few feet away and put her fingers in her mouth and let out a whistle that would have awakened the dead. She bent and clutched her side again. "That was a mistake."

A horse whinnied in the distance.

Isa straightened. "That's Adelita. I hope she brings the others back with her."

"I imagine they'll stay together, as spooked as they were." Blue stuffed her hands in the pockets of her linsey-woolsey vest, trying to hide her trembling. "If I can get one of them back, I'll be able to find the rest a lot easier. I don't fancy walking in this heat."

"If they don't return with Adelita, you can ride her. Just let her have her head. She'll go right to them." Isa's smile seemed a mixture of satisfaction and pride.

"You go rest on your blanket," Martha said. "You've done enough for one day." She took the rifle from Isa. "Go on now."

Isa touched Blue's shoulder as she walked past her. "I'm glad you weren't bit. Adelita will be along in a few minutes."

Blue heard the horses before she saw them. Adelita was in front of Traveler, followed by one of the mares. She breathed a sigh of relief and adjusted her hat. "Well, I'll have to go after the others. At least Traveler came back, and my best mare. I hope nothing's happened to the stud. I can't afford to replace him." Adelita slowed and walked into camp. Blue patted her neck and took hold of her halter rope, then grabbed Traveler's. The broodmare nestled up against Traveler. She handed the ropes to Martha. "I'll check the other side of those rocks again, then set a tie line. I'll have to water Traveler before we leave. No telling how long I'll be gone." Why didn't they come back with the others?

Blue saddled and mounted Traveler, then leaned down toward Martha, who was stroking the side of his face. "It's best we stay here for the night. The horses will be skittish from all the commotion."

Martha nodded and backed away. "Mind yourself. I'll set up camp."

Isa approached Blue, the scabbard in her hand. "You can use this now."

Blue moved her leg to let Isa fasten it into place underneath the stirrup strap.

Isa patted Blue's thigh. "Mind your safety. They shouldn't be too far away."

Martha handed Blue the rifle, and she slipped it into its sheath.

Blue reined Traveler and headed west, following the horses' tracks.

"Dang!" she said to herself. "What doesn't that woman do? She sews. She shoots. She's good with horses." And she was the most beautiful woman Blue had ever laid eyes on.

Forty minutes later, she smelled water and heard a frantic whinny. The terrain had changed from hard rock and sand to more trees, shrubs, and roots. She spied one of the wagon team, the stud, and two mares in a gulley, drinking from a stream. The other puller and a mare were missing. "Now what?" The sound of a horse in distress grew clearer. She followed it, urging Traveler down the rough bank and past the horses that were drinking. She went around the bend and stopped short. The other two horses lay near the water's edge, one dead, the other writhing. "Hell fire."

She eased Traveler toward them. From the position of the dead gelding, it was easy to guess what had happened. He must have been in the lead when they went into the gully, stumbled, caught his front legs on the terrain, and tumbled the rest of the way down, breaking his neck. The mare had followed and most likely also got tangled in the tree roots and had broken her left foreleg. It appeared shattered. Blue dismounted and tied Traveler to a tree root.

The mare continued to call out. Blue went behind her and held her head, then stroked her neck. "Poor girl." She inspected the leg. "You won't be able to get up. Not with that break. Damn it."

She went to Traveler, drew her rifle from the scabbard, then cocked it. "What a waste." Her future depended on her horses. If she lost them, how would she manage?

The animal continued to fight to get up.

She brought the rifle to the mare's forehead and aimed, then lowered the weapon. She inspected the mare once again, hoping the situation wasn't what she thought. But it was, and it had to be done. She repositioned, digging her boot into the sand for a more balanced stance. She gritted her teeth and aimed the rifle.

Traveler jerked his head at the sharp report of the gun. The sound echoed into the gully. And then silence.

After checking to make sure the blood wouldn't run into the stream, and that the carcasses wouldn't slide into the water, Blue settled onto the rocky bank in disgust. Now what? She was down two horses, both important, and none of the breeding mares were trained to pull.

She glanced one last time at the two dead animals. They were good horses and had served her well. She said a quiet thank you, then got to her feet and brushed herself off. She slid the rifle back into the scabbard and led Traveler to the other horses. She retethered them together and made her way out of the gully.

Isa and Martha were standing by the wagon when she returned.

"You've been gone a long time. We were worried," Martha said. "And from the looks of it, we had cause."

Blue dismounted. "We lost two of the horses—Old Dan and one of the mares. I figure they got tangled when they went into a gulley. Old Dan broke his neck, and the mare shattered her foreleg. I hated to put her down, but I didn't want her to suffer. The stream's a good one. I think we should move the camp up ahead about five miles. We need the water, and I could use a bath."

Martha's expression tightened. "How are we going to pull the wagon with only one horse?"

"We'll have to lighten the load. I can pack two of the mares."

Isa came forward. "Adelita can do it."

"Are you sure? I wouldn't want to use her if you have a fear of it."

"She'll be fine." Isa started to walk to where Adelita was tied.

"I can get her," Blue said. "You should rest."

"No. I'll need to help you in order to settle her into the harness."

"These horses are well watered," Blue said, leading the runaways. "Make sure Adelita gets a good drink, and then we'll leave." Blue fastened the mares' and the stud's leads to the wagon and put the puller into position. "Jake here is pretty mild. They should get along all right."

Isa led Adelita to Jake, in the right-side position, and Blue began to fasten the rigging into place. Isa held her side every few minutes as she helped adjust the tack.

"I can do it," Blue said.

"I'm all right. I've been enough of a burden."

Blue was too tired to argue or insist that Isa rest. If she wanted to be stubborn, so be it. She'd pay for it later when the pain got worse. "Suit yourself."

Martha patted Blue's arm. "You look spent."

Blue nodded. The emotion of what she'd had to do had drained her of her strength. She checked the tie-down on the mares and then mounted Traveler.

The problem of the wagon was solved for now. But what about tomorrow? Would Isa be leaving them? Always something to get in the way. Nothing easy. The weariness of the struggle sank deep into Blue's bones.

CHAPTER FOUR

The wagon swayed and bumped along the dry, rutted terrain. The scent of stale flour floated through the air as Isa lay on the half-empty sack, her knees up to ease the pain. The incline of the wagon made it harder to get comfortable. They'd been going up the mountain for almost half a day, already three days past where she needed to head toward her uncle's ranch. The farther north they went, the longer it would take her out of her way.

They'd passed several ranches in the last two days. Blue had tried to bargain for horses to replace the one that pulled the wagon, but no one had any to spare. It couldn't be Isa's concern, except that Adelita would have to keep pulling the wagon until Blue obtained one or they reached their destination. Could Isa leave before that? Blue had said they could manage by packing the other horses. Isa didn't have to stay. So why did she? Obligation? Guilt? Debt? If they hadn't helped her, she'd most likely be dead by now. She owed them at least something. But once they reached Blue's property, her obligation to help would end. Now fit to ride, she just needed to go slow. Mounting and dismounting Adelita would be painful, but she'd deal with it. Time to move on.

The ponderosa pine spread over the landscape. As evening approached, the air became moist and cool. It was a pleasant change. Isa gazed through the opening at the back of the wagon, watching the clouds gather as the sky became a deeper azure.

"Ho!" Martha eased the reins and leaned back. "Are you ready to stop, Isa?"

"Yes." Isa scooted to the back and gingerly climbed out, then carefully stretched. The intense spasms in her ribs had become a dull ache.

Blue came beside her on Traveler and dismounted. "This is a level enough spot."

"I'll help get the horses settled," Isa said. She approached the team and began to unhitch the animals.

"You're moving better." Blue led the mares to a shaded spot and set the tie-downs. "Do you think you'll ride tomorrow?"

"No. I'll sit with Martha so Adelita can continue to pull." She secured Jake and then Adelita, running her hand over the horse's chest, back, and hips, checking to see if she had any tender spots from the weight of the harnesses. The horse flinched when Isa ran her hand firmly over her right hip. "Easy." She gently rubbed the area. "How many more days?" She could feel Blue watching her.

"I checked the map a little while ago before we stopped. As far as I can tell, we should reach Carson City sometime tomorrow, and then another full day to the ranch. Is she all right?"

"She's a little sore but nothing to be alarmed about."

They finished the chores and set camp. A chill seeped into Isa's arms when the sun went down. She moved her bedroll closer to the fire.

Blue sat with her legs crossed, stirring the stew on her tin plate.

"You're not eating, Blue. Are you ailing?" Martha asked.

"No. Just used up." She sighed.

"It's been a long day," Martha said. "I 'spect we'll need to get supplies before we head out of town."

"The quicker we leave Carson City, the better I'll like it." Blue squirmed and set the half-eaten plate of food beside her.

Martha stopped eating. "Why?"

"Isa, I imagine the men who attacked you are from the area around Carson City," Blue said, watching her.

"I thought that myself." Isa returned her gaze.

Blue's expression changed. Her brows furrowed, and she rubbed her chin. "If they recognize you, it could mean trouble."

Why would she care? For herself? Martha?

As if Blue read her thoughts, she said, "I wouldn't want any more harm to come to you. Perhaps it might be best if you and Martha bypassed town and I took two horses and met you once I secure the supplies."

"I think we need to take the wagon in and get it repaired, then stock up as much as possible," Martha said. "We don't know what condition the ranch is in."

Blue shifted. "I don't know. I think it's asking for trouble if they see Isa."

"I think I know how to remedy your concern," Isa said.

Blue's sincere worry showed in her eyes, but they became softer and more intent when she looked at her.

"In the morning I'll change into a dress and bonnet. They won't recognize me. They'll be looking for a man, not a woman."

"Clever girl," Martha said.

Blue picked up her plate and began to finish her meal. "That's good, but still…I want to get out of there as soon as possible. It'll be a strain on the horses to pull a loaded wagon. I'll pack two of the mares with some of the new supplies."

Isa watched Blue. She'd averted her eyes when she'd said it. Was she trying to hide something?

The next day, the sun not quite above them, they reached Carson City. The noise of the city was almost deafening. Groups of men lingered near the entranceways of every building—talking, laughing, spitting. They stopped their conversations and observed each of them as Blue led the way through town. They must have been an odd sight—the three of them, alone without any men, and the rickety, worn-out wagon. Isa surveyed each cowboy as they passed, hoping to find the men who attacked her, yet concerned she would.

Carson City was bigger than she'd imagined. The town bustled with the activities of the day. Shoppers. Men gathered at the gun shop and the barber's. Women at the dry goods store.

Blue stopped. "Let's head to the livery and get another wagon wheel. We should do it before we load supplies."

Martha guided the team to the edge of town toward the large, planked building with *Livery* painted in red above the double barn doors. The sound of hammering steel against steel grew louder as they approached. Wagon wheels, metal rims, leather harnesses, pitchforks, pails, and other merchandise were piled against the front wall. Before Blue could dismount, a large, dark-haired man with a ruddy-bearded face came out to meet them.

"Howdy." He smiled, a tooth missing near the upper left front of his mouth. "I'm Luther. Luther Henderson. From the sound of it, you need a new wheel." He surveyed the wagon, squinted, then scratched his beard. "Or two or three." He laughed.

Blue got down from Traveler. "Howdy. Can you replace that one?" She pointed to the worst-offending wheel.

"Yep. How loaded is your wagon?"

"We haven't gotten supplies yet," Blue said.

Luther scratched his head and inspected the wheel. "I can manage it. I'll give you a good deal on two more. I'm guessing those two, he pointed, won't make another twenty or thirty miles."

"What kind of deal?" Blue asked.

They agreed on a price for three wheels instead of one.

"It shouldn't take more than a little while. Why don't you ladies go over to the Morris store," he pointed down the street, "and order your supplies. I'll send a boy for you when the wagon's ready."

Isa scrutinized Luther. Not one of her attackers.

"Where you headed?" he asked.

"About another day's ride," Blue said.

He nodded. "All right then. Won't be but a bit." He moved to the wagon and assisted Martha and Isa.

"I'll pay half now and the other half when the job's done," Blue said.

"Fair enough, but it's not necessary. I'll take full payment after I finish." He strode to Blue. "I 'spect you're the boss of this outfit." He grinned.

Blue half-smiled. "Yes."

"How far you come?" he asked.

"Texas," Martha said, smoothing the sides of her dress.

"Where's your men folk?"

"We're meeting them," Blue said, looking straight into his eyes.

Isa knew Blue would say what she must to protect herself and the others. The less said and the faster they left town, the better for all of them.

"You can tie your horse stock beside the barn, just there." He pointed and then eyed the coal-black stud. "That's a mighty fine animal. Any chance he's for sale?"

Blue shook her head.

"What's his blood? I've never seen a finer stud in these parts."

"He's Steeldust with Copper Bottom mix. I bred him to be quick, hardy, and go a far distance."

Luther stroked the stud's neck, then rubbed his chest and front knees. "He's a beauty. Did he cover your mares?"

"Yes. They should foal sometime early spring."

"You're welcome to put him and the mares in the small pen, just there." Luther pointed to a smaller corral next to the main barn.

Isa walked behind the wagon and helped Blue lead the breeding mares.

"I'll unhitch your team and keep them in the main corral until the wagon's ready, then re-hitch them. It's included in the price."

"Do you have any wagon stock?" Blue asked. "We need one more."

"Over there. They're already trained. I'll give you a good deal," he said.

Blue laughed. "You seem to have a lot of good deals."

Luther smiled broadly. "I'm prepared, that's for sure."

"I'll look them over and pick one. Thank you," Blue said.

"Let me know, and I'll add it onto the cost." He returned to his work.

Blue discussed with Isa which one she thought would be best suited.

Isa patted the neck of the bay with a star on its forehead that Blue had admired. She ran her hand down its front knees. "He's a good choice."

They took their poke and moved along the dusty storefronts to Morris Dry Goods, Feed, and Supply, directly across from the Carson City Bank and the surveyor's office.

Isa scrutinized each man as they passed them, tipping their hats, some greeting, some nodding, some ogling. None were her attackers.

She and Blue entered the store and stood beside Martha, who was inspecting the displayed china.

It took a moment for Isa's eyes to adjust to the change in the light.

A tall, thin man, with a pleasant smile, greeted them. "Afternoon, ladies. May I be of assistance?"

Martha spoke without hesitation as she handed him her list. "Good day. Everything on the list. If you please."

"An organized female. How refreshing." He rubbed his hands on his white apron and came out from behind the counter, studying the paper. "My, this *is* a list. It'll take a while. Would you like to have your man pull your wagon around to the back, and we can load from there?"

Blue shifted. "It's getting new wheels and will be ready shortly."

"Very good. We'll start working on your order." He turned and called to the back room. "Thomas, come out here.

"Meanwhile, you ladies help yourselves to some refreshments, and I'll let you know when your supplies are ready to load." He pointed to an adjoining room with a few round wooden tables and chairs. "Mrs. Morris, my wife, is in there and she'll wait on you. I'm James Morris."

Martha nodded and thanked him, then introduced their small group. They started toward the next room.

Isa hesitated, pulling her bonnet closer around her face. Could they tell she was Mexican? Would they speak to her?

Martha wrapped her arm in Isa's. "Come. No need to be shy."

The scent of coffee, baked bread, and homemade goods filled the air. Isa's stomach growled loudly as she breathed in the delicious aromas. Baked cookies and pies were lined up on glass shelving.

A stocky woman with a huge smile and rosy cheeks, probably in her forties, greeted them. "Come in, come in. Sit down. Welcome. I'm Mrs. Morris. You call me Nettie. Can I get some coffee or lemonade, or a pastry?"

Martha surveyed the room. Blue stared at the baked goods.

Isa cleared her throat. "I'm afraid the wonderful scents have overtaken us."

Nettie laughed. "Aw, 'tis a rich experience indeed. While Mr. Morris fills your order, I'll get you some coffee and a treat. What would you like? Pie, cookies, some homemade sweet bread perhaps? We have apple pie, oatmeal and ginger-snap cookies, and johnnycake."

Blue licked her lips. "I'll have one of those oatmeal cookies."

"I'll have a piece of apple pie," Martha said.

"Apple pie for me also," Isa said, her stomach rumbling once again.

"Wonderful. You ladies look like you've traveled far. Where are you hailing from, and where are you going?" Before anyone could answer, Nettie waddled to the stove, brought back a pot of coffee and three mugs, and began to pour the dark liquid. "No cream, I'm afraid." She left, then returned with their plated requests on a tray and placed them on the table. "Now tell me, will you be staying or moving on? I hope you'll be staying."

Blue took a bite of her cookie. Martha forked her pie.

Isa couldn't wait to get the dessert into her mouth. When the flavor exploded on her tongue, she savored every tart, delicious morsel.

Blue cleared her throat. "We're moving on."

"Where to?" Mrs. Morris's eyes lit with interest as she leaned forward. "Not far, I hope."

"About a day's journey south, near the Genoa area," Blue said.

It surprised Isa that she'd given such specific detail.

"I know that part of the country. It's beautiful. There was a Mormon settlement there but has since been taken over. You can get a few supplies there, but they don't offer much. Might I ask if you're going to your people, or are you new settlers?"

"Hutchings," Blue said between bites of her cookie.

"Silas Hutchings?" Nettie blurted. "Are you related to Silas Hutchings?"

"I am," Blue said. "My uncle. He was settling the land for my father."

"Nice man. It's a shame what happened to him."

Blue stopped eating. Her gaze darted to Nettie.

"Shot, you know. Shot right out there beside the bank." She pointed through the window, across the street.

Isa followed her gesture. A small alley ran between the bank and the hotel.

"Right there," Nettie repeated, continuing to point.

"He wasn't shot," Blue said. "He died of consumption."

"I beg to differ." Nettie huffed. "I saw his body. Mr. Morris and two of his helpers carried him to the undertaker's. He was shot. Right through the chest."

Blue paled.

"Please, Mrs. Morris. Can't you see you've upset her?" Martha said.

Isa touched Blue's arm, feeling her tremble.

"Oh! I'm so sorry, my dear. I meant no disrespect. But he did not die of consumption. I can assure you of that. Now you three enjoy your desserts." She left quickly and went to the far end of the room and began to busy herself.

Martha placed her hand on Blue's. "I think she's telling the truth. Someone lied, but I don't think it's her."

"I'll find out what this is all about," Blue said. Her face tensed, and her lips pursed.

Martha squeezed Blue's fingers. "It's a shock, I know. We'll get to the bottom of it."

Nettie returned a short while later with more coffee. "I reckon the Hutchings place is about ten miles or so southeast of the Genoa settlement. It'll take all of a day by wagon to get to where you're headed. You should camp for the night at the river, about a half-day's journey southeast of here. You can set up comfortably, but tell your men folk to be watchful. Sometimes there's not the best of sorts around those parts."

Martha nodded. "Thank you. We're meeting them just outside town, and we'll let them know."

Nettie nodded, then returned to her tasks.

Isa watched Blue intently. Was Blue taking on more than she could handle? Would she be able to make a go of it? Should Isa stay with them for a time? Would they need her help?

CHAPTER FIVE

The scrubs and trees became denser. The horses began to snort and picked up their pace. Water.

Blue didn't like not knowing what might lie ahead. "I'm riding on," she said. "Just keep coming."

"Shall I go with you?" Isa asked. She patted Adelita's neck and sat more upright, probably to position herself on the horse for the least amount of pain.

Blue admired her grit. It wasn't easy to ride hurt. "I'd rather you stay with Martha. I'd feel better if you accompanied her. I suspect water's less than a mile away."

"*I'd* rather you stay with us," Isa said. "I think it'd be safer."

Blue brought Traveler to a stop, and Isa reined Adelita next to her.

Isa could be right. There was safety in numbers, and no real need to go ahead of them. And if someone was already there waiting to do them harm, Blue couldn't prevent it. "All right. If you think it's better." It surprised her that she'd given in so quickly. Normally she'd have bucked at someone telling her what to do. But she didn't feel that way toward Isa because her tone was easy and kind. Or was it something else?

Once at the riverbank, they traveled south until they found a convenient spot and made camp. The remains of old campfires, matted-down grass, wagon tracks, and discarded items gave the telltale signs that this must have been the place Nettie had talked about. No other wagons were in the area. They made a fire, cooked their meal, and settled in for the night as darkness engulfed them.

The sound of running water on the current of the river eased the ache of the day's journey from Blue. A light breeze and moisture in the air brought the scent of the junipers along the riverbank, a welcome relief from the many arid and dusty days and nights they'd traveled.

Part of another day and they'd be at the ranch. The excitement of what waited ahead chased the needed sleep from Blue. She stretched out on her blanket and tried to rest. Should she go down to the river's edge and bathe? The water would be cold, but it'd be a welcome relief.

Isa sat upright, catching Blue's attention.

"What is it?" Blue asked.

"Someone's out there," Isa whispered, lifting her rifle and cocking the lever. She stood. "I'm going just beyond the camp. Arm yourself."

Before Blue could protest her leaving, Isa had disappeared into the blackness.

Blue unlatched the tie-down to her pistol in the holster hanging on the saddle horn just above her head.

"What is it?" Martha's voice was anxious. "What's going on?"

Blue quieted her.

A deep male voice boomed, "Hello in the camp."

It broke the silence like a clap of thunder. The sound of several horses and riders grew louder as they approached.

"Sorry to disturb you." The man who'd spoken and two other riders halted just before they reached the wagon. The glow of the campfire lit his silhouette, but Blue couldn't make out the other two men and their exact features because they seemed to purposely avoid the light from the fire.

The speaker was beefy, ragged, and dirty. His hat sat low on his forehead, making it hard to discern his features. He dismounted without permission, handed the reins of his horse to the rider beside him, and walked toward the fire, holding out his hands as if to warm them over the heat of the flames. All the while he scanned the camp, halting on Blue, then darting back to Martha. One of the men eased his horse behind the wagon and started to lean down to peer inside.

Blue had seen enough. "Stop right there, mister." She drew her pistol.

"Easy. No need to get riled," the big man said.

Blue repositioned the handgun and pointed it at him.

He raised his hands. "No need to be hostile. We're just ridin' through."

"Then keep on riding," Blue said.

"Well, derned if you aren't a feisty little thing." He began to lower his gun hand.

"Keep 'em high," Isa shouted from the shadows. "Or I'll make you a left-handed shooter."

The man turned toward her voice and squinted, but Isa remained out of sight.

"We don't mean no harm," said the dismounted rider, still peering into the night. "Just thought we'd stop and say howdy."

Blue cocked the pistol. "Be on your way. All of you."

The man turned again to Blue and began to back away. "All right. Don't want to stay with this unfriendly group of women anyway." He mounted his horse. "I'd think twice about being so unsociable if I was you." His mouth curled into a half grin. He tipped his hat to her, then to Martha.

Blue spied his nicked ear.

"Eve-nin' ladies." He reined his horse, and the three men left.

Isa returned a few minutes later. "I didn't get a good look at them, but they're trouble," she said, warming her hands at the fire. "They rode back toward Carson City, but we better set watch the rest of the night."

Blue agreed. "No telling what they're up to, but I'm sure it's no good. You try to get some sleep. I'll take first watch. The big man had a nicked ear."

Isa nodded. "I thought it might be him, but I wasn't able to see him clearly. I'll spell you in a couple of hours."

Blue grew more restless as time passed. She stoked the fire, then strode a short way from camp. She could see a fair distance under the light of the full moon. If the men were coming back, they'd be here soon. She settled into a crouch and listened intently. Only the sounds of the critters along the riverbank caught her attention. Suddenly, it grew quiet. Too quiet. She strained to see but detected no shadows or movement. Her heart raced and her mouth went dry. Should she return to camp and wake Isa? Just as she started to rise, she saw their silhouettes. Three men bunched together and leading their horses. One stopped and took the other's reins. Two continued to walk closer. Blue could make out their features. One was the man who'd been in camp earlier.

She heard soft footsteps and spun, ready to aim the rifle.

Isa knelt beside her, dressed in her pants, shirt, and vest, her hat pulled low. "It's me," she said, grinning.

"You 'bout scared the life out of me," Blue whispered.

"Sorry. I figured you'd need some help."

Blue repositioned and watched the two men walk closer, then leaned toward Isa. "Now what? We can't shoot 'em, but I'll be dammed if I'll let them come into camp."

"Martha's waiting under the wagon with a pistol," Isa said.

She was so close, her breath caressed Blue's cheek, sending a chill down her arms.

"We gave them a warning when they were here the first time," Isa said. "If they're coming back again it's because they mean us harm. I say we shoot 'em."

Blue was shocked that Isa would feel that way, but who could blame her?

"And I'll bet he's carrying my husband's rifle," Isa said. "Damn bushwhackers."

Blue took in a steadying breath. They had to be stopped. "Well, if they want trouble, they've got it. They didn't see you, only me and Martha. Whatever you do to convince everyone you're a man, do it now. We have to end this, or they'll keep coming after us."

"All right. Give me your rifle."

Blue surrendered her weapon.

"Stay here and cover me with your hand shooter," Isa said. "If the big fella doesn't go down right away, shoot him in the leg. We won't kill them, but we'll spook the horses so they'll have to walk until they can catch them. That'll give us enough time to pack up and hightail it out of here. Don't hesitate to shoot him if he doesn't go down. They can't have the advantage over us. Watch for the third man. You'll have to take care of him. I'll be busy with the other two." She pulled the dark bandana from around her neck and placed it over her nose and mouth and stood.

She ran full speed toward the two men. When she got close, they must have heard her because they drew their weapons.

In a deep voice she yelled, "Damn bushwhackers." Running full speed, she lunged at the big man with the nick in his ear, jabbing him in the belly with the rifle barrel. When he doubled over, she struck him full force in the jaw with the rifle butt.

He went down with a grunt and lay motionless on the ground. Before the other man could focus his aim on her, she whipped the barrel of the gun to the side of his knee, sending him to the ground. Then she stood over him, pointing the business end of the rifle at his face.

"You were told to stay away. Now you've been warned twice. You come back again, or anywhere near us, and I'll shoot you dead. And just to show you I mean what I say…"

"No!" Blue yelled. Was Isa going to shoot him? Which one? Or both?

Blue strained to see the third man, desperate to find him. Did he take off? Was he trying to sneak up on Isa? Sound carried in the still of the night, so he had to have heard the commotion.

Isa pointed the rifle at the dirt next to the man's face and fired.

The bigger man moaned and started to sit up.

She knocked him again in the side of the head with the rifle. He went down with a thud.

Suddenly the third man appeared, his weapon aimed at Isa.

"Watch out," Blue warned, and fired.

The man staggered backward. His rifle fell out of his hand as he grabbed his right shoulder. "You damn near kilt me," he yelled.

Blue came forward. "Yeah, well, what would you three have done to us?" She walked closer. "Sit down."

The man awkwardly squatted, then collapsed onto the ground.

"Toss that shooter here," Isa said.

He squinted. "I know you."

"Yes. You do. You robbed me and left me for dead."

"We were going to come back. We felt bad about it."

"Shut up, Yates," said the man Isa had her gun aimed at.

Isa pointed the rifle at his face again. "What's your name?"

He didn't speak.

"Tell me your name or I'll shoot your ear off." She moved the rifle closer to his ear.

"Gawd, mister, you're a tough customer."

"Name."

"Bill Evans."

"And his?" Isa motioned to the big man lying unconscious.

Evans eyed him. "Is he dead?"

"No."

"It's Travis. Travis McCoy," Yates said. "We didn't mean no harm."

Blue had had enough. "Oh, shut up. You did too. I think we should shoot all of them and bury 'em right here."

Isa glanced at Blue. "That's not a bad idea. They would have killed us for sure."

Yates raised one hand. "Please, don't."

"Put your hand down and be quiet," Isa said.

Blue walked to her, continuing to point the gun at Yates, who held his shoulder. "I'll go with Yates and bring in their horses."

Would Isa kill the other two men while she was gone? Surely not. "Let's go." Blue ordered Yates to his feet as she peered at Isa. "We'll be right back. Don't do anything rash."

Isa stabbed the rifle barrel toward Evans. "That's up to them."

Blue walked behind Yates a few steps, distancing herself so he couldn't turn and attack her before she could shoot him.

"Honest. We weren't going to hurt you womenfolk, just have some fun. We didn't know any men were around," Yates said.

"You're disgusting. Shut your mouth and hurry up."

They retrieved the three horses and returned.

Isa picked up the rifle McCoy had been using and handed Blue hers.

Blue disarmed the three men of two more rifles and three pistols and checked their rigs to make sure they didn't have any more hidden. She holstered her handgun and aimed her long gun at Evans, clearly more of a threat than Yates.

"Now what?" Evans asked, staring at Isa as McCoy began to stir.

Isa motioned to McCoy. "Take him and start walkin' to whatever hole you crawled out of." She fired the rifle twice. The three horses took off. She turned to Evans. "Don't you ever come near me and mine again, or I'll kill all of you."

"But what about our horses and guns?" Yates asked. "You can't leave us without anything to protect ourselves."

"That's your problem," Blue said.

"You didn't much care what happened when you left me for dead," Isa said.

"Well, we didn't kill you," Yates said.

"Shut the hell up," Evans ordered him.

Blue stood closer to Isa, almost against her arm, watching Isa's hands tense around the silver-plated rifle reflecting in the moonlight.

Yates and Evans struggled to lift McCoy, then started walking in the direction of Carson City.

Blue stood motionless. Her knees felt weak. What had happened finally began to sink in. They just took on three men and won. At least this round. "Do you think we should have let them go?"

Isa started to gather the weapons from the ground. "No, but what choice did we have? I don't know about you, but I couldn't have justified killing them. They're going to be back. Carson City isn't that far from here, and from what you've said, we're not far from your ranch. There's going to be another run-in sooner or later. They're like weeds in the garden. No matter how many times you pull them out, they always come back. I'm worried for you."

Isa's words went into Blue's heart. She worried for her too. Isa must feel something for her, even if it was only a little. It felt good for someone to be concerned for her—for Isa to care.

When they returned to camp, Martha battered them with questions. "Are you sure they won't be back tonight?"

"Well, they won't have any weapons," Blue said. She tried to reassure her. "We're going to hitch up and move on. We're not waiting." The darkness began to ebb. They had about an hour before daylight. "We may as well get started." She yawned. "No reason to stay here any longer than we have to."

They broke camp, Blue's excitement growing with each task. Today they'd arrive at the ranch. Finally, after over two and a half months of travel. What kind of shape would it be in? Could they get the help they'd need? Could she and Martha make a go of it? The questions swirled in her mind as the anticipation of the answers swelled. And the one that seemed to sink the deepest—would Isa stay for a while or leave?

CHAPTER SIX

Isa sat quietly in the saddle enjoying the expression of pleasure on Blue's face as she got off Traveler and took in the view of her property, a vast expanse, from the cleared and developed land to the far mountain ranges. The ranch house faced southeast and was better constructed than Isa expected. A porch ran the length of the front and west side. Pieces of a rocking chair lay scattered underneath one of the two window frames, like someone had slammed it against the wall.

The circular corral to the right of the house had large pieces of fencing missing, and some of the poles were split and lay piled on top of others, like they'd been purposely broken. The barn, north of the corral, appeared sturdy enough, but portions of the roof were caved in. A large pile of cut logs lay stacked just beyond the barn. Probably for buildings that were never completed.

Now the time had come to decide whether to leave. If she stayed and helped Blue settle, the work would be endless. She should go now.

Blue went to the well, primed it, and pumped the handle. She raised her hands in triumph as water gushed out. She removed her hat and filled it, then poured the contents over her head and gasped as the water cascaded. "I'm home," she said, holding her hands out and twirling.

Isa couldn't help but laugh. The sight of Blue drenching herself and dancing at the water pump was something to remember.

Martha went to Blue and hugged her, and then they swung each other in a circle.

"We did it, Martha. We did it." Blue kissed her cheek.

Isa joined them. "It's a fair spread. Good water, plentiful trees, and a mountain range behind. Well suited for what you want. I'm happy for you, Blue."

Blue smiled and went to her. "We wouldn't have made it without your help." She took her in her arms. A full embrace. And all-consuming.

Isa couldn't stop herself. She wrapped her arms around Blue, drawing her in. She was soft, and the feel of her sent a shiver through Isa. In that moment, the ache of loneliness and need was replaced with a deep, abiding comfort. Their cheeks touched. Isa wanted to whisper in her ear. She didn't know what, but she wanted to. Perhaps to speak of her beauty or to tell her she longed to touch her.

Blue stepped away but slid her hand down Isa's arm and clasped her fingers.

Now was the time to speak. "I wouldn't be alive without you and Martha," Isa said. "You taking me in saved *my* life."

Surprisingly, Blue nestled into her once again and whispered in *her* ear. "I owe *you*. Please stay."

And there it was. The decision that had to be made.

She forced herself to step back, separating from Blue. "I'll give it proper thought," she said, holding Blue's gaze. Their hands parted, and the emptiness surged inside Isa once again.

"We've got plenty of daylight left. Let's see the cabin." Blue took off almost at a run.

"Don't get your hopes up," Martha shouted after her. "There'll be wagonloads to do with it being empty for so long." She put her arm around Isa's shoulder as they followed Blue.

"Lord, this is going to be a lot of hard work," Martha said.

Isa nodded. "I hope she didn't take on more than she can handle."

Martha dipped her head. "We'll see."

Blue poked her head out of the opening of one of the windows. "It's not as bad as I expected. Come look."

Isa supposed it was a matter of perspective. Beauty truly was in the eye of the beholder. Dirt, dust, cobwebs, a whole lot of repairs, and scorpions caught her attention. And most likely snakes were holed up under the chimney frame out back.

"It's perfect," Blue said.

Who was she trying to convince?

"I see a lot of repairs," Isa said.

Martha used more diplomacy. "It has possibilities, but Isa is correct. We'll need to do a lot of cleanup here."

"Work is good for the soul," Blue said, running her fingers along the edge of the long, dirt-caked wooden kitchen table.

Isa walked to the fireplace. The hearth was wide and solid, the actual size probably one and a half times the normal width.

Blue stepped beside her. "We'll need to clear out the critters in here first, then start a fire." She rested her foot on the hearth. "I don't see any snake holes. Uncle Silas built a fine fireplace. If they're here, they'll most likely be out back, under the chimney. We'll have to deal with them quickly."

"I'll build a fire with plenty of smoke and take care of what's in here," Martha said. "You two mind where you tread out there and give them serpents plenty of room before you shoot 'em. We'll have snake for supper."

"After we do that, we'll tend to the rest tomorrow," Blue said. She pulled her pistol and checked the load.

No one questioned Isa about if or when she'd be leaving. Clearly, they didn't want her to go. How long was it proper to stay? A few days? A few weeks? She'd feel better if she didn't leave until she knew they were safe and had a decent place to settle into.

She and Blue went to the horses. Isa drew her rifle from the scabbard and followed Blue to the back of the cabin.

Blue eyed the rifle Isa had taken from the men. "Is that your husband's?"

Isa nodded.

"It's a well-made weapon," Blue said. "Your aim is better than mine, but we best wait for the smoke to do its job." She walked about ten yards from the structure and sat. "Isa, I want to talk with you." She patted the space beside her.

The conversation about her leaving was going to happen sooner than Isa had thought. She took a seat on the ground beside Blue and leaned on her rifle. "I imagine you want to know my plans."

Blue nodded. "I hope you understand how badly I want you to stay."

Isa drew a deep breath, feeling the tug of Blue's words, the choice harder than she'd imagined it would be. Where did her future lie? Could she work for Blue and be satisfied? That was the real question. She hadn't seen her Uncle Juan in seventeen years. She had no reason to think he and his children wouldn't welcome her. But they had a large family, with many grown offspring now and families of their own. What if they didn't need her? And how would she earn the money to get there?

Blue interrupted her thoughts. "I can't pay you much, and the work will be from sunup to sundown, but you'll have a place to stay, food to eat, and be among friends."

"I need to go," Isa blurted. "If it doesn't turn out the way I'd hoped, I'll come back." Her words surprised her. Why did she say them? Was it out of fear?

The disappointment on Blue's face showed how much she wanted her to stay.

Blue rose slowly. "I'm sorry to hear that. I wish you'd change your mind."

Isa could say nothing. She knew what would happen if she didn't leave. She already felt the longing and yearning for Blue's affection and touch. She had to go soon, before it was too late, before she became too attached. Loving Blue would only bring heartache and disappointment. She wouldn't spend her life pining after another woman she couldn't have.

"Stay at least a few days." Blue walked away. "We best get to the snakes."

After they'd killed four rattlers, Blue skinned them like she'd done it a thousand times. It was the one thing Isa wouldn't do, couldn't do. The memories forced their way in, almost making her retch. At eight years old, she and her family were traveling home from a trip to see one of her father's family members. They'd stayed four days and were returning. A half-day's journey from their meager ranch they came upon a bloody scene. The more she thought about it, the more vivid the images grew. A family of five had been attacked and left mutilated and dead, their wagon burned, their bodies smoldering. The woman and three children had been skinned. From the tracks and evidence, most likely a small band of marauders had done the deed. She'd found the father about one hundred yards away, gutted, his tongue and eyes cut out. Isa rubbed her forehead, forcing the images to fade.

She left Blue to her chore and went to the pump, washed her face and hands, then walked to the barn. She rested her foot on one of the rails of a stall, placing her arms on the top of the gate, then lowered her head and closed her eyes. Was it a mistake to stay? Or was the mistake in leaving? She was free to do whatever she wanted. She answered to no one. Where did her future lie? In California or here? What did she want in her life? She'd been so focused on getting to her uncle's ranch, she hadn't thought about the deeper questions. Suddenly a twinge of pain streaked through her side. She massaged it gently, keeping her eyes closed. More images from her past began to drift in. Crying on the bed she'd shared with her husband, her tears for Margarette. Her husband's crumpled body as the raiders galloped away. The pain of the bullet in her arm. The weight of her guilt rushed in. She jerked her head up. "No."

Blue's laughter startled her.

"I haven't asked the question yet," Blue said.

Isa turned.

In the cool of the barn, the evening sun offering its last glimpse of light, Blue's smile faded, and the muscles in her face tensed. "You look a fright. Are you well?"

Isa didn't want to hide it, not from Blue. For some illogical reason she wanted to tell Blue everything. Every thought. Every dream. Every disappointment and heartache. But she'd never talked about how she felt or how she wanted to be with a woman more than a man. Or how she wanted to be with her. Was now the time, or would there ever be a proper time? "I just need a good night's rest."

"I'm sure we'll all sleep better tonight. What do you think of the ranch?" Blue's expression intensified. She was serious. She wanted Isa's opinion.

Blue's interest in what she thought settled Isa, calmed her like the sound and feel of a gentle breeze in the pines.

She inspected her surroundings. Leather hitching, an anvil, pitchfork, shovel, and an overturned worn wooden box of tools lay scattered on the dirt floor. Several old hay bales were stacked against a wall. Straw, once in the stalls, had been carried by the wind to wherever anything resisted it—boards, slats, old buckets, the edges of the barn itself. And then she looked at Blue.

The start of a smile formed on Blue's face, then grew into a full grin. "I think you'd be very happy here."

The last rays of the setting sun held Blue in their embrace. She tucked a strand of runaway hair behind her ear. Her eyes seemed to dance as she continued to gaze at Isa, drawing her in, holding her captive.

Could Isa leave?

"Won't you change your mind and stay?" Blue stepped closer, her eyes widening. "Please." She spoke in a half-whisper, full of pleading.

The wind suddenly whipped through the barn and carried the

sound of her voice deeper into Isa. It entered with intensity, sweeping through her. The barn sparrows chirped Blue's plea, shouting it over and over. *Stay! Stay! Stay!*

Should she tell Blue why she shouldn't? Could she explain her hesitation? Her doubt? Her fear?

Silence permeated the space around them. Even the birds stopped their chatter.

Was it better to show her? Then she'd know, and there'd be no doubt.

Isa inched toward Blue. Then closer. She rested her hand on Blue's waist. They were so near, the warmth of Blue's breath caressed Isa's cheek.

Blue's pulse beat rapidly in her neck. The intensity of her gaze penetrated Isa's hesitation.

Isa leaned near and risked it all. She kissed her. Lips warm and wet. Inviting. She kissed deeper.

Blue wrapped her in an embrace, pressing into her, sending heat and need racing in a thousand different directions.

Isa's nipples hardened, aching to be touched.

"Stay," Blue whispered.

Another kiss. This time more heated. Passionate. Desire surging for release.

A startled voice. "Oh, Lord!"

Isa froze.

Blue jumped back.

Martha ran from the barn.

The look of panic on Blue's face burned into Isa.

"What are we going to do?" Blue's question was pleading, overflowing with desperation and confusion.

Isa had no words of solace.

Blue began to pace, wrapping her arms around herself, then covering her face in her hands. "I don't know what to do. What will she think? How can I ever face her?" She ran her hands through her hair. "How can I ever explain this? Damn it."

What could Isa do? Martha had seen them kissing. Would she understand? She'd run from the barn, which meant she must have been shocked at what she'd seen. Of course, it was unexpected.

Isa took a deep breath, forcing it out.

Blue had panicked.

But what should Isa do? She tried to think. How could she help

Blue? "I think it's best if we give Martha a few minutes." She touched Blue's elbow.

Blue recoiled, burying her face in her hands again. "I shouldn't have…We shouldn't have done that." She said it like she'd spit out something vile. She looked afraid and concerned. "I'm sorry. I have to talk with Martha."

When Blue reached the entrance of the barn, she grabbed the frame and glanced back but didn't speak. What was she thinking? She hesitated for a moment, then kept walking.

Isa felt the emptiness and the deafening silence. She could do only one thing now. She went to the wagon, gathered her meager belongings, and carried them toward Adelita.

Decision made.

She unlashed the saddlebags from the horse's back and began to pack. Darkness and uncertainty now covered what had moments ago been hopeful and bright. She retrieved her rifle from behind the cabin and secured it in the scabbard, under the stirrup strap, then watered Adelita.

Self-doubt and guilt flooded her with regret and remorse. Run away! That's what she always did. That's what eased the pain.

CHAPTER SEVEN

Blue's heart pounded as she hurried to the cabin. What would Martha think? What would she say? What did she do? And why did she do it so easily? Yes. She'd wanted to kiss Isa for days. She'd dreamed about doing it. Who wouldn't want to kiss her? She was beautiful, and graceful, and… She grabbed the latch to the door but stopped short of entering. She glanced back toward the barn. She'd left Isa without saying anything. She'd left her standing alone, her eyes full of pain. Should she go to her?

But what could she say? *I don't want you to leave, but let's pretend this kiss didn't happen and life will go on as before.* Her life would never be the same. The world fell off its axis when Isa kissed her. Only a kiss, yet it had changed everything about her. For the first time ever, she didn't feel alone. Isa was there, filling her with want and hope and a sense of belonging.

But what about Martha? If she had to choose, who would it be? It wasn't that simple. Martha was a treasured friend and had been since the time of Blue's youth. But if Martha's husband hadn't been killed cheating at poker, or hadn't gambled their store away, she wouldn't be with Blue.

And Isa? If they hadn't come upon her when they did, would she have died? Even if she hadn't been hurt so badly, they still would have helped her, and then she'd have gone on her way. Circumstances or fate or luck had placed them in that situation.

And now, how should she proceed? She just wanted a decent ranch where she could raise her horses in peace. Why did she have to fight to the death for everything she wanted? Why did it have to be so hard? Now this on top of all of it. Blue's heart sank as she pushed on the door, swinging it open, not knowing what to say or do.

Martha stood at the stove, her back to Blue, fry bread in the pan and a plate of rattlesnake meat beside it on the clapboard. She didn't turn or make a movement of any kind. Would she speak to her? Did she hate her now? Would she want to pack up and leave as soon as possible?

"Martha? Can we talk?" Blue struggled to get the words out. They hung in the air like cobwebs in the corners of the room.

Martha put the spatula down, took the skillet off the stove, and faced her, wiping her hands on her apron. "Sit."

Blue obeyed. Here it came. She braced herself.

Martha poured a cup of coffee and set it in front of her, then sat next to Isa's place setting, reminding Blue someone was missing in this conversation.

"I'm sorry I interrupted your privacy." Martha folded her hands in her lap.

Blue stared at her. Had she heard correctly? *She* was sorry? "You aren't upset?"

"It caught me by surprise, but I'm not upset."

Blue cleared her throat. "I'm sure it did. It surprised me."

Martha chuckled. "No doubt."

The silence grew thick. Blue wanted to swat it away, like flies around honey.

More uncertainty filled Blue's heart. She sucked in a deep breath. "I don't know what to do."

"I don't imagine there's anything you can do," Martha said. "It happened for a reason. The way you two have looked at each other, almost since you met, told me something was afoot."

"Is it strange, Martha. Am I tainted?"

"Tainted?"

"You know…different?"

"Well, it's different, but not unheard of. I've known lots of women who felt like you do. Remember Rebecca Sterling and Annabel Ramsey? They've lived quite happily for as long as I can remember. And Mrs. Hardgrove, over in Clarkston. That wasn't her cousin who lived with her."

"What?"

Martha laughed. "I suppose the rules don't mean a hoot and a holler when it comes to who you want." She took Blue's hand. "We're in for a lot of adventures. My guess is you'll write your own rules. I want you to be happy, Blue. I want you to live a rich, full life. You deserve it. And if Isa makes you happy and brings you the love you've longed for, then I can't fault you for it. This is your home. You say what does and doesn't go on around here."

Blue fought back the emotion. She'd never felt so free. "I don't know what this is that I feel for Isa. I just know I want her here with me."

"I imagine it's the beginnings of love, in one form or another."

"I want to talk to her. I'll eat later." Blue stood and kissed Martha on the head. "My dear friend."

Martha patted her arm. "It's almost dark. I believe I'll call it a night. I managed to clear some space for us to sleep in here. We can make plans in the morning."

Blue nodded and opened the door. "I don't know how long we'll be."

"Don't hurry. Best take your time about things like this."

Blue closed the door behind her, anxious to get to Isa.

The barn was quiet. The fading light cast shadows into every corner. Blue strained to see. "Isa?"

No answer.

She called again, louder this time. Fear gripped her.

Still no answer.

She left the barn and went to where the horses were tied. "Isa?" Her voice rose with her desperation. Then she saw the evidence of what she'd dreaded. Adelita was gone.

"Isa!" She screamed it, her ears aching to hear Isa's response.

"No! No! Isa, come back. Don't go."

But it was too late. She sank to her knees and wept, burying her face in her hands.

Warm fingers touched her shoulders.

Her heart skipped a beat and she whipped around. "Isa?"

There was sadness in Martha's eyes.

Blue's hope drained from her heart like water from the pump.

Martha helped her to her feet and led her inside.

During the long, lonely night, each sound brought an unfulfilled yearning that Isa might return.

The next day dragged on, then stretched into two, then five.

Weeks passed.

Martha and Blue worked from sunup to long past sundown, just as Blue had told Isa they would. But Isa wasn't there. Blue's heart grew harder with each passing day. The more hours she worked, the less pain she felt. But the nights brought longing and dreams of their kiss, the passion, and the feel of Isa close to her.

Blue sat at the kitchen table, staring into her coffee, the morning sun shining through the window. "The barn roof's almost done."

"It's not good for you to labor this hard," Martha said. "You're going to work yourself to death. It's time to go to Carson City and hire some help."

Blue rubbed her blistered hands. "I suppose you're right. The barn needs to be ready for storage, and the stalls need to be repaired for the mares. I'm hoping the foals won't be born later than February or March. We'll leave tomorrow."

A day and a half later in town, Blue stopped by the blacksmith to get some ideas for hired hands. She couldn't believe what Luther told her. "What do you mean no men will work for me?"

He scratched his beard. "Frank Anderson put the word out."

"Why?"

"He's probably hoping to run you off."

"But why? I don't understand."

"Folks are saying you're looking to build up your spread, and he's the he-bull around these parts. He doesn't want any competition."

Blue slapped her hat against her pants. "I'm not competition. Hell, at best I have a few pregnant mares and a run-down ranch. What kind of competition is that?"

Luther shook his head. "I'm telling you, Blue. No one will go against him. And don't bother with any of the other ranchers. He's got them locked up in his pen. Most of them won't buck him."

"Damn him. I've never even met him."

"And you don't want to. If you come across him, you better be ready for a fight. He doesn't care you're a female. I'm surprised he hasn't sent his men to stir you up."

"I think he did when we passed through here on our way to the ranch. At the campsite by the river."

"That was *you*?" He grunted a laugh.

"Yes."

"Well, hell. Those three men work for him, and they never heard the end of it. Travis McCoy, the big fella with the nicked ear, is still complaining about his jaw. You watch your back, 'cause you sure stirred the hornets' nest. Yates said a man was with you. Where is he?"

Blue didn't want to explain that it was Isa. "He's gone. Went off to California." She and Isa had only protected themselves. *Isa.* She dismissed the thought and hurried to the dry goods store. Martha and Nettie were discussing cloth with one of the other female customers.

Martha immediately came to her. "What's wrong?"

Blue pulled her to the side. "We can't get any hires because of Frank Anderson."

"What? Who's he?"

Blue explained.

Nettie looked up and immediately approached them, most likely listening in on part of their conversation. "I heard about that," she said. "Two of his hands were in here last week crowin' about it. Said you'd be stupid to stay in the area and might as well go back to where you came from."

"Well, we'll see about that. I need some paper and a pencil," Blue said.

Nettie fetched the requested items and handed them to her.

Blue wrote what she wanted, then gave it to Nettie. "Post this on your board, would you?" She turned to Martha. "I've got to go to the telegraph office."

Nettie read the ad, then frowned. "I'll post it, but there's going to be trouble."

"There's already trouble," Blue said. "I'll be damned if I'll let Frank Anderson push me around."

Martha snatched the ad from Nettie and read it aloud.

Women wanted for ranch work and such.
Must be able to ride and willing to work.
Fair wages.
Contact Blue Hutchings, Carson City, Nevada

"Well, hell. Just what we need, Blue. What are you doing?" Martha asked.

"The best I can under the circumstances."

Blue would tackle this setback just as she'd done all the rest. She was getting used to taking things head-on.

CHAPTER EIGHT

It'd been six weeks. Isa worked at the Wyman spread, a half-day's ride from Blue. She couldn't bring herself to go any farther. Every day she told herself as soon as she had enough money she'd go on to California, but as time passed, her ache and longing for Blue grew deeper. She wanted to settle things between them, at least talk to Blue, explain why she'd left, and then she'd head on.

She and two of the hands made the day's ride to Carson City for supplies. When she entered the dry goods store, Blue's post caught her eye. What had happened? Why was she hiring women?

"She's something," Nettie said as she passed Isa. "I reckon you men folk caused this."

"How so?" Isa asked, pulling her hat lower.

"She had no choice. No women have inquired so far, but as soon as someone asks, I'm sending her to Blue's. I don't care what Anderson does."

"Frank Anderson?"

Nettie told her the entire story.

Isa and the others loaded the wagon with the supplies and left the store, hearing more gossip than she knew what to do with. Would it hurt to ride to Blue's and see for herself? She might need help. Isa scoffed at the thought. She should be on her way to California. She'd already wasted too much time pining after her. What if she went there and Blue kicked her off her property? Or Martha did? But Blue needed women to work for her. Isa had skills. She could do the job. Why not hire her? It was a big *why not.* The thought of Blue not wanting her there gnawed at her stomach for hours.

She made her decision when she got back to the Wyman ranch, said her good-byes, and headed for Blue's.

Each hour on the trail brought her closer to Blue but filled her with greater dread. Would she be welcome? What would Blue say? What would Martha do? How would Blue manage with Frank Anderson determined to drive her out?

Anderson and six of his men had passed by the Wyman ranch two weeks before. Isa didn't know what Anderson and Wyman were talking about, but it had ended in a heated argument.

All ranch hands, no matter their feelings or situation, sided with their employer. So, when the argument broke out, Wyman's four ranch hands, including Isa, gathered around him, guns at the ready.

Anderson and his men rode off, but not before he gave Mr. Wyman a clear warning. "Do it, or you'll find yourself on the wrong side."

"The hell I will," Wyman yelled back. "I won't do that to another rancher."

Now Isa had a fair idea of what had gone on between them. Anderson had ordered Wyman to stay clear of Blue's ranch and offer no assistance.

She needed to see her, if only to make sure she was all right. Then, if she wasn't welcomed, she'd go on to California.

She stopped Adelita on a small rise above Blue's ranch, immediately seeing Blue by the barn. In that moment she realized how much she'd missed her. Her heart raced, and her hands began to tremble. She took a settling breath and urged Adelita forward. Whatever happened, she'd have to accept it.

As she got closer, she forced her gaze from Blue and took in her surroundings. Blue's three mares and a dozen or so other horses were in the repaired corral. The barn roof looked half-patched.

When Blue saw her, she stopped mid-step and stiffened, as if she'd suddenly transformed into a stone statue.

Isa halted and dismounted. She held Adelita's reins and walked forward, uncertain and ready to run.

Blue walked toward her, stopping about two steps in front of her. Was she glad to see her? Or so mad she had to keep her distance? Isa couldn't tell.

Blue removed her hat, and then, to Isa's surprise, Blue smiled, and her green eyes sparkled in the sunlight.

"Isa, you're back." She stepped closer and embraced her. "You're here."

Isa let go of Adelita's reins and threw her arms around Blue. "I couldn't stay away any longer. I'm sorry I left. I didn't know what to do."

Blue hugged her tighter, her arms strong and reassuring. "It's all right. You're here now. I can't believe it. I thought you'd left for good. I'm so glad you're here." She stepped back and held her at arm's length, inspecting her.

Isa laughed. "I'm a fright."

"No! You're beautiful, even dressed as a man. Come in. Let's get you something to eat."

Isa tied Adelita to the corral post.

Blue wrapped her arm around her waist as they walked to the cabin. She stopped. "You're staying, aren't you? You won't leave?"

Isa hugged her. "Yes. I'm staying, if it's agreeable."

Blue's smile widened.

"Will Martha be opposed?"

Blue laughed. "No! I'll tell you later all about what happened after you left. For now, know everything's good." She led her by the hand into the house. "Martha, look who I found."

Martha turned from the stove, and when she recognized Isa, a huge smile washed over her face. "Oh, Isa, you've come back. How grand." She set the wooden spoon on the side of the stew pot and came to her. "How wonderful." She hugged her.

Being welcomed and feeling like she belonged filled her with peace. This was where she needed to be—not in California but with Blue.

"Thank you, Martha." Isa turned to Blue. "You've done well."

"It's only a start, and it's slow going," Blue said. "Sit. Martha, what can we feed this hungry wanderer?"

Isa laughed.

Martha brought her a biscuit and some hot stew, and Blue sat with her as she ate.

"As usual, your food is delicious, Martha," Isa said.

Blue sat quietly, not taking her eyes off her. What was she thinking?

After Isa had eaten her fill, they talked about her experiences since she'd left them.

Blue stood. "I want to show you around the property."

Isa grabbed her hat as Blue took her by the hand and led her outside.

Blue saddled Traveler, and they rode northwest for a time.

The beauty of what Isa saw struck her deeply. The fading pink and azure of the sky, mountain ranges, thick ponderosa pine. The property was abundant with pasture and water.

Blue pointed to the mountains. "I filed with the surveyor's office in Carson City to make sure the paperwork and deed were in order before Martha and I left Texas. There's been rumors of land-grabbers trying to take over illegally." She hesitated. "I've had some problems. There's a rancher named Frank Anderson. Remember the three men we had trouble with?"

Isa nodded.

"I was informed they work for him."

Isa touched her arm. "Nettie Morris told me about it when I stopped by the dry goods store in Carson City. I saw your notice."

"Did she recognize you?"

"Not at all."

Blue nodded. "I don't know how it'll turn out, but I need some help."

"I'll help you."

Blue took her hat off and laid it over the saddle horn, then ran her fingers through her hair. She studied Isa.

"What is it?" Isa asked.

"I'd welcome your help, of course." Blue surveyed her property. "This land makes you hard. I imagine it will weather me into an old woman by the time I'm forty. I can't afford to waste what precious time I have." She rubbed her thigh, then looked directly at Isa. "I have a feeling for you. I couldn't get you out of my mind. It's only been in the last couple of weeks I've been able to sleep. Does that offend you?"

Isa placed her hand on Blue's. "No! Not at all. I like that you thought about me. You were on my mind, also."

"Why did you leave?"

Isa took a breath, then shifted in the saddle. She avoided Blue's watchful eyes. How open should she be?

She'd never get where she wanted with Blue unless she told her what was in her heart. "Because I was afraid."

"Of what? I've never met any woman with the kind of grit you have."

Was it time to be completely honest, or should she hold back? They'd both suffered from being apart. Blue had told her how she felt. Could she do the same? Could she be as bold as Blue? The risk of being hurt sent a chill to her bones. She'd been alone for so long. Was she ready to open her heart?

The only way she'd know was if she told Blue. "I have a tender feeling for you also." She forced the words out. "I felt it the moment I saw you. And the thought of you not feeling that way in return sends terror into my heart. I don't want to scare you off, but I think it's best to tell you how I feel."

"I'm open to it," Blue said.

They urged the horses onward.

"I left because I worried there'd be backlash. I didn't want to cause you any trouble. I knew if I stayed, I'd have to face how I felt about you. I didn't think I was ready. Being away forced me to admit how I feel." Isa halted Adelita and turned to Blue. "I can't dismiss my emotions about you. I don't want to hide them."

They rode without speaking, not in an uncomfortable silence, but more like an unspoken interlude for the needed time to come to terms with what they'd both revealed. A respite for it to settle in and take hold. They stopped at the edge of a grouping of pine trees. Blue got off Traveler. Isa dismounted and followed. They walked the horses into the small forest, the pine needles soft beneath their feet. The birds sang, and the afternoon sun streamed in. The rich scent of foliage hung in the cooler air.

Blue stopped and tied Traveler to a branch. Isa did the same with Adelita.

Blue sat on a thick bed of pine needles and patted the space beside her. When they were settled, she took Isa's hand. "I don't know what's going to happen between us. Whatever this is, I want it. I somehow need it. All my life I've had an ache I couldn't stop, a deep feeling of loneliness that no man could fill. I knew what I needed when you kissed me. Every night I saw you in my mind. I thought about our kiss and the feelings I had when you were close to me.

"Life is short, and Lord knows it's not easy. I don't want you to leave again. Stay with me. I have a big dream for myself, and I want you in it. We can work this land together. We'll build an honorable, good life here. I don't know about love and such things. All I know is I don't want to be away from you. Throw your truck in with mine, and we'll make a go of it."

Isa couldn't believe what she heard. It was reasonable to hope Blue felt something for her, that she'd be welcomed and not thrown off her property, but this was beyond anything she'd imagined.

Blue laughed. "Did you lose your ability to speak?"

Isa smiled. "You've stunned me."

Blue repositioned and pulled her close. "I want you here with me. Don't say no. I couldn't bear it."

"What will Martha say about it?" Isa asked.

"Martha? Lord, Isa. She's the one who set me straight about how I feel about you. She told me it was my life, my property, and my rules."

"Blue, I'd hoped you'd feel as I did, but I…"

Blue traced the contour of Isa's cheek with her fingertips. "Will you stay with me?" she whispered.

Desire and yearning swept over Isa. She brushed her lips over Blue's and longed to be closer, to touch, to caress. "My beautiful Caroline, I will."

Blue cradled her in her arms. "Things will work out. You'll see." She stood and lifted Isa by the hand.

Isa kissed her, the wet of Blue's mouth drawing her in, deepening the need to be with her.

Blue returned her kiss and pressed into her, her mouth hot and demanding, but then she withdrew. "We best ride back."

Isa caught a breath. She didn't want to stop, but they needed to return. "We'll have good days and bad. One thing's certain, though."

"What's that?" Blue asked.

"Heaven help anyone who stands in your way."

They laughed and strolled side by side from the woods.

CHAPTER NINE

With Isa's return came the high desert heat of July.
As the weeks passed, the labor and temperatures demanded all they could give, but Blue was pleased with the progress of their work at the ranch. She sat on a wooden bucket in the shade of an oak tree.

The first woman to answer her ad, Henrietta Scottsboro from Carson City, sat next to her on a log. She was dressed in a new pair of dungarees and a gray cotton shirt. She'd arrived on a roan gelding that had bad knees and looked like he'd run out of steam long before noon.

"How much did you pay for that animal?" Blue asked. She didn't want to embarrass Henrietta but needed to know how much horse sense she had.

"Twenty dollars. And I paid fifteen for the saddle and rig."

"Well, I hate to tell you this, sister, but you got took. The rig is pretty beat-up, and from the looks of the horse, it'll last one day on a roundup, maybe."

Henrietta put her elbows on her knees and plopped her face into her hands. "I suspected ol' man Peterson wasn't being honest. I should've known better. That damn horse did nothing but stumble and lollygag all the way here."

"It's because he's exhausted, and his knees are aching. I imagine he can't tolerate much. You're lucky you made it this far," Blue said.

Henrietta sighed heavily.

"How much ranch experience do you have?"

Henrietta sat straight. "I can cook fair enough. Mostly I've been on my back."

"What?"

"Look, Miss Blue. I've got to be honest with you. I worked at Mrs. Victoria's place on the edge of town."

"Oh! Um…Have you ever ridden?"

Henrietta cackled. "Sure, plenty of times."

Blue couldn't help herself. The sound of Henrietta's laughter made her chuckle. "I mean a horse. Have you ever ridden a horse—cow-punching, driving, or on a roundup?"

"No. But I grew up on a farm and did plowing with my pa. And I can ride a horse." She pointed to the roan. "Just not that one."

Blue tried to hide her exasperation. If Henrietta was any indication of the type of women who were going to show up for a job, she'd never get any work done. "I'd like to hire you, but you don't have the experience I need."

"I can learn, Miss Blue. Give me a chance. I'm a hard worker. I can sew and cook some, and I can drive a team."

"I appreciate that, but I need riders."

Henrietta's eyes filled with tears. "I got nowhere else to go, Miss Blue. I can't go back to the whorehouse. I won't. Men have pawed and snorted after me all my life. I won't let them do it anymore. I promise I'll do whatever you ask, and I won't make a fuss or be bad tempered. I'm a fair shot. One of my customers taught me in exchange for a roll in the hay."

Blue rubbed her chin. Henrietta was probably in her early twenties. Her long, brown hair strayed from being tucked under her new brimmed hat. She seemed determined enough, but she had dark circles under her eyes and a worldly look about her, like life had beat her down and dumped her on the side of the road. Would she have a full day's work in her? Would she be worth her salt?

Blue pointed to the ranch house. "Why don't you go inside and visit with Martha and get something to eat? I'll think on it for a spell."

Henrietta stood. "Thanks, Miss Blue. And would you call me Etta?"

"Sure enough."

She waited until Etta entered the house and then went to the back of the barn where Isa was shoeing one of the new geldings.

Isa laid the hoof nipper into the dilapidated wooden supply box and stretched, then rubbed the small of her back with both hands.

"Are you about done?" Blue asked.

"Just ready to put on his last shoe. Traveler and Adelita were easy. This boy is giving me fits. He's dancing around like he wants a partner."

Blue stroked the buckskin's neck. "He's going to be a fine addition. Do you need some help?"

"If you've got time, stand there and calm him for me. How'd the job interview go?"

Blue tripped on her words when she tried to explain.

"That bad." Isa continued her work. "She doesn't look like she's got much meat on her."

"She's got spunk, that's for sure. But I don't know if she's cut out for the type of work we need her to do."

"What's her experience?"

"None."

"Hmm."

"That's it? That's all you've got to say? I was hoping you'd help me decide."

"I can't decide from nothing. Tell me about her," Isa said.

Blue reviewed what she'd learned about Etta.

Isa stuck the hoof nails in her side pocket and positioned herself, lifted the foreleg of the gelding, and began to fit the shoe. "Sounds to me like she'll be a mercy hire."

"I know. I think I'll try her on a temporary basis. If she doesn't work out, she's gone."

"This is your outfit, plain and simple," Isa said. "You'll have to ride roughshod over whoever you hire. Your word is law. Are you going to be able to cut her from the herd if she doesn't get the job done?"

"Oh, Lord, I hope so."

Isa chuckled.

"But you're my partner in this. I was hoping you'd take the lead in such things."

Isa finished the horse's shoe and then lowered his hoof and patted his chest. She swiped the dripping sweat from her forehead with her shirtsleeve.

Blue went to the bucket and brought her a ladle of water.

Isa drank it all, then wiped her mouth and handed the scoop back to Blue. "Well, I say give her a try. It's not like we have a lot of women lining up for the job. By the way, we're going to need to get someone to do the farrier work in the future. It's going to take too much time. The more horses we get, the more we'll need the help."

Isa was right. They couldn't do everything by themselves. Had Anderson gotten to the tradespeople also?

"The bunkhouse will need to be done soon," Blue said. "I'm hoping we can get a crew in here from one of the ranches Frank Anderson hasn't gotten to yet. If there are any. It shouldn't take more than a couple of days with a few men. But it's not going to be easy with him riding roughshod over every man in the area."

"I met some good hands at the Wyman ranch," Isa said. "But I'm not sure if they'd be willing to go against Anderson. I know Mr. Wyman won't allow him to dictate what he does or doesn't do. I doubt they'd mind working for a woman, especially you." Isa smiled. "They'll be shocked when they find out I'm not a man."

"There's some advantage for you to keep on posing as one," Blue said.

Isa shrugged. "I'm sure, but it's hot in all that extra clothing. I don't fancy pretending." Isa stopped her work and looked at Blue, her gaze going into her. "Unless you really need me to."

Blue saw through her. Isa didn't want to, and Blue wasn't about to make her do something she had no interest in. Besides, she liked seeing her as she was. "No. You dress the way you like. We'll deal with whatever comes our way just as we are. I'll need a six-bed bunkhouse built."

"*Six*? Not four?"

"I don't want to be putting up another one in the next several years. We've got a lot of work ahead of us. Right now, I can't afford anything but building a place for workers to stay in and finishing the repairs on the barn. I'm hoping once word gets out about my stud, I'll be able to hire him out. I imagine we can barter for most of what we need for the rest of the year. The garden and the fruit trees Uncle Silas planted should yield a good crop. I'll bless his efforts the rest of my life."

"The irrigation system looks solid," Isa said. "If we don't have any trouble, we should manage."

Blue patted the horse's rump as she walked past. "If you need any help, give a holler. I'm going to go hire someone who doesn't have any experience but wants to learn. I think I'll lend her one of the other horses until she can get a better one. She can work it off. She can't go riding around on the pitiful one she came in on."

"Careful. She may end up wanting to work it out on her back." Isa laughed.

"Oh, you're funny!" Blue grinned as she left for the house.

She stopped by the corral and inspected Etta's horse. She unsaddled him and looked at his mouth, felt his knees, and ran her hand along his spine. He flinched. He needed to have his shoes pulled, his hooves trimmed, and his knees treated.

"I think with a little rest and some good feed and care, you'll be a lot better in a week or two." She rubbed his head and then led him to the corral, unbridled him, and shut the gate. She leaned on the railing and watched.

He walked to the lead mare and nuzzled her. She nipped. He moved away to the others. The herd would need to be led to pasture to graze and get acclimated to the land. They needed the freedom to roam, exercise, and adjust. She inspected the house and the barn. So much work still to be done. But Isa was here, and it brought comfort knowing she would be here to share it. But would she stay if everything became too much of a struggle?

She went to the house and got a cup of coffee.

Etta sat at the table, eating the last of a plate of beans and cornbread.

"When you're finished, Etta, come out to the porch."

They sat on the steps.

Etta remained quiet, her face muscles tense. She clasped both hands around her cup.

Would Blue regret hiring her? What if Etta ended up more trouble than she was worth? She watched her for a few minutes, then decided that she'd never know unless she gave her a chance to prove herself. "You're hired on a temporary basis for one month."

Etta's shoulders relaxed.

"You'll get paid at the end of the month, or I'll give you what's owed if it doesn't work out. If you don't measure up, I'll have to let you go."

Etta jumped up, slopping her coffee onto the planks. "That's fine, Miss Blue. Just fine." She wiped her hand on her pants.

"You can start now. I want you to clean up your saddle and such. What you need is in the barn. Your leather rig needs soaked and soaped. I imagine with a few weeks' rest that horse of yours will perk up a bit. Meanwhile, you can ride one of the others. My partner, Isa, is around the back of the barn. Go introduce yourself and get acquainted. Help her with anything she needs. You'll also help Martha. You can stay in the barn for now. Once the bunkhouse's built, you can claim which bed you want. Martha will ring the dinner bell when it's time to eat."

"Thanks, Miss Blue. I'll get to it right away." She handed Blue her remaining coffee. "You saved my life, Miss Blue." She dashed off the porch and headed for the barn.

Blue went inside and sat at the table.

Martha's hands were covered in dough as she made bread. "Don't look so worried. Etta's going to be a good addition. You'll see."

"I hope so. I can't afford to waste a penny. She said she could shoot. I forgot to ask her if she brought a pistol."

"What's bothering you so?"

"Just thinking." Blue looked at the ceiling, then the walls and into the rooms. The house was sturdy and built to add on to. Part of the frame was stone. Martha slept in the bedroom across from the fireplace. Blue wanted her to have it so she'd feel a part of the ranch. Eventually, they'd have other bedrooms. But for now, Blue and Isa slept in the loft. It was an arrangement Blue enjoyed. Isa's soft sounds while she slumbered comforted her, and on occasion they talked long into the night.

Martha kept the house clean and inviting. A china cabinet, filled with Blue and Martha's wares, stood against the kitchen wall. The pantry was next to it. Martha had managed to collect about four dozen of the new Mason jars with screw-on rings and rubber lids. Blue didn't trust them, but Martha had unwavering faith in their safety.

To the left of the fireplace were two rocking chairs and a wooden case filled with books. Martha's collection always fascinated Blue. One in particular stood out. *Miss Beecher's Domestic Receipt Book.* Martha didn't do anything without consulting it. The large dining table had a bench on each side, and there was a worktable in front of the stove. Someday they'd have the water inside the house. Martha had also brought three knotted rugs from Texas. Blue went to the bookcase and pulled out the writing pad and pencil. She sat and began a list of their inventory.

July 18, 1868

　　　Six pullets, one rooster, a milking cow, three broodmares—foals due in early spring, a stud, eight stock mares, five geldings, Traveler and Adelita. One two-bowed wagon with rigging, various and sundry barn tools, eight fruit trees—four apple, two cherry, and two pomegranates.

"Martha, what do we need to get through the rest of the year?"

Martha filled the loaf pans with dough, covered them, and set them aside. She washed her hands in the bucket, then poured herself a cup of coffee and sat at the table next to Blue. "We'll need to buy more stores, especially beans, dried beef, flour, sugar, salt, and such. I'll need more canning jars. The garden was planted late but hopefully will yield quite nicely. I'll make the list of what we'll need to purchase. How many should I plan to feed?"

"I 'spect not more than six or seven, including the three of us."

Blue checked the leather pouch inside her shirt.

"You can keep that in the cabinet or in one of the books. It'll be safe," Martha said.

"I'm so used to carrying it around I'd feel naked without it."

Martha patted her hand. "I'll watch over it."

"I'd feel better if I hid it somewhere outside."

"Are you expecting trouble?"

Blue stretched her neck, then her shoulders. "I think we should be prepared."

"You can use one of the tin coffers on my dresser in the bedroom if you'd like."

Blue nodded. "I saw some loose stones on the far side of the house. I imagine that would be a good spot for it. That way you'll know where it is in case you need it."

Martha nodded. "I suppose it's best. Although I don't like to think of such things as me needing it without you."

Blue took her hand. "We're building a dream, Martha, and it won't be easy. Trouble is sure to come our way." Blue stood. "But we can hold our own. First of the week I'll be going to the Wyman ranch and try to arrange for workers to build the bunkhouse, then on to Carson City and get supplies. I'll take Etta with me. We'll probably be gone three or four days."

"You and Isa go. I can take care of things here with Etta."

"Best not," Blue said. "Isa worked for Wyman. She'd be recognized."

"I still think it'd be better if Isa went with you." Martha said. "You never know what kind of trouble is underfoot." Martha's facial expression tightened, and her eyes narrowed. "Please reconsider, Blue."

"Etta can help me," Blue said. "She needs to learn what's expected of her before she gets too comfortable and takes us for a slippery group." She patted Martha's shoulder. "Besides, I'd rather Isa be here with you, in case *you* run into trouble. I trust her with your life. And mine."

"All right then. I'll make the list."

Blue went behind the barn and watched as Isa and Etta completed their chores. Isa tied the buckskin and started cleaning the mess from shoeing. Etta mucked the stalls.

"I 'spect Miss Blue will get on well with this ranch," Etta said. "But she'll have her hands full with Frank Anderson. He's mean-tempered and likes to throw his weight around. I saw him draw down on a man because he didn't get out of the way fast enough to his liking. All of us girls ran for cover when he wanted a poke. He rode us hard. The only good thing was that he didn't last but a second." Etta laughed.

"I imagine you're glad to be done with that sort of thing," Isa said. She tossed the hoof pick into the wooden box, untied the buckskin, and led him toward the corral. She grinned when she saw Blue.

"Gawd knows it," Etta said, continuing her work.

"Etta," Blue called.

Etta stopped raking abruptly and straightened. "Yes, Miss Blue?"

"You'll be coming with me on Monday. We'll be gone several days. Pack accordingly. You'll drive the wagon," Blue said.

"Yes, ma'am."

"Are you going into town?" Isa asked.

"I'm heading to the Wyman ranch to see if I can get some hands to build the bunkhouse, then on to Carson City for supplies."

"Would you like me to come with you?"

"Yes. I would. But I think it's best you stay here with Martha in case there's trouble."

Isa nodded. "I see your point." She strode past Blue and smiled. "You never know what Martha's going to get into."

Blue laughed. "We'll attach the bows on the wagon to cover the supplies."

The buckskin reared and pulled on his halter. Isa tightened her grip on his rope and circled him. "He's still a little skittish. I'll work him some while you and Etta are gone. He should be a little more settled by the time you get back. He's going to be a handful when we saddle-break him."

Blue stroked his neck. "Probably, but he's a fine animal. I'll need help with the rest of the fencing around the orchard. The horses will be ready to be turned out when we get back, and I don't want them getting into the fruit."

"Sure enough. And while you're gone, I'll start repairing the stalls. Adelita and Traveler will fare better in there. I don't want them picking up any bad habits from the herd. They can stay in the corral once we let the group out."

Isa turned the buckskin into the corral with the rest of the horses. She and Blue leaned on the rails and watched them.

Blue eased next to her. "I really wish you were going with me, but I do need you here."

"I know," Isa said. "I understand. You watch yourself, though."

"I will."

The dinner bell rang.

The day had brought change to the ranch. A new worker— hopefully. And the possibility of getting the bunkhouse built. It was a good day. Blue wished she didn't have to leave Isa. She didn't want to be separated from her again, even for a short while. But it was best she remained at the ranch with Martha. Trouble was sure to show up at their door.

CHAPTER TEN

Blue and Etta left at sunup. By afternoon, the light easterly wind blew puffs of dark-gray clouds toward them.

Etta inspected the sky. "Looks like rain."

"I imagine so," Blue said. "We should get to the Wyman ranch soon."

Etta was more capable than she appeared, which had surprised Blue. She looked pale and weak, yet she drove the wagon with skilled hands. They stopped for lunch and ate the cornbread and dried beef jerky Martha had packed.

"How many women do you think will come looking for work?" Etta asked.

"I'm not sure. I hope at least a couple more. There's a lot of work to be done."

"Are you a widow, Miss Blue?"

Blue found her question disturbing. Did it imply she looked like a widow? Old? Worn out? At twenty-five she sometimes felt beyond what she reckoned a twenty-five-year-old female should feel. All she really knew were men's perspectives. Her father's. Businessmen who came to trade or buy. Other cattlemen. She'd rarely had contact with younger females growing up. She'd admired other women, found them beautiful and longed for their company, if for nothing more than to exchange ideas and thoughts. Isa was the first she'd taken a sure interest in. *Their kiss.* The thought of it appeared full force to center stage. The want and hunger to touch her and explore the unknown-yet-imagined pressed into her. She yearned for more, but all the work left no time or energy. She'd have to wait. The calm of a deep breath shoved the thoughts away. "No. I've never married. You?"

Etta snorted. "I've had plenty of opportunities, but to tell the truth, the thought of being with a man, sharing a life with him, just never appealed to me." She smiled. "I know what you're thinkin'. If I don't like men, why'd I do what I did?" She bent her knees and wrapped her arms around them, then rested her chin. "It just kind of slipped up on me. I was born in Ohio." A pensive expression crossed her face. She surveyed the expanse above. "We had a good farm, and we had a good life. We laughed a lot and sang, but everything changed when the war started." She drew her knees closer and scowled. "Like everyone else, we struggled to make ends meet. I had a little sister and brother, but they died of typhus. Then Pa was killed at Yorktown in the spring of '62.

"After the war, everywhere I looked, people were crying and angry. My ma remarried. But within a year he was drunk most of the time. One night he took a liking to me, and when he tried to force himself on me, my ma went after him. Her reward was a beating so bad she died the next day." Etta's voice filled with anger, and she stiffened. "There ain't no justice for womenfolk. No one cared what he did. Once I realized it, I got on a locomotive and came west. I kept riding that train until I couldn't go no further. Then I bought a ticket on a stagecoach and ended up in Carson City. I tried to find work. First as a seamstress, then as a maid in a boardinghouse. I finally gave up and went to Mrs. Victoria's. She was glad to feed me, clothe me...and put me on my back." Her countenance changed from anger to something else. Despair?

"You didn't give up, Etta. You did what you had to do to survive."

"You don't think poorly of me, Miss Blue?"

"I won't judge you, Etta. I'm just glad you found your way to us."

Etta smiled. "Me too."

"How old are you?" Blue asked.

Etta sighed. "Twenty."

So young to have had so many harsh experiences already. "We best move on," Blue said. "We have some long days ahead of us."

They prepared to leave.

Would Etta judge her or Isa? They'd only kissed. Yet it wasn't just a kiss. It was more like a declaration of their feelings for one another. Isa's voice and the softness of her touch filled Blue as her thoughts drifted.

The sun was a little past mid-sky by the time they reached the Wyman ranch. Mr. and Mrs. Wyman welcomed them. Their ranch was well established, with corrals, a barn, bunkhouse, and blacksmith shop. The ranch house was large, but not as large as Blue's.

They sat at the kitchen table, coffee cups in hand.

"So, you're Silas Hutchings's niece?" Mr. Wyman asked.

"Yes. I only met him once, years ago when he came to visit us in Texas."

"He was a good man. Kind and generous. It wasn't right what happened. You watch yourself. Anderson will do whatever he wants. We all know it was him that did Silas wrong."

"Why hasn't anyone held him responsible, Mr. Wyman?"

"Call me Jacob," he said. "You've got to understand these parts. Local law has barely taken hold. We were just made a state a few years ago. Up until then we were part of the Utah Territory. We have federal marshals, but it takes forever to get them here. Since the war ended, the country's trying to find its balance again. And a strong local law and government are what's going to steady us. Until that happens in these parts, those that can, do what they want.

"It takes God-fearing, strong people to make a go of it," Jacob said. "Anderson is bullheaded. He has money. And he's mean. He's got himself some men, and he thinks he can do whatever he wants. There's a group of us ranchers who will stand together. We'd be pleased for you to join us, Blue."

"I'm in favor of what's right and fair, and if that's what all of you are trying to do, then I'll stand with you."

"Good. That's very good. Now, about your bunkhouse. I can't spare any men. I only have three. One left not too long ago, a hard worker, but I don't know where he went."

Blue knew he was talking about Isa.

"Virgil Pettiman, about seven miles southwest of my spread, can probably help you. He has four strapping boys. You plan to range your horses?"

"Yes. As soon as I can I'll turn them out. Why?"

"You best brand them. My guess is Anderson will run you out any way he can, and stealing your horses isn't beneath him. Virgil also does metal work, and he can make you a brand if you need one."

"I brought my own brand from Texas. My father had it made for me a few years ago. Why does Anderson hate me so much?"

"It started with your Uncle Silas. From what he told me, it has to do with the size of your property and what's on it. You have the best water this side of the Truckee River, and the tributary runs right through your boundaries. Anderson threatened to dam up the creek, but he never went through with it."

Blue stood. "Thank you for your advice and friendship, Jacob."

"We'll do what we can to help you, Blue, but I'm afraid most of the ranchers around these parts have troubles of their own right now. Watch your back. And if you get into a desperate situation, send someone, and we'll come a-runnin'." Jacob grinned and shook her hand.

Blue and Etta made their way to the Pettiman ranch. Another fine spread with several buildings and a large ranch house.

Etta stopped the wagon, and Blue dismounted Traveler.

A stocky woman with strands of gray hair sticking out over her ears and a full smile on her face greeted them from the porch. She wiped her hands on a white cotton apron. "Afternoon. Don't see many women traveling alone in these parts."

Blue introduced herself and Etta and asked to speak to Mr. Pettiman.

"I'm Pearl, his wife. He's out back in the shop." She pointed.

Two young girls, about six and eight, joined her on the porch.

Blue said hello and introduced herself and Etta.

The girls giggled.

"These are my tads, Sabrina and Sally." Pearl motioned to Blue. "I 'spect you have business with my husband. Etta, would you like to join us in the kitchen?"

Etta nodded and went with Pearl, as Blue made her way to the shop.

She heard hammering and then a man's voice.

"Not with that length, son. Wider and smoother."

She entered the building to find three boys and the man who Blue assumed was Virgil Pettiman.

One of the boys, about fourteen, with a tuft of thick, brown hair, held a hammer in his hand and stopped working on a metal strip. The other boys, both taller in size, stood next to him.

"It's because he's left-handed, Pa," the older boy said. "He can't get the angle."

The young man next to him laughed.

"He'll get it. He just has to adjust," the man said. He glanced at Blue as she entered and motioned for the young man with the hammer to stop. "Howdy."

He seemed gentle and friendly. Blue liked him instantly. "Mr. Pettiman?"

His smile grew wider. "Yep. Virgil. These are my boys—Sam,

Ben, and Nate. Morgan's out with the horses." He beamed with evident pride in his sons by the way he introduced them. Each nodded and greeted her.

"I'm Blue Hutchings. Jacob Wyman sent me. He said you might be able to build my bunkhouse."

"When do you need it done?" He took off his gloves and walked over to her.

"As soon as you can."

He scratched his head. "How far away are you?"

"Almost directly west, about half a day's ride."

"Did you say Hutchings?"

"Yes. I'm Silas Hutchings's niece."

"Well, I'll be derned. So, you're at the Hutchings spread."

"Yes. My uncle homesteaded it for my father."

"Is your father there now?"

"No. He passed a while ago. I've come to make a go of it."

"Well, good for you. Are there any menfolk about?"

"No. Just me and a few other women. I tried to hire men, but no one will work for me. I'm hoping you can help. I'll pay you a fair wage to put up the building." Blue grew anxious. If he wouldn't do it, she'd have to find a way herself, and she wasn't experienced enough to take on that kind of job.

He looked her over for a long time. "It takes a lot of grit to do what you're doing without any menfolk. I imagine you've got your hands full." He turned to his boys. "You gents finish up here and then go help your brother with the horses. Supper should be ready soon."

The air filled with the words, "Yes, Pa."

Virgil walked Blue to the house.

She and Etta were invited for supper and to spend the night. Virgil and Blue agreed on a price to build the bunkhouse. He said they'd leave for her ranch the next morning. She paid him half the agreed-upon price and told him she'd give him the final payment when the job was completed. He complimented her on her business sense.

On the way to Carson City the following day, she and Etta stopped at the campsite she'd stayed at on the way to the ranch. Two other wagons were already camped. They said their pleasantries and passed the night without incident.

When they arrived at Carson City the next afternoon, it was a different matter.

She'd managed to order the supplies they needed. Etta had pulled the wagon to the back for loading. Halfway through the job, Frank Anderson rode in. A big man, strong arms, a full head of dark hair, jet-black eyes. And he wasn't alone. Two of the three men who'd accosted Isa and Blue by the river were with him. And they recognized her.

"She's the one," said Travis McCoy, the man with the nicked ear. Bill Evans rode beside him.

Where was the third man? Yates? The one she'd shot.

Mr. Morris checked off Blue's order list as she and his hired assistant, Thomas, continued to load the items.

Anderson moved his horse closer to Blue's wagon where Etta was seated. "Morris, I thought you and I had an understanding."

All activity stopped.

"And I thought I made it clear that I will sell to the public, no matter who they are," Morris said.

So, not everyone yielded to Anderson's demands. Blue straightened and faced him. They were at eye level, she on the dock, he on his horse.

"You've got your uncle in you," Anderson said. He moved his mount closer to Etta and tipped his hat "Well, look at you, pretty pants. Didn't expect to see you here. Why don't you run on along to Victoria's and take those men's clothes off? I'll be there shortly to show you what a real man can do." He grabbed himself and laughed.

Evans and McCoy howled.

"Go to hell," Etta spit out.

They were in it now. If Blue gave even an inch, Anderson would have the advantage.

He raised his hand to strike Etta.

Without thinking, Blue drew her pistol and aimed at him. "Mister, you either back away or I'll shoot you dead."

Evans and McCoy drew their weapons and aimed at Blue.

Mr. Morris and Thomas froze.

"Well, what are you going to do now?" Anderson said, a smug expression on his face. "Three to one isn't very good odds."

"They're better than you think," Etta said. She sat rigid, the pistol in her hand pointed at Anderson's manhood.

The blood surged through Blue. She didn't know Etta well, but she knew her enough to know she had a short fuse. If Etta pulled the trigger she'd be hung for murder, because no gun was pointed at her. All Anderson had done was gesture to slap her.

Blue, on the other hand, faced two guns. And Anderson was sure to draw his. She could fire at any time but wouldn't be able to hit all three men without being shot or without Etta getting shot.

Etta aimed the gun surer, then cocked the trigger. "I'd say the chances of you dying today, Frank, are pretty good."

"You crazy whore." Anderson sat motionless, the sweat beading on his forehead.

Did he think Etta would do more than just talk?

Blue saw an opening and went for it. "Back your horse away and ride on. We don't want any trouble."

"Oh, you've got trouble." Anderson motioned for his men to leave. He backed his horse, and before he turned, he gave Blue a steely eye. "I want you off that property."

"The hell I'll leave. It's mine, legal and proper. And not you or anyone else can take it from me."

Anderson pointed at her. "I'll give you a fair price."

"It's not for sale."

"I'll give you more than anyone would offer."

"It's not for sale. Ever."

"So be it." He jerked the reins and kicked his horse into a dead run.

Blue slipped the pistol back into the holster. Etta laid her gun in her lap.

Mr. Morris sighed and put his hand on Blue's shoulder. "Oh, my dear, what have you done?"

What *had* she done?

Etta stared at her.

All Blue could think about was putting the supplies in the wagon as fast as she could and getting home.

"You won't be safe on the trail after dark. Spend the night here with us," Mr. Morris said. "If you leave early in the morning and push, you can make it home not long after sunset."

Blue nodded. It was the best plan. But what about Isa and Martha? Would they be safe? Would Anderson and his men ride there before she could get home?

Was this all worth the risk?

He'd offered her more than the property's value. She could settle somewhere else with that kind of money. Far away from here. But it was her home. A piece of her family. And now a piece of *her*. Her father had purchased it years ago. It was all she had left. But was it worth dying over? Or worth someone else getting killed because she wanted to hang on to a dream?

She turned to Etta. "You should go if you want. There's going to be trouble."

CHAPTER ELEVEN

Isa led Etta's horse from the stall, fastened his lead to the rail, and began to groom him. His ears perked, and when she curried him, he lowered his head and blew. All signs he had a gentle nature. She removed his shoes and trimmed his hooves. After four days of extra feed, his coat had brightened, but his ribs were still showing. He was a typical American saddle horse, probably a mix of the Narragansett Pacer and a Thoroughbred. He was tall and graceful, and appeared to have an easy gait. The abuse he'd suffered from overwork and poor diet had disguised his better qualities. But now that he'd somewhat improved, she could see he'd make a fine riding horse. Not a cutter or built for stamina, but he'd be useful. "You'll be ready to earn your keep in no time." She reapplied the liniment to his front legs and rewrapped his knees. The swelling had gone down, and he walked without tenderness.

As she stabled him in a fresh bed of straw, she heard Martha greet someone.

When she left the barn, she saw a young girl, no more than ten or eleven, standing by the porch. She was dressed in tattered pants and shirt and covered in dust. Isa couldn't tell if her face was tanned or just dirty. Her horse, an ebony mare with two white legs, appeared as travel worn as she did.

Isa approached.

"How far have you come?" Martha asked.

"Four days' ride, ma'am. Is Miss Blue about? I'm in need of work."

"That's a long way for a job prospect," Martha said. "I 'spect you're plumb wore out."

"It weren't too much trouble. Mostly I been in a powerful hurry to get here. Hope the job's still open."

"Blue isn't here right now, but we expect her back anytime," Martha said.

The girl crossed her feet, took her hat off, and looked down. "Oh!" she said, her disappointment evident.

"Hello! I'm Isa. Blue's partner. Why don't you come in, and we'll talk?"

"I'm Gertrude Tuttle. Gertie. That'd be fine, ma'am." She tied her horse to the rail and placed her well-used hat on the saddle horn.

Gertie's stomach grumbled as Isa guided her onto the porch.

"This is Martha," Isa said.

Martha smiled and led the way into the house. "Come in and get something to eat."

Gertie nodded eagerly. "I'd be mighty obliged."

Martha pointed to one of the benches.

Gertie slipped onto it.

Isa poured herself a cup of coffee and sat on the opposite side of Gertie, while Martha fixed her a plate of potatoes, green beans, and ham, then set it and a cup of coffee in front of her.

"Thank you, ma'am. That's awfully kind."

"Please call me Martha." She looked at Isa and tilted her head toward Gertie.

Martha must have been just as taken with this young girl as Isa was.

She was thin as a starving calf. Her dark hair, partially tied back with a red bandanna, clung to the sides of her head. Her dirt-smudged face contrasted with her deep-blue eyes. Her shirt, two sizes too big and ripped at one shoulder, was tied together with string where the buttons had once been.

Gertie picked up her fork and began to eat with vigor.

Isa tried not to smile as she watched her barely come up for air.

Martha handed her a napkin.

After Gertie had devoured the last morsel, she wiped her mouth, then her face. She carefully laid the soiled napkin near her empty plate and picked up the cup of coffee. She had a strong odor of sweat and horse, and she'd certainly been in her clothes for more than one barn dance.

She ducked her head when she found Isa watching her. "I'm sorry. I ain't et in a while."

Martha cringed. "How long has it been?"

"Two days. I had a few coins, but I used them to buy feed for my horse. I figured I better arrive with a good mount."

Isa felt an immediate bond to Gertie. She'd sacrificed her own needs for her animal and was concerned about being able to perform her work. And she was just a kid.

She asked the pressing question she knew Martha wanted to know. "How old are you?"

Gertie's eyes darted from Martha to Isa. "I'm fourteen."

Martha frowned. "Honesty is important on this ranch."

Gertie hung her head, then fixed her gaze on Martha. "Sorry. I'm going on twelve before fall comes. But I can handle any work and won't stop till the job gets done."

Martha slid onto the bench beside her. "You're awfully young to be on your own."

"It don't matter none. I've been fending for myself since I was knee-high to a grasshopper. My pa got kilt in the war. Then my ma got discouraged and run off with some damned banjo-playin' sonofa-bitch."

Martha put her hand to her mouth and turned her head.

Isa bit her lip and tried not to laugh. It wasn't meant to be funny, but the way Gertie had said it made it sound like it'd been an everyday occurrence that had caused her a considerable amount of annoyance.

Martha cleared her throat. "Where are you from?"

"Other side of the big lake."

"The big lake?" Martha asked.

Gertie pointed northwest. "Yes, ma'am. Lake Bigler or Tahoe, or whatever they're calling it. I heard it called different names. No one can seem to agree. Don't matter to me. I call it Lake Tahoe. I like the way it feels in my mouth when you say it. Kind of sings, don't you think?"

Martha nodded. "Yes. It does. You're absolutely right."

"I like the way you talk, Martha. If Miss Blue hires me, and I stick around these parts, would you teach me proper words? Ma taught me some learnin,' but it weren't much."

Martha smiled. "I'd be happy to, Gertie."

This young girl, who seemed to have been robbed of her childhood, was a curious mixture of youth and experience—much too young to have gone through what many others didn't experience by the time they were twenty, let alone twelve. Yet here she sat in Blue's kitchen.

"How did you hear about this job?" Isa asked.

"I passed through Carson City, and the dry goods store owner's wife told me about it when I asked her if there was any work about. And I come a-runnin'. I got a good horse. She's strong and sure on the trail."

"What's her name?" Isa asked.

"Name? Don't have a name. Never saw a need to name her."

"Where'd you get her?" Martha asked.

Gertie stiffened and stretched her neck. "There's a fine story in that question."

Martha leaned forward, closer to Gertie. "You didn't steal that mare, did you?"

"Well. No. Not exactly."

Isa's stomach soured. They couldn't hire a horse thief, no matter how young.

"I sort of claimed her," Gertie said. "There's a wild herd that passes through every now and again near where we had our cabin... Shack." She took a breath and her face muscles tensed. She might have acted like she didn't care about her mother, but she obviously did. "One afternoon I followed their trail to see if I could find where they went. They were bunched in a canyon, and I managed to trap three of them. Two escaped, but that one," she pointed toward the door, "hung out near the back of the canyon wall. I threw my rope around her, and that was that."

"Wait," Isa said. "You're saying you caught her from the herd, broke her, and then trained her?" She couldn't have done that. She was too small, too young, and too inexperienced.

Gertie stiffened and locked eyes with Isa. "'Twern't nothing. She gentled up right fast. All I had to do was take a firm hand. Once I got her settled, I thought about going after more of the herd and selling them to the locals, but I was too dern scared of my own shadow back then to do it."

"How long ago was that?" Martha asked.

"Last summer sometime."

"You were ten when you did it?" Isa asked in disbelief.

"Yeah, about that."

"How long have you been on your own?" Isa asked.

"Two summers, maybe three. It's hard to recall."

Martha pressed her lips together, and her eyes grew moist.

It was hard not to be astonished at what was coming out of Gertie's mouth. You knew it was truth just by the way she'd said it.

"You'll stay here with us," Martha said. "And when Blue gets back, she can decide about you working here or not."

Isa stood. "Come on. Let's get you settled."

Gertie nodded.

Martha reached for her arm. "When's the last time you had a bath?"

"To be honest, ma'am, I don't recall."

"I'll fill the tub this evening, and you'll take one. And we'll burn those clothes you have on. We'll find something else for you to wear."

"I don't want no dress. I can't wear dresses. They make me itch, and my legs feel all scared from the wind. And I can't work in that attire. Do you know most catastrophes are caused from a woman's dress?"

Isa could no longer hold back a laugh. This young sprout was going to be a very interesting addition to their group.

The next morning, the day after Blue had left, Gertie was almost unrecognizable from the night before. Martha had managed to fit her with not-so-baggy pants and a shirt. Gertie had protested for an hour when Martha tried to get the knots out of her hair. She'd ended up cutting parts of it and then trimmed the rest the best she could.

There'd even been freckles under all that dirt. And today she looked her age.

They had a good start on the second corral and were working on repairing the other stalls in the barn when Isa heard a wagon and horses.

A man and two young boys on horseback, and two even younger boys in a wagon, stopped in front of the barn.

Isa and Gertie greeted them.

"Howdy! I'm Virgil Pettiman, and these are my lads. Miss Hutchings hired us to build your bunkhouse."

Blue had worked fast. "I'm glad you're here," Isa said.

Gertie moved slightly behind her. Was she afraid of them or just shy?

Isa introduced herself and Gertie, and then she showed Mr. Pettiman where Blue wanted the bunkhouse.

Virgil surveyed the area, and he and his boys got right to work.

Gertie whispered in her ear. "Does that mean they'll be staying a while?"

Isa nodded. "A couple days at least. You'll sleep in the loft with me until they're done."

Virgil and his boys worked until dark, then had their supper and spent the night in the barn.

They were up early the next morning. Pleasant and efficient, they made fast progress.

Martha insisted Gertie help her with the meals. Gertie pouted, but in between her chores, she assisted Isa with the horses.

She had a natural way with the animals and worked hard. She had confidence and seemed to sense the horses' needs. But she was so young.

On the fifth day since Blue and Etta had left, Isa grew more concerned. They should have been back the evening before. The day waned and still no sign of them. Isa grew restless and unable to focus.

She decided to ride the area where she and Blue had determined to release the horses. Evidence of several recent riders caught her attention. One set of tracks left a deeper indentation than the others. The hoofprints weren't extraordinarily large, so it had to have been the weight of its rider that had caused the impression in the ground. Could it have been McCoy and his friends? She followed the tracks southeast back to about a quarter of a mile from the ranch house, and then the trail led east. The riders had dismounted and walked in the area. What were they up to? From this vantage point, she could clearly see the ranch and the Pettiman family working on the frame of the bunkhouse. Her concern grew.

The sun had slipped over the peak of the western mountain range by the time she returned. She marveled at how much of the building Virgil and his sons had completed while she'd been away.

"You're making fast work of it," she said.

Virgil nodded. "We should be done tomorrow evening. Would you like the bunks made? We can get them completed by the time we're finished with the walls."

Isa was sure Blue would approve. "Yes. That would be fine. Six, please."

Virgil nodded. "I'll have two of my boys do it while the rest of us finish. We'll put the stove in after we finish this third wall."

She stabled Adelita next to Etta's horse and then went to the house, noticing Gertie's horse wasn't in the corral.

"I've been wondering when you'd get back," Martha said. "You've been gone a long time." She dipped the stew onto a plate and set it and a slice of bread on the table in front of Isa. "Virgil and his boys, and Gertie and I, had supper a couple of hours ago. They sure work hard."

Isa agreed as she began to eat. "He said they'd probably be done by tomorrow evening. I imagine they'll be on their way as soon as they finish. Where's Gertie?"

"She's out somewhere on her horse. Said she wanted to go for a ride. It's hard not to treat her like the child she is. She's been on her own for so long she doesn't think or act like an eleven-year-old." Martha sat opposite Isa, a cup of coffee in her hand. "I'm worried about Blue and Etta. They should have been home by now." She took a sip of her drink.

Isa placed her fork on her plate and wiped her mouth with a napkin. "If they aren't here by morning, I'll ride toward Carson City. I can't stand this waiting."

"I don't imagine neither one of us will get much sleep tonight." Martha patted Isa's arm.

Gertie arrived a short time later.

Under a full moon, Isa sat on the steps of the porch, listening, hoping to hear the wagon as it approached, but nothing. Only the sounds of the crickets, and the horses as they moved in the corrals.

Martha joined her a few minutes later, dressed in her night clothes. "They should have been home yesterday."

"I don't like this." Isa kicked her foot against the side of the step.

"Waiting's always hard," Martha said. "Especially at night. I don't think I'll ever get used to it."

Something moved in the distance. A reflection of trees in the moonlight? Isa strained to get a better look. "I think it's the wagon."

Martha moved closer to her and peered into the darkness. "I don't see a thing."

Isa pointed. "There, just over the rise. I think it's them. I'm going to ride out to meet them."

"In the dark? You better stay here."

"There's plenty of moonlight." She went to the barn, bridled Adelita, and rode out bareback.

Blue was on Traveler in front of the wagon. She waved.

Isa couldn't hold back her smile. It'd only been days, but it seemed like a month since Blue had left. How had she become so attached to her this quickly? Did Blue feel the same? "We've been worried. What took you so long?"

"I've got a lot to tell you, but we're wore out. We've been on the trail since early this morning."

"You didn't camp at the river halfway?"

"No. We spent the night at the Morris store, then left at daybreak. We had a run-in with Frank Anderson when we were loading supplies yesterday and felt it was best not to be out in the dark." Blue yawned and covered her mouth. "I'll tell you the rest tomorrow."

"I'll take care of the horses and wagon," Isa said. "We can unload in the morning. We made room in the loft for Etta. Virgil and his boys are staying in the barn."

Blue nodded and smiled, then reached for Isa's hand. "It's good to be home."

"It's good to have you back." How could she explain about Gertie? "Um, we have another worker. Well, with your approval, of course."

"Really. Do you think she'll be a good fit?"

Isa cleared her throat. "Yes. But she's young, awfully young. She's also sleeping in the loft. You're bunking next to me." Isa smiled.

Blue squeezed her hand.

They unhitched the team. Blue hugged Martha and went straight into the house with Etta.

Isa fed and watered the horses, then turned them into the corral. By the time she returned to the house, Blue had already gone to bed.

She washed and then climbed to the loft, carefully weaving her way between the sleeping figures until she stood beside Blue. She slid under the covers and moved close, feeling the warmth of Blue's body and the rhythm of her breathing. The inclination to wrap her arm around her and bring her as close as possible overpowered her. She breathed deeply, her hands aching to touch the soft curves of the wonder beside her. But should she? It was her last thought before slumber overtook her.

CHAPTER TWELVE

Blue woke suddenly in the haze of an early dawn's greeting and, for a moment, thought she was dreaming. Isa lay next to her, wide awake, watching her. More like gazing. Deeply. And the expression on her face was full of…What? Peace? Contentment?

She stroked Isa's cheek with the back of her fingers. "Good morning." She wanted to kiss her, to touch and caress.

Isa placed her hand over hers and held it there. She brushed Blue's lips with her fingertips. "Good morning." And as if she knew her thoughts, she said, "We're not alone. Remember?"

Blue scanned the loft. She saw Etta and then another figure. "Who's that?"

Isa moved closer and whispered. "Gertie. Your new hire."

"I've missed you. When did I hire her?"

Isa smiled. "A few days ago, but it's not official until you say it is." She rolled to her back and stretched her arms above her head.

Blue swallowed. How much longer until they'd touch? This morning would be a perfect time to explore Isa's gifts. She could see the outline of her full breasts and hard nipples beneath her cotton gown. Would she welcome her? She was sure she would. But when?

Martha rattled pots in the kitchen. The sound of sizzling bacon and its strong scent wafted into the loft, driving Blue's hunger.

Etta and Gertie began to stir.

Isa rolled toward Blue. She grazed her lips against Blue's cheek without uttering a word and then got out of bed, graceful, like a butterfly taking flight. She faced Blue and, without hesitation, slowly and deliberately lifted her nightgown, revealing her treasures, all the while her eyes fixed on Blue.

Awestruck and overwhelmed by the splendor of the sight before her, Blue couldn't even gasp. Was she dreaming? Would she wake any moment to find herself alone? No. She'd never been more awake.

The corners of Isa's mouth lifted slightly, like she'd discovered a secret no one else could guess and wanted to keep it hidden.

Blue stilled, helplessly watching every exquisite movement, the graceful way she held herself, the rich contours of flesh over bone.

Isa loosely bound her breasts.

Denial and disappointment crashed in around Blue. It couldn't be over. Was this glimpse of pure joy and exuberance gone, like a star shooting across the sky revealing one momentary, glorious illumination?

Isa slipped on her underclothing over the full nest of thick, dark hair between her long, slender legs. She eased her shirt over her shoulders and, with nimble fingers, buttoned each button. She started at the bottom and worked her way to the top, sliding each disc into its designated position, her hands floating in the air as if she were placing each planet in the universe in its proper order. She eased into her pants, one leg at a time, tucked her shirt in, and then buttoned the fly of her dungarees. She hovered over Blue, still watching her. Her smile broadened. And then she left.

Blue sucked in a breath, vaguely aware she'd been holding it. Her breasts were full and hard. An unyielding want and need to be repeatedly touched deep within her summoned her attention. She felt warm and wet, and her face flushed. If her heart beat any faster, it would explode. What had Isa done to her?

She dressed while Etta and the new hire slept.

She sat opposite Isa at the table, unable to take her eyes off her.

Martha brought her a cup of coffee, then set heaping plates of biscuits and bacon on the table. "Good morning. Are you rested?" She went to the stove and returned with two eggs for her and Isa.

Blue kept her gaze fixed on Isa. "Good morning. Yes. I rested well. How are things here?" She wrapped her fingers around her cup and sipped the hot liquid, never looking away from Isa's eyes.

"I'm glad you're rested," Isa said. "We need to ride to the spot I found to release the horses. It'll take all day by the time we get there, scout the area, and get back." She locked eyes with Blue, then reached for a biscuit and two slices of bacon.

Blue's heartbeat surged. Was she going to get to spend the day alone with her?

Martha sat across from Blue. "You better eat. You're a little flushed."

"What?"

Isa's smile widened.

Martha pointed to Blue's plate. "I said you're *flushed*. Eat."

Blue had lost her appetite. All she wanted to do was ride as far away as she could with Isa. She took a biscuit and buttered it, set it on her plate, then drowned it in honey.

"Blue, what are you doing?" Martha asked.

"What?"

"You're smothering that biscuit. Give me that." Martha snatched the jar of honey from her. "What's gotten into you?"

If she only knew. "I imagine I'm still a bit addled from my trip."

"What happened?" Martha asked.

Blue told the story of Frank Anderson.

Martha rubbed her hands. "What kind of trouble are we in for?"

Out of the corner of her eye, Blue saw a girl, who she thought was Etta, descend the ladder and quietly sit on her side of the bench, but near the far edge. She paid little attention.

"Morning, Gertie. This is Blue," Isa said, still smiling, like she'd finally caught her prey. Which she had.

"Morning, Miss Blue," Gertie said.

Blue choked on a swallow of coffee and almost dropped her cup. "Good Lord, you're just a child. What are you, ten?"

"I'll be twelve come fall. I'm a hard worker. Can I have some coffee?"

"Give that baby a sugar tit," Etta said as she settled between Blue and Gertie.

Gertie scowled. "I ain't no baby."

"All right, that's enough," Martha said. "Coffee and eggs are on the stove. Get them yourselves."

Etta went to the stove and placed an egg on her plate, then returned to the table, getting two biscuits and a generous portion of bacon. "I'll tell you what. I'll go fill a bottle with the cow's milk, and you can suck it down." She laughed as she sliced a biscuit and slathered it in butter.

Gertie pursed her lips as she jumped up from the table, stomped to the stove, and poured a cup of coffee.

She *was* a child. But if she was going to work here, she'd have to hold her own. Blue watched to see what she'd do before she intervened.

"What's your name?" Gertie asked.

"Etta."

"That's not much of a name. Sounds like someone spit out something they didn't like."

Blue laughed. That was good, but she could see where things were headed. "Martha's right. Both of you settle down. You either get along or get going somewhere else."

To Blue's surprise, Gertie brought two cups of coffee to the table and set one in front of Etta. "Truce?"

"Fair enough," Etta said.

"She'll do," Isa said.

Martha nodded. "I agree. She's a hard worker and quick to learn."

"All right, it's decided," Blue said. "You're hired. Same wage as everyone else. You get paid at the end of the month."

Etta scoffed. "No probation?"

Blue shook her head. "She came highly recommended." She winked at Isa.

The sound of hammers broke the morning. "Well, the day's wasting away," Blue said. She stood.

"Gertie can stay with me today," Martha said. "Lots of things to get done."

"Dern. I wanted to be outside."

"None of that," Martha said. "You'll work where you're told. That's how it runs around here. Now give me a *yes ma'am* and let's get to it."

"Yes, ma'am."

"Etta, I want you to muck the stalls and anything Martha wants you to do," Blue said.

"And I want you to turn your horse out in the corral today," Isa added. "He's coming along nicely. You'll be surprised. Blue, when do you want to leave?" She grinned.

"As soon as possible." Blue's heartbeat increased again. "Martha, would you pack us a lunch? I imagine we won't be back till late."

"Sure enough. I told Virgil they could take their supper with us each night they're here."

"That's fine," Blue said. "I'm sure they'll appreciate it. They're good people. They live about a half-day's ride east of our property. They're fine neighbors. When does he think they'll be done?"

"He said probably late tonight."

"That's fast work. I'll go check with him before Isa and I leave. Have a good day, all of you."

"You also, Miss Blue," Etta said.

While Isa saddled the horses, Blue talked with Virgil and inspected his work. "It's a fine job."

Virgil instructed one of his sons, then pointed to the far wall. He returned his attention to Blue. "Gone a little easier than I thought. We'll be on our way come morning."

"Martha said you'd probably be finished by this evening."

"Yep."

Gertie came out of the house carrying a plate of biscuits, a jar of honey, and a butter knife, and set them on the wooden table by Virgil's wagon. "Miss Martha said to say good morning." She scurried back into the house.

"That Gertie seems like a spry little thing. My younger boys like her," Virgil said. "There's a traveling farrier that comes by about once a month or so. A big fella named Samuel. He's good with the horses. If you like, the next time he comes through, I'll send him your way."

"Thank you for that. I appreciate it."

Despite Frank Anderson, things were working out. But Blue knew deep down that trouble was coming her way. She needed to talk with Martha and Isa about it. But it could wait. She had other things more important to discuss with Isa. And do!

It seemed like they rode the better part of the morning until Isa pointed to the spot where she thought the horses should be released. The mountain base was about a mile away and was a natural barrier to contain them. The lake was large, with an abundance of juniper and cotton woods near it. The open spaces were adequate for roaming and had ample pasture for grazing.

"It's a great spot," Blue said.

Isa pointed to the cluster of pines. "We can rest over there."

They rode to the area, dismounted, and secured the horses.

Isa pulled a blanket from her saddlebag and spread it atop a bed of pine needles. She sat, then fixed her eyes on Blue.

Blue's heart pounded at the thought of being close to Isa again. Her cheeks burned from the sudden rush of blood. Was this what it felt like to want someone so badly they consumed every thought? Her strength waned, and she grew weak in the knees the moment she stepped onto the blanket. She sank onto the soft bedding. The scent of pine and fresh air, and the feel of the sunshine as it peeked through the trees, were intoxicating. She stretched out on her back.

"Do you know how to swim?" Isa asked.

"No," Blue said, forcing herself to focus on the question. "I never liked being in the water. It's hard enough to get a bath."

"Is everything all right?" Isa asked. "You seem distracted."

Blue lifted her hand to block the sun that had suddenly made its way through an opening in the branches. Her hand trembled. Things were happening to her body she had no control over, and she didn't know if she liked it or not.

Isa lay beside her, propped up on her elbow, watching her.

Blue refused to look at her because she knew if she did, she'd somehow fall. Isa was a well of desire and want, and if Blue peered into her eyes, she'd tumble into her. Whether Isa knew it or not, she had a power over Blue. And Blue feared it. At this moment, she would do anything Isa asked of her. There were no bounds. She wouldn't be able to tell her no, even if she wanted to.

Breathe. Blue risked it all and looked into Isa's eyes, and it happened—she fell. Deep and fast, and strong. Yet she felt suspended in slow motion as Isa called to her without speaking. She turned and laid her hand on the curve of Isa's waist. It felt familiar and pleasurable and only increased her desire to touch.

Isa didn't stop her.

Blue trailed her finger tips up her arm, then over her neck and cheek.

Isa leaned closer.

Blue had never loved before. Would she be a good lover to Isa? Could she please her? Could she be understanding and considerate? How could she do it when her own body craved to be touched? To take.

Isa slid her hand around Blue's side and pulled her closer.

They kissed.

There was a freedom in their joining, a release of emotion, as if Blue opened to her.

Isa began to unbutton Blue's shirt, then slid it off her shoulder and kissed bare skin. She managed it with confidence. Had she done this before?

Chills and tingling surged through Blue. She fumbled to undo Isa's shirt. She unbuttoned her pants and tugged at the waistband, feeling the material spread apart, reminding her of the sight she'd beheld that morning.

The birds in the trees warbled louder.

Isa slid Blue's shirt completely off, then lifted her undergarment over her head. She touched her breasts, her hands warm and gentle as she caressed.

Blue's breath caught. She pressed into Isa.

Isa kissed her again, entering, her tongue probing, demanding.

Blue didn't have to ask if it was right. It felt right. It felt natural and good. And oh, so pleasurable.

Isa stopped. She unwrapped the binding around her own chest, then lay against Blue, their breasts pressing into each other. Firm, hard nipples rubbing against nipples.

Blue realized then that she'd closed her eyes. All she sensed was Isa against her—soft, warm. She heard a familiar noise, and her eyes flew open. "Horses!"

"What?" Isa pushed herself up.

"Horses. I hear horses," Blue said. She frantically began to button her shirt. "To the north somewhere."

"Oh, hell. I hear them too."

They were now in a race to see who could get dressed the quickest.

Blue was winning. She stood and watched, then tilted her head toward the sound, continuing to button her shirt. "I don't see anything, but I know they're close."

Isa finished and got to her knees. "Two, maybe three riders?"

"Probably," Blue said, straining to see. She untied Traveler and stood quietly beside him. His and Adelita's colors blended into the surroundings.

Blue checked her sidearm.

Isa slid her rifle from the scabbard and cocked it.

Blue touched her arm. "Whoa." We don't know who it is."

"I found tracks leading toward the ranch the other day when I was scouting where to release the herd. These could be the same men."

Blue's stomach tightened with dread, but she didn't want to overreact. "They could just be passing through. The lake's just there. Maybe they need water."

"Everyone always needs water," Isa said.

"I don't like it," Blue said. "Not after what happened in town and what you found." Blue pointed. "There, four riders along the base of the mountain, just past the lake."

"I see them," Isa said.

"Let's mount up," Blue said. "We can get a better view from atop the horses. I won't give them the benefit of the doubt. Let's follow along the tree line and see where they go."

They eased their way through the trees.

The four men rode along the mountain base for a time, then turned and disappeared into a canyon.

"Why would they go that way? There's nothing there but mountains," Blue said. "I've ridden up to the base, beyond the lake. It's only canyons. My property ends past where they turned."

"Let's sit awhile and see what they do," Isa said.

Blue nodded.

As the moments passed, Blue's nerves began to calm.

Isa glanced at her and smiled.

"What?"

Isa shook her head. "Nothing."

Isa didn't appear like she was thinking about the men they'd seen. Blue squirmed in the saddle, remembering what she and Isa had been up to.

Should they talk about it? Blue took a deep breath. She didn't know of such things. Should she bring it up or let Isa? What could Blue say? Her feelings for Isa were powerful and strong. And it scared her.

CHAPTER THIRTEEN

Isa sat quietly for an hour as she and Blue watched for the men to come back through the canyon, but they never returned. "I want to show you something before we head back," she said.

She led Blue to the tracks she'd found the day before. "I think one of them is McCoy."

Blue dismounted and touched the deeper imprint, then inspected what remained of the others. "What do you think? Four sets?"

"That's my guess."

Blue mounted her horse. She sighed heavily and rubbed her chin. "It could be the same four we just saw. If we let the horses loose, how safe will they be? We'll need to brand them, which I don't want to do, but I know it's necessary."

"We could also have a couple of riders herd them out during the day and bring them back in the evening," Isa said.

"But how long can we go on like that and still get anything done?" Blue asked. "The barn needs repaired. There's work on the house. I need to visit some of the other ranchers and build up my stock. And other things need taken care of. Repairs. The animals. Getting ready for winter." Blue hung her head. "I suppose the best thing to do is brand them and then turn them out every day with riders. It stresses them, though. I don't like it."

"It'll be worse for them if they're penned all the time."

"I know."

"We can figure it out." Isa patted Blue's leg. The distress was evident in her face. Was some of it caused by what they'd done a few hours before? Blue didn't act like it had bothered her. On the contrary, she'd acted like she enjoyed it. And her expression earlier in the morning when Isa had disrobed in front of her told her volumes about what Blue had felt. She smiled, thinking about the delight in her eyes.

Isa couldn't believe she'd done it. And she had no idea why. An impulse? She didn't think about it ahead of time. She just stood and did it. The more intently Blue watched her, the more enjoyable it became for Isa. She sensed Blue needed time to work through her feelings, so she didn't press her on the subject.

They arrived at the ranch just before sunset. Etta and Gertie sat on the porch talking with another woman. Blond and fair, in her early twenties and with a pleasant laugh.

They dismounted. Blue took Adelita's reins from Isa.

"I need to talk with Virgil," Blue said. "You take this one. I don't think I can face another disappointment. If she isn't up to the standard, don't hire her." She led the horses to the barn.

So, it would be Isa's responsibility whether to hire this woman. She seemed sturdy enough. Her pants and shirt were well fitted. A new hat. A strong-looking gelding Quarter horse tied to the rail, well suited for the work that needed done. The saddle was worn but in good condition.

When Isa approached, the small group stopped talking.

"Evening," Isa said. "I 'spect you're hoping for work?"

The fair-haired woman nodded and stood. "Yes, ma'am. I'm Rosemary Coghlan." She straightened. Her intense expression hinted of exceptional awareness of her surroundings. It caught Isa's attention.

"I'm Isa. Blue's partner. Let's go over here and talk." She led Rosemary to the bench beneath the tree near the barn, and they sat.

"Did you come far?"

"Virginia City. A long couple of days."

"We need riders. And if you're thinking it's going to be an easy job, then you're mistaken. I'm telling you this so you'll know up front. It's hard work."

"I heard in Carson City the reason Miss Blue needs women folk. Mrs. Morris, from the dry goods store, said no men will work for her because of Frank Anderson. I know of him. He's had dealings in Virginia City. I don't like him. My father had run-ins with him doing business at the bank."

"Then you know what Blue's up against?"

Rosemary nodded.

"Are you still interested?"

"Yes. I believe I am."

Whoever Rosemary was, she was well-spoken, had self-confidence, and seemed intelligent. Why was she here?

"Tell me about yourself."

"I'm twenty-two and have never married. I've had opportunities, but it's not something I care to do. My family owns a ranch east of Virginia City. They supplement their earnings by helping with the stagecoach line. My folks told me if I was going to be an old spinster, I at least needed a profession. It was either work on my father's ranch or be a schoolteacher. And since I had no desire to continue to be under my father's thumb, I chose to teach. But it's not something I want to spend my life doing either. I saw Miss Blue's ad on the board at the telegraph office in Virginia City. I can ride. My roping's decent. I know how to use a hammer, and if I read how to do something, I can usually figure it out."

"Can you use a pistol?"

"Yes. My brother taught me. Point and shoot! I'm a fair shot. Not great but fair."

"Do you own a gun?"

"I have one in my saddlebag. It's not much, but it'll get the job done."

"Pay's at the end of the month. You best go into town and get yourself a pair of chaps. You're going to need them."

"I already have a pair in my saddlebag."

"Good."

Isa stood and Rosemary followed.

"Welcome to the Hutchings ranch. We start branding horses first thing in the morning. Have you eaten?"

"Yes. Martha kindly offered me a meal when I arrived about two hours ago."

"I'll find out where you're sleeping and let you know."

"Thank you for the opportunity, Isa. I won't let you down."

Isa nodded. "I'm sure you won't."

Rosemary joined the others on the porch, and Isa went to find Blue.

She was with Virgil and his boys by the campfire. The bunkhouse looked completed.

Virgil and his sons stood when Isa came near. "Evening, Isa," he said.

Isa said hello to him and the others. "Is the bunkhouse ready?"

Virgil smiled. "Yep. The hires can sleep in it tonight."

It was easy to see Blue's excitement. "I went in it. It's good and will meet our needs nicely. Etta and Gertie's things are already in there. How about the other woman?"

Isa nodded. "I think you'll like her. Her name's Rosemary Coghlan."

"I wonder if she's related to Earl Coghlan in Silver City?" Virgil asked.

"She said she's from Virginia City," Isa said.

"Probably kin somehow. Decent people," Virgil said.

"Good to know," Blue said and stood. "I'm ready to eat and turn in. Virgil, you and your boys did a fine job. Thank you. Have breakfast with us in the morning, and we'll settle up before you leave."

The family stood. "That'd be agreeable, Blue. Thank you," Virgil said.

The boys echoed their good-nights.

The small group of women was still on the porch talking and laughing as Blue and Isa walked to the house.

"Do you think Rosemary will do well?" Blue asked.

"Yes. She'll do nicely. And I think we're lucky to have her here."

Blue's eyebrows raised. "That's encouraging."

"And she's a schoolteacher to boot. Maybe Gertie can get some lessons."

Blue laughed. "And Etta?"

They both laughed.

"Rosemary?" Isa called.

Rosemary stood. "Yes, Isa."

"The bunkhouse is ready for you and the others to sleep in. Put your horse in the corral and your tack in the barn."

"Etta gets first bunk pick," Blue said.

"We already picked, Miss Blue," Etta announced.

"Well, get to it then," Blue said. "It's going to be a long day tomorrow. Good night."

The women said their good-nights and walked toward the corral.

Blue touched Isa's arm as they climbed the steps to the porch. "I'm wore out."

Isa laughed. "Yes. It was a hard day's work."

Blue laughed.

The sound danced on the evening air and filled Isa with joy.

Martha had their hot meal ready when they came into the house.

Isa sat in her spot, across from Blue, her back to the kitchen stove.

Martha took a seat beside her. It felt familiar, secure, like a home should be. Peace and fulfillment surrounded her, a contentment she'd never known before. Did Blue feel it? She hoped she did. She wanted her to.

That night, as she lay near Blue, alone in the loft, listening to the sound of Blue's even breathing, Isa thought of the last few months. How she'd felt when she started for her uncle's ranch. Full of uncertainty and fear. Anger and bitterness. Regret. Life had gone in a completely different direction now. If she hadn't taken the risk, she would have never met Blue. But she did. And she would try to make a life here with her.

She wanted to move to Blue and wrap her in her arms, but should she? Blue hadn't made any gestures toward her when they lay down. Isa knew it was best to let it happen when Blue was ready. She also realized Blue had never known a woman or a man. She was shy and withdrawn in that area, unsure of herself.

Margaretta flashed in Isa's mind. She and Margaretta were fifteen when they went into the valley exploring, trying to find rocks and birds, and anything that could spark their interest and imagination. For an entire summer they were together as often as they could get away. Then, one afternoon, on a beautiful October day, they stopped under the shade of an ahuehuete tree. The cempasúchil were in bloom. Margaretta took her hand. And they knew each other. They touched and caressed, and delighted in each other's bodies. Then, not long after, Margaretta was sent away. Isa's heart broke. She pleaded to know where Margaretta's parents had sent her, but she never found out. And Isa was treated like she had leprosy. How had they known? The following year she was sent to her grandmother's, a two-day journey from the home she loved. She never returned until she married.

How would she and Blue fare if they continued on this path they seemed so unable to control? Would they have to suffer wagging tongues and steely stares, pointing fingers? Did Blue know what people were capable of? Or was she naive and unaware of the actions of supposed Christian men and women? Blue was strong, but was she strong enough to withstand what could happen when others felt they were on higher ground? Maybe it was better for her and Blue if they no longer pursued their feelings for each other.

CHAPTER FOURTEEN

B lue bent over and rested her hands on her knees.
     Isa led the next mare to the inside of the corral fence. She pinned the horse and handed the rope to Gertie.

Blue grabbed the hot iron brand her father had made for her. An *H* with a *C* over the top, like a hat. She approached the animal. "Gertie, if you don't move closer to her shoulder, you're going to get kicked for sure."

Gertie jumped into the correct position.

Blue quickly applied the brand. The horse jerked. The stench of burning horse flesh smoked in the air. "Get some cold water on that."

Gertie led the mare to the water trough.

"Bring me the buckskin," Blue yelled, making her way to the fire once more. They were almost halfway done.

Rosemary led the horse to the fence. Isa penned it against the rails, and then Rosemary took the correct position, stroking the horse's neck. "Easy, boy."

Blue approached its hindquarters. She wanted the brand to be in a similar position on all her horses. Left side of the upper thigh, just below the rump. Easy to see from a distance. She applied the brand evenly for just a moment. "Go."

The horse kicked out as Rosemary led him away.

The next gelding brought a different story. The minute Etta led him into the corral, he began to buck and pull. He was too much for her inexperience to handle. Before Blue could say anything, Rosemary handed her horse's rope to Gertie and went into the corral to help Etta.

"Let me," Rosemary told Etta. "I've got this. He's seen what's happening and is refusing."

She removed her bandanna from around her neck and slipped it under his rope halter. Next, she led him to the fence and then covered his eyes. Isa pinned his hindquarters against the rails.

"If this doesn't work and he won't stand, we can use a twitch," Rosemary said.

"I don't like to do it if we can help it," Blue said.

Rosemary was skilled and a good worker, and Blue already trusted her. Isa was right. She was a fine addition.

Blue heated the brand and approached the horse. "You watch yourself."

"I'm ready," Rosemary said. "Let it rip."

Rosemary grabbed her bandanna from the horse's eyes as soon as Blue removed the hot iron.

He pawed the ground and shook his head.

"He's a fine animal," Rosemary said, leading him to the trough.

Martha stood by the corral gate. "Your lunches are ready over there under the trees. I thought you might like to stay outside and rest in the shade."

Blue waved her acknowledgment and called the women to eat.

They gathered around the wooden table, where Martha had put ham sandwiches, apples, and water.

"Miss Blue, do you reckon we can practice shooting tomorrow?" Gertie asked.

Blue stopped eating. "I imagine so. Isa, would you supervise it?"

Isa nodded. "Pistol? Or rifle?"

"I only have a pistol," Gertie said, "and a poor one at that." She left the group and returned a few minutes later, holding a revolver.

"Good Lord, Gertie. That's bigger than you are," Etta said.

Gertie held it up with both hands.

"Don't point that at anyone," Blue said. "Have you ever fired it?"

"Nope. I took it from that banjo-playin' sonofabitch when he was in a drunken stupor."

Laughter erupted.

Gertie glared at the others. "What's so funny? I did take it."

"What is it?" Isa asked.

"Some kind of revolver," Gertie said.

"No. What's the make or model?" Isa asked.

"It's a Colt," Rosemary said. "Actually, an 1860 Colt Remington six-shot revolver, the most common weapon used in the war. Total length is fourteen inches, and it weighs two pounds, eleven ounces." She stood and took it from Gertie, spun the cylinder, and sighted it toward the ground. "It's in fair condition, but it's in need of a good cleaning and oiling." She handed it back to Gertie and sat down. "Etta's correct. It's too much weapon for you, Gertie. I suggest getting a Colt Pocket five-shot. Not a lot of distance, but a lot smaller and lighter. Easier to handle. Besides, wearing that six-shooter on your hip will weigh you down so much you'd be aching by suppertime."

Etta and Isa laughed.

Blue was impressed. "How'd you know what kind of weapon that is?"

"Because my father sold guns. And he sold about two hundred of the Colts like Gertie has after the war," Rosemary said. "My brothers and I had to take them apart, clean them, and fire them all."

"What's the best rifle?" Isa asked.

"In my mind, it's a Springfield. Quick-firing, dead accuracy, fast-loading," Rosemary said. "They're coming out with some new models, but I haven't seen them yet."

"You should see Isa's rifle. It's a beauty," Blue said. "Bring your weapons tomorrow evening after supper, and we'll do some shooting out by the tree line." She stood to go back to work. "Oh, I almost forgot. Virgil Pettiman told me there's going to be a social and dance at the Wyman ranch in a few weeks. You're all invited. We'll take the wagon and stay two nights at the Wymans'."

Talk started like a clap of thunder.

There'd be complications. Blue was sure of it. Isa, for one. Wyman knew her only as a man. How would his ranch hands act when they saw her as a woman? Would she even want to go? Since she didn't want to disguise herself any longer as a man, sooner or later she'd have to reveal she was female. And the other most likely problem—Frank Anderson and his men might be there.

By suppertime they were ready to stop. All the horses had been branded and taken care of. They cleaned up and were ready to eat when two riders approached.

Blue watched as they came closer. Isa stood beside her.

"They're women," Blue said. "If they're wanting work, we have a problem."

"Why?"

"Because I can only afford one more hand," Blue said.

"I'll let you handle it this time," Isa said.

"Thanks a heap." Blue managed a laugh.

Martha called them to supper.

Blue remained outside and waited for the riders.

"Evenin'," the woman to her left said. She sat taller than the other. Red hair, freckles, and, as far as Blue could guess, somewhere in her late teens or early twenties. She wore her hat low, locks of fire-red pushing out under it like sagebrush trying to break free. "We're looking for Blue Hutchings."

"I'm her. Are you interested in work?"

"Yes, ma'am," the other answered. "I'm Abigail Saunders and this is Laurel Winfield."

The woman who'd introduced herself as Abigail ducked her head. The right side of her face caught the evening light, revealing a large mass of rippled scar tissue from her ear to the edge of her chin and down her neck. How had it happened? Most likely it was a burn of some type.

Now Blue had a dilemma. Two. And she only needed one!

"Why don't you come inside and have some supper. Then we'll talk."

They thanked her and dismounted, tied their horses to the rail, and Blue led them into the house.

The others made room at the table.

As they conversed with the group, Blue learned they'd come separately to Carson City and decided to ride together to the ranch. They didn't know each other before they met in town. That was a relief. At least they weren't related or good friends. She needed to be up front about the situation. But how to decide? Because of competition, she would pick the best one.

"As you can see, we already have three hires. I'm sorry to say I need only one of you."

Silence filled the room, all eyes on Abigail and Laurel.

Gertie held her fork in her hand and stopped chewing. "Miss Blue." She swallowed. "I'll take a half-wage if it'll help."

Etta shushed her. "It's best for Miss Blue to handle this."

"Did I say something wrong?" Gertie asked.

Blue stood. "It's fine, Gertie. Abigail, as soon as you and Laurel finish your meal, I'd like to see you outside."

They came out onto the porch a little while later.

"Laurel, why don't you sit here and visit with the others when they're done? Abigail, let's you and me go over by the shade trees and talk."

Abigail sat on a stump, sliding toward the right, revealing more of the left side of her face than her right.

Blue sat on the bench.

"Tell me about yourself," Blue said.

"I'm from Silver Springs. I grew up on a ranch, like most folks in these parts. My ma and pa own a small parcel of land just outside town. I'm nineteen. I can rope and ride, and I know how to farrier somewhat, at least the basics. I helped build our barn and corral."

"Why did you come for the job?"

"To be honest, I can't stay any longer with my folks. Too many mouths to feed. I tried to get work in town, but no one would hire me full-time. I worked at the dry goods store part-time for a spell, but it was only temporary, and they had to let me go. So many men are looking for work, it's hard to get anything. And with my disfigurement, people are hesitant to be around me. I saw your advertisement and left the next day."

"Can you shoot?" If there was going to be trouble like Blue expected, she'd need the gun hands.

"I've never liked the idea of it, but I can. My little sister, brother, and me used to shoot quail and varmints. I got pretty good at it."

"Rifle or pistol?"

"Pistol."

"Do you have a firearm with you?"

"I brought a Colt revolver my pa gave me. He said it was from the war."

"You'll need chaps."

"I have some. They're worn hand-me-downs, but useable. I ain't afraid of hard work, Miss Blue. I've done men's work most of my life."

She appeared capable.

"Miss Blue, I know my appearance may be disturbing. I was burnt in a fire when I was young."

"I'm more concerned with your abilities to do the job than your appearance."

Abigail's expression relaxed. "Thank you for that."

Blue was curious about the incident that had caused the deep scarring but decided not to pry into the matter. She stood. "I can't give you my answer right now."

"I understand."

"Would you send Laurel?"

"Yes, ma'am."

Abigail went to the porch and talked with Laurel, who immediately came over.

"Miss Blue. I want to tell you right off that I can ride and rope, but I'm not good with a shooter."

Blue nodded. "How old are you?"

"Seventeen. I come from a family of eight up in the High Sierra. I left home 'cause food was scarce, and I didn't want to be a burden to my folks. I made my way to the stagecoach line and rode to Carson City. I bought me a horse when I saw your advertisement. There weren't no prospects of marriage where I'm from. Only old men and little boys. It's a sad tale."

"So, you're wanting to marry?"

"Yes, ma'am. I aim to marry well, and in the meantime, I need to provide for myself. I'm willing to do most any work. I have a strong back, good sense, and a clear head. I'm good in the kitchen too. You name it, I can cook it."

Martha would be glad to hear that. "I'm sure you'll be a fine companion for someone."

Laurel nodded.

"Do you have a gun or chaps?"

"Yes, ma'am. I bought both secondhand in Carson City with the last of the money I had."

Blue tried not to sigh too loudly. What was she going to do? Turn one of them away to starve to death or end up as a prostitute at Mrs. Victoria's in Carson City? This was harder than she'd imagined it would be. And then she had a thought. If she hired them both, chances were that Laurel would be married before the year was out. She had a pretty face and good features. There were plenty of eligible men in the area. She could make sure Laurel did the Carson City runs and went with them to any surrounding farms. The word would get out, and then Blue's dilemma would be resolved. In the meantime, she'd be able to get as much work out of her as she could. They both would benefit. Problem solved! But she wanted to discuss it with Isa first.

She and Laurel returned to the porch, and then Blue went into the kitchen and asked Isa to go for a walk with her.

They strolled southeast of the house, through the trees, and along the creek.

"What did you decide?" Isa asked.

Blue told her the plan.

"I knew when they showed up together, you'd want to hire them both. You've got to learn to say no, Blue. Because you're so easy, that means I have to be hard."

"No, it doesn't."

"Yes. It does. You think those women can't see you're as easy to tip as an unsuspecting cow?"

"Now, wait a minute!" Blue shot her a teasing glare. "I left *you* alone for five minutes, and *you* hired an eleven-year-old."

Isa blushed and her lips quirked. "But she has a big gun!"

Blue nudged her shoulder and hid her smile.

"I don't mean it in a bad way," Isa said. "It's just you need to be stronger. You can't show any weakness with these women or with the area ranchers, especially if you want to grow your ranch like you said. You need to have a reputation of being hard, yet fair."

"I thought I was doing that." Did Isa see who she really was? Or was her view distorted by how she felt about her? "I'm building my life the way I feel I can live with it. I want to be able to sleep at night, knowing I'm doing the best I can."

"That's all well and good, but what happens when you run out of money? You won't be able to pay these women, or your taxes on your property, or put food on the table for you and Martha."

"You mean me, Martha, and *you*?"

Isa put her hand around Blue's waist as they walked. "Yes. Of course. But what I'm saying is, I don't have much money to help you, and from what you've said, Martha's funds are almost depleted. What's going to happen when the banker is at the door with his hand out demanding payment?"

Isa was right. But so was Blue. She alone had to make the decision.

"If we get to the end of the year and Laurel hasn't married, I'll decide then. Who knows? I might have to let most of them go by then. Hell, Isa. If I don't get this problem with Frank Anderson solved, I may not be around by the end of the year."

Isa stopped mid-step. "Don't say that, Blue."

But Blue spoke the truth. Isa hadn't been with her at the store that day. She didn't see the hate and anger in Anderson's eyes. Whatever his problem with her, he wouldn't stop until she left or one of them was dead. And she wasn't leaving. They were like two trains headed toward each other on the same track. Why was he so desperate to get rid of her?

He had to have a reason. "With five hires, we can have guards with the horses. I'd feel better about that. We can't lose the herd. It's our future. They'll be ready to turn out the day after tomorrow."

They started back.

"So, there'll be five then?" Isa asked.

"Yes. Will you stand by me in this?"

Isa stopped and caught her gaze. "Of course, I will. By the time we're through with them, they'll be hell bent for leather!"

Five! Each different. Each as desperate as Blue. What had she gotten herself into?

CHAPTER FIFTEEN

After supper the next day, Isa walked behind Etta, watching as the group lined up and shot at a pile of rocks on a tree stump about a hundred yards away. Only Rosemary had hit her target. It was a disappointment. "All of you stop and put your guns on the ground."

Gertie laid her revolver in the dirt, picked up a rock, and inspected it.

"This target practice isn't for pleasure," Isa said. "Any one of us could be killed because of your lack of skill. I've seen jackasses kick a tin can with better aim."

"Jackasses are closer to a tin can than we are to our target," Gertie mumbled, continuing to play with the stone.

"Gertie," Isa said.

Gertie startled and looked at her.

Isa wanted to be stern, especially after what she'd told Blue the night before, but she had to stifle a smile. "Did you hear a word I said?"

"No, ma'am. Did you see this rock?"

Etta grabbed it from her.

The other three women gathered around her and Gertie, inspecting the rock.

"I believe it's got silver in it," Rosemary said.

"Could be granite," Abigail said. "I've heard there's lots of it in these parts."

Isa grew more frustrated. They had the attention span of a new foal. Were they tired? They'd put in a full day's work. How could she make them understand the importance of being able to shoot? "Stop it! Drop the rock and pay attention. Gertie, get your weapon."

Gertie tossed the rock and picked up her revolver.

Isa stood squarely behind her. "Aim at the target."

Gertie aimed her gun with both hands. She fired. The gun kicked back and almost knocked her off balance. She didn't come close to the tree stump.

"You've got to squeeze the trigger, not pull on it like it was a cow teat. All of you come stand behind Gertie."

After an hour of instruction and practice, Abigail, Etta, and even Gertie were improving, but clearly Gertie's weapon was too much for her.

"I'll talk to Blue about an advance so you can get something easier to handle, Gertie."

"Many thanks."

Isa softened. Something about Gertie tugged at her heartstrings. Maybe because she was so young or that she'd already had such a hard life. Whatever the cause, they all seemed to feel it. Even Etta, as brassy as she acted toward her, was attached to her.

But it was perfectly clear that Laurel showed little interest in learning to shoot. Had it been a mistake to hire her? Isa would never be able to convince Blue of it. She had a tender spot for strays and a sad story.

Gertie stared off into the distance.

"Gertie, what's the matter?" Isa asked.

Gertie shrugged. "Nothing."

"All right. That's it for the night. You all wore me out," Isa said.

The group dispersed.

Isa went to the bench where Martha and Blue were and sat beside Blue. They'd been watching for most of the hour.

"Rosemary and Abigail look pretty good," Martha said.

"Lord help us if we run into trouble. They're not ready," Isa said. "Gertie can't use that gun. She'll kill herself or one of us."

Blue elbowed her gently. "They'll get better. I imagine we can take a couple of days and make a run to town at the end of the month. I'm sure all of them will want to get some things before the social, and Gertie can trade for a smaller one."

"I worry about them being able to protect themselves and each other," Isa said.

"Rosemary seems to be an exceptional shot," Martha said. "I like her. She's sensible. I've asked her to teach Gertie some better English and math. That's a powerful scar Abigail has on her face. Did you find out how it happened?"

"No. Not yet," Blue said. "She only said it happened when she was young. Some type of burn. I don't want to bring it up unless she does."

Martha nodded. "Best to wait until she tells us on her own."

Laurel came around the barn, making a beeline for them. "Something's wrong with Gertie."

Martha stood. "What?"

"She's back behind the barn, crying. She said she's dying." Laurel's face was red and strained.

"Did she hurt herself?" Martha asked. "She didn't shoot herself, did she? I didn't hear a gunshot."

They quickly followed Laurel toward the barn and found Gertie curled up in a ball so tight she could have rolled down a hill.

Martha sat and put her arm around her. She pushed Gertie's hair out of her eyes. "What's wrong, child? Did you get hurt? What happened?"

Gertie raised her head, sobbing. "I'm dyin', Martha. I'm dyin' for sure."

"Where are you hurt?" Martha asked.

Gertie's sobs grew louder. She wiped her runny nose on her sleeve. "I can't rightly say. I'm bleedin' all over, and it won't stop. I hurt like I been stuck."

Isa kneeled beside her, trying to see if she had blood anywhere. She couldn't find any signs of a cut or wound.

Martha had a wry smile on her face.

Gertie grabbed Isa's arm. "Help me. I'm dyin'. I most likely won't make it through the night." She cried harder and then began to rock back and forth, distraught.

And then it dawned on Isa what Gertie was going through. She stood. "I think we best let Martha handle this." She touched Blue's elbow and eased her away from Gertie's sobs.

"Evidently, Gertie wasn't expecting company," Blue whispered. "No wonder she's crying." She laughed. "I'll bet you a greenback no one explained to her anything about such goings-on."

Gertie was in for an eye-opening experience. Everything would change. No wonder she'd been moody and grouchy. What would have happened if she still lived alone? How would she have coped with the changes in her body? Who would have been there to explain to her she was only growing up and this was natural, not a death sentence? Although sometimes it did feel like it.

Isa chuckled. "It's been a long day, and I'm bone tired. I think I'll take a hot soak tonight."

"Are you sure? That sounds like a lot of work. I'll put some water on the stove for you."

Isa slipped her arm around Blue's waist as they walked toward the house. "That's sweet, but I'm sure you're as weary as I am."

"It's no bother."

A flash of orneriness streaked through Isa. "Would you like to take one with me?"

She watched as the blood rushed to Blue's cheeks. She loved her innocence and hoped Blue would never lose it.

"I...I...don't think I should. Could I?"

Isa grinned. "Most likely Martha wouldn't approve. But think what fun it would be."

Blue laughed. "Yes. It might be."

Blue did heat the water for her, two buckets full, while Isa pushed the tub into the corner of the kitchen and drew the curtain. As Isa soaked in the metal tub, her mind filled with Blue. She remembered the taste of her lips and feel of her skin against her fingertips. And the way her eyes danced when she looked at her in the morning light.

Breakfast was hurried the next morning.

"Laurel, you'll be in the kitchen with me today," Martha said. "We need to take inventory and organize the stores."

"I need to see how the rest of you fare with a rope and the horses," Blue said. "Bring your rigging and wear your chaps. I'll meet you at the corral." She set her empty cup on the table and went outside.

Gertie took the last bite of her biscuit and swilled it down with coffee. She wiped her mouth with her napkin and took her plate, fork, and cup to the wash bucket. "Isa, do you think Miss Blue is pleased with us?"

She must have gotten all her concerns worked out with Martha because she didn't seem addled.

"I think she likes it when you work hard and do your chores correctly," Isa said. "Come on now. Let's get to it."

By the time the sun was fully up, the corral fence had four females sitting on it, ropes in hand.

"I need that piebald cut from the herd," Blue said. "The one with the black mane and white spots. Abigail, get your rope."

Isa watched closely. Today she and Blue would find out who was worth their salt.

Abigail hopped from the fence and threaded her lariat through the knot. She stalked the piebald until he was in position. Then she twirled the rope and threw. Missed!

Loud moans filled the air.

"Come on, Abigail. Try it again. You can do it," Rosemary shouted.

Abigail adjusted her loop.

Isa watched her process, but before she could correct her, Blue spotted her problem.

"This time," Blue said, "let your arm swing directly at him, and line your shoulder with it."

Abigail nodded, flung the lariat, and landed it around the horse's neck.

Everyone cheered.

"Pick up the slack or the horse will break free," Blue yelled.

The piebald bucked and threw his head. Now it was getting good. How would Abigail get him under control? The other horses in the corral bolted away from the caught animal.

Abigail jerked the rope tight and walked toward him. "Steady," she said. "Easy."

She slowly let the rope out and forced him into a circle. Each time he threw his head or bucked, she made the circle smaller. She drew him in slowly, then made a halter with the rope and settled him. She led him to Blue. "Where do you want him?" she asked.

"Good. Put him in the other corral. Who wants to go next?" Blue asked.

Rosemary raised her hand. "Which one, Miss Blue?"

"Get the buckskin," Blue said.

Each demonstrated her ability. As small as Gertie was, she handled the rope like she was born to it. She'd probably been doing it since she could walk.

"What about Laurel?" Isa asked. "How will she do with a lariat and around the horses? It's not fair to the others if she doesn't pull her weight. Each one needs to do their job. Some are better than others, but they all have to rope, ride, and shoot. Otherwise, they'll put themselves and each other at risk."

"That's true," Blue said. "But I'm thinking she'd fare better doing other things. Martha needs the help. Gertie is more suited for this work than Laurel. And Gertie can hold her own with the others. There's plenty to do with Martha, and she'll keep her busy."

She addressed the group. "I want you ready tomorrow to turn the herd out. We're taking them a couple hours northwest of here and then letting them loose. Use the rest of the day to practice and get ready. We'll need to have a constant guard on them. I want you to change partners every few days so you can get used to working with each other. Rosemary, set the schedule."

Rosemary nodded and jumped from the fence.

Etta left and brought the General from the barn.

That's what she'd named her horse. He was fit and ready to ride. He'd never be the quality of the others, but he was good-tempered and trail smart. He would do to make the trips back and forth to the herd and to town.

"Remember, horses don't stand still to be roped," Blue said.

"Isa, could you help me get a little better at this?" Etta asked, holding her rope.

They worked hard throughout the day, honing their skills, and by evening they were as ready as they'd probably ever be.

Blue and Isa went for a walk after supper, which was turning into a nightly routine. It provided an opportunity to discuss the day and especially to be alone together.

"I look forward to this time with you," Blue said.

Isa touched her arm. "I do as well. It's good for both of us. The days are going by so fast."

They walked on in silence.

"Do you think they'll be ready tomorrow?" Blue asked.

Isa peered at the sky. Sunset was casting a palette of pastels across its canvas. Ribbons of pink, yellow, and purple hung in the heavens. It was magnificent. A feeling of peace and contentment swept over her. She turned to Blue and brought her close.

They kissed.

"You always surprise me," Blue said. "I like it when you kiss me."

Isa brushed Blue's cheek. "It's hard to keep from kissing you, but I know we need to be careful. When we sit by the campfire with the others, or when we're in the house getting ready for the day, I want to take you in my arms. And the nights are the worst."

Blue slipped her arm in Isa's and nudged her forward. "I know I don't say much about it, but I do think about you. Sometimes I can feel your arms around me." She kicked the dirt with her boot. "I'm not sure where we go from here."

Isa laid her hand over Blue's arm as they continued to walk. "Let's do whatever feels right."

"I like that idea," Blue said. "I'm going to stay with the herd tomorrow night. I think you or I should be with the others for a while, at least until we have more confidence in them."

Isa agreed.

They strolled along the creek.

"Does the water look low to you, or is it just me?" Isa asked.

Blue separated from Isa and walked closer to the bank. "It does seem down, but I don't know how low it gets in the summer. It's been dry."

They turned at their usual spot and headed home.

The morning light had barely peeked through the window in the loft when Isa woke fully. She'd heard Blue rise long before daybreak. She dressed and descended the ladder.

Martha and Laurel were busy preparing breakfast.

"Did Blue eat already?" Isa asked.

"I don't think so," Martha said. "I thought she was still sleeping."

"She left a while ago," Isa said. Where had she gone? "I'll check on her."

She went to the barn and found Blue had placed the bows and cover on the wagon and was loading supplies.

"You're up awfully early. You'll wear yourself out before the day's through."

"It's better if we have cover instead of a packhorse in case of bad weather. I want to leave as soon as possible." Blue continued to load the items.

Isa felt her worry. "Hey, ease up for a minute. What's troubling you?"

Blue stopped and turned toward her. She removed her gloves and leaned on the wagon boards, scrubbing her face. "Have I made a mistake thinking these women can do the job? What if something happens to them?" Her jaw muscles tightened, and her eyebrows furrowed.

Isa moved closer to her. "You forgot. You didn't have a choice to hire females. Yes. There's always a risk someone could be injured. I've seen plenty of cowboys get hurt doing the job. Sometimes because of accidents and sometimes because of others' mistakes. It happens. You've tried to prepare these women the best you can. It was their choice to come here. I think they all understand the danger, even Gertie. Probably especially Gertie. Would you feel this way if they were men?"

Blue breathed deeply. "No. I don't think I would."

"Why?"

"Because they'd be men. But these are women."

"No," Isa said. "It's not that. It's because of what you expect from them."

Blue quieted and stared at the ground.

Isa could tell she was thinking about what she'd said. "Rosemary, Abigail, and Gertie are well skilled in what you want them to do. It's true, Etta needs some work. But she's smart and learns fast. They can do the job. Don't cut them short because they aren't male. Plenty of men are incapable of the work you need these women to do."

Blue nodded. "I suppose you're right. It's a way of thinking that's hard to get my mind around. There's been a lot of that lately. Sometimes I feel like I'm trying to cross a creek bed full of slippery stones."

Isa wrapped her arms around her and held tight.

Blue rested her head on her shoulder.

Suddenly Etta appeared and stopped short.

Isa saw her surprised expression and moved away from Blue, not for her own sake but for Blue's.

"Martha sent me to get you two."

"We'll be right there," Blue said, not looking at her.

Etta left.

Blue grabbed Isa's arm. "Do you think she saw anything?"

"Yes. She saw me hugging you. Is that so bad?"

Blue slipped on her gloves and busied herself loading supplies. "You go in. I'll be along in a minute."

"Blue, don't hide it. I'd bet everyone sees how we feel about each other. If they don't like it, they can move on."

Blue threw a blanket into the wagon, then raked her hand along the boards. "You know how people talk."

"Let them talk."

Blue stared into the wagon. "Go on. I'll be there shortly."

It was clear she wanted to be alone. Isa knew Blue well enough to understand she needed time. It wouldn't be easy for her to face this situation. "I'm right here with you. It's going to be all right."

Blue pursed her lips, picked up a lantern, and put it into the wagon.

There was nothing more to say. Isa touched her arm and returned to the house.

CHAPTER SIXTEEN

Blue watched from a distance while the others maneuvered the herd. She rested her leg on Traveler's neck, in front of the saddle horn, her elbow on her thigh. Traveler shifted his weight and snorted. She stroked his neck. They'd gotten the horses where she wanted them, and now the herd was settling in and seemed content.

Abigail and Gertie stopped at the base of the mountain. Gertie waved her hat.

Blue repositioned in the saddle, slipping her boots into the stirrups. What had they seen? She urged Traveler into a canter, then stopped by Rosemary. "You and Etta stay here with the horses." She reined Traveler away and took off.

Isa caught up with her. "What is it?"

"I don't know, but I think they want us over there."

Gertie had dismounted and was bent over inspecting the ground when they reached them.

"What's wrong?" Blue asked.

Gertie pointed to the dirt. "Lots of horse and wagon tracks here."

Blue dismounted and kneeled by the tracks. They led toward the mountains and canyon. "More horses, and now wagon tracks, deep, like something was being hauled."

Isa came beside her. "There were no wagon tracks before."

"Let's follow them and see where they go," Blue said.

"I'll lead, Miss Blue," Gertie said. "I've tracked lots of animals and such."

Blue nodded. "Mind your surroundings."

Gertie rode about a hundred yards in front of them and continued northwest. A half hour later she dismounted and squatted. She motioned to the group. "They stop here," she called.

The others gathered by her.

"What do you mean they stop? That's not likely." Blue got off Traveler and stood beside her, searching the area. But Gertie was right. The tracks had disappeared.

"That's not possible," Abigail said. "They couldn't have just vanished into the air."

"Spread out and search. They have to be here somewhere," Blue said.

They fanned out in different directions.

About three hundred yards from the others, Abigail called to them. "Over here!"

Wagon-wheel marks were etched into the rocks.

"That doesn't happen without repeated use," Blue said. She surveyed the area. Nothing. "What's going on?"

"Is this still your property, Miss Blue?" Abigail asked.

"Yes. For another mile."

"Let's keep looking," Isa said.

"Gertie, you go west with Isa. Abigail and I will go north," Blue said.

They split and went in their designated directions. Blue and Abigail rode for another ten minutes before they saw what they might have been searching for. A mine shaft in the side of the mountain. Blue drew her weapon and fired into the air to signal the others.

She and Abigail secured their horses and began inspecting the outside of the opening. Clumps of large rocks and boulders were piled to the side. Deep grooves from wheels were dug into the dirt.

"Someone's mining something," Abigail said. "And from the sight of it, they've done a lot. Is this your property?"

"Yes. It is," Blue said slowly, not disbelieving what she was seeing. She started to enter the shaft.

"I wouldn't do that without first knowing what's in there, Miss Blue. There could be cougars, or worse."

"Worse?"

"Yeah. Sinkholes or snakes. That shaft doesn't appear none too stable. It might collapse. We best wait for the others."

Blue agreed.

Isa and Gertie arrived a few minutes later, their horses lathered.

"Everything all right?" Isa asked.

Blue nodded. "We found a mine."

The others got off their horses and walked to the shaft.

Isa peered inside. "I can't see much in the dark."

Blue took a few steps in.

Isa grabbed her arm. "Be careful."

Blue saw three torches piled together. She grabbed one and lit it with a stick match from her pocket. The smell of kerosene filled the air around her. She called the others.

Abigail and Isa lit the remaining torches.

The walls became visible. A few picks and shovels with broken handles and rotted wooden buckets lay against them.

Abigail touched the wall and ran her hand along the pick marks. "I suspect someone was mining for silver. See the way the marks are formed?"

"Was?" Isa asked.

"It's been a spell," Abigail said. "Maybe a year or two. If this is your property, Miss Blue, you've been robbed."

The shaft was almost ten feet wide and went into the mountain about fifty yards.

When they'd seen what they could, they smothered the torches and left the mine. Blue shaded her eyes from the sudden sting of sunlight.

They gathered by their horses.

"Let's get back," Isa said. "I'm sure Etta and Rosemary are worried about us."

They mounted and began the journey. Isa rode beside Blue.

Blue didn't know what to make of it. Who did it? How long had they been at it? How much silver did they get? If the shaft hadn't been worked in a year or two, why were there fresh wagon tracks near the mountain? Whose were they?

She had so many questions her head hurt. They traveled in silence back to the herd.

Rosemary rode out to meet them. "Everyone all right?"

Blue nodded.

They built a campfire, and while they prepared supper, Blue told Rosemary and Etta what they'd found. "Rosemary, you and Etta will have watch tonight. Gertie, Abigail, and I will stay with the herd while you two and Isa leave for home at first light. Spell us in two days. Tell Martha I'll be here a while."

As they gathered to eat their meal, she hoped Isa wouldn't sit beside her. She wasn't sure why. She chided herself. That wasn't true. She knew perfectly well why. She'd lied to herself. She didn't want her to sit by her because Etta would be watching, and she'd judge her. Isa could go back with Rosemary and Etta in the morning. There was no point in her being here if Blue was going to stay. Blue hated herself for feeling this way. Why did she react like this? The feelings grated against her, rubbing her heart raw.

"Who were the riders, and why a wagon?" Abigail asked.

"I saw riders' tracks before," Isa said. "They went toward the ranch and then headed northeast."

"Maybe from Carson City," Gertie said.

"Frank Anderson lives a little east of Carson City," Abigail said, then took a bite of beef jerky.

A sinking feeling shot through Blue. What if it had been him?

Isa watched her from across the campfire.

What was she thinking? Could she feel Blue's turmoil? Blue wanted to talk with her about what had happened earlier in the morning, but she felt too unsettled. Would Etta say anything to the others? Had Isa spoken the truth? Had they all noticed? What if she and Isa did stand too close, or lingered too long together?

It was her ranch. They worked for her. Should she care what they thought? Etta had been a prostitute. She had a lot of nerve judging her.

Blue stood. "I'll keep first watch. The rest of you get some sleep." She mounted Traveler and rode out of camp to the herd. They were quiet and settled. Unlike her. She slowly circled, keeping her distance, watching the terrain. A few of the horses looked up and perked their ears when an owl hooted in a distant pine. She stopped and listened. The night sounds stilled.

Isa appeared on Adelita, whispering when she neared. "It's quiet, isn't it?"

"Yes. Why aren't you asleep?"

"Why aren't you?" Isa asked. "Rosemary and Etta are perfectly capable of standing watch."

A cutting silence distanced them. The insects around the lake began their serenade once again.

How could Blue admit to her what she felt when she couldn't acknowledge it herself? She wanted to be with her, yet she didn't.

They rode in silence. When Blue was sure no one could hear, she decided to try to explain how she felt. Isa deserved that much. But before she could say anything, Isa spoke.

"You're bothered by what the others may think, aren't you?" Isa reined Adelita to a stop.

"Yes, but I'm confused if I should care what they think."

A few of the horses started moving. Two whinnied.

Blue stopped talking and listened, straining to see.

Etta appeared and guided her horse to them.

Isa backed Adelita away from Traveler. "I'm going to camp. You two should talk."

And then she left.

The blood rushed to Blue's cheeks and neck. Could Etta see it in the darkness? How could Isa ride away and leave her there alone to face Etta? What was she thinking?

A deafening silence surrounded her. She wanted the night to engulf her, consume her, help her disappear.

And then Etta spoke.

"Miss Blue, I know what you're feeling. I've had the same stirrings myself a time or two."

Blue glanced at her but didn't speak.

"I guess what I'm saying is I understand. Except I haven't been as lucky as you. I haven't found someone who looks at me the way you and Isa look at each other. I wish I had. I'd give anything to have what you two have."

Blue's cheeks grew hotter. She wanted to turn Traveler and gallop away.

"It's all right, Miss Blue."

The words still wouldn't come. Blue tried but they weren't there.

They sat on their horses in silence, the thick darkness hovering around Blue until she could hardly breathe. Etta remained beside her in the stillness.

Then, in the quiet, everything seemed to settle. A soft breeze, carrying the faint scent of pine, touched Blue's face. She glanced at Etta, who was watching the herd. Should she say it? Could she say it? She mustered what little courage she had left.

"I'm afraid," she said, choking on the words.

Etta peered at her with soft eyes. "I know. But don't ever be afraid of love. Lord knows it doesn't come often. I know about the darker side of desire, Miss Blue. And believe me, what you and Isa have is something special. If I was you, I'd grab onto it with both hands and hold on like your life depended on it. Because it just might."

In that instant, Blue wanted to ride back to camp and gather Isa in her arms. "You're a lot younger than me, Etta. How'd you get so wise?"

"I suspect most folks learn what love isn't before they know what it is. I've had a sack full of what isn't. Believe me, Miss Blue, at this point in my life, I'd settle for kindness and friendship. Why don't you head back to camp and rest? I imagine you're full spent. Wake Rosemary. We were supposed to be on watch anyway."

"Thank you for your understanding and kindness, Etta." Blue turned Traveler and started toward camp.

"Miss Blue?"

Blue stopped and looked back. "Yes."

"I appreciate what you've done for me. I won't let you down. And I'm grateful to you for fixing the General." Etta stroked his neck. "He's a fine horse."

"I didn't do much. Isa was the one who doctored him. Be safe tonight. Keep a close watch, especially toward the northeast."

Blue could see the glow of the campfire in the distance. The closer she got, the more she wanted to talk with Isa. Would she be awake?

She settled Traveler, then woke Rosemary for her watch. Abigail and Gertie were sound asleep near the wagon. Isa was alone on the other side of the fire. Blue decided not to disturb her. Better to wait until morning.

Her heart lightened, and relief filled her mind. She put her bedroll as near to Isa as she thought proper in case the others woke in the night, but she wanted to be closer. What would Isa do in the morning?

CHAPTER SEVENTEEN

Isa woke suddenly, hearing someone call her name. Or was it only a noise? She peered through the bleakness of pre-dawn. The campfire coals were nearly out. Gertie and Abigail must have been on watch because Rosemary and Etta were asleep on the opposite side of the fire. Where was Blue? Had she changed her mind and left for home? Relief washed over Isa when she discovered her close by, near her feet.

Isa lay on her back watching the stars as they began to lose their visibility, hoping Blue wasn't upset with her for telling Etta to talk with her. Had she been able to get things clear in her mind? No matter how Blue felt, at least she'd stayed and remained close by. All positive things.

Isa slipped from her bedding and stoked the coals, placing more wood on the fire as quietly as she could.

Blue stirred, then rolled toward her. "Isa," she called softly. "Come here."

Isa went to her and knelt, glad for the invitation.

Blue lifted her blanket and took Isa's hand, guiding her toward her. She slid her arm around Isa's neck and pulled her close, then kissed her.

Isa lay beside her as they continued to kiss. The warmth of Blue's body, and her encouragement to be with her, sent a clear invitation. But Isa was keenly aware of their surroundings. "The others will be up any minute."

"Yes. They will," Blue whispered. "I just wanted to let you know I wish we were alone."

Isa couldn't stop her smile. "You feel better about things, then?"

"Much. Will you stay here with me today instead of going back to the ranch? Rosemary and Etta can handle things there."

Isa kissed her again. "Yes. We can go for a ride later and talk."

"Good."

Blue seemed to relax, and a contented expression brightened her face.

"I don't know what you and Etta discussed, but it must have helped," Isa said.

Blue nodded but said nothing.

Blue would talk to her when she was ready, so Isa changed the subject. "It's not easy to do a four-hour watch and then stand guard all day. With two, they can at least take turns catching up on their sleep. And the teams can go back to the ranch every two days."

Blue grazed Isa's cheek with her lips.

Desire raced through Isa, lodging in her deepest parts. She wanted to roll over onto Blue. Touch her. Caress.

"It's not an unreasonable situation," Blue said. "And I feel comfortable about them being here with the horses."

Isa took a deep breath, trying to settle herself. "You have a lot invested in your animals. I know it's important to you. We better get up." She forced herself from Blue, then rose and began to pack her things.

Blue stretched and yawned. "Rosemary and Etta will stay until later in the morning to give Abigail and Gertie time to sleep, and then they'll leave for the ranch."

In the afternoon, after lunch, Isa and Blue managed to get time alone.

Isa was curious about Blue and Etta's conversation and hoped Blue would tell her soon, but she'd have to let her decide when.

They rode to the silver mine, scouted the area more thoroughly for any clue as to who might have trespassed, and then started back to the herd. They hadn't found a single trace of evidence to identify the trespassers.

"Whoever mined it probably came back when they found out I was on the property," Blue said. "Then they cleared everything out, and I helped them."

"What do you mean?"

"I gave them plenty of time when I wrote to the surveyor's office and let them know I was coming. You know, if we ride into town and ask around, we might find out who the surveyor spoke with about it."

"That may not work," Isa said. "I'm sure he talked with lots of people. It's big news, and especially that you're a woman taking over the ranch. The entire town probably gossiped about it with him."

Blue grew quiet.

Was she ready to discuss her and Etta's conversation?

Isa adjusted in the saddle, waiting.

"Did you tell Etta to come talk with me?" Blue asked.

Isa gripped the reins tighter and hesitated to answer. What if Blue didn't like that she'd told Etta? But the deed had been done, so she couldn't do much about it now. "Yes. I mentioned you were upset and suggested she have a conversation with you."

Blue reached for Isa's hand.

Isa grabbed it, relieved.

"I'm glad you did," Blue said. "It was hard but the best thing that could have happened."

"So, you got it settled in your mind?" Isa asked.

Blue nodded. "I did. I…" She looked toward the direction of the herd and let go of Isa's hand. "Did you hear that?" She tilted her head. "It's gunshots." She urged Traveler into a full gallop.

Isa followed close behind.

The shots became more distinct as they narrowed the distance to camp. Three…then four. Pauses. Then more.

Isa drew her rifle as she rode.

"Fire northeast into the air before we get there. Maybe it'll scare them off," Blue yelled. "Bastards."

Isa saw the dust rise from the herd before she saw the horses. They were scattering and headed toward them. Gertie and Abigail were nowhere to be found. "Where are they?"

Blue pointed toward the lake. "There, by those rocks."

Abigail and Gertie were firing in the direction Blue had predicted.

The herd began to veer toward the base of the mountain range.

Isa and Blue thundered toward Abigail and Gertie's position.

"Fire toward that clump of pines," Blue shouted, shooting her weapon.

Isa aimed and rapid-fired directly into the trees. Gertie stood and waved her hat.

They kept riding, straight past her and Abigail, toward the trees.

"That's right. Run, you bastards," Abigail yelled toward the pines. "You picked on the wrong women."

She and Gertie mounted their horses and beelined behind Isa.

Blue didn't slow until they got to within a few feet of the trees.

"They hightailed it when they saw you two," Gertie said.

"Isa, you and Gertie go south around the tree line. Abigail and I'll meet you on the other side." She pointed to Isa. "You watch yourself."

Isa nodded and took off with Gertie.

They searched the timber, guns at the ready, but saw no sign of the shooters.

They met Blue and Abigail on the other side.

"There." Gertie pointed northeast.

They could still see rising dust from the running horses, but the riders were nowhere in sight. They turned and tracked their trail through the woods to the disturbed pine needles and footprints where they'd been.

"We best get the herd before they go too far," Isa said.

They rode from the woods.

"No!" Blue cried and galloped away.

There, on the ground, struggling to get up, lay her prized stallion. Blue dismounted on the run and went to him. "No…No!"

Isa managed to get to her and held Blue out of the way of the stud's flailing hooves. He had two shots in his neck and one in his belly and was gasping for air. Even if she and Blue wanted to save him, which they did, it was hopeless. He had to be put down.

The task fell to Isa. Blue wasn't capable of it.

Isa returned to Adelita and reluctantly drew her rifle. She stepped to the stallion and aimed at his head. But before she could fire, he gasped his last breath. She breathed a sigh of relief, knowing she didn't have to shoot him.

Blue dropped to her knees. "Why? Why would they do this vicious thing? Why?"

Isa handed her weapon to Gertie, guided Blue to her feet, and took her in her arms.

Blue trembled so hard she felt like she would break apart.

There was nothing Isa could say. It made no sense why they would do it. Only that whoever did it was out to destroy Blue, and they'd stop at nothing.

"Abigail, you and Gertie go get the herd. Slow-walk them back," Isa said.

Blue started to collapse in her arms.

"Let's get you to the wagon," Isa said.

She walked Blue to Traveler and helped her mount, and then they rode to the campsite.

Isa tied the horses and reached into the stores and brought out the bottle of whiskey. She sat Blue beside the wagon, poured some of the alcohol into a tin cup, and handed it to her.

Blue grasped it with shaking hands. "Why?" she said, trying to catch her breath. She took a big drink and choked.

Isa rested her hand on Blue's shoulder. "It's sipping whiskey, not gulping whiskey."

Blue shook her head. "I don't understand. Why?"

Isa knew whoever did it couldn't have hurt Blue more. It'd been a calculated move. The stud and the mares were Blue's future, and her success depended on their survival.

Blue took another drink from the cup. Her hands had stopped trembling. She stared at the ground, then threw the cup in the dirt and stood abruptly. "The mares?"

"I'm sure they're fine. The herd should be back in a little while. We can check them then."

She clutched Isa's arm. "I want them at the ranch. We need to protect them. They're my only hope. Nothing can happen to them."

Her face was pale and drawn.

Isa took her in her arms again. "We will. We'll guard them with our lives. They'll be safe."

The herd came over the rise.

"They're back. Look!" Isa said.

Abigail and Gertie walked them to the lake. The horses were a little flighty, but in general, they seemed to be in good condition.

"I want to check them more closely," Blue said. She took Isa's hand. "Come with me?"

They rode to the herd and inspected each of the mares, paying closer attention to the remaining three Blue had brought with her from Texas.

"They seem healthy and strong. I don't see any injuries or marks on them," Isa said. She left Blue and went to the other riders.

Blue lingered with the mares before she came to Abigail and Gertie. "Tell me what happened."

"Everything was fine," Abigail said. "Then, out of nowhere, we heard three shots. The stallion went down. We fired our pistols as we took cover in those rocks yonder." She pointed toward the lake.

"How many were there?" Isa asked.

Gertie shook her head. "We couldn't tell. They hit us too fast. We kept firing. Don't know if we hit any of them. Then you two started shooting, and they stopped and ran off. If you hadn't come back when you did, I don't know what would have happened."

"I hope you shot the hell out of them," Blue said.

"We didn't see any blood trails, so we probably didn't," Abigail said. "I'm so sorry about the stud, Miss Blue."

"It's not your fault," Blue said. "Whoever they were knew they'd only get one chance at him. You did the best you could. I'm glad neither of you were hurt. Thank you for doing what you did."

"How do you want to handle this, Blue?" Isa asked.

"I'd like to pick up their trail and hunt them down and shoot them in the balls. But I need to get my three mares out of harm's way. Isa, can we talk a minute?"

Isa rode with Blue a little distance from the others.

"What do you think is the best way to get the mares back to the ranch and still keep all the other horses and us safe?"

Isa wanted to remain with Blue wherever she went, but it probably wasn't the best plan. It would be wisest to split up since they were the best shots and had the most experience. Blue was vulnerable and needed to be at the ranch where she could control her surroundings and better protect the mares. They'd be safer in the barn and not exposed out in the open. She could put them in the corrals during the day and in the stalls at night. There'd be plenty of room at the ranch with the rest of the herd here by the lake. And it would certainly be less worry for Blue.

"I think it's best if you and Gertie take your three prized mares back home, and Abigail and I can keep the rest here. Once the others have more experience and things are well in hand, I'll come back to the ranch. I don't know how long it'll be. I won't leave unless I know they can handle the situation."

Blue nodded. "You're right. If you aren't home in a few days, I'll come see you."

"I'd like that. I know we didn't get to finish talking."

Blue touched her arm. "There's more to be said, but it'll have to wait. We'll start for home soon. I know this probably sounds silly, but could we bury the stud?" She took a stuttered breath. "I don't think I could stand thinking about him lying out here on the open ground with the birds and critters picking at him." She drew her arms around herself. Her hands were trembling again. "I know it's…I need to do it."

"Of course. The other horses won't go around him anyway, and it'll make them nervous if we don't do something about the carcass."

Blue squeezed her hand. "Thank you."

They dug a deep pit near where he'd been shot and buried him.

Gertie and Blue left in time to arrive at the ranch by dark.

Isa was relieved to know Blue and her mares would be safe.

She and Abigail stayed by the herd, not wanting to go to camp.

"Who do you think would do such a thing, Isa?"

"We all know who did it. We just don't have any proof."

"Anderson? I wouldn't put it past him," Abigail said. "You know what I think?"

"What?"

"He's most likely the one who mined Miss Blue's property, and he's trying to run her off so no one will find out about that. He didn't come here with money. Word is in Silver Springs he was about ready to give up his property several years ago."

Isa perked up.

"Then, next thing we hear, he paid his debts and his back taxes and bought more land. Sounds suspicious to me. Don't you think?"

Not only did it sound suspicious, but it also sounded very plausible. "Did you say he bought more property?"

Abigail nodded. "Yes. And his neighbor to the north never wanted to sell it. I know that for a fact because his son, Albert, was sweet on my sister for a while and told me everything. That's one of the things I didn't like about him. He gossiped like an old woman. Never could shut his mouth."

Isa sat quietly on Adelita.

Abigail went on to talk more about her family. After what seemed like an hour, Isa wished she'd stop talking. She told Abigail she'd go make supper, just to get away from her jabbering.

After they finished their meal and dusk approached, Isa rebuilt the fire and lay on her bedroll. Abigail had taken first night watch. They decided to do two hours alone and then a two-man watch through the rest of the night, in case the raiders decided to come back.

The stars in the clear night hung over her like a canopy. Three shooting stars, one after another, streaked across the sky. She thought of making love with Blue under these stars. Was she there at the ranch thinking of her? Or was her mind too full of what had happened to the horses?

Blue's situation still held hope. She had three mares that would foal in the spring. If one of the births was a colt, she could use it as a stud in two to three years. He'd have the fine qualities of his sire. It would set her back, but eventually she'd have a stud she wanted. And if she had more than one colt, she could sell them at a good price. With any luck, the other stock mares had also been covered by the stud. Although those mares weren't the quality of the other three, they'd produce good foals.

Anderson? How could they get the evidence to prove he did it? And once they had it, would the law stop him?

Blue!

Isa drifted off with thoughts of her kiss and the taste of her lips.

Chapter Eighteen

F our days had passed since Blue had brought the mares back or seen Isa. In that time, she and the others had extended the corral and made larger stalls in the barn for the mares when they were ready to foal.

Each time the others had left to stand their watch with Isa and the herd, Blue wanted to go with them, but the situation at the ranch had grown more troublesome. The tributary had now slowed to a trickle, and two nights in a row she'd seen the distant light of a campfire along the creek bank. She waited anxiously for the riders to report. Isa's last message was that the herd had adjusted and all was quiet for now.

She decided to go with Etta and Abigail in the morning when they left for their assignment. She wanted to see Isa, but more than that, she needed to tell her the situation. Martha could oversee the work for the day.

"Put those posts wider apart," Blue said.

Etta and Abigail had worked tirelessly since finishing their watch with the herd.

Now, only a few weeks until September, the weather was comfortable and pleasant, but it would turn cold soon enough. They had accomplished a lot on the property since they'd first arrived. The house and barn had been repaired, the bunkhouse built, the corrals were being extended, and they had five capable workers. Her situation had greatly improved, yet sometimes it felt bleaker than ever. Losing the stud had devastated her, and the depletion of the water in the creek grew more dire each day. Would she ever feel safe and content or get away from the worry of it all?

The garden flourished, and Martha and Laurel would get a fine yield from it. Rosemary had managed to kill an elk by the creek, and Laurel had butchered it, salted and smoked a part of it, and managed to can the rest. She'd proved a valuable help to Martha, which had surprised Blue the most.

She leaned on the corral fence and watched Abigail and Etta dig the postholes.

Martha came out of the house and stood beside her with a cup of coffee in her hand. "Are you ready to go to the herd tomorrow?"

Blue nodded. "I've decided to stay just for the day. It's best. Two riders can manage the herd now. They've all adjusted pretty well, and I need Isa here."

Martha watched the women toil. "They're hard workers. When will you stop guarding the herd?"

Blue kicked the rail with her boot. "Soon, I suppose."

"I imagine snow will be here in late November or early December," Martha said.

Blue had never been in large amounts of snow and didn't know what to expect. But Martha was right. The weather would eventually change, and they'd best be prepared. "Don't rush it. It's only late August."

"It'll be here soon enough," Martha said. "Time is slipping by. "We've been here almost four months already."

Blue's worry for the group's safety wouldn't leave her.

"I imagine all the girls will want to go to the social." Martha's referral to the hires as *girls* showed how attached she was to them. It was in her nature to mother them, and Blue was glad. They all needed it.

"Except Etta. She's made it clear she wants no part of the event," Blue said.

"Why?"

"She didn't say. Let's ask her. Etta, come over here."

Etta stopped her work, pulled off her gloves, and walked to Blue.

"Why aren't you going to the social?" Blue asked.

Etta wiped her cheek with her sleeve and leaned on her shovel. "Miss Blue, I've been on my back with half the men in this territory. I don't want to have to dance with any of them."

Martha laughed. "Fair enough."

"Besides, I imagine it'll be good to have someone here while all of you are away," Etta said.

"You won't mind staying behind?" Martha asked.

"No. I'd rather not be with any of them. They'd be wanting a poke. And I'd be a mind to pull out my pistol and give them a poke of my own!"

Martha cackled. Blue couldn't help but laugh.

"I'll hold down the fort while all of you go." Etta went back to work.

Blue took a drink from Martha's cup and returned it. "Smart woman."

"What about Abigail?" Martha asked. "Will she be comfortable going?"

Blue shrugged. "She said she'd go. I'm sure some folks will stare, but she has to get on with her life, scarred or not."

"Did you find out how it happened?" Martha asked.

"She didn't tell me, but she told Rosemary. Evidently, when she was eleven, her baby brother's night clothes caught fire when he was playing in front of the fireplace. She grabbed him up and put out the fire but got burnt in her effort."

"How tragic. I admire her even more now," Martha said.

The night trudged on.

Blue tossed and couldn't get settled. How was Isa? Did she miss her? She went to the barn loft and once again saw the light of a fire in the distance. Who was out there? Dread crept up her spine. Should she go on her own to investigate? No. Better to wait for Isa to come back.

At dawn Etta and Abigail loaded the packhorse and prepared to leave.

Blue saddled Traveler and tied him to the rail, then returned to the house. "I'll be back by nightfall. Gertie and Rosemary should be home by lunchtime. If Laurel will bake one of her cakes, I'm sure they'd enjoy it."

Martha hugged her. "I'll see to it. You watch yourself. We'll be leaving for town Thursday late and camp at the river."

"Rosemary can drive the wagon home this afternoon," Blue said.

They said their good-byes, and Blue left with the others.

The closer they got to camp, the more eager she grew to see Isa. She spotted her by the wagon rooting around for something. Gertie waved her hat and started toward them. Rosemary waved from the far side of the herd.

The horses appeared good, content.

Abigail tied the packhorse, and then she and Etta rode over near the lake with the others.

Isa stopped her task. A huge smile appeared, and her eyes brightened. "You're finally here."

Blue dismounted Traveler and rushed to her. She threw her arms around her, hugging her as tight as she could.

Isa laughed. "I think you missed me as much as I missed you."

"I'm sure I missed you more." Blue pushed Isa behind the wagon, so the others couldn't see, then kissed her, full-on without any restraint.

Isa reciprocated, soft and full of promise of things to come.

"Let's go somewhere so we can be alone," Blue said.

"We can ride west, to the pines where we were before," Isa said. She got a blanket, then mounted Adelita. "Race you there." She took off.

Blue grabbed Traveler's reins and gripped the horn. She let him start before she mounted, then took two hops forward and let the momentum swing her up into the saddle.

Adelita was fast, but Traveler caught up quickly and, to Blue's surprise, overtook her before they reached the trees.

They eased to a walk.

"Is it just me, or has Adelita gotten fat?"

Isa patted Adelita's neck. "She's not fat. She's healthy. Look how her coat shines."

"I swear she looks fat to me." Blue said. "She's getting lazy standing around watching the other horses."

Isa smiled and dismounted. She laid the covering over a bed of pine needles. Before she could get all the way seated, Blue grabbed her and pulled her down onto the blanket with her.

"You *are* glad to see me." Isa chuckled.

Blue held her face in her hands and gazed into her eyes. They were a vivid amber, rich with color. "I've hardly slept for thinking about you." She kissed her, long and deep, unhurried, and full of wanton pleasure.

Isa moved to Blue and pressed into her.

Blue embraced her and buried her face in her neck, refusing to let go. She didn't want to spend another moment away from her.

They lay together without speaking.

Blue's heart beat wildly, and she ached to be touched. Isa made her feel this way. Isa excited her. No one had ever stirred her like this. She breathed in her scent. Campfire. Horse. And her body. "Isa," she whispered.

Isa somehow held her closer, kissing her neck and cheek, and then her lips.

"Please, touch me," Blue said. The words came out in a pleading whisper, her desperation surprising even her. She closed her eyes. All she wanted to think about was now. Not about the horses, or the ranch, or all the things that had happened. Or the future or the past. Or even who was camped by the creek. Only this moment.

"I've wanted to touch you since the first day I saw you." Isa spoke in a hushed tone, her breath in Blue's ear.

Rivulets of desire and need surged through Blue.

Isa hesitated. "But I'm afraid something's wrong." She slipped from Blue and propped herself on her elbow, watching her. "What is it? What's happened?"

Blue flinched, then pulled Isa to her. "I don't want to think of anything but you and me. Here. Now."

Isa tensed. She sat, lifting Blue with her. "What is it? Tell me what's happened."

Isa wasn't going to give her this time together. *Why?* "Please? Can't we just be here now?"

"Yes. We could," Isa said. "I've thought of nothing but you since you left. And I want to do this, but I can tell something's wrong."

Isa had shown Blue her gifts. Revealed her wonders. And Blue wanted her. All of her. And she wanted Isa to touch and caress every part of her. So why not take it?

Blue began to unbutton her own shirt. She slipped it over her shoulders, then took off her undershirt, exposing her hard, erect nipples.

A moan passed through Isa's lips.

Blue breathed out her name, then gasped, pressing into her, unable to restrain herself. Her need to be touched raged. Did Isa know how much Blue needed this?

Isa guided her down onto the blanket.

Blue wanted more. Much more.

Isa lifted slightly and handed Blue her undershirt. "I'm sorry. I promise we will have time to love one another, but not today. Talk to me."

Blue lay stunned, the ache of frustration coursing through her. She wanted to be angry, but the pleasures Isa promised her overshadowed all other emotion. *Would* they have time?

Isa remained close. "Get dressed and tell me what's troubling you."

After Blue covered herself, Isa took her hand and kissed it.

"I want to be angry with you, but I can't. Not after what I just felt," Blue said.

Isa smiled, licked her lips, and swallowed, but she remained quiet.

Blue took a deep breath. Isa was right. They needed to talk. And as much as she wanted her, she shouldn't use them being together as an escape. They both deserved more than that. "The creek is down to hardly a trickle, and I've seen a campfire light the last couple of nights in the distance by the bank."

Isa stiffened. "Has anyone approached the property?"

"Not that I can tell. How have things been here? Any sign of anyone?"

Isa shook her head. "Not a soul. Every day I've ridden north and east and haven't seen a thing. No new tracks. No disturbances. Nothing."

"Do you think we can leave the riders alone with the herd, and you could come back with me to the ranch? We need to find out what's going on with the creek, and I think it's best if you and I do it together."

"They're ready. I trust each of them to do her job. I'm confident they can handle it. If there's trouble, one of them will ride back to get us."

Blue stood and pulled Isa up with her. They wouldn't be together like she'd wanted. That much was clear. "Let's get started. I don't want to be away from the ranch any longer than I have to."

They rode to the herd, and Blue eyed the horses carefully. They seemed good. "That chestnut with the star on its forehead, is she the lead mare?"

"Yes. She's guided them to water and pasture, and seems to be doing a good job. How are your mares?"

"We keep them in the corral during the day and stall them at night." Blue inspected Isa's horse more closely. "Isa, do you think Adelita might be pregnant? She seems wider, and she's slower than before."

Isa dismounted and handed the reins to Blue. She stepped back and looked at Adelita. "She's not cinching tighter than usual, but now that you mention it, I haven't noticed her in heat in a while. I'll check her when we get back to the ranch. If she is pregnant, she'll have a fine foal from your stud."

"I'd like it if she was pregnant by him. It'd be a good legacy," Blue said.

"I would too. He was a fine stallion." Isa got back on Adelita. "If it's all right with you, I'd like to ride the buckskin just in case."

"That's fine. He's yours if you want him."

Gertie rode over to them. "Miss Blue, Rosemary and I will be leaving now. Will you be staying here?"

"Why, Gertie, I believe your English has improved," Blue said.

Gertie smiled. "Yes, ma'am. Rosemary has been learning… teaching me."

"Isa and I will be riding back today. Martha needs the wagon. If you and the others would get it ready, I'd like Rosemary to drive it home."

Gertie nodded. "Sure thing." She turned her horse and went to the campsite.

Rosemary and Etta had already put up the canvas tent, unloaded the supplies, and released the packhorse into the herd.

"It won't give them as much protection as the wagon, but at least it's some shelter from the elements."

"It's been fine weather. This is pretty country," Isa said. "I don't imagine the winters will be too miserable, although I'm curious to know what the snow will be like."

"I'm concerned about it. I'm sure there'll be more than we're used to," Blue said. She couldn't focus on the months ahead, only now. "We need to go north along the creek bed and try to find out what's going on with the water."

Isa nodded. She checked her rifle and slipped it back into the scabbard. "Gertie," she called. "Cut the buckskin from the herd and put a lead on him."

Gertie waved and moved toward the horse.

Isa would be coming back with Blue. She'd be there, riding beside her. Blue already felt relief. Was it Anderson that had already caused her so much heartache? She had a feeling she'd know soon.

CHAPTER NINETEEN

Isa saw the tension in Blue as she rode. Her fingers gripped the reins, her legs were stiff, and the muscles in her face were drawn.

Should she have made love to her like she'd asked? Was it right to hold off? She wasn't sure now, only that it'd felt right at the time. She hated second-guessing herself. They had to let it go for a while longer. They had too many unknowns to resolve. But when *would* it happen? Blue was beautiful, and her charms were more than Isa had imagined. She breathed deeply and tried to clear her head.

They reached the ranch by noon. Laurel had prepared a delicious meal of elk, cooked apples, green beans, and potatoes. She'd even made a spice cake. Isa had never eaten such a fine meal.

After they rested a few hours, Isa gathered the bronc saddle, harness, and rope, and tethered the buckskin. She took him into the corral and lunged him for a few minutes to settle him.

Gertie and Rosemary climbed onto the fence and watched.

Martha, Laurel, and Blue came out to see the show.

"I'd be pleased if you'd let me break him," Gertie said.

Isa waved her over. "Are you sure? He's going to be a handful."

"I'll give it my best," Gertie said.

"Be careful." Isa blindfolded the horse, positioned the blanket and the riding saddle on his back, then cinched it.

Gertie slipped on her gloves, pulled her hat low, and ambled up beside her.

Isa adjusted the stirrups to the first opening. "Up you go," she said. "Seat him deep. He's all muscle. He'll buck high and to the right."

Gertie was barely tall enough to reach the stirrup and get on. She positioned herself in the seat and grabbed the ropes on each side of his neck as Isa handed them to her.

"You ready?" Isa asked.

Gertie nodded and lowered her chin. "Let him buck."

"Ride him," Rosemary yelled.

Martha cupped her hands to her mouth. "Be careful, cowgirl."

The others clapped.

Isa removed the blindfold, then darted to the fence and hopped up on it.

The buckskin kicked out a back leg and swished his tail. Gertie circled him hard to the right.

"He's trying to get into position. Get ready," Blue yelled.

The horse dug his front hooves into the dirt, reared, and then hopped. He bucked, lifting his hind end to the right as Isa had predicted.

"Keep his head up," Blue yelled. She put her hand on Isa's thigh. "I think he's too much horse for her. He's going to toss her like she was a fly."

"I don't know. She's a determined little sprout," Isa said.

The horse spun and bucked. He hopped again, trying to get height, then kicked his hind legs in the air.

Gertie stayed with him until he dipped his head and bucked higher. She lost her balance and went sailing over his head. She landed on her bottom and slapped the ground. "Damn it." She leapt to her feet, brushed herself off, and reset her hat. "I'm going again."

Isa grabbed the back of her shirt as she went by. "No, you don't, rough rider. You go over there to the fence. You did good, but he's too much horse for you. I'll finish him."

Gertie stomped off and climbed up beside Rosemary, who gave her a quick hug.

Isa held the ropes and calmed the horse, then immediately went into the saddle.

He began to buck, twisting and turning. He was strong and coordinated, every bit the horse she thought he'd be. She pulled as hard as she could on the ropes, trying to keep his head up and rein him where she wanted him to go.

She lost track of time.

The dirt and dust swirled around her. Then she felt him give way beneath her. He was breathing hard. He'd given her all he had. He half bucked and then settled into a walk. Each time he started to kick out she pulled him hard in a circle. They both were soaked in sweat by the time it was over. She rode him around the pen several times, then stopped next to Gertie and dismounted.

She handed his ropes to her. "I want you to walk him out and clean him up, then give him a good feed. Tomorrow you start working him. I want him trail-ready by the end of the week."

Gertie jumped from the fence. "Yes, ma'am. He sure is a fine animal. What are you going to call him?"

"You name him," Isa said.

"Me?"

Isa nodded.

"Thanks. I'll think of something special." Gertie led him away.

Isa reached behind herself and brushed her own backside as she walked toward Blue.

"That was fine riding," Rosemary said. "I've never seen better." She left the corral and went back to work.

Isa leaned on the fence beside Blue and Martha. "Lord, I'm spent."

Martha laughed. "I imagine so."

Blue patted her shoulder. "Well done."

"You get the next one," Isa said.

They walked to the house, Isa a little slower than the others.

Martha poured coffee for the three of them.

"Are you still up to riding the creek bank later?" Blue asked.

Isa nodded. "Give me some time to recuperate, and I'll be ready." She rubbed her backside once more. "He gave me a run for my money, but I think he's going to make a good trail horse. He's smart and sure-footed."

"We better take Rosemary with us," Blue said.

"That's probably a good idea. What about Gertie? You know she'll be mad as a poked badger if we leave her here," Isa said.

"She's too young to go off into trouble," Martha said. "It's one thing to ride up on it. Another to trot directly into it."

"I agree," Blue said. "She's stays here, no matter how much she protests. And besides, it may be nothing to fret about."

"The creek didn't just dry up by itself, not that fast," Isa said. "Most likely it's been dammed somehow, either natural or manmade. Either way, we've got our work cut out for us. I believe I'll wash up. I feel like I've been in a Texas dust storm." She went to the well pump, cleaned herself, and returned to the house.

Within a short time Blue began to pace. Then she left the house.

"She's nervous about what she might find at the creek," Martha said.

"I know. These months haven't been easy on her, especially since she lost the stud. She's worried about her ability to hang on."

"We're here with her," Martha said. "And we won't leave her. She'll make it through no matter what. Even if she ends up with a small herd. She may have to let all those girls go, but she can make do. She's come too far to give up."

Isa set her coffee cup on the table and stood. "We won't let her give up. Hold the fort."

"Mind your biscuits," Martha said with a smile.

Isa laughed. "Mind yourn. Don't know when we'll be back, but try not to fret too much while we're gone."

"I'll try, but it won't do much good."

Their horses were saddled and waiting at the corral. Rosemary and Gertie were arguing in the barn. Isa could hear Gertie yelling the loudest.

"I don't see why I can't go. I'm a fair shot. I can ride."

Isa stood at the entrance of the barn watching the ruckus.

Blue stood beside them and put her arm around Gertie. "Yes. You are. But you aren't coming. I don't want to hear any more about it. You watch over Martha and Laurel while we're gone. I'm counting on you to keep them and the mares safe."

Gertie stuffed her hands into her pockets. "I wish you'd reconsider, Miss Blue. I can be of help."

"You are helping by staying here and doing what I've asked."

"All right. I guess I don't have a choice."

"I've got enough worry without adding the ranch to it. I'm counting on you, Gertie."

Gertie nodded, conceding.

Blue had a way of calming her and helping her see other sides of a situation.

Gertie walked them to the corral, and they mounted their horses.

"Did you name the buckskin yet?" Isa asked, trying to distract Gertie.

"Biscuit," she said. "I'll call him Biscuit."

Isa laughed. "Well then, Biscuit it is. Be sure to tell Martha. She'll enjoy that."

Gertie waved to them, her eyes moist.

"She's taking this hard," Rosemary said.

"Better she do that than get shot," Blue said. "I don't think we're going to like what we find."

Blue was right. Isa could feel it.

They didn't see any sign of anyone when they got to the remains of the campfire and walked around the area. The ash was cool to the touch. Whoever had been there were pigs and hadn't cared what they left—strewn tin cans, horse dung, and human waste.

They didn't find any clues as to who they were or why they were there. But from the looks of it, there were three or four of them.

Isa closely examined their tracks and noticed one of the horses' imprints was deeper into the soil, just like those she'd found when she rode Blue's property. And one set of boot prints was larger than the others, just like before.

"Let's keep going," Blue said.

They rode another mile or so and found the problem with the water. A dam. Quickly constructed but built well enough to stop a significant flow. The water was diverted to a gully on the other side of the creek.

They dismounted and walked the area.

Blue sat by the bank, picked up some rocks, and threw them at the dam.

Isa sat beside her. "Well, now we know."

Blue shook her head. "I'm not sure how I'm supposed to fight this."

Rosemary sat on the other side of Blue. "When you can't go through something, you go around it, Miss Blue."

Blue shrugged. "I have no idea what that means."

Rosemary threw a pebble at the dam. "You've got a well and a lake. You can get by for now. Whoever did this came after you, but others will be affected. Let them fight the battle for you. You've got enough to deal with. You don't have to take this on by yourself. Sooner or later someone's going to have to do something. If Anderson is responsible, which he probably is, he's making more trouble for himself than he realizes. People are fed up with what he's doing. When the pot finally boils over, the other ranchers will be on your side." She threw another pebble. "And those are powerful allies. You'll see."

Blue nodded. "That's an interesting theory."

Isa was impressed with Rosemary's clear thinking.

They sat on the bank of the creek, settling into a cadence of silence, watching the water flow into the gully. Isa hoped Rosemary was correct, that the other ranchers would side with Blue. If not, how would Blue manage to protect herself?

"Why do you suppose those men camped back there, but the dam was built here?" Rosemary asked.

"What do you think?" Blue asked.

"Probably to get your attention," Rosemary said. "I figure Anderson is baiting you. He knew if you looked hard enough, you'd be able to see their campfire."

Blue didn't respond.

They returned to the ranch.

Isa took time for a hot soak. She couldn't see her backside but was sure it was bruised. She climbed the ladder to the loft and slid into her bed, moaning.

Blue laughed, then got up and started to go down the ladder.

"Where're you going?" Isa asked.

"To the barn. I want to see if they came back and built another fire."

"Would it matter if they did?"

"I suppose not, but I want to find out."

Isa watched her descend the ladder. Blue would make herself sick if she couldn't find a way to relax.

The next morning, Isa felt the ride on Biscuit all over again. She dressed with care. Every muscle in her body was sore. Even her fingers ached.

Blue was awake but didn't speak.

"Lord, that horse gave me a ride."

Blue closed her eyes. "I'm glad it was you and not me."

It was clear Blue didn't want to have a conversation.

Isa went to the kitchen and poured herself a cup of coffee and sat at the table. Rosemary and Gertie came in a few minutes later, and then Blue joined them.

Laurel brought the breakfast food to the table, then sat next to Gertie.

"What time are we leaving for Carson City?" Laurel asked, grabbing a slice of ham from the plate, then some scrambled eggs.

"I'd like to shop for a new hat," Gertie said. "Mine's about wore out."

Martha brought the coffee pot with a hot pad and filled everyone's cups. "As soon as the morning chores are done, we'll leave. Gertie, you're getting a dress."

Gertie's face grew dark. "I don't want no dress."

"I'll hear no more about it," Martha said.

Gertie lowered her head and stabbed her fork at her food.

"I'll be staying here," Blue said. "Someone needs to be at the ranch at all times."

Isa stopped buttering her biscuit. "I'll stay. I wanted to work with the buckskin anyway."

Blue shook her head and sipped her coffee. "You go. Martha knows what we need."

Isa watched Martha, then Blue.

Blue's mood was sour.

"I'll stay. I don't need anything," Isa said. Maybe if they were alone, Blue would talk with her.

"It'd do all of us good to go to town," Martha said. "This is the last time we'll get supplies before winter sets in. And dresses and frills need bought for the social." She pointed her finger at Blue and then Isa. "And you're both going to that social. Etta's staying here, so there's no excuse. I swear you're all moodier than a squirrel with his last nut."

Blue slammed her cup on the table and stood. "I'll be damned if I'll go to that social. I've had nothing but trouble since we got here."

Everyone stopped eating.

Martha glared at her. "You know there's plenty of good folks in the area who will always do right by you. Just because there's a few rotten ones, you shouldn't shun the whole lot."

Blue stomped out the door.

Isa stood to go after her, but Martha stopped her.

"She needs to be alone to have a good cry. I've seen her get like this before. She's overloaded with emotion. You go with us today, Isa. Give her the time she needs to get herself together."

"Do you think she should be left alone for that long? We'll be gone three days," Isa asked. Maybe Martha was mistaken.

"She won't get rid of her feelings unless she can cry them out. And she won't do it unless she's by herself. That stud and those mares were all she had left from her father. She raised them from babies. She lost everything but them. And now the stud's gone. She just needs some time to adjust."

Was Isa thinking more about herself than Blue? She drank her coffee.

The others went back to their meal.

She'd have to trust Martha for now. Blue was probably going through almost more than she could bear. And Isa realized she'd caused some of it. All Blue wanted was for her to love her, and she wouldn't do it. And she'd left her for weeks when she could have used the help.

They started for Carson City.

Martha drove the wagon, Laurel beside her. Rosemary, Gertie, and Isa rode alongside. It was hard to leave Blue behind. Isa didn't get to say good-bye to her because she'd ridden off on Traveler before they'd left. Three days that Isa could have been alone with Blue. More than enough time to make love and share their thoughts and feelings.

They camped by the river and reached town by noon the next day. The Morrises were glad to see them. They got the supplies they needed, and Rosemary purchased a new dress and frills for Abigail, as she'd promised. Isa breathed a sigh of relief that neither Anderson nor his men were anywhere in the vicinity. The nearest thing to a problem occurred when Martha took Gertie into the back room to try on a calico dress with ruffles. Gertie protested so loudly people could hear her out on the loading dock. Martha emerged from the room red-faced and her hair slipping out from under her bonnet, but she had a satisfied expression. Gertie, on the other hand, came out pouting, her arms folded tightly against her chest. The battle had evidently been hard fought.

They returned home in late afternoon the following day.

Isa searched for Blue but didn't see her. Traveler wasn't in the corral. Did she ride out to check on the herd and Etta and Abigail? Isa decided to see if she could find her. She went to Martha, who was instructing Rosemary, Gertie, and Laurel where to put the supplies. "I'm going to meet Blue. I imagine she's with the herd or on her way back by now."

Martha nodded and continued her task.

About halfway to the herd, Isa spotted Blue. She reined Adelita and waited. Did she have her cry? Had she been able to work things out?

Blue took her hand when she got beside her. "I'm glad you're back. Did things go well? Any trouble?"

"Everything went well, except for Gertie throwing a fit about the dress Martha insisted she buy."

Blue laughed. "I'd have liked to see that."

"Gertie was pretty cantankerous. How are you? Did you get things worked out in your mind?"

Blue nodded. "I'm glad I had the time alone. I needed it."

They rode in silence for almost a mile before Blue spoke again. "I can see a lot of things more clearly now. Martha was right about you and me going to the social. We need to be with our neighbors and build our friendships." She stopped Traveler. "And you were right about us holding off making love. I'm not ready. I need to get things clear about what's going on. Then we can focus on us. I think it will be much better then. Don't you?"

"Yes," Isa said. "It's a beautiful thing to happen, and I don't want anything to hurry or spoil it."

Blue leaned over and kissed her. "But I hope it's not too long. Will you be with me from now on at night? In the same bed? I fear we'll have some hard days ahead before it gets better, and I want you as close as possible. I'll sleep better."

Relief washed over Isa. It was good Blue had said these things. Good for her and good for Isa. Their feelings and commitment to one another were growing. "I'd love to sleep beside you. Just being around you helps me feel stronger. How are Etta and Abigail holding up?"

They urged their horses forward.

"Good," Blue said. "They're looking forward to coming back tomorrow. I feel comfortable leaving the herd without a guard for the days we'll be at the social. They're well adjusted. The lead mare's doing a fine job."

"I think you're right about Adelita being pregnant." Isa stroked the horse's neck. "I've decided to ride Biscuit to the social."

"That's good. No sense in stressing her just in case."

Isa eased in the saddle. Blue seemed much more settled. She only hoped the social would be good for her. If Anderson and his men were there, that could be a problem. But it made no sense to borrow trouble. Heaven knew they had enough on their own.

CHAPTER TWENTY

B lue grew more nervous the closer they got to the Wyman ranch. Her palms were sweating, and her underarms were damp. Silly, really. Anderson wouldn't be there tonight. No one'd be there to cause her any discomfort. But still.

Isa rode beside her. Rosemary, Gertie, and Abigail were in front of them. Martha drove the wagon. Laurel, already dressed in her finery, sat beside Martha. Evidently, her search for a husband was in full swing. The others would dress for the social tomorrow afternoon. No sense in soiling good clothes before it was necessary.

Wearing a dress? Like Gertie, Blue wasn't thrilled with the idea, but if she didn't set the example, there'd be no chance in Hades Gertie would wear anything other than pants and a shirt.

The social would be a fine event. In preparation, Martha and Laurel had cooked the entire day yesterday and early this morning. The scent of the apple pies had filled the house, and now, as the sun started to set and Blue's hunger grew, the aroma wafted from the wagon.

It took a half day to reach the Wyman ranch. They planned to spend the night, relax, and the next day gather for the social, stay one more night, and then leave the next morning for home. Etta being at the ranch gave Blue a measure of peace. At least someone would be watching over it while they were away.

Jacob and his wife were waiting for them, smiling and waving.

They walked out to the wagon as soon as Martha slowed.

"Welcome. What a fine group you've brought, Blue," Jacob said.

Blue started to introduce everyone.

He surveyed Martha and Laurel in the wagon and those on horseback but stopped when his eyes fell on Isa.

Isa dismounted and shook his hand. "I know what you're thinking, Mr. Wyman. I can explain."

"I'll be damned." He slapped his knee and turned to his wife. "Did you know, Cora?"

"Know what?"

"Did you know Emanuel here was a woman?"

"Why, no. Of course not," Cora said.

"It's Isabel. Isa, Mr. Wyman. Again, I apologize for the deception, but I was trying to get through the territory."

"No harm done, although the boys may have something to say about it."

Cora smiled. "As pretty as she is, they'll probably have a lot to say about it."

"I'm only sorry you left. You were a damn fine hand," Jacob said.

"That's very kind. Thank you," Isa said.

Jacob clapped his hands, then rubbed them together. "All right. Let's get all of you settled."

They set up camp by a huge bonfire. Martha made sure they were as far away as they could get from the men's bunkhouse.

"No sense in asking for trouble," she told Blue.

Three large wooden tables with benches were placed side by side for as many people as possible to have their meals together. The festivities were going to be something special, and Blue was glad she'd realized the importance of her being there.

She, Isa, and Martha sat on the front porch with Jacob and Cora and watched the others as they gathered by the fire. Rosemary was particularly subdued. Laurel, on the other hand, seemed to attract the men like bees to clover. Once they'd gotten over the shock of Isa being a woman, they started falling all over themselves to get Laurel's attention.

"I imagine Laurel is pleased," Blue said.

Isa and Martha laughed.

"She's a pretty little thing," Cora said.

Blue told her about Laurel's plans.

"She's well on her way." Cora sighed. "Jacob and me could never have any children of our own. I suppose we've adopted every stray hand that's ever worked for us."

Jacob patted her hand. "How are things coming along, Blue?" he asked.

"Not as well as I'd hoped," she said.

Jacob stood. "Let's go for a stroll." He pointed toward the steps.

He and Blue walked to the corrals. He put one foot on the bottom rail, then placed his arm on the top one and rested his chin. He pointed to the horses. "See that roan there, the one with the star and two white legs?"

Blue focused on the mare and nodded.

"Darndest thing about that horse. She was born scrawny and the clumsiest filly you'd ever find. Tripped over her own shadow. Then, as a yearling, she started running and wouldn't stop. She's four now, and the best horse I have."

Blue wasn't sure what his point was.

He must have seen her puzzled expression. "Sometimes, things look hopeless. Then, you wait it out, and things change."

"I think Anderson's men shot my stud."

Jacob lowered his boot and kicked the dirt. He straightened, one hand on the fence, as he watched her. "That's tough to swallow. Are you sure it was his men?"

"I have no proof, but I'm almost positive he had his hand in it. I had a run-in with him at the dry goods store in Carson City a while back. He made it clear he wants me off the property. And I suspect he stole silver from a mine on my property."

"*You* have a silver mine?" Jacob asked.

"Not anymore." Blue scoffed. "That mine might have been why my uncle was killed."

"If it was over silver, you're probably correct," Jacob said. "There's not a greedier man around these parts than Anderson. We all wondered how his finances turned around so fast. If he did strip your mine, he went a far distance to make the exchange, because no one ever saw him with it."

One of the men began to play a guitar and sing. The soft sound of his voice carried in the wind. Blue turned to listen.

"That's Adam. Mighty fine voice. He can sing those cattle to sleep like no one I ever heard."

His voice was rich and smooth as honey, low and gentle.

"I suppose Anderson will be here tomorrow sometime?" Blue asked.

"Most likely. This is a big event. We've held it for going on ten years. It's always after we sell the herd and before we move the others to winter pasture. Everyone comes from miles around. Even get some folks from as far away as Virginia City and Silver Springs. Had someone about four years ago come in on the stage from somewhere east of here and stayed for three days. His name was Bigelow. A cattleman."

"Jacob, what's the law like in these parts?"

"Harman Tudsdale is the sheriff in Carson City. Aaron Jenkins is the US marshal for this territory. Aaron works with the judge, Clive Ruggles, who comes into Carson City every three months, give or take. That's the only law we have in the area. They're good men. Fair and reasonable."

"I might need some legal advice," Blue said.

"Then you want to talk with Jeremiah Hawthorne in Carson City. He and his wife, Elizabeth, will be here tomorrow. I'll introduce you."

❖

By mid-morning the next day, a hundred people were at the ranch. And by noon, when the festivities started, it came closer to two hundred. Most were crowded into the barn. Tables of food were placed everywhere. Blue mingled with the area ranchers she hadn't met and tried to remember their names. Most were cordial. A few, who she found out later were close friends of Frank Anderson, were a little standoffish.

She never wandered very far from Isa, who seemed to enjoy meeting the others. Martha and Cora had become fast friends. As expected, Gertie pitched a fit, but Martha managed to get her into her new dress. Rosemary mingled but acted reluctant, not like her. Usually she was affable and pleasant. Abigail seemed content. And Laurel gloried in the attention of the men.

Virgil and Pearl Pettiman arrived with their brood. Morgan, the oldest son, immediately caught Laurel's attention. Tall and strapping, he had dark hair and beautiful blue eyes the color of a sunny December sky.

When the square dancing began, almost immediately a man with a thick head of blond hair approached Blue.

"Would you mind?" he asked.

As they walked toward the dance floor, strewn with cornmeal, she caught a glimpse of Isa. One of Jacob's cowhands had escorted her to the center of the floor with a group of six. And when he put his arm around Isa's waist to swing her, Blue wished she could be her partner.

Samuel, another of the Pettiman boys, asked Gertie to dance. Blue laughed as she watched.

Gertie stood like a tree in the woods, her arms rigid against her sides. She was adorable in her dress with ruffles on the sleeves, her hair tied back in a bow, her freckles highlighted in the sunlight streaming in.

"Dance?" Gertie asked.

Samuel nodded. "Yes, ma'am. I'd be pleased."

"Me?"

He pried her hand away from her side. "Come on. It's easy, and fun. I'll show you."

To Blue's astonishment, Gertie followed him without resistance.

Where was Isa?

Blue searched the crowded room as her partner held her hand and circled her.

She found her again, laughing and smiling as her group promenaded.

Blue wanted to be the one to make her laugh and smile.

The dance ended.

"Thank you," Blue's partner said. He tipped his new, freshly shaped cowboy hat. "Jimmy, ma'am. Jimmy Conners."

"Blue Hutchings," she said.

"Pleased to meet you."

He didn't leave, only stared at her. If he expected an invitation to remain, he was in for a big disappointment.

"Are you from these parts, Miss Blue?"

Blue nodded. She didn't want to have a conversation. Where could Isa be? She'd left the dance floor. Where had she gone? Had she left for a walk with the handsome cowboy? A sadness overtook her. Where was she?

A light touch brushed her shoulder. She turned. Isa!

She handed Blue a glass of punch and smiled at the man beside Blue. "Hello. I'm Isabel."

Jimmy tipped his hat. "Jimmy Conners, ma'am." He remained, evidently determined to rope someone. And from the way he ogled both Isa and her, it didn't matter which one.

Now what?

Blue had who she wanted. Now if Jimmy would just leave.

Isa took Blue's hand. "Excuse us, but we need to get some pie before it's all gone."

The music began again. Before Blue and Isa reached a food table, Jimmy had his sights on Rosemary.

"Clever you," Blue said.

"Thank you, ma'am." Isa laughed.

Jacob came to them in the company of a dark-haired man with bushy eyebrows and a mustache.

"Blue, I'd like you to meet Jeremiah Hawthorne, the attorney I told you about. This is Blue Hutchings and Isabel…?"

"Aguilar. Isabel Aguilar," Isa said.

Jeremiah bowed slightly. "Charmed. Jacob tells me you may be in need of legal advice. Why don't we go for a walk outside where the air is cooler and it's less noisy." He offered Blue his arm.

Jacob and Isa followed as their escorts a few paces behind.

The fresh air was a welcome change from the stifling heat inside the barn from the press of people. Others lingered in small groups around them, talking and laughing.

"How may I be of service, Miss Hutchings?" Jeremiah asked.

"Please call me Blue."

He nodded. "Of course."

"I think I've been robbed."

Jeremiah stopped.

Isa and Jacob stilled, keeping their distance.

"How so?" Jeremiah asked.

Blue explained the killing of her stud, what they'd found at the silver mine, and Anderson's threat.

Jeremiah rubbed his chin and darted his gaze at the ground, as if mulling over what she'd said.

She liked him. He thought before he spoke. He seemed intelligent and genuinely interested in what she'd shared.

"Do you have any proof? Can you identify the shooters if you saw them again?"

"No to both questions."

Disappointment crossed his face. "Well, without that, I'm afraid legally you have no recourse."

She sighed in frustration.

"I'd like to help you, Blue. You're not the first to complain or suspect Frank Anderson of foul play. But legally your hands are tied for now. Is the mine claimed and registered in Carson City?"

"I have no idea."

"I'll look into it for you," he said.

"Would you also check to make sure everything is in order with the deed to my property?"

"I'd be happy to. The next time you're in town, come by my office, just beside the bank."

"I will. And thank you," Blue said.

They turned and walked to Jacob and Isa, who were deep in conversation.

"Ladies, shall we return to the dance?" Jeremiah asked. "I'd like you both to meet my wife Elizabeth. I know she'll be pleased."

Cora, Martha, Pearl, and a young woman heavy with child stood near the entrance to the barn.

Jeremiah slipped his arm around the pregnant woman. "My dear, I'd like you to meet some new friends."

She smiled, blushing slightly. Her blond curls lay soft on her shoulders. She was a small woman, graceful and lithe. Her emerald-green eyes sparkled. A beauty to be sure.

Jeremiah introduced her to Blue and Isa.

"How wonderful to meet you, Blue. I've already heard so many good things about you from Martha, Cora, and Pearl. And Isabel, it's a pleasure." She touched Blue's hand and then Isa's.

"How soon?" Blue asked Elizabeth.

She smiled again. "Not for about two months, I'm afraid. This is our first, so I'm unfamiliar with the process."

As Blue listened, a shiver ran through her. She scanned the room. Anderson stood in the far corner, glaring at her, the group of men around him talking and laughing.

The muscles in his jaw tightened.

She wanted to look away but didn't. They were already in a standoff. Who would flinch first?

Not her.

Isa touched her arm. "What is it?"

One of the men in Anderson's circle asked him a question, and he broke eye contact.

Blue turned to Isa. "It's nothing."

Anderson remained on the far side of the room until the music began again. He crossed the floor toward her with a few men from his circle.

She stiffened. Surely, he would not. He wouldn't have the nerve.

"Would you like to dance, Miss Hutchings?" He smirked.

The men behind him laughed.

Isa shifted, standing closer beside her.

Blue cut in front of her and locked eyes with Anderson. "I don't believe I would."

He took a step back. The corners of his mouth lifted.

It wasn't a smile, more like a sneer. He'd had no intention of dancing with her. He merely wanted to see what she'd do.

"I'm sure you'd like to," he said, reaching as though to put his arm around her.

She recoiled at the thought and then pushed him away. "I said no!"

"Beggars can't be choosers," he said.

The men behind him released what could only be described as a raucous laugh. And this time Anderson grinned, full-out with teeth bared.

She slapped his face, hard, his whiskered stubble rough against her hand.

Those around them grew silent and turned in their direction.

He narrowed his eyes, like an animal on the hunt. He fisted his hands. "Who do you think you are?"

"See here, Anderson." Jacob pushed his way through the crowd. "You're way out of line. I'll have none of this."

"You say," Anderson said.

Jeremiah and Virgil stood shoulder to shoulder with Jacob.

"We all say," Virgil said.

Jacob pointed toward the barn door. "Leave immediately."

Anderson studied Blue, then surveyed the crowd around him. "Fine."

He started to leave but hesitated. "This isn't over."

She glared at him. "Not even close."

Several men left with him.

Blue took a seat on the bench.

Isa sat beside her as the crowd began to disperse. Rosemary and Abigail stood by her side, next to Martha.

Blue took a steadying breath.

"I've never seen such horrid manners from a man," Elizabeth said. "Never."

"There's absolutely no excuse for his behavior," Jeremiah said. "He's a scoundrel." He put his arm around Elizabeth.

Virgil appeared with a glass of punch and offered it to Blue. "Here. This will settle you."

Blue thanked him and took a sip. She gasped. "Virgil, what's in this?"

He laughed. "Just a little something to help."

Pearl poked his ribs. "Virgil. Shame on you."

They all laughed.

The music started to play.

"Come on, Pearl. We don't want to waste any of this music." Virgil clasped her hand and led her away.

The longer Blue sat, the more apprehensive she became. "I think I'll get some fresh air." She handed her punch glass to Martha.

What if Anderson headed for her property, knowing she was away? What if he tried to burn her out? He was capable of it. She froze. Etta! Etta was there alone.

CHAPTER TWENTY-ONE

Isa looped her arm through Blue's when they left the barn. The late-afternoon sun beat down on them as the music faded into the background with the crowds and the noise.

"Isa, I'm afraid Anderson will go to the ranch and try to do something while we're here. We need to go home. Etta's there alone." The worry on Blue's face covered her like a shroud.

"You don't want to wait until morning?"

"No. We need to go now. Martha and the others can leave in the morning."

Blue's concern filled Isa with dread. It would take hours to get back to the ranch. Anderson had a head start on them, and if he was planning something, she and Blue might not get there in time. "All right. Let's change into our riding clothes and leave."

"I need to explain to Jacob and the others," Blue said.

Jacob and Virgil wanted to send a few of their riders with her, but Blue refused. "It's probably nothing, but I'm uncomfortable staying here any longer."

Blue talked with Martha, and then she and Isa changed and left.

They rode as quickly as they could, desperately trying to get home before nightfall. They took a break about halfway and rested the horses as long as they dared.

"I feel like the devil is walking over my grave," Blue said.

Isa wrapped her in her arms and held her for a moment. Nothing she could say would ease Blue's worry. They started homeward again as fast as their good sense would allow.

Distant gunshots rang out in the evening stillness. They galloped full speed. By the time they reached the ranch, no one was there.

"Etta?" Blue called. "Etta, where are you?"

"Etta?" Isa yelled.

They heard noise in the barn loft above them.

Etta poked her head out in the fading light, holding her upper arm. "I'm here. Can you help me? I've been shot."

Isa dismounted Biscuit and went into the barn before Blue could get there. She climbed the loft ladder and steadied Etta as she came down.

Blue turned a bucket upside down for Etta to sit on.

"I don't think it's too bad," Etta said, trying to inspect the wound.

"What happened?" Isa asked.

"I was in here trying to finish up with one of the stalls, and I heard riders." She sat. "I peeked out and saw four of them, guns drawn. I figured they were up to no good, so I made a beeline for the loft. I got to thinking yesterday about being alone, so, in case something happened, I put two rifles up there with some extra shot."

"Smart thinking," Isa said.

"It was, wasn't it?" Etta smiled.

Isa laughed.

"I scampered into the loft and fired the first shot to let them know someone was here." Etta winced in pain. "That only stirred the pot. Then all hell broke loose. They started firing. I shot a few rounds, then managed to get to the other rifle and fired from a different direction. I shot as much as I could. I didn't care where I aimed. I just let 'em have it. Every so often I'd change rifles and positions. After a while my plan must have fooled them because they scattered like rats."

"We're losing the light. Let's get you into the house so I can clean that wound," Blue said.

Isa followed them, making sure no one was lurking in the shadows.

Etta sat on the bench in the kitchen, still holding her upper arm. "They took off, and I fired a couple more shots for good measure."

"Those must have been the ones we heard," Blue said.

Isa lit the lanterns, and Blue retrieved Martha's medical kit.

"I don't think it's bad. It probably went through the flesh," Blue said.

"It doesn't feel like it," Etta said. "Damn, that hurts."

"It's going to be sore for a while." Blue finished the dressing and sat beside her. "I don't suppose you got a look at them?"

Etta sighed and rested her arm on the table. "Those bushwhackers had bandannas over their faces. *That* I could see."

Blue lowered her head and frowned. "Sleep in Martha's room tonight, Etta. I don't want you out in the bunkhouse by yourself." She stood. "We best check the property and get the horses bedded."

"I'll help you," Etta said.

They unsaddled the horses and gave them water.

"We ran them pretty hard," Isa said. "Best wait for a while before we feed them."

"I'm spent," Blue said. "I'm going to bed as soon as we're done."

"Why don't you go on in? I can finish up," Isa said.

Blue touched Isa's shoulder. "Thanks." She trudged to the house.

Isa eased into a rocking chair on the porch. She put her head back and closed her eyes. Like Blue, she was exhausted from the ride and the events of the day.

Etta sat on the porch steps. "I'm glad you came back, but why did you?"

"Blue had a run-in with Frank Anderson. He tried to force her to dance with him and got slapped for his trouble. It was quite a scene."

Etta gasped. "Miss Blue slapped him?"

Isa nodded, too tired to open her eyes. "Yes. Then Jacob Wyman, Virgil Pettiman, and some of the others told Anderson to leave. He finally did, but not before he spewed some angry words. Blue stayed for a while after that but told me she had a bad feeling and wanted to come home. She was worried about you. We changed clothes and left shortly after that."

"What about Martha and the others?"

"They'll be along sometime tomorrow."

They sat in the quiet of the night, only the sounds of the cicadas and night birds serenading them.

"Isa. Wake up."

Isa woke suddenly, drowsy and momentarily unsure where she was. Then she remembered she was on the porch.

Etta stood over her. "I fed the horses. Everything's fine. Go to bed."

Isa groggily climbed the ladder to the loft. She undressed hurriedly and washed herself with the water in the basin. She slipped into her night clothes and lay beside Blue, who was breathing deep and even.

Isa woke in the morning to the noise of metal clanging against metal, and then the words "Damn it to hell."

She rolled over to see if Blue was in bed. Finding herself alone, she dressed and scurried to the kitchen.

Blue was stoking the fire in the stove. Eggs were in a basket on the clapboard, ham in the frying pan, and a huge pan of coffee sat on the back burner. She glanced at Isa. "Sorry. I hoped to give you breakfast in bed, but I only got as far as starting the fire and heating Martha's steeped coffee." She was pale and had dark circles under her eyes. "Thanks for taking care of Traveler last night. I'm sorry I left you with it."

"Etta finished up because I fell asleep on the porch. How can I help?" Isa stepped beside her and slid her arm around her waist, the scent of her skin filling her with a need to be closer. She heard Etta in Martha's room and reluctantly removed her hand from Blue, feeling her slip away.

"Would you pour some of that coffee into the small pot so we can heat it?" Blue asked.

"Why is there so much in the big pot?"

"That's Martha's secret. She steeps the grounds in cold water for a day, then strains the grounds with cheesecloth. Then she heats the liquid in the coffee pot for us. No matter how hard I try, I can't make it like she does."

Martha's door opened. Etta came out dressed for the day, yawning. "Morning. Martha has a mighty fine bed." She gently rubbed her wound.

"How's the arm?" Blue asked.

"It's sore as fire but no blood."

"That's good," Blue said.

The three of them sat together and ate their breakfast.

Blue took a sip of her coffee and hurriedly put her cup on the table. "I don't know what Martha does to *her* coffee, but mine is awful. I'm sorry."

Isa took a drink and forced herself to swallow. She didn't want to hurt Blue's feelings, but she spoke the truth. The bitter flavor left a bad aftertaste.

They finished and went to inspect the barn. The area around the loft was riddled with evidence of the gunfire.

"Good Lord, Etta. You were lucky you weren't shot to pieces," Blue said. She balled her fists. "This has got to stop." She took a deep breath, as if to settle herself.

Isa's inclination to protect Blue rose to the surface. She had a sudden urge to ride to Anderson's and shoot him. In her frustration to help her, she realized there was one thing she could do. "I'm going to ride to the herd and check on them."

Blue seemed to perk up a bit. Maybe this would ease her mind.

"I'm sure things are fine," Isa said as an afterthought, not wanting to alarm Blue any more than she already was.

"I'll watch over Miss Blue," Etta said and winked at Isa.

Isa took Blue by the elbow. "Walk with me a bit before I leave."

They strolled toward the creek as always.

The songbirds' chirp seemed sweet and clear, the blue sky a deeper hue than the days before. A few white, puffy clouds meandered lazily directly above, seemingly unconcerned with the cares below.

"I know you're addled about what's happened," Isa said.

Blue remained silent, as if no words were left in her.

Isa couldn't read Blue's expression but felt her discontent. She wanted to understand her, anticipate what she needed. They continued, serenaded by the sounds of the morning. Could nearby animals sense Blue's heartbreak? Or her need for comfort?

Isa stopped.

Blue halted, looking puzzled.

Isa wrapped her arms around her and kissed her cheek.

Blue trembled.

"You aren't alone," Isa whispered. "We're all going to help you get through this."

Blue threw her arms around Isa's neck and held on like she was being pulled in the opposite direction.

Isa grasped her tighter.

They stood in the morning sun, locked in each other's embrace until Isa could feel the strain in Blue's body subside.

They held hands as they returned to the barn. Isa didn't care if Etta saw, and evidently neither did Blue.

Isa bridled and saddled Biscuit.

Blue stood by her, still silent.

"It'll be good for him," Isa said. "He did well going to the Wymans'. I think I'll ride him regularly now instead of Adelita."

Blue moved closer. And, to Isa's surprise, she kissed her—not a short "I'll see you later kiss"—but long and lavish.

"I'll expect you back by evening," Blue said. "Mind you return in one piece." She kissed Isa again, then stepped back.

Something was going on with Blue, but Isa wasn't sure what it might be. She enjoyed her display of affection, yet her behavior concerned her. It had a disturbing air, like when everything grows still before a storm. Isa couldn't name it, for it was more like a general dismay. It appeared one way when she studied it in separate pieces, then different when she put the parts together and a pattern emerged. She decided to return as quickly as possible.

Biscuit had a pleasant gait and behaved well. He sensed his surroundings, naturally avoided any hazards, and responded quickly to her subtle cues. She checked the herd, rode the perimeter, and looked for any signs of recent riders. None.

By the time she returned in late afternoon, the wagon was near the house, and Martha and the others were gathered on the porch. They must have already had their evening meal. Blue wasn't with them. Perhaps she was in the barn or out for a stroll. Isa dismounted, tied Biscuit to the fence, and eyed the corral. Traveler wasn't there. Where could Blue have gone? Then she had a disturbing thought. Nausea swirled in her stomach.

She went directly to the porch. "Where's Blue?"

Martha stopped rocking. "She told me she was going to Carson City to discuss some business with her new lawyer friend, Jeremiah Hawthorne. She packed enough truck for three days, and off she went."

"The hell she is. She's going to Anderson's." Isa jumped from the porch. "I need three days' food for the trail, Martha. Gertie, fill two canteens with water and get me enough grain for five feeds. Don't skimp."

Isa went to the barn and retrieved her long riding slicker and an extra box of ammunition.

Martha brought her the food and stuffed it into one of the saddlebags. Gertie hung the water containers on her saddle horn and placed the feed in the other pouch.

Isa secured the slicker behind the saddle and swung up. "Set a guard at night, Martha. I'll be back as soon as I can. If Blue comes back, don't let her leave again. I don't care if you have to tie her down."

Martha patted her thigh. "Mind yourself. I don't know what Blue's up to, but bring her back safe."

"How long ago did she leave?"

"A couple of hours," Martha said.

"Did she say anything before she left?"

"Nothing much. She was quiet."

"That's what worries me." Isa reined Biscuit and took off.

Blue had about a two-hour head start on her. Which way would she go? Carson City or Anderson's? She followed her tracks northeast toward the river. Maybe she'd camp there for the night and go on to Anderson's or Carson City in the morning. Maybe she just needed some time alone. Maybe she intended to see Jeremiah like she'd told Martha, although it was doubtful.

Isa now had a feeling like Blue had had at the Wyman ranch. It pressed down on her, twisting her gut, permeating her mind until she could think of nothing else.

She followed Blue's trail until it became too dark to see it clearly. From the way her tracks led, she would most likely camp for the night along the river. She kept the thought in her heart and headed in that direction, searching for the light of her campfire, hoping she'd find her, determined to do what was necessary to protect her.

CHAPTER TWENTY-TWO

B lue poured coffee into a tin cup, then set the pot on a small boulder beside the campfire. She leaned against her saddle and sipped, staring into the flames. After going to Anderson's to warn him to stay away from her and her property, she'd head into Carson City to talk with Jeremiah again. And while in town, she could get the explosive to blow up the dam they'd found. How much would it take? She'd never handled it before. Could she do it? Was it safe? She took another drink of the strong brew. Far from Martha's, it tasted like someone had thrown a horseshoe in it.

This was only the second time she'd been on her own for any length of time. Martha or Isa had always been with her. She missed them. Isa! The thought of her lips against hers sent a surge of want through her. Would Isa approve of what she planned to do? Most likely not. That's why Blue had left before she got back. Isa was a decent, good person, and she wouldn't want Blue to go looking for trouble. But this was necessary.

Traveler pawed the ground and snorted.

Blue tensed. Had he heard something? She set down her cup and gripped her pistol, peering into the darkness. Should she have had a fire?

Then Traveler nickered.

Blue quickly moved beside him and used him for cover. Watching. Waiting. Someone was out there.

"Blue, don't shoot. It's me."

Blue couldn't believe it. "Isa?"

"Tarnation, Blue. Who else would it be?"

Blue released her hold on her gun and stepped to the campfire.

Isa appeared in the light.

"I don't know if I'm glad to see you or mad because you're here," Blue said.

"Well. At least you're talking again." Isa sidled up to her. "Damned if you didn't scare the life out of me." She led Biscuit beside Traveler, unsaddled him, slipped off his bridle, and tied him. She pulled his feed from the bag and laid it out for him. Then she brought her saddle and set it beside Blue's, tossed the blanket over it, and sat down. "I didn't know if I'd be able to find you."

Blue sat beside her and handed her the cup of coffee. "Here. You might as well drink some. It's not very good."

Isa took a sip and made a face. She swallowed hard. "You're right. It's pretty awful."

Blue laughed. "What are you doing here?"

"The question is, what are *you* doing here?"

Did Isa have a right to know what she planned to do? Did she come here to stop her? Did it matter now? "I'm going to Carson City to talk with Jeremiah."

"The hell you are. You're going to Anderson's."

Blue stood and folded her arms tight against her chest, inclined to defend herself. Isa had no right to stop her from doing what she felt she needed to do. She wouldn't back down about this.

"Don't try to stop me, Isa. I've made up my mind. I won't stand by and watch that man destroy my life. You saw what he's like. You know what he's done as surely as I do. He'll keep on until someone does something about it."

Isa rose and grasped Blue's shoulders. "Easy. I'm not here to stop you. I'm here to make sure you don't get killed doing whatever it is you're planning."

The words were like Isa had lifted her and swung her around, then breathed life into her. She would support her in what she wanted to do, and it meant everything to Blue.

"I *am* going to Anderson's. I'm going to warn him. And then I'm going to Carson City, buy some explosive, and blow the hell out of that dam."

"Well. That'll sure get his attention. Do you think it'll stop him?"

"It might. It could." Blue took a deep breath. "Probably not. But I've got nothing to lose by doing it. Maybe if I stand up to him, he'll back down."

"Are you trying to convince me or yourself?"

"I don't know."

They both laughed.

"I just know I have to do something," Blue said.

"All right then. But it might be better to go to Carson City first, get the explosive, go to Anderson's, and then blow up the dam. That way we can hightail it home and be ready if he sends his men after us. Which he most likely will. And you know as well as I do, he'll get his men to do his dirty work."

It was a reasonable suggestion, and Blue agreed.

They left at dawn and reached Carson City by afternoon.

Jeremiah assured Blue the documents for her property were in order. They ate lunch at his home, visited with Elizabeth, then later went to the hardware store and requested an explosive. Morris said he didn't stock it. "It's too dangerous. But Jon Hanover, the gun shop owner, carries it. What do you need it for?"

"Boulders," Blue said. She looked at Isa.

"Yes. Boulders," Isa said.

She and Isa left.

Hanover was short, bald, and wore his metal-rimmed glasses too far down his nose, causing him to sound like he had a cold. "It's an unusual purchase. I don't carry nitroglycerin. It's too volatile and dangerous. Do you ladies know what you're asking for or how to use an explosive?"

Blue did not. Did Isa?

Isa leaned into her and whispered, "I have no idea."

"How about gunpowder?" Blue asked.

Hanover nodded, and his face brightened. "Yes. I have gunpowder."

"Could you give us a brief review on how best to use it? We have some boulders on the property that have to be removed."

"Well! In that case." He left for a moment and returned carrying a box with sticks of something a few inches long and about an inch wide, wrapped in thick, brown, waxy paper. In his other hand he had long lengths of what appeared to be heavy, braided string. He set the items on the counter and then picked up one of the sticks and came over to them.

He held the item in the air and ogled it like it was made of gold. "This, ladies," he said, "is the greatest invention since tin cans. It's versatile, easy to manipulate, and can cause great destruction." His eyes danced as he described it. "I have in my hand the tool that conquers nature. We will never be able to build the rails for the Iron Beasts without it."

Blue wasn't sure, but the man might have lifted himself on his toes.

"It's the latest thing. Developed in Sweden by a man named Nobel. It's called Nobel's Safety Blasting Powder, or Dynamite, named thusly after the ancient Greek word for powder." He seemed so pleased with himself he could barely contain his excitement.

Blue listened, though she had an exaggerated inclination to rip the stick out of his hand and make a run for the door.

"It must be kept dry, out of direct sunlight, and not jostled about. You need matches and a fuse." He reached on the counter and grabbed the braided rope. "I suggest you use long ones. Give yourself a lot of time to get a safe distance away. How many boulders do you plan to remove?"

"Four," Isa said. "Huge ones."

"Indeed," he said. "Are they near or far apart?"

"Close together," Blue said. "Very close together."

He nodded. "I see. Then I think two would be sufficient. Definitely two. I think at least a twenty-inch fuse should be enough. Each inch is one second. Estimated, of course."

Isa rested her hand on Blue's shoulder. "Thirty seconds at least."

Blue nodded. "All right. We'll take two sticks and thirty inches of fuse. Show me how to set it."

He held the stick in one hand, the fuse in the other. "Bundle the sticks together with twine, then take a knife and make a slit in the top of one of them. Gently, with as little friction as possible, push the fuse about one inch into the dynamite. Position it at the base of the middle of the boulders. Light the fuse, and run like hell." He laughed.

Blue didn't appreciate his humor. All she pictured was lighting the fuse and it going off before she and Isa had a chance to scatter. They had to climb down into the stream, place the dynamite sticks where they'd be most effective, climb out again, and then get quite a ways from the blast and flying debris. She envisioned logs and rocks raining down on them. They'd need more than thirty seconds. Maybe this wasn't such a good idea after all?

Isa must have been thinking something similar. "Best give us sixty inches of fuse."

A minute would be better. Then again, maybe two. "Make that one hundred and twenty," Blue said.

The clerk nodded and scurried behind the counter, prepared their request, and told them the price.

Blue handed him the coins, and they left. She carefully wrapped the package in some cloth and placed it in her saddlebag.

"I hope we don't blow ourselves up before we get to the dam," Isa said.

Blue took a deep breath and mounted Traveler, gingerly swinging her leg over the saddle. "Lord, I hope not too."

"Are you sure you want to do this?" Isa asked. "You don't have to."

"Yes. I do," Blue said. "I have to show him he can't push me around."

They left town and headed southeast to Anderson's ranch, stopping several times to check the explosive.

"I don't know why we keep checking it," Blue said. "I wouldn't know if something was wrong."

Isa laughed. "I suppose if it starts getting sweat on it, that's a bad sign."

"I'll be glad when this is over," Blue said.

Anderson's ranch was situated across the river between some hills.

They stopped at the crest of one of them and looked down on his land. His cattle were scattered in the valley, and there were at least four riders.

"It's not a bad spread," Isa said.

"It should be nice. He made it with my silver."

"Maybe he's got some stashed that we can take?" Isa smiled.

Blue laughed. "Yeah. I'm sure he'll hand it over."

Isa chuckled. "We should bury the explosive. I don't want to go down there with it in your saddlebag in case the bullets start flying. It's too much of a risk."

"He won't shoot. He's too much of a coward. But you're right. We should stash it before we go. And when we come back this way, they'll think we're headed for town or back home."

They buried the dynamite and then rode directly to his ranch.

He stood on the porch, leaning against a post, smirking. He stepped off it in front of them. "Did you come to apologize?"

Blue rested her hand on her pistol grip. "Anderson, I'm here to tell you if you or any of your men step one foot on my property again, I'll kill you."

He adjusted his hat and laughed. "That's supposed to intimidate me? You ride up here with your Mexican wants-to-be-a-man and expect me to give a damn what you think? Go back to Texas before you bite off more than you can chew."

"You've been warned. Stay off my property and away from me and my people."

"Your *people*?"

His riders eased over, dismounted, and started to fan out around her and Isa.

Blue drew her gun and pointed it at Anderson. "Stop right there. All of you go over to the porch where I can see you."

They stilled and eyed Anderson.

He nodded.

They sauntered to the porch.

Blue recognized Evans and Yates. McCoy wasn't with them.

Evans moved his hand to his pistol.

Isa drew her rifle from the scabbard and cocked it. "Get your hand away from your gun," she said.

Evans smirked and gripped the handle.

Isa fired, hitting the post next to his head.

Evans snapped his hand away.

"All of you throw your weapons on the ground," Isa said.

They didn't.

She fired again, this time shooting Evans's hat off.

Each of them hurriedly removed his pistol from his holster and tossed it in the dirt.

"You too, Anderson," Blue said.

"Who do you think you are?"

Isa immediately shot the leather strap at the bottom of his holster.

He jumped back.

"Ease it out and throw it in the dirt," Blue said, continuing to aim at him.

He picked it out of the holster with his finger and thumb and let it drop.

"You," Isa said, pointing at Yates. "Pick up those guns and put them in the water trough."

He scurried and gathered the guns and dumped them into the wooden bin.

Blue motioned with her pistol. "All of you walk over to the barn. Including you, Anderson."

When they reached the building, and Anderson followed, Blue called to him. "I won't hesitate to kill you, Anderson. Leave me alone."

She nodded to Isa and they galloped away.

Maybe her warning would work and he'd leave them alone. If not, she'd do what she had to.

When they reached the back of the hill, Blue recovered the dynamite. She brushed the dirt from the cloth and inspected the sticks. "They look fine."

"Let's get to it," Isa said. "We have a long ride home." She glanced to where they'd been. "I don't imagine he's very happy right now."

"Wait till he finds out what else we do," Blue said. "That was so audacious." She couldn't help her smile. "You should have seen his expression when you shot his holster." She laughed.

Isa didn't.

Blue watched for some reaction. Was she mad? Or worried?

"Let's get this done," Isa said.

They rode as long as they dared in the dark and then camped by the river for the night.

It took two hours in the morning to reach the dam. Blue inspected it closely. They dismounted, took what they needed, and climbed into the creek bed.

"I think here," Isa said. "It's in the middle, like Hanover said."

Blue agreed. "You go on to the horses and wait."

Isa shook her head. "I'll stay here."

"No. As soon as we get the fuse prepared, go up to the bank and be ready. I don't want to have to worry about you too."

Isa retrieved her knife from her pocket but stopped. "Did we just need one fuse or two? We have only one."

"One. Remember? He said to bundle the sticks. I imagine the blast will set off the other. Don't you think?"

"I'm sure it will."

Blue secured the string around the dynamite.

Isa made the hole in one of the sticks.

Blue wedged the fuse carefully into the opening and held the explosive away from her. "I don't think this dam is too well constructed. It should blow pretty easily. Remember, we need to move like hellfire as soon as I light it."

Isa nodded. "Put it in the driest spot you can find at the base."

Blue searched until she found the best location. "I forgot how many minutes we have."

"About two."

Blue's hands began to shake. "Okay. I'm ready. Go now."

Isa climbed from the bank, got on Biscuit, and grabbed Traveler's reins. "Ready," she yelled.

"Oh, Lord, help us." Blue took a deep breath and held it. She lit the fuse and took off running, almost falling down the bank. She jumped into the stirrup, and they took off at a gallop. They ran the horses for what seemed like two minutes but didn't hear anything. They stopped and peered back.

"Did the fuse go out?" Isa asked. "Maybe the water doused it."

"I don't—"

The explosion shook the ground. The sound of the blast caused Blue's ears to pop. Both horses reared. Rocks and logs spewed into the air and then landed in the water, on the bank, some flying two hundred yards toward them. One minute the dam was there, and the next it was gone. Obliterated.

"Hanover wasn't kidding," Blue said. It was the most fascinating thing she'd ever witnessed.

Traveler hopped, then shook his head and snorted. Biscuit bucked, but Isa quickly got him under control.

Blue couldn't wait to see what was left. "Come on."

They rode to the creek. Nothing remained of the dam but a few logs on each side of the bank and along the edges. Water thundered through the debris.

They dismounted and walked closer.

Blue wanted to jump up and down. They'd done it. They blew the hell out of it. She grabbed Isa and kissed her. "By God, I wish I could see Anderson's reaction when he discovers this."

"I'm afraid you poked the bear."

"Do you think it was too much?" Blue asked.

"The dam would have been plenty, let alone going to his ranch. He'll come after you, Blue. You can't expect him to do nothing after what you've done...*we've* done. You chopped off his manhood. I'm not saying he didn't deserve it. I've seen men like him. They lose their reason."

Her words went through Blue like a dagger. Wasn't she on her side? "You think what he did before was reasonable? He killed my stallion. He shot at my riders. He's pushed me around. He stole my silver. He's tried to get rid of me from the moment I got here."

Isa raised her hand. "I'm not saying you don't have cause to do what you did. I'm saying we better be ready for the consequences."

"You think I was wrong?"

They mounted their horses and headed toward home.

"Not wrong," Isa said. "Just be ready. Because he's coming after us." She reached for Blue's hand. "I'm standing with you. And so will Martha and the others. But it's not going to be easy."

"None of this has been easy," Blue said.

Was all she'd been through worth it? She realized that her actions might have put Isa, Martha, and the others in danger again. But weren't they already in peril because they were with her? What now? Watch Frank Anderson destroy her and take everything she had? Her stepbrother had already done that. No! She wouldn't stand by and let it happen twice.

CHAPTER TWENTY-THREE

Isa grew more nervous as time passed. It'd been five days since she and Blue had gone to Anderson's and destroyed the dam. He and his men hadn't caused them any more trouble. But Isa suspected he was out there plotting, squatting like a toad in the mud.

She curried and brushed Adelita until her coat shone. Her belly hadn't started to expand, but she hadn't been in heat and seemed to have a larger appetite. She'd produce a fine foal if she was pregnant.

She tossed the tools into the wooden box, cleaned Adelita's hooves with the pick, and then led her to the stall.

Gertie loped into the barn with a piece of straw hanging out of her mouth. She climbed onto the top rail of Adelita's stall. "I finished with you and Miss Blue's saddles and bridles." She whipped the piece of straw out from between her teeth. "I soaped them good and washed the blankets like you said. They're drying on the corral fence."

"And the wagon rigging?" Isa asked.

"It's done. I stored it in the back of the wagon by the bunkhouse. Isa, why do you think that Anderson man hates Miss Blue so much? She didn't do anything to him. He's the one that done something to her."

"It's 'did something,' not 'done something.' And get off the rail before you break it." Isa gave Gertie's knee a pat.

Gertie jumped down and returned the straw to her mouth. "Why do you suppose that is?"

Isa scooped out Adelita's ration of feed and slipped the bucket into her stall. "Frank Anderson is a hard man. Somewhere in his life he started on his path to the way he is."

"He weren't born like that?"

"You're doing better with your words but watch your tense. It's 'wasn't born like that.' No. It was a choice."

Gertie followed her to the end stall. "But some menfolk are born like that. Mean as little boys and meaner as big men. Take my neighbor, Tom something-or-other. Why, he'd just as soon shoot you as look at you. And his son was just like him."

Isa patted the mare and rubbed her ears. The horse nickered and blew. "Gertie, you'll find in your life that choosing makes all the difference."

"You sayin' Tom could have choosed to be nice?"

Isa cringed at Gertie's language. How much should she correct her? She didn't want to discourage her. "It's 'chosen.' Yes. I'm saying you can choose how you act. No matter what you feel."

"You mean when I'm spittin' mad I don't have to throw somethin'? That don't make any sense."

"Yes. That's exactly what I'm saying. We can choose how we act. When our feelings come upon us, we always have a choice."

"That's a hard thing to understand."

"Well, you think on it while you muck out this stall." Isa handed her the pitchfork. "And make sure all the mares have plenty of water in their buckets. Who has first guard tonight?"

"Rosemary and Etta. I saddled their horses in case there's trouble. Abigail and I have second watch."

"Finish up and then get some rest."

Isa left the barn and stopped at the corral. Biscuit immediately came to her and nudged her hand. She reached into her pocket and gave him a piece of carrot, then went into the house and sat at the table.

Martha poured her a cup of coffee as she sipped her own.

Isa rubbed the back of her neck. Her shoulders were stiff from strain. "Gertie's a chatterbox this evening."

Blue leaned over the loft rail and yelled down. "She's always a chatterbox."

"That child talks more than Abigail and Etta put together," Martha said. She smiled. "But she's a sweet thing. Full of energy and ready to discuss any topic. Rosemary's already taught her every math book she has. And she wants to read from the house books any chance she gets. We probably should think about getting her into a real school."

"I doubt she'd go," Blue said, descending the ladder. "The first time you told her she'd have to wear a dress, that'd be the end of it."

Isa laughed. "That's for sure."

"I suppose." Martha sighed and sat across from Isa. "There's nowhere to send her around here anyway. All quiet out there?"

Isa nodded. "I feel like we're waiting for the storm to get here. Everyone's on edge. Abigail told me Etta accidentally knocked over the water bucket in the bunkhouse, and Rosemary jumped all over her."

Martha raised her eyebrows. "Rosemary did? She's always so calm and even-tempered."

"I know. It surprised me too," Isa said. "Goes to show how everyone's on edge."

Blue walked behind Isa and massaged her shoulders.

Isa put her head back, closed her eyes, and moaned. "That feels so good."

"Want a hot bath?" Blue asked. "I'll heat some water."

"Did you two ever hear of hot springs?" Martha asked.

Isa opened her eyes and glanced at her. "Hot springs?"

"Yes," Martha said. "There's places on the earth that have hot water coming out of the ground. It's supposed to be very healthy for you. Stimulates your skin and organs and such."

Blue massaged deeper, causing surges of chills and tingling to sweep through Isa. If Blue didn't stop soon, Isa wasn't going to be able to restrain herself from reaching around and taking her in her arms. She'd had about as much stimulation as she could stand. She grabbed Blue's hand and squeezed it. "Thank you."

Blue patted her shoulder. She filled a pot with water and put it on to boil, then sat beside her.

Martha finished her coffee and yawned. "I believe I'll get ready for bed."

"It's still daylight," Blue said.

Martha walked toward her bedroom and waved her hand. "I'm tuckered out."

Blue filled the tub with the hot water and called Isa to check it.

"Perfect," Isa said.

Blue pulled the curtain, enclosing them. She moved close to Isa and began to unbutton Isa's shirt.

"Blue, what are you doing?"

"I'm undressing you."

Isa touched her hand. "We can't."

"Why?" Blue looked into her eyes with an expression of desire and want.

Her gaze was penetrating and captivating and full of heat, and Isa was drowning in it.

"Why?" Blue asked again.

"I…I don't know."

Blue kissed her.

All Isa wanted to do was let Blue undress her as she would her.

Someone outside screamed, and then the sound of horses and riders descended upon them.

"Anderson!" Isa yelled, buttoning her shirt.

She and Blue grabbed their rifles by the door and ran outside.

Six men on horses were thundering toward them. Two had lit torches in their hands. One threw his into the loft of the barn, and the other tossed his into the entranceway. Two men fired at Blue and Isa.

Isa dove for cover on the porch. Blue managed to duck behind the water trough. They returned fire as best they could. Rosemary came around the side of the barn and fired at the two men who had thrown the torches. One of the them was McCoy. She hit the other man square in the shoulder. He slumped forward on his horse. Yates!

Smoke poured from the barn.

Blue yelled to Abigail. "Get the mares out."

Flames began to flash from the loft.

Evans raced toward Blue. He fired three shots and then jumped the trough and circled back toward the others.

She fired, but none of her bullets hit him or the others.

Isa couldn't get a decent aim on him. She fired twice but missed.

More smoke and flames billowed from the barn, making it difficult to see their attackers. The men were shooting so fast, Isa and Blue were pinned down and unable to return adequate gunfire. Abigail and Gertie were cross-firing as they tried to get into the back of the barn to let the horses out. But every time they attempted to move, three of the men zeroed in and peppered them with gunfire.

Martha came out of the house armed with a shotgun and fired, hitting the man beside Evans. He fell to the ground. His horse turned east and galloped away.

"Let's go," Evans yelled.

They took off, not bothering to get their wounded man who lay bleeding on the ground.

On their way past, Rosemary did an unbelievable thing. She jumped onto Yates's horse and pulled him off, then struck him with her rifle. His horse took off with the other four men as they galloped away.

Blue immediately ran for the barn, but the flames and smoke had already engulfed it, and she couldn't get in.

Isa let the other horses out of the corral and then ran around to the back. Gertie had managed to get only two of the four horses out—Adelita and one of Blue's mares. The flames were so high, and the heat so intense, no one could reenter to save the other two.

Blue pushed past Isa and Abigail and tried to get into the barn.

They grabbed her and held fast, dragging her away as more flames shot up the side of the building.

The trapped horses screamed and kicked at the stall boards, struggling to get free.

Blue wrestled her arms free and tried to run toward the trapped animals.

Isa gripped her with all the strength she could muster. "It's too late, Blue. There's nothing we can do to save them."

"No! We can't let them die." She writhed, kicking and flailing her arms, trying to get loose.

Abigail clasped Blue around the waist and dragged her away from the scene.

"We're going to lose the ranch house if we don't get it soaked," Martha yelled.

"Hold her tight," Isa told Abigail.

"I've got her. Go," Abigail said.

Isa, Rosemary, Martha, Etta, and Gertie ran to fill buckets and started dousing the log walls of the house. As Isa raced to the trough, she saw Laurel with Martha's shotgun standing over Yates and the other wounded man, daring them to move.

Isa circled behind the house and found that Abigail had taken Blue away from the barn, which was now nothing but burning rubble. Blue was collapsed on the ground, sobbing.

Isa kneeled and gathered her in her arms, holding on with all the energy she had left. Adelita, Traveler, Blue's remaining mare, and the other horses from the corral grazed near the apple orchard.

Nothing more could be done but to let Blue cry herself out and wait for the fire to burn what remained of the barn, which didn't take long.

As the pile of black charred remains smoked and sputtered, Isa led Blue to the porch and gave her water. Rosemary, Abigail, and Laurel had taken the two men to the corral and tied them to the fence.

Gertie had bridled her horse and was guarding the herd.

Anderson's men had left devastation in their wake. Her and Blue's planning hadn't considered that they'd come in daylight or be so bold. They'd swooped down on them and were gone in minutes. With all the gunfire, it was a miracle none of the women were shot, or the horses in the corral. But the barn and two of Blue's prized mares had been lost.

As dusk settled, the others gathered at the porch around Blue, Isa, and Martha. The smell of smoke clung to everything. It lingered in the air, outside the house, inside, on their clothes, hair, and skin. You couldn't get away from it no matter where you turned.

"What now, Miss Blue?" Rosemary asked.

"Hitch the wagon," Blue told Abigail and Etta. She drew her pistol and stepped from the porch. Isa immediately followed her.

Blue went to the men tied to the fence. She pointed her pistol at Yates.

Was she going to shoot him?

"Blue? No!" Isa said. "You can't do that."

Blue cocked the lever. "I can do anything I damn well want. My property. My rules."

She aimed at Yates's forehead. "Anderson seems to think he can do anything he wants. So can I."

Yates's eyes widened.

Blue trembled. She lowered the gun, then raised it again. "You filthy trash. What do you have to say for yourselves? You like working for a man who's a bully, a thief, and a horse killer? You think it's fun? You poor excuse for human beings."

Her eyes grew cold and dark. Her jaw clenched.

She was going to do it. She was going to shoot both of them. Right here. Right now.

Isa slipped her hand between the hammer and barrel of Blue's gun and moved the pistol downward.

Blue began to shake.

Isa took the weapon from Blue's hand, released the lever, and stuck it in her own belt.

Rosemary stepped beside Blue and put her arm around her.

Blue stood stoic, unmoving, staring at the two men.

Yates's eyes were huge.

Abigail and Etta walked toward the wagon.

"What are you going to do?" Yates asked.

"I think Blue wants to do a Texas two-step," Isa said. "Shoot you, and then take your stinking corpses out into the mountains and bury you. Convince me she shouldn't."

"Anderson just wanted us to burn you out. That's all," he said. "Pup and I know things."

The other man called Pup nodded. "We do know things. I swear."

"What kind of things?" Isa asked.

"Like who shot the stud," Pup said.

Yates sat straighter, holding his shoulder. "Yeah. And who dammed up the creek, and what Anderson did with the silver from the mine."

Blue pushed Rosemary's arm away and stepped closer to the men. "I want to hear all of it."

Yates and Pup spewed out what they knew.

It was no surprise to Isa that Yates said Anderson had ordered his men to do all those things, or that he'd traveled almost a hundred and fifty miles to Stockton to exchange the silver he stole.

Isa listened intently to what they had to say and then consulted with Blue.

Blue seemed drained and exhausted, too consumed by her sorrow to argue or disagree. Isa was sure she would do the reasonable thing.

"I think it's best if we toss them in the wagon and cart them to the sheriff in Carson City," Isa said.

Blue nodded.

Isa ordered Rosemary and Abigail to take the bows off the wagon and then guard the men. "We'll leave at first light. Keep them here until we're ready to go. Give them something to drink. Etta and Gertie will spell you in a couple of hours. I want you two to go with us. Abigail, you drive. Rosemary, you guard them once they're in the wagon."

"Ain't we goin' ta get somethin' for our wounds and some vittles?" Pup asked. "My leg's powerful hurt, and I ain't et since this mornin'."

"I don't care if you bleed to death or starve," Blue said.

Yates poked him with his elbow. "Shut up! You want to get us kilt?"

Yates had changed since their first meeting by the river. He was harder, more steeped in his chosen profession.

Blue walked toward the house, then called over her shoulder to Rosemary. "Shoot them if they give you any trouble."

Isa knew she meant it, but more importantly, so did Yates and Pup.

She followed Blue inside. Martha had prepared some ham and biscuits. Blue pushed her food around her plate without speaking and ate little, then went to the loft.

Martha watched her climb the ladder. She lowered her voice so Blue couldn't hear. "I'll be relieved when you get those varmints to the sheriff. Not for us, but for them. Blue's in a state, and the sooner you get them away from her and in his care, the better I'll feel."

Blue's silence and withdrawal was disturbing, and Isa wasn't sure what to do, or if she could do anything. Blue had been gut-churned inside, like she'd been shaken so hard the reason and good sense had been forced out of her. Isa didn't know if she should go to the loft and be with her or stay away. She needed to do something. But what? She remained downstairs with Martha for a time, but neither of them talked. She got a couple of clean rags from the stores and took them out to the men. She threw the cloth at them. "Here. That's all you'll get for bandages."

She returned to the house and bathed in the water Blue had prepared for her, now cold and void of comfort. Everything had changed again. It'd all happened so quickly. What would become of Blue now? What would they all do? More questions and concerns without answers.

She dried and slipped into her nightclothes, climbed the ladder, and lay beside Blue. Should she reach out to her? She knew she wasn't asleep. She was too still. She slid her arm over her waist.

Blue immediately stiffened.

Would she listen to Isa's words? Could she feel them? Or would they trickle over her heart, like water over stone?

"Blue," she whispered.

Blue clasped Isa's hand, her shoulders trembling as she wept in silence.

Isa moved closer and embraced her.

Blue turned toward her and reached out, molding into Isa.

Blue's tears flowed freely. Unrestrained. Down Isa's neck, sliding into the cleavage of her breasts, cascading over her.

Isa said nothing more. There, in the dark, foreboding night, she caught Blue as she fell.

CHAPTER TWENTY-FOUR

Blue woke exhausted, barely able to lift her arm from Isa's waist. The stars were somber from the hint of morning. The smell of smoke permeated her clothes and the bedding. Isa must have bathed before she came to bed, because the scent of beeswax and lavender soap they'd bought at the dry goods store lingered on her skin. Blue kissed her neck and breathed in the aroma.

Isa stirred.

For a brief moment Blue enjoyed Isa next to her, the soft contours of her body, the gentle rhythm of her breathing. And then the memories of the day before came crashing in. What would she do? How would they survive now? She told herself it wasn't all gone. But they were bitter thoughts, lying in her mind like coffee grounds in the bottom of the pot.

She'd lost the mares. The thought gouged at her heart, ripping, shredding.

She couldn't afford to replace the barn. They'd have to build a shanty and make do the best they could. *Make do.* The weariness of the words overwhelmed her.

She left Isa and descended the ladder.

Martha was already up and busy in the kitchen. "Did you sleep at all?"

"A little. How about you?"

"I think I did," Martha said. "It went by so fast I'm not sure."

"Isa, Rosemary, Abigail, and I will be leaving soon to take those two worthless reprobates to the sheriff," Blue said. "Would you pack some food for us?"

"Already did. I imagine you'll be driving straight through to town?"

"Yes."

"I have some ham and such for those varmints," Martha said.

"That's fine. They can have it this morning. They won't get anything else but water from me."

Martha put her arm around her shoulder and kissed the top of her head.

Blue leaned into her. It was the best she could do. She appreciated Martha's affection, but she didn't have the wherewithal to think about it. Numbness from the turmoil of the day before engulfed her. She took the two plates of food and carried them outside.

The stench in the air hit her the moment she went onto the porch. Smoldering burnt wood mixed with the scent of charred horse flesh. She wanted to vomit.

Etta and Gertie were standing guard on the men.

"Morning, Miss Blue," Gertie said. "I reckon you'll be leaving soon with the prisoners?"

"As soon as everyone's up and ready." Blue glared at the men. "I hope you slept well. Here's your breakfast. It's all you'll get." She handed the plates to Etta, who in turn gave them to the men.

They grabbed at the food and stuffed themselves.

Pup wiped his mouth with his arm. "This here rag is mighty bloody. Could I have another for my leg, if you please?"

His pant leg and the cloth were red where Martha had peppered his thigh with shot. It wasn't life threatening.

"No. Make do with what you've got. That's what you expect us to do," Blue said.

Yates had stuffed his rag inside his shirt against his shoulder. He didn't ask for anything.

A good thing because Blue wouldn't have given him anything anyway.

Gertie came beside her. "That one," she pointed to Pup, "wanted loose last night to take a piss. I told him to wet his pants for all I cared. I finally gave in and untied one hand. The thanks I got was that he opened his pants, pulled out his dingle, and tried to douse me."

"What'd you do?" Blue asked.

"I whacked it with Abigail's rifle. He cried like a baby. I doubt he'll be able to piss this morning. I'm sorry, Miss Blue. I lost control of myself. I know I could have chosen differently."

Blue stifled her laugh. "Don't you worry about it, Gertie. I might have done the same thing myself. You go wake Rosemary and Abigail and tell them we'll be leaving shortly."

"Yes, ma'am."

"Gertie."

Gertie skidded to a stop and turned toward her.

"I'm sorry about your saddle and tack."

Gertie shrugged. "It's all right, Miss Blue. At least we have some of them. I'm glad Isa's was saved. It's a mighty fine one."

Blue felt the loss even more as Gertie ran to the bunkhouse. Pure luck had saved the wagon and rigging. And her and Isa's saddles and tack were on the corral fence. Rosemary and Abigail's horses had been saddled and ready in case they were needed. But Gertie, the one who'd saved it all because she'd done her chores like she was told, lost everything in the fire. And so did Martha, Etta, and Laurel.

The putrid taste of the unfairness gagged Blue. She spat as she returned to the house.

Isa was eating breakfast.

Martha poured Blue a cup of coffee and set a plate of food on the table beside Isa's. "You eat now so you can keep up your strength. It's going to be a hard ride to Carson City. I doubt you'll be there before dark."

Blue managed to choke the food down with the coffee.

Isa finished her meal and started to stand.

Blue grabbed her and held on. She needed to tell her how she felt, even if Martha was standing beside them. "Thank you," she whispered, "for holding me last night. It meant everything to me." The tears welled again, and she forced them back.

Isa brushed her cheek. "It meant as much to me." And then she left.

Martha walked Blue to the wagon and hugged her. "Mind yourself." She turned to the others. "All of you be careful."

"I don't expect any trouble while we're gone, but keep a ready eye," Isa said. "Set the guns where you can always get to them."

"Don't you and Miss Blue worry about us," Etta said.

"We'll take good care of Martha," Laurel said.

Gertie helped Etta prepare the wagon and hitch the team. Rosemary and Abigail loaded the two men into the back. They sat them across from each other and tied their hands to the posts, then bound their feet.

Pup complained about the pain in his leg.

"If you don't shut your yap," Abigail said, "I'm going to gag you."

Pup drew his knees up. "Don't you speak to me, you devil monster. Look at you, scarred and ugly."

Rosemary immediately stood over Pup. She raised her rifle butt and slammed it into the side of his face. Blood splattered onto the sideboard. "You shut the hell up, you piece of shit. Don't you say another word, or so help me God, I'll cut your tongue out." She turned away and touched Abigail's arm as Abigail climbed into the driver's seat.

Isa and Blue looked at each other.

Isa shrugged.

Yates didn't speak.

They left a little after sunup. Abigail drove, and Rosemary sat in the back, her rifle ready to fire if the men gave them any trouble.

Blue and Isa rode beside the wagon.

When they stopped for a break, Blue checked the men's ropes. Abigail held the canteen to their mouths and let them drink as much as they wanted.

Pup remained silent, the side of his face swollen and smeared with blood.

When they stopped for supper, Blue untied their hands and feet and let them take care of what was needed.

"Shouldn't we have some type of a restraint on them?" Rosemary asked.

"No!" Blue said. "If they try anything, we'll shoot them." She drew her pistol and pointed it at Yates.

Rosemary kept her rifle aimed at Pup.

He gave her an icy stare as he hobbled a few steps and relieved himself, groaning the entire time.

Yates walked a little farther, then did his business. They both returned voluntarily and got into the wagon.

Blue and Isa bound them as before.

Blue couldn't make herself eat. She stood guard on the men while the others had their cold meal.

They were back on the trail a little while later.

They arrived in town at dusk. They pulled the wagon in front of the sheriff's office, and Blue and Isa got off their horses and secured them to the post.

They went into the building, but no one was there.

"Where do you think he is?" Isa asked.

"Most likely home," Blue said. "You stay here with the others, and I'll ask around town. Mr. Morris will probably know where he is."

"You want Abigail or Rosemary to go with you?"

Blue shook her head. "I shouldn't be too long."

She returned her rifle to the scabbard and readjusted her gun holster. She didn't feel like herself. She'd thought about it all the way there. Maybe because she didn't feel fear anymore. Or because anger prevailed and clouded her emotions. She still had a lot to lose. She'd come to the conclusion that Anderson would pay for what he'd done one way or the other. Maybe she didn't feel herself because she'd accepted what had happened. She felt calm about things. And she hadn't felt this settled in a long time. Isa had made the difference in the night.

She went to the dry goods store and saw lights in the upper windows. She banged on the door.

Someone descended the stairs.

Mr. Morris appeared with a dinner napkin tucked under his chin. He unlocked the latch. "Blue, come in."

"Good evening, Mr. Morris. I'm sorry to disturb your supper, but do you know where the sheriff is?"

"Yes. He lives just at the end of the street." He pointed. "Has there been trouble?"

"Yes. I need him right away."

"Oh, my. That's unfortunate. Can I be of assistance?"

"Thank you, but no. Down there, you say?"

"Yes." He pointed again. "Just past the gun shop."

Blue hurried on her way. The sheriff's house was small but tidy. Wooden boxes underneath the two windows facing the street were filled with yellow, blue, and purple flowers. She could see a man and a woman sitting at a small table, drinking cups of something.

She knocked.

A wooden chair scraped the floor.

A big-shouldered, six-foot-tall man, probably in his late thirties, swung the door open. He had a thick mustache and a mass of sandy-brown hair. He didn't say anything. No greeting. No question as to what Blue wanted. He just stood there like a massive oak.

"Sheriff?" Blue asked.

"He cleared his throat. "Yes. Who might you be?"

"I'm Blue Hutchings."

He smiled. "Of course. Of course. Come in." He stood aside and waved her to enter.

The house felt warm and inviting. A stout woman with long, braided brown hair stood as Blue entered. She smiled. "We've heard so many good things about you, Miss Hutchings. Please sit down. May I get you some tea or coffee?"

"Thank you, ma'am, but no. I have pressing business with the sheriff."

He put on his hat, and then his holster and gun. "I'll be at the office, Melly." He kissed her forehead.

Blue followed him outside, and they walked toward his office.

"What's this about?" he asked.

Blue explained what had happened and that she had two men to turn over to him.

He stopped short. "You brought them here? All the way from your ranch?"

"Yes. My partner and I and two of our hires."

"Did they give you any trouble?"

"No. They're in need of medical attention. One has a wound in his shoulder, and the other got his leg peppered with a shotgun. We kept them tied up."

They resumed walking.

"It sounds to me like you took care of business. I'm Sheriff Harmon Tudsdale, by the way. Let's get them settled, and then we can talk."

Rosemary and Abigail climbed down from the wagon. Isa untied the men and directed them to get out.

"I've been treated mighty poorly, Sheriff," Pup said. "Mighty poorly." He held the side of his face.

"Of course you have, Pup," Sheriff Tudsdale said. "And Yates, I suppose you have a word or two to say?"

"She about kilt me," Yates said.

"From the sound of things, you're both pretty lucky she didn't." The sheriff pushed them through the door and pointed to the cells. "You know where they are, Pup. Each of you get in one."

Pup took the first of the three connected, barred cells, about eight feet by six feet, and Yates the second. The sheriff locked them in. The heavy wooden outer door had metal bars in the shape of a window at the top, probably to keep an eye on the prisoners.

He slammed it shut, then bolted it.

"We're powerful hurt, Sheriff," Pup yelled. "Can't you see we've been shot? Those crazy women tried to murder us. We need help."

The sheriff peered through the barred opening. "The doc will be along directly, if he's not out on a call."

"And I'm hungry. She wouldn't feed us nothing," Pup said.

"Shut your mouth, Pup. You'll be taken care of in a while." The sheriff tossed the cell keys onto his scratched wooden desk and sat in his chair.

"Isa, would you see to Abigail and Rosemary?" Blue asked. "We'll head back as soon as I'm done here."

Isa nodded and left.

"All right. Let's hear the whole story," Tudsdale said.

Blue gave as much detail as she could. "I want them prosecuted. It's not right what Anderson and his men did, Sheriff."

Tudsdale removed his hat and reached back and hung it on the rack behind him.

Blue admired its sleek, stiff edges.

He caught her looking at it. "It's called 'Boss of the Plains,'" Tudsdale said. "A man named Stetson made it up East somewhere. Morris, at the dry goods store, is supposed to get a bunch of them in with his next shipment. If I were you, I'd put in an order for one. It's the best hat I've ever had. It's waterproof and holds the rain and sun off your neck." He folded his arms across his chest. "Now, about your problem. This is how it works. You live in the US marshal's territory. That'd be Aaron Jenkins. I only have jurisdiction within the city limits. He's out in the territory now and should be back in a day or two."

He continued. "Our judge is Clive Ruggles. He lives just outside of Virginia City. He comes every three months and holds court. So Pup and Yates won't go to trial until then." He reviewed the calendar on his desk. "And His Honor won't be here for another"—he pointed to the squares on the paper—"four to six weeks. Now here's where it gets sticky. Because we can't hold their trial for a while, they can be out on bail as long as someone pays it. And Frank Anderson always pays for his boys."

"You mean they'll be let go?"

"Well, not really. They'll be signed over to Anderson's custody, and they'll have to appear in court. Then the judge will decide what punishment fits the crime."

"Anderson can come and get them, and they'll be back at his ranch, under his orders again? Like before?" Blue asked.

The sheriff didn't say anything, just watched her.

"How long until they can get out on bail?"

"Any time after two days."

Blue stood. "This is horseshit, and you know it."

He unfolded his arms and stood. "I'm sorry. My hands are tied about this. The trial will be set for one o'clock, October second, at the courthouse. You'll need to be here with your witnesses and any evidence you have to present to the judge."

Blue gritted her teeth. She had to talk with Jeremiah before she left. She had to know how to deal with this. She couldn't go all the way home without resolving it.

"I'll be back in town tomorrow," Blue said.

"Miss Hutchings, I'm sorry for your trouble. We got some mighty fine people around here. Don't let a few bad men discourage you. From what I've heard, you have a good head about you and want to help build a decent community. We need you, more than you know. You can pull your wagon at the end of the street. There's a pump with good water and a nice area to set up for the night."

His kindness took the edge off her anger. "Thank you, Sheriff. I'll see you tomorrow."

She left his office and told Isa and the others her plan to stay the night. They moved the wagon to the edge of town and set up camp.

Blue was at Jeremiah's office the next morning by the time the pendulum of his tall case clock struck nine.

She recapped what had happened.

"Blue, you can't prevent the men from their right to bail. I suggest you return home and gather your evidence as the sheriff instructed. I'll go with you to court. Also, I'd like to write down your statement and have you sign it. Can any of the others write?"

"A few."

"Have someone take their statements and have them dated and signed. We'll present those in court also."

Why did she have to go through all of this? And why would Yates and Pup get to walk free? It wasn't right or fair.

He took her hand. "Don't worry. You have a good case. The judge is a reasonable man, and I'm sure he'll do what's right."

Jeremiah took her statement, and she signed the paper.

"Will you and your party stay for supper this evening? I'm sure Elizabeth can prepare enough for all of you."

"Thank you, but we need to stop at the hardware store to replace as many items as I can afford. Then I want to get back to the ranch."

He walked her to camp. "I'm so sorry for your loss and trouble." He said hello to Isa and the others, then left.

His words were of little comfort. Blue knew perfectly well this wasn't the end of it. Isa had been right. She should have left it alone. But how could she? She'd picked up one end of the stick, and now she'd have to deal with the other.

CHAPTER TWENTY-FIVE

Isa wiped the gritty sweat from her face with her neckerchief. It was grimy work. For two and a half days they'd shoveled and dug and carried debris from what remained of the barn. What they couldn't salvage or finish burning, they threw in the pit they'd dug on the far side of the outhouse. She didn't want Blue to help with the cleanup but insisted she busy herself with the horses and other things. She was quiet again and stayed by herself most of the time.

Isa leaned the shovel against the wheelbarrow and sat on the only bucket that had survived the fire. The hardest part was removing the charred remains of the broodmares. They were Blue's future. And now, once again, her prospects were bleak. She'd spent every cent she had replacing what little equipment she could afford. She'd reluctantly accepted what scant amount of money Isa and the others had given her after they'd bought replacement saddles, blankets, bridles, and other tack. But the scarce amount didn't cover everything needed.

Isa stood to shovel more debris and realized the work had been completed.

Gertie leaned on the pitchfork. "It's a fine job. I know Miss Blue will feel better knowing it's done." Her face was smudged with soot, and her clothes were filthy.

Rosemary and Etta stood together talking.

Rosemary stopped and pointed. "What is that?"

Massive clouds of dust swirled in the distance.

Isa stood and strained to see.

Gertie climbed on the bucket and shaded her eyes. "It's wagons. Lots of them."

The others gathered near Isa.

"Is it a wagon train?" Abigail asked. "I've never seen one this far out."

"Maybe they're lost," Etta said.

Martha, Laurel, and Blue came out of the house and watched from the porch. Isa walked to them and stood beside Blue.

"Do you think they're going to Carson City?" Blue asked no one in particular.

"I don't know, but I think they're headed this way," Martha said.

"Grab your guns," Blue called. "Be on the ready."

Everyone scattered to get their weapons and then returned to the porch.

"I count ten," Laurel said.

"Where on earth are they going?" Martha asked. "I can't imagine."

Gertie stood in front of Isa. "Maybe they're on their way to California. It's not that far."

"They would have turned long before this," Rosemary said.

As the wagons neared, Isa recognized one of the men in the lead. "It's Jacob Wyman."

"I see Virgil Pettiman and his sons," Blue said. "Oh, Isa. They're coming here."

As the company neared, their purpose was revealed. Lumber stuck out the back of most of the wagons, and others were filled with more people. Jeremiah Hawthorne, James and Nettie Morris from the dry goods store, Luther Henderson, the livery owner, and many others Isa didn't recognize.

Blue sat on the porch steps, shaking her head. "I don't believe it."

Martha put her hands to her face. "Mercy sakes."

Virgil and Jacob waved, smiling as they approached.

Blue, Isa, and Martha led the way as they walked out to greet them.

Jacob and Virgil dismounted and removed their hats.

"We heard you had trouble, and we're here to help. If it's all right, once we unload, we'll circle the wagons over there." He pointed past the corrals.

"I don't know what to say, Jacob," Blue said. "I'm speechless." Tears wetted her cheeks.

Jacob laughed.

"Everyone wanted to help, Blue," Virgil said. "Don't you worry about a thing. We'll have that new barn up by sundown tomorrow. The womenfolk came along to cook the meals and, I suspect, to visit with your ladies. Morgan can't stop talking about Laurel." He laughed.

Jacob directed the wagons as Virgil inspected the cleanup Isa and the others had completed.

"We were going to get that done first," Virgil said. "But since you've already taken care of it, we'll jump in and get started. Do you want the new barn built where the other one was, Blue?"

Blue nodded and smiled. "That'd be fine, Virgil."

It was good to see genuine relief in Blue's eyes. It'd been a long time.

Everyone unloaded supplies. Virgil and Jacob organized the workers and began construction. The chatter and voices of those giving instructions and the sounds of hammering and sawing filled the air.

Some wagons held replacement items that had been lost in the fire. There were buckets, pitchforks, farrier tools, bales of straw and hay, and other necessities for the barn.

Pearl Pettiman, Cora Wyman, and Nettie Morris gathered around Blue and Isa.

"There was such excitement when Jacob came into town and met with the others," Nettie said. "I thought my husband would burst with enthusiasm."

Blue laughed. "I still don't know what to say. It's overwhelming." Her eyes sparkled, and she smiled constantly.

Each of the women hugged her.

Martha's tears flowed from the corners of her eyes.

Blue needed this spark. Even if the neighbors and townspeople had only come to say hello and tell her they were thinking of her, it would have been enough. No wonder she felt overwhelmed. Isa did too. The outpouring of friendship and care was beyond words.

They worked on the structure and prepared food until darkness overtook them. They ate supper by the light of candle and campfire. They sat on the grass, on the porch, in the house, or wherever they could find a seat. After the meal, musical instruments suddenly appeared, and everyone enjoyed one another's company.

Isa accompanied Blue and Martha as they went from person to person and thanked them. She spied Laurel and Morgan Pettiman holding hands as they walked by the creek. She caught Blue's eye and winked.

Blue smiled.

When everyone had gone to bed, and Blue lay with Isa in the loft, Isa kissed her.

"My heart is full," Blue said and wrapped her arms around Isa. "Never have I seen such a grand act of service. I know it sounds odd, but today I feel like I'm home."

Isa held her close. "That's not odd. Home is where love is."

"I feel a stronger sense of belonging than I ever have," Blue said. She kissed Isa. "And I know I wouldn't feel most of it without you."

They held each other as they drifted off into sleep.

Virgil's prediction had been wrong. The barn wasn't completed by sundown the next day. It was finished by afternoon. Then they covered the stalls with straw, stored the equipment, and led Adelita and the remaining broodmare in.

Everyone cheered. Their friends and neighbors then ate, packed the wagons, exchanged good-byes, and left.

The others gathered around Blue, Martha, and Isa and watched until all that remained were the dust clouds in the distance once again.

Martha retired to one of the rocking chairs on the porch. "This was the grandest time I've ever had. I believe we've just experienced what heaven is like."

"Of a truth," Abigail said.

Laurel bounded onto the porch. "I have an announcement."

"Huh. I bet you do," Etta said.

"What is it?" Blue asked.

Isa knew, and so did everyone else. Blue was being polite so as not to spoil Laurel's big reveal.

"Morgan Pettiman has asked me to marry him. And I've accepted." Everyone congratulated her.

"I'll sure miss your cookin'," Gertie said. Her face turned red. "Not that Martha isn't a fine cook."

Everyone laughed.

"I know what you mean," Martha said. "Laurel does have a gift in the kitchen."

"But no one makes biscuits like you do," Gertie said.

Martha chuckled.

"Isa, there's still plenty of daylight left. Let's ride out and check on the herd," Blue said.

"I believe I'll go along," Gertie said. She started to step off the porch.

Etta grabbed the back of her shirt. "No, you don't, little lady. You need to scrub yourself and your bunk area, and get your laundry done."

Rosemary patted Gertie's back. "She's not kidding. If you don't take a bath soon, we're going to throw you in the creek with a bar of soap."

Isa and Blue saddled Traveler and Biscuit and left.

The ride was pleasant. No wind, and the temperature was comfortable.

"It's beautiful here, isn't it?" Blue asked.

Isa surveyed the landscape. "I always enjoy looking at it."

Blue touched Isa's thigh. "When I saw those wagons were for us, I couldn't believe it. I'd forgotten there are good people in the world. All I've been able to think about lately is the bad."

"That's understandable," Isa said. "You've certainly had your share of it."

When they reached the herd, they circled and inspected them carefully.

"They look good. Really good," Blue said.

Isa agreed.

"Isa, do you have a blanket in your saddlebag?"

Isa laughed. "Yes. Would you like to go over to the pines and sit awhile?"

"Could we go over by the lake?"

"If that's what you want."

They rode the short distance and secured Traveler and Biscuit. Isa spread the blanket near some large boulders and sat.

Blue stood in front of her with a mischievous grin.

Isa glanced at her, but the sun, directly behind Blue, momentarily blinded her.

Blue moved slightly.

Isa shaded her eyes, and when she was able to focus, Blue was unbuttoning her shirt.

"What are you doing?"

"I'm going in the lake."

"I thought you didn't like the water."

"Today I do." Blue stripped her shirt off.

Isa kept her eyes glued to her, not wanting to miss one second of this big moment. "It's going to be colder than you think."

Blue continued to undress. She slipped her pants off and stood in her long-sleeved undershirt and underwear. The top had a tear in the shoulder where she must have caught it on something, and the edges of the sleeves were frayed. Isa became aware that her clothes were just as tattered as Blue's.

She wasn't sure if Blue would remove it. She leaned back on her elbows. Would she? If she did, Isa decided she'd join her.

Blue suddenly turned and ran toward the water.

Isa jumped up and followed her.

Blue lifted her top over her head as she ran. She stopped only for a moment, hopped out of the bottoms, then made a dash for the water, laughing the entire time.

Isa stilled to watch, craving more of the scene before her. Sleek and nude, Blue slid effortlessly into the water. The sun danced on the pale skin of her back and her firm, rounded buttocks. She broke the surface facing Isa, her hands raised to her cheeks, her fleshy pink breasts pert and her muscled stomach tight.

She gazed at Isa. "You're right. It's terribly cold but refreshing." The color of her eyes seemed to deepen.

Isa stripped as fast as she could and walked to the water's edge, hesitating before she started to make her way toward Blue. The water wasn't cold—it was liquid ice. She shivered and tried to keep her focus on Blue, but the pain and shock of the sudden drop in temperature locked her knees. In spite of it, she dove in.

Blue must have sensed her experience because she hurried toward her, pulled her up, and wrapped her arms around her. "Your lips are turning purple."

Blue's body was cold, but her breasts pressing against Isa sent chills into her, and she couldn't tell which was the stronger sensation.

She tried to speak, but her teeth chattered. "Let's go…back…to the blanket."

Blue's smile changed to an expression of alarm. She guided her out of the water and onto the blanket.

Isa shook so hard she couldn't grasp the covering to wrap herself in it.

Blue tucked it around her. "I'm so sorry."

Isa tried to nod, but she couldn't move her head.

Blue retrieved their clothes. "Put your top on."

Isa fumbled to get it on as Blue helped her.

Blue stood and dressed. "I'll get some firewood and make a fire." She got her starting kit from her saddlebag and had a fire going in a matter of minutes.

Isa's disappointment flooded her. She'd waited all this time to experience Blue, and in a few chilling, tormenting minutes, the possibility had vanished. She could hardly remember seeing Blue. But what she could remember was delightful.

Blue sat behind her and encircled her in her arms and legs as they faced the fire.

Isa began to feel the heat. She stopped shivering.

Blue whispered in her ear. "I'm sorry I spoiled everything."

The warmth returned fast. Isa opened her legs and let the heat from the fire radiate to her inner thighs and female parts. She now could feel Blue against her—warm, strong. She leaned into her.

Blue moved to the front of her and began to undress again.

"Are you sure, Blue?"

"I've never been more sure of anything in my life."

Her movements were slow and deliberate. Now naked, she went to her knees in front of Isa.

Isa let go of the blanket, removed her shirt, and raised her arms. Her nipples had hardened before Blue could remove her top.

"Isa, you're so beautiful."

Blue moved toward her until she was against her and guided Isa onto her back. She kissed her with lips full of wanton heat. She lifted herself on her elbows and gazed at her.

No one had ever looked at her that way. Blue's gaze penetrated, and liberated, and consumed her.

"I've dreamed so many nights about touching you," Blue said.

The sound of her voice took Isa's breath away, and when Blue covered one of Isa's nipples with her mouth, Isa arched and cried out for her.

Blue caressed each breast, then rubbed hers against them, sending rivulets of desire and need through Isa.

She trailed her fingers over the inside of Isa's thighs.

Isa moaned. Anticipating, she raised her hips and moved toward Blue's fingers.

"I'm not sure what to do," Blue said, "but I know I want to touch you."

"Yes," Isa pleaded, desperate for her.

The instant Blue entered her, Isa opened.

"You're so hot and wet. It's wonderful." Blue kissed her, sliding her tongue and lips over her, down her neck, onto her breasts, licking.

She went deeper into her and began to thrust.

Isa's need to touch Blue surged through her. She cupped her hand over Blue's breast and squeezed gently. Blue's nipples were inviting and hard. She lifted Blue enough to suck the nipple as she caressed the other, moaning and writhing.

"Isa," Blue called.

Isa caressed her thigh and then spread her. She entered slick folds of hot flesh. She thrust in unison with Blue.

They tensed, and arched, and joined together.

Blue's breathing increased. She panted. She delved deeper into Isa, her fingers tender and firm, and perfectly positioned.

Blue pushed her hips into her, grinding as she released.

Isa couldn't hold back any longer.

They writhed in ecstasy, wave after wave of pleasure.

Their pace slowed, and then Blue collapsed on her, showering her with kisses.

Isa took Blue's breast and sucked, then the other.

They kissed.

Blue gazed at her, smiling. "What just happened?"

Isa laughed. "We'll have to ask Etta what it's called, but your body was fulfilled."

"Fulfilled?"

"Yes. Like when a stud enters a mare and ejaculates."

"Women can do that too? Whatever happened, it was wonderful."

Isa threw her head back and laughed. "Yes, it was. What's good for the stud is good for the mare."

Blue kissed her, then eased away. "Has that ever happened to you before?"

Isa hesitated. "Yes."

Blue tilted her head to one side. "Really? With who?"

Should Isa tell her? The last thing she wanted was to hurt Blue in any way. But wouldn't a lie hurt her more than the truth? "When I was fifteen, I had a dear friend named Margarette. We fell in love and explored each other the way a boy and a girl would."

Blue pouted.

Was she jealous? Isa touched her face. "But it wasn't as strong as this."

Blue's smile returned. "Someday I'll want to hear more. But for today, I just want to be with you."

Isa pulled her close. "You're who I've searched for. You are who I want. There'll never be anyone but you."

They lay in the sun by the fire, talking, touching, and knowing one another.

And then it was time to return to the ranch.

Blue remained quiet on the way back, occasionally taking Isa's hand.

"Are you well?" Isa asked.

"Mmm. Just..." Blue inhaled deeply. "Just enjoying this. You. The ranch. The horses. Everything. I'm thoroughly content, and it's indescribable." She reined Traveler to a stop. "You're well, aren't you?"

"Oh, yes!"

Blue smiled and rode on. "I can see now what all the fuss is about."

Isa laughed, glad Blue seemed content. She needed the release. They both needed it. It'd been a long time since she'd experienced it herself. And to be honest, in her heart, she'd never felt it as fully as she had with Blue. She was sure both of them glowed. And most likely, if the others were still up when they got home, they'd see it. She knew Martha and Etta might even be happy for them. Gertie would be clueless. But what about the others? Did it matter? Was it any of their business? No, it wasn't.

"What are you thinking about? You're frowning," Blue said.

"I imagine what we did is written all over our faces, and I'm wondering if any of the others will figure it out."

Blue readjusted in the saddle. "I don't give a damn. My property. My rules."

They both laughed, but then Blue grew solemn.

"Isa, I can't afford to pay the hires any more. I'll have to let them go, and I don't know how to do it. How can I throw Gertie out into the world? Or any of the others, for that matter? What am I going to do?"

Isa thought for a moment. Blue underestimated the others. "I think you should sit them down and talk with them about it and see what happens." She already knew the probable outcome. All of them had grown attached to Blue, Martha, and her. And their options were limited. But no matter what happened, it would be a hard decision.

They arrived home just after sundown and took care of the horses. Isa didn't realize how hungry she'd been until she smelled the stew. Her stomach growled.

"Will you talk with the girls?" Blue asked as they walked toward the house.

"No. This is something you need to do. But I'll be beside you."

They entered the kitchen. All eyes shifted to them. Or did it just feel that way?

Gertie stopped eating. "What took you so long?"

Etta snickered.

Neither Blue nor Isa answered. They went to the stove and dished out the stew, then the cooked apples, and grabbed a biscuit.

"After supper I need to talk with all of you out on the porch." Blue said it like she didn't expect an answer.

"Did we do something wrong?" Gertie asked.

"Mind your manners and eat your supper," Martha said.

"No. I just need to talk with you," Blue said.

Rosemary, Abigail, and Etta looked at each other.

Isa sat quietly and ate. Did they suspect what was coming? They knew Blue was now penniless. Had they discussed it already among themselves? It would be hard on all of them if they had to leave. What would become of them?

CHAPTER TWENTY-SIX

Blue's stomach began to churn halfway through her meal. It'd been such a wonderful day. Did she want to spoil it by telling the hires she couldn't pay them and they'd have to leave?

When the others had gathered on the porch, Blue finished her coffee and stood.

"I think they know what's coming," Martha said. "They've been quiet all evening."

"It has to be done," Blue said. She touched Isa's shoulder as she walked past her.

Isa grabbed her hand and squeezed.

Blue sat in the rocker, while the others stood, leaned against the posts, or sat on the steps.

How could she tell them? They'd all showed their loyalty and been through so much with her. But it wasn't fair to expect them to stay without being paid.

"I don't have any money left, so I'll have to let you go."

The women were silent as they looked at each other.

Rosemary stood straighter and cleared her throat. "Miss Blue. We've all talked about it, and we want to stay on, even though you can't pay us. Most of us have nowhere else to go, and if you'll have us, we'd like to work off our living expenses here. You, Martha, and Isa have been mighty good to us."

The others nodded.

Blue studied each of their faces. Gertie had tears in her eyes. Abigail had an earnest expression, as if anxious to hear Blue's answer. Etta looked serious. Blue had a hard time reading Laurel because she ducked her head. Rosemary's shoulders were squared like she was filled with confidence.

Each one was familiar, no longer a stranger or a passing

acquaintance, or even a hired hand. They were more like family. Sisters. They'd somehow found each other and made their way into Blue's heart. She had no idea if they got along with each other in the bunkhouse. Were they friends? Or did they only tolerate each other? She'd heard them quarrel occasionally.

"You do know that it's not over with Anderson," she said. "I'm afraid there's going to be more trouble before it's done. Are you sure you want to stay?"

Gertie stood. "Yes, Miss Blue."

"Yes," Laurel said.

"Laurel, you're going to be married soon," Blue said. "I'm sure you can find someone to board with in town, where it's safer, or even at the Pettiman ranch. I know you'd be welcome there."

"No, Miss Blue. I'll remain here if you'll have me."

"Please change your mind and leave, Laurel," Blue said. "Your life is full of hope and a future." Staying here might cause her a loss Blue could never justify.

"If you're ordering me, then I will. Otherwise, I want to stay."

What could Blue say? Should she order her? She hung her head and sighed.

The others remained quiet.

Laurel spoke again. "I want to be here, Miss Blue. I need to learn from Martha, you, Isa, and the others."

"We all need to be here, Miss Blue," Abigail said. "We've gotten more from you than we ever gave."

"It seems like all I've ever given you is trouble," Blue said.

Tears ran down Etta's cheeks. "That's not true, Miss Blue. You saved my life. No amount of money you could ever pay me is worth more than that. If you never give me another cent, I'd still be in your debt."

"We all feel that way, Miss Blue," Rosemary said. "Let us stay."

Blue looked into their faces once again.

Each nodded in response.

The weight of what they were asking fell heavy on her heart. What if they remained and Anderson came back? They could be shot, or killed. She couldn't bear that responsibility. But was it her decision to make? If she forced them to leave, what would become of them?

They remained silent, their eyes fixed on her.

She breathed deeply. The decision was made. Stand or fall, they'd do it together. "All right. Stay until you feel you've got something better to move on to. I'll pay you when I can."

They all smiled.

"That's good enough," Rosemary said. "We best get to bed."

Each said their good-nights and left the porch.

Blue went into the house.

Isa patted the bench beside her. "Well done."

"I'm afraid they don't know what kind of trouble they've asked for."

"Maybe Anderson has had enough," Martha said.

Blue rubbed her face. "I doubt if he's had his fill."

Gertie stood at the entrance. "Miss Blue, may I talk with you?"

Blue waved her in. "What is it?"

"I've been thinking terrible hard about the herd. I'd like to propose an idea."

"Sit," Isa said.

Gertie sat by Martha across from Isa and Blue.

"Now that I know my numbers and ciphers, I reckon in one swoop we can get over one hundred and fifty horses."

Blue's interest perked up.

Isa leaned forward.

"I know where they run. I know the passes well. We can ride in, gather them up, and herd them back here."

"I like your idea, Gertie, but there's one small problem," Isa said.

"What's that?" Gertie asked.

"They're wild, and most likely they'll want to roam, and they'll head right back where we found them, taking our herd with them."

"I doubt they'd risk the mountains," Gertie said. "Those passes are snowbound most of the time. They'd have good feed and water right here."

"She has a point," Blue said.

Isa nodded. "Maybe. But it's still a risk."

"What if we only took some of the best of the herd?" Blue asked. "Not the lead mare or the stallion. We could leave a few prime ones to continue the line. And if we had a buyer in advance, we could drive them directly to an agreed-upon spot and not risk the other herd."

"I think that would work," Isa said.

"There's a hitch," Gertie said. "It's too late in the year to do it. We'll have to wait until spring. The snows will close the passes soon."

"Thank you, Gertie. It's good information, and we'll consider it," Blue said.

Gertie left.

Blue's enthusiasm grew. "Do you think we can do it?"

"It's worth a try," Isa said. "Gertie knows that area, and if anyone can find those horses, she can."

"It would definitely boost our income," Martha said. "There were postings all over in Carson City for large numbers of horses."

"Let's keep it between ourselves for now," Blue said.

Martha and Isa agreed.

That night, as Blue lay in Isa's arms, she felt hope. If a buyer made a contract with her she wouldn't get paid until after they delivered the horses, but the idea grabbed hold in her mind. Something to hang on to. They had enough riders to do it. They had Gertie to lead them to the herd, and they had the skills. They just needed to get through the winter.

Two days later Martha, Isa, and Rosemary were going through the stores, making an inventory. Blue left the house and started helping the others split and stack needed firewood.

Mid-afternoon painted the sky a vivid, cloudless azure, and a gentle breeze swept over them.

Blue's arms were aching from the repeated motion of her swings. "Gertie, please bring the water bucket and ladle."

Gertie stopped stacking wood and took three steps toward the barn. A shot rang out. The bullet missed her head by inches and slammed into the side of the building.

Blue dropped the ax, reached for her rifle propped against a log, and yelled for everyone to take cover.

Gertie and Abigail grabbed their weapons and rushed to the barn loft. Etta reached for her rifle, and Rosemary pulled her pistol as they both dove behind the wood pile.

"Raiders," Blue yelled to Isa in the house. "Anderson."

Three riders came at a full gallop between the corral and barn. Blue dove for the only cover she could get to—the porch, behind the rocking chair.

She heard more riders behind her and to the right. Two. Coming fast. Exposed from that angle, she swung the rifle in their direction, aimed, and fired.

Yates fell off his horse.

She fired again, and he stilled on the ground.

A shot whizzed above her head.

Isa returned fire from the window.

Two more riders were coming from the south, making a wide circle.

Blue had to get better cover.

Isa shot in rapid fire. "Get in here," she yelled.

Blue dashed for the doorway.

Shots rang out.

Before she could close the door, bullets riddled the table, the wall, and stove.

She had no idea how Rosemary and the others were doing. Were they hit? Were they able to get any of the other riders? No time to think. "I need ammunition." She pulled her pistol and started firing. Out of the corner of her eye, she saw Laurel reach for a box of bullets from the shelf, but then she screamed and grabbed her hand, dropping the container. Blood dripped around her fingers. She kicked the container to Blue.

Blue could hear men's voices.

"She's in the house," one of them yelled.

She eased up to the window and peered out. She could see a man on the ground by the barn. Pup. Anderson was off his horse and behind the corral post, trying to aim at the loft, but he was pinned down by Etta and Rosemary.

Isa shot again. A rider fell backward off his horse. Evans.

Another barrage of shots came into the house.

Isa crouched lower.

Martha stood and started moving toward the window, the shotgun in her hand.

Isa called to her to stay back, then started firing as she sprang toward Martha to stop her.

Blue saw it all as if in slow motion.

A bullet went into Isa's left shoulder, and then another ripped through her side. She fell with a thud and lay motionless. Pools of blood began to soak her shirt.

"Isa!" Blue tried to get to her but couldn't because of the spray of gunfire. She scooted to another position and returned fire, hitting one of the remaining men out front. Before he could get away, one of the other women put another shot in him, and he fell to the ground.

Blue crawled to Isa and dragged her to the corner.

Martha threw the shotgun down and belly-crawled to Isa. "I've got her."

Blue ran toward the rear window, dove out, and slipped around the side of the house.

She fired at Anderson. The bullet hit the post, just missing his head.

"You sonofabitch," she yelled. "You're a dead man."

She looked at Etta and Rosemary by the woodpile and held up two fingers, then motioned for them to go around to the far side of the house.

Anderson and two of his men were the only ones left.

"Go now." She started shooting, giving them enough covering fire to move.

She aimed at Anderson, hitting him in the upper arm. He flinched. She shot him again in the same arm.

She heard more gunfire.

One of the two men in front of the house slumped in the saddle. McCoy. He and the other man raced away.

Blue kept firing at Anderson.

He tossed his rifle and raised his hand. "I give up. Don't shoot. I give up. Hold your fire. I'm unarmed."

"Pick it up, Anderson. You made your bed, and now you'll die in it."

He crouched behind the post. "Don't fire."

"Go to hell," Blue said. She kept firing as she walked closer. She couldn't focus but continued to pull the trigger. No recoil. She became aware the chamber had emptied. She took the bullets from the leather holder on her belt and tried to load the gun as she walked. Two slipped from her trembling fingers and fell to the ground, but she kept on. Another dropped. She managed to shove two into the chamber.

She felt a hand on her arm. "Miss Blue, that's enough."

She jerked her arm away from Rosemary's touch. "He's not dead yet."

She could barely aim. Her strength had left her. She shot the post. Wood splintered by Anderson's ear.

"Blue. It's over." Martha came toward her, her dress covered in blood. Isa's blood.

"No. It's not over." Blue aimed.

Martha grabbed her arm and lowered the gun. "I need your help with Isa."

Blue dropped it and ran to the house.

She knelt beside Isa. Martha had stuffed cloth into her wounds. She was pale. Blood was everywhere.

Blue slipped her hand under her head and held her. "Isa. No! No!" She kissed her cheek. "Don't leave me."

Isa reached for her but didn't speak.

Laurel was near the stove, wrapping her wound.

Martha, Rosemary, and Etta rushed into the room.

"We've got to get her up into the light so I can see better," Martha said.

They moved Isa with a blanket and laid her on the table.

"Etta, get my medicinal bag from the pantry. Help me get her shirt off."

Etta left them, and Rosemary and Blue did as instructed.

The cloth slipped from the wound in Isa's shoulder. The blood still leaked but had slowed. The tissue was torn and ragged.

"I'll have to get the bullet out," Martha said. "I think the one in her side went all the way through."

Blue sat on the bench and held Isa's hand.

Etta came back with Martha's bag.

"I need a pan of hot water and more cloth and sheets," Martha said.

Gertie and Abigail crowded into the room.

"We've tied Anderson to the post," Abigail said. "His arm's bleeding pretty bad. I wrapped it. What do you want us to do now, Miss Blue?"

Blue didn't answer.

"Etta, Laurel needs help," Martha said.

"Gertie, you and Abigail come with me," Rosemary said.

Blue glanced at them. Gertie's arm was bleeding. "Gertie, were you shot?"

Gertie inspected her arm. "Aw. It's nothing. Just a scratch. I'll be fine."

Blue tried to focus. All she saw was Isa. But there were things that had to be done. How many men were lying dead outside? She didn't care. "How's Laurel?" she asked.

"She'll survive," Martha said.

"Isa," Blue said, barely able to speak her name. What if she died? How would Blue go on?

"Blue, you're no good to me. Go help the others," Martha said.

"I won't leave her." Blue grasped Isa's hand tighter.

"Go take care of things outside. Rosemary can't do it with only Gertie and Abigail. I promise you if I see any problems, I'll call you in. She's lost a lot of blood, but it's not hopeless."

"No!" Blue said.

"Damn it, Blue. This is no time to be stubborn. If you insist on doing this, then stick the poker into the fire and get it red-hot."

Blue glared at Martha. She knew what Martha was going to do. Cauterize the bullet hole once she dug the bullet out of Isa's shoulder.

"If you can't help, then you need to leave."

"I can help. I can do it," Blue said.

Etta moved beside Martha, holding strips of cloth and a sheet. "I helped Laurel dress her hand. I cleaned it with whiskey, wrapped it, then gave her a stiff drink. She's resting. The water's almost ready."

Martha nodded.

Blue stoked the coals in the fireplace and jammed the poker in. Anderson. He did this. All of it.

Isa screamed.

Blue ran to her.

Martha dug into Isa's shoulder as Etta held her arms down.

Blue squeezed Isa's hand "Hang on."

Isa moaned.

Martha held the bullet in the tweezers and dropped it into the pan. "I need the hot iron."

Blue grabbed the metal bar with the pad and twisted it deeper into the coals. She waited a few seconds until the tip became fiery red hot, then took it to Martha.

"Hold her shoulder, Blue. Etta, don't let her hands loose."

Martha applied the hot iron to the wound.

Isa screamed and then went still and quiet.

"Isa," Blue cried.

"She's passed out. That's all," Martha said. "It's a good thing. She won't fight me anymore."

Martha continued her work.

Once Isa's wounds were cleansed and bandaged, they washed her and slipped a gown on her. They moved her to Martha's bed and made her as comfortable as possible. Etta and Martha left the room.

Blue sat beside Isa and held her hand for a long while. Isa was the color of a snow owl, and her breathing was shallow.

How could this have happened? Of all of them, why Isa?

Laurel came into the room, her right hand in a sling. "I'll sit with her."

Blue didn't want to leave, but a lot of things needed her attention. "Let me know when she wakes." Reluctantly, she went to the kitchen.

Martha and Etta had cleaned the blood from the table, but it remained where Isa had lain on the floor.

"I'm going to check on the others," Blue said. She grabbed a handful of bullets, stuffed them into her pocket, and left before Martha could say anything.

The sun was beginning to set.

Rosemary came to her. "There's four dead. McCoy was wounded, but I don't know how badly. I think he might have been gut shot. He got away with the other one. That makes six, plus Anderson." She glanced toward the corral. "He's quiet."

"None of the others survived?" Blue asked.

"Just the two who got away, and him. Do you think they'll come back?"

"I don't think so, but we better set guards," Blue said.

"What should we do with the bodies?"

"We'll have to take them to town," Blue said. "I recognized Pup, Evans, and Yates, but not the other one. And I don't know who left with McCoy."

"We're going to have to leave soon. They won't last long in this weather," Rosemary said.

"I want to wait until I know about Isa. I don't care how badly they stink. We'll wrap them in canvas and put them in the back of the wagon."

By the time they loaded the last body, it was long past dark.

"What should we do about him?" Abigail pointed to Anderson.

"Nothing. Let him stay there," Blue said. "I don't care what happens to him."

Abigail nodded.

The others gathered around Blue.

"All of you get cleaned up and rest while you can. You did good. I couldn't have asked for better hands. Rosemary, at first light I want you and Abigail to take the wagon to Carson City and hand those bodies over to the sheriff. Tell him everything that happened."

"What about Anderson?" Abigail asked.

"I'll take him myself as soon as I know more about Isa."

"Miss Blue, you reckon Isa is going to make it?" Gertie asked.

"We don't know yet," Blue said. "But if she doesn't, there'll be one more body to take to town." She glared at Anderson. "I don't know what the sheriff will want to do, but you get back here as fast as you can. We'll figure the rest out later."

Blue washed at the pump and then went into the house and straight to the bedroom to see Isa.

Laurel sat in a chair beside the bed. She stood. "Would you like to sit a while?"

"Yes. How is she?"

"She's sleeping and hasn't moved." Laurel left the room.

Martha came in with a cup of coffee and handed it to Blue, then touched Isa's forehead. "She's warm. I cleaned her wounds the best I could and put yarrow in them. It should help draw out any infection. Blue, Anderson has been tied to that post quite a while. Someone should at least give him water and let him relieve himself."

"No one goes near him."

"Blue."

The rage in Blue burst. "He'll get nothing," she yelled, "until I say so."

Isa flinched as Martha left the room.

Blue sat and clasped Isa's hand.

"Water," Isa said weakly.

Blue jumped from the chair and ran into the Kitchen. "She wants water, Martha."

Martha poured a cup of the liquid from the pot on the stove. "Give her this. It's full of herbs and will help her much more than just water."

Blue took the cup and went to the room. She supported Isa's head and offered the liquid. "It's good for you. Drink it."

Isa swallowed and grimaced.

"Take a little more," Blue said.

Isa drank, then weakly pushed it away.

Blue settled her and then returned to the chair, placing the cup on the stand beside the bed. She watched her sleep.

"Blue?" The voice got louder. "Blue?"

Blue opened her eyes.

Martha was beside her. "Rosemary and Abigail are ready to leave."

Blue immediately looked at Isa. Her eyes were closed, and her breathing seemed labored. She touched her forehead with the back of her hand. "She feels hot, Martha."

Martha touched Isa's flushed face. "It'll take time before we know if she's going to make it through this."

Blue went to the wagon. The bows and covering had been positioned on the top. She peered inside and saw the straw covering the corpses.

Abigail was seated with the reins in her hand. Rosemary was sitting on her horse.

"Rest when you need to," Blue said. "But mind your surroundings, and keep a ready eye."

"We will, Miss Blue," Rosemary said. "We'll be back as soon as we can."

Blue watched their shadowy image as they slipped through the haze of pre-dawn.

Anderson called to her. "Water."

"Go to hell," Blue said, and went into the house and continued her vigil beside Isa.

Martha brought Blue a plate of food, but she refused to eat.

"You've got to eat something. Please."

Blue finally relented and managed to get the egg and a piece of bacon down.

Isa stirred and then tried to move to her side. She cried out and reached for her shoulder.

"Martha," Blue called.

Martha flitted into the room. "What's the matter?"

"I think she wants to move, but I don't know what to do."

Martha left and returned with a roll of cloth. She positioned it cautiously behind Isa's back. "That will help relieve some of the pressure. It's time to wrap that arm to keep her from straining her shoulder."

Blue helped her.

Isa's face seemed to relax, and her breathing became less labored.

"Why don't you let Laurel sit with her, and you go try to rest for a while?"

"I want to clean up," Blue said. She climbed the ladder to the loft and washed in the basin, put on a clean shirt and pants, then lay on the bed. She had no fight left. Within seconds she was asleep.

CHAPTER TWENTY-SEVEN

Blue woke suddenly. How long had she been asleep? Isa?
She climbed down the ladder to find Gertie, Etta, and Laurel at the table, eating. "What time is it?"

"A little after noon, I imagine," Laurel said.

She walked past them and into Martha's room. Martha spoke as she sat in the chair.

Isa was awake. Her eyes held pain and something Blue couldn't discern. Fear? Worry?

Blue knelt beside the bed and took her hand. "You're awake?"

Isa's mouth tensed. Did she want to speak? Ask her a question?

"Stay for only a few minutes," Martha said. "She needs to rest."

She appeared pale and weaker than before. But she was awake. Blue tucked Isa's hand between hers and kissed her lightly on the lips, dry and still hot from the fever.

"Blue." Her voice was barely above a whisper.

Blue leaned in to hear her. "Yes, Isa. I'm here."

"Give him water."

Blue straightened. Had she heard correctly?

"Get him to the sheriff." Isa's brow wrinkled. She squeezed Blue's fingers and then closed her eyes. Her expression relaxed.

Blue held her breath and immediately put her hand on Isa's chest, afraid she no longer remained with her. Relief washed over her when she felt Isa's breasts rise and fall in rhythm.

How could Isa know Anderson was even there? Did she hear the conversation between Martha and her?

Martha came in. "She needs to rest, Blue."

"Did you tell Isa that Anderson was tied up in the corral?"

"No. She called for you when she woke, and I told her you'd be there shortly. Then I called you."

Blue rose from her knees, kissed Isa's cheek, and left the room. She grabbed a piece of ham from the skillet on her way out the door and stuffed it into her pocket.

The others watched as she passed by.

She went to the barn, got a bucket of water, and took it to the corral. She stepped to the post where Anderson was secured and poured water over him. "Here's your drink," she said.

Anderson groaned and licked the liquid from around his mouth.

She walked to the pump, filled the bucket, and this time she threw the water in his face.

He gasped.

"Would you like some more?"

She returned to the pump, half-filled the bucket, and set it in front of him. She hobbled his feet, untied his hands, then threw the ham on the ground beside him. "Enjoy your breakfast." She pulled the pistol from her holster. "I hope you try to leave the corral."

He clinched his jaw and remained silent.

She called to the house. "Etta, get out here."

Etta appeared immediately. "Yes, Miss Blue."

"Get a shovel and a wheelbarrow of lye from the barn."

Blue climbed onto the fence and toyed with her gun as she watched Anderson's every move.

He drank from the bucket, washed the ham, then ate it. He picked up his hat, put it on his head, then relieved himself. He nodded to Blue, then sat and waited for his hands to be tied.

It made Blue sick to her stomach. He ate, drank, and pissed. But Isa lay in bed barely alive because of him. "Not so fast. You have some work to do."

Etta came out of the barn with the shovel and wheelbarrow of lye.

"Take them to the bloody dirt there." Blue pointed. "Then put your gun and holster on the porch."

Etta did as she was told, then returned to Blue.

"Make a noose and slip it around his neck, tighten it, and stand back."

Laurel and Gertie came out on the porch and watched.

"Gertie, saddle Biscuit and bring him here."

Gertie jumped from the porch and ran to the barn.

Blue continued to watch Anderson's eyes and movements. "Now you stand real still, Anderson, because if I see any sudden moves, I'm going to shoot you in the foot."

Etta completed her task and stood back, holding the rope.

"Is it tight?" Blue asked.

"Yes, Miss Blue."

Gertie brought Biscuit and handed his reins to Blue.

She swung into the saddle. "Etta, hand me the rope, open the corral gate, and put your gun on."

Etta did as instructed.

"Anderson, walk out here and over to the wheelbarrow."

He shuffled to the designated area.

"Put that lye on every bit of blood you see."

"I can't. My arm's shot to hell."

"I don't care," Blue said.

"I can't," he shouted.

Blue drew her gun and fired next to his boot. Biscuit shied, and she reined him back. "You will, or you'll lose more than that arm."

"You're crazy."

"Maybe. But I know one thing. You'll do what I tell you, or I'll kill you." She fired again, on the other side of his boot. "Now get to it."

He took the shovel and started the task, groaning and complaining as he did.

Martha came to the door, watched for a few minutes, and then went back inside.

When he'd covered the area, Blue moved him and made him do the same at each of the sites his men had bled. Then she walked him back to the corral and held Etta's gun while she tied him to the post.

"Take the noose off. I want you or Gertie standing guard on him. You're not to go in the corral under any circumstances. If he gives you any trouble, come get me."

"Yes, ma'am," Etta said.

Blue got off Biscuit and handed the reins to Gertie. "Unsaddle him and put him in a stall. Make sure he gets a good feed tonight."

Gertie nodded.

Blue went to the house and had a cup of coffee. She heard Isa make a sound and went into the room.

She was awake.

Blue sat in the chair and took her hand.

"I heard gunshots," Isa whispered.

"Nothing for you to worry about. Everything's fine. How are you feeling?"

"Like I've been shot." She smiled weakly.

Blue gave her more of Martha's herbal mixture.

"That's horrible."

"Keep drinking."

Isa took a few more swallows and waved it away. She'd almost finished the cup.

"I'll be leaving in the morning," Blue said. "I'll most likely be gone a few days."

Isa's face tensed. "Where?"

"I'm taking Anderson to Carson City. I expect Rosemary and Abigail will be back by late tomorrow. I'll probably pass them on the way."

Isa drifted back to sleep as Blue sat with her through the rest of the evening. Then Blue went to the creek and bathed. She thought about their time at the lake and their lovemaking. And then yesterday's scene crashed into her mind and played over and over.

She took a walk along the bank like she and Isa had done so many times before, but it brought no comfort or peace without Isa beside her.

She returned to her, watching her sleep, pain evident on Isa's face.

Evening passed and turned to night, but this time the darkness overpowered Blue, filling her with a bitterness of soul that consumed every thought, every feeling. Isa lay in peril, and Blue couldn't do anything but stand by and watch.

The impressions of death were all around her. She lit the lamp, hoping it would ease her mind. But the shadows in the room only cast reminders that whatever she had could be taken in a heartbeat. Nothing was safe.

Martha had told her if Isa could get through the night she had more than a good chance of living. Would she make it?

Blue felt Isa's face. The fever still raged.

The night dragged on, holding its secrets in the darkness.

Isa became agitated and began to moan. A sheen of sweat formed on her forehead.

Blue repeatedly washed her face with a cool cloth.

Isa mumbled something, but Blue couldn't understand what she'd said.

She held Isa in her arms, put the herbal drink to her lips, and encouraged her.

Isa managed to take a few swallows, then seemed to go into a deeper sleep.

Blue woke at daylight, before the rooster crowed.

Isa was asleep but restless.

Blue checked her skin. Warm, but not as hot as it had been. She leaned in and kissed her. "Isa. Stay with me."

Martha came in and touched Isa's skin and asked how her night had been.

"She started sweating and moaning a couple of hours ago. She seems a little more restful now."

Martha inspected Isa's dressings and then repositioned her. She listened to her breathing. "I like what I'm seeing, Blue. She's not bleeding any more. Her breathing is deeper, and I think her fever has broken." She patted Blue's shoulder. "These are all good things."

Blue grabbed Martha's hand and breathed a sigh of relief.

When Martha left, Blue whispered to Isa, "I have to go, but I'll be with you in my heart." She kissed her forehead. Then she went into the kitchen, had a slice of bread and cold ham, and washed it down with yesterday's coffee.

She walked to the barn and fed Biscuit and then saddled him.

Gertie was on guard and sauntered in. "Morning, Miss Blue."

"Morning." Blue motioned toward the corral. "Did he behave himself?"

"Yes, ma'am. Not a peep out of him."

"Everything else okay?"

"Yes, ma'am. Quiet as a mouse. How's Isa? I've been saying my prayers through the night for her."

"I think she's going to make it, Gertie."

"Oh, that's mighty happy news, Miss Blue. Mighty happy. Why aren't you riding Traveler?"

"Biscuit needs the workout." Blue led him from the barn, put her rifle in the scabbard, and got on. She checked her pistol and inserted two more rounds. She tied a noose and tossed it to Gertie. "Give me your gun, then put that around Anderson's neck and make it tight. Remove his hobble."

Gertie complied. "I reckon you'll be taking him to Carson City? Which horse would you like me to saddle for him?"

"None. He's walking." She tucked Gertie's gun behind her belt.

Gertie stared at her.

"You heard me, Gertie."

"All the way to Carson City?"

"Untie him."

Gertie unbound his hands and came outside the corral but kept glancing at Blue.

"Anderson, do your business. We're leaving."

He rubbed his wrists and stood facing Blue. He unbuttoned his pants and urinated, smirking at her the entire time.

"The last man of yours to enjoy that pleasure was whacked in his dingle," Gertie said.

"Shut your mouth, you whelp." He fastened his pants and reached for his neck.

Blue jerked the rope, looped it over the horn, and backed Biscuit, dragging Anderson to the fence.

He choked and gagged.

She slacked the rope and let him breathe. "Gertie, tie his hands behind his back."

When Gertie approached him, Anderson grabbed at her.

She kicked him in the shin.

Blue flipped the noose tight again and dragged him halfway over the fence. He flapped like a fish out of water, pulling at the rope, trying to get free.

"You keep struggling, and eventually you'll hang. Doesn't matter to me one way or the other." Blue backed Biscuit another two steps.

"All right," he croaked.

Blue slacked the rope, and he fell to the ground.

"On your knees," Blue said.

He didn't move.

She pulled Gertie's gun from her belt and aimed it at him. "I said on your knees."

He hesitated, then got into position.

"Put your hands behind your back." She cocked the pistol. "Tie him good."

He groaned when Gertie grabbed his arms and knotted the rope.

"Check it."

"The knots are secure, Miss Blue."

"Open the gate."

Gertie swung it open and then hurried out of the way.

Blue tossed Gertie's five-shot to her, then drew hers and aimed at Anderson. She motioned him to go forward. "Move. And if you won't walk, I'll drag you all the way."

Anderson continued to glare at her but started walking.

"I'll be praying for you too, Miss Blue," Gertie said.

Blue raised her hand. She needed prayers. Her heart was so full of bitterness and hatred it didn't have room for anything else.

Anderson walked in front of her for three hours and then stopped and faced her. "I need water. And my arm is throbbing. I need to get it up so it won't hurt so damn bad."

Blue reined Biscuit. "You don't seem to understand the nature of our relationship, Anderson." She took a long drink from her canteen. "Let me see if I can clear this up." She wiped her lips. "I don't give a rat's ass what you need or don't need. I don't care if you drop dead right here. Either way, you're going to get moving. On your own or I'm going to drag you. Now what's it going to be, on your feet or on your belly?"

He swallowed, glowered at her, then turned and started walking.

Another hour went by.

"I know you must be thinking of ways to get loose, but let me assure you, any attempt at anything other than walking forward will get you a demonstration of my roping and marksmanship skills. My partner Isa, you know, the one your men shot, who's lying back there at my ranch fighting for her life, she's the one who can shoot. Lord, she can hit a fly off a pile of shit and not make a splatter. Speaking of a pile of shit, you do know you're a coward and a thief? Do you have a wife so I can tell her what kind of an animal you really are?"

Blue glanced at the sky. "You may ask what my goal is in all of this? And I think that's a legitimate question, so I'll answer it. I aim to make sure you never hurt another human being for the rest of your pitiful, puny life. Did you ever, in your pathetic existence, do anything other than rain down misery and chaos on others? I think not."

They continued until they arrived at a creek. Blue slackened the rope. "You can climb down there and get all the water you want. If you can't make it back up the bank with your hands tied, I'll be happy to pull you up. Just let me know if you need any help."

Anderson started down the embankment but tripped and fell the rest of the way, losing his hat as he landed at the water's edge.

Blue sat on Biscuit and watched.

He rolled over and began slurping the water, then lay quiet. Blue let him rest in that position. She dismounted and stretched. While she was walking, Anderson popped up from the ground and started running downstream.

She grabbed the line and jerked hard. He flew backward and landed in the water. She led the horse to the creek bank. "You know, Biscuit is newly trained, and I'd hate to see him spooked and take off running, especially with the end of this rope tied to the saddle horn. That could prove a very unfortunate ending for you." She mounted Biscuit and looped the slack on the rope. "I think you've rested enough. Time to get moving."

Anderson struggled to his feet and trudged through the water to the bank. He got halfway up, then slipped and fell back down.

"It makes it hard because your clothes and boots are wet. I'm sure it's frustrating. Why don't you stand, and I'll be glad to help you?"

He shook his head. "Please don't do that."

He tried to come up the bank again but only got about a third of the way.

Blue backed Biscuit and pulled the line taut.

"No, please," he shouted.

He began choking but moved faster until he reached the top on level ground. His face was dark red. He gagged and bent over, then coughed and threw up.

Blue dismounted and loosened the rope around his neck.

Speckles of blood covered raw skin where the rope had rubbed. She thought of Isa and all the blood on the floor. "That was scary." She mounted Biscuit. "Well, we better get going. I want to be halfway before dark."

Anderson watched her every move. "I need my hat."

"Oh, that's right. Would you like to go back down there and get it? I'll wait. You can pick it up with your hands tied behind your back. I'll even put it on your head for you. And it'll be a pleasure to help you back up the bank."

He stared at her.

"Make your choice," she said.

He turned and started walking.

By early evening he was staggering. He wouldn't last much longer. She guessed they were almost halfway, so she stopped. She untied his hands and allowed him to do what he needed, pointing the gun at him the entire time. When he finished, she tied him to a tree and hobbled him. She built a fire and lay near it.

None of this helped her feel better, no matter what she did to Anderson. No matter how she treated him, she couldn't get any comfort or release from the anger and rage inside her. Would she feel better if she killed him? Would it help in any way?

She'd expected to see Rosemary and Abigail by now. Most likely they'd traveled a different route, and they'd missed each other by a mile or so.

To her surprise she slept a few hours. She allowed Anderson his necessities at daybreak, and they continued on their journey.

Anderson was barely on his feet by the time they reached the outskirts of Carson City in late evening. He wasn't going to make it, and Blue refused to put him on Biscuit. She got off her horse and took the noose from around his neck. She looped it under his arms and made a harness around his chest. "Make no mistake. You're going to the sheriff."

She got back in the saddle. "Giddy-up, Anderson."

He staggered forward.

When they got within eyesight of the sheriff's office, people had gathered on the boardwalk and in the street watching them come in.

Anderson dropped to his knees. "I can't go any farther."

"Sure you can. We're almost there," Blue said.

He shook his head. "I can't." He fell to the ground.

"No problem," Blue said.

She took up the slack and rode forward at a slow, steady walk.

A silent crowd had gathered as they watched her near, dragging Anderson in the dirt behind her. She dismounted and tied Biscuit to the hitching rail. She didn't check to see if Anderson was still breathing. She made her way through the press of people, all of them solemn-faced, many with tears in their eyes. Some she knew. Most she didn't.

Tudsdale met her at the entrance. Another man—as tall as Tudsdale, with dark hair, cold blue eyes, and a small scar on his left cheek—stood beside him.

The sheriff nodded and tipped his hat. "Blue, this is Aaron Jenkins, US marshal for the territory."

Jenkins nodded and tucked his hands in the belt of his gun holster.

"Good evening," Blue said. "I have Anderson outside. Did my people report to you?"

Jenkins nodded. "They gave a thorough accounting. Is he alive?"

His deep voice caught her by surprise. The sound of it calmed her for some reason. Maybe because this part of the journey had ended? If Anderson was dead, would they arrest her for murder? Could they? A thought swept through her. Only Anderson's men had been killed. They couldn't hold him for murder, or could they? She should get Jeremiah and let him help her. She turned to the crowd that continued watching the events unfold and saw James Morris and his wife Nettie, from the dry goods store. Both nodded when she made eye contact.

She stepped toward them. "Would you ask Jeremiah Hawthorne to come over here?"

Morris took off his hat and touched her arm. "Of course, Blue. Right away." He scuttled off.

Nettie patted Blue's hand. "God bless you," she said, tears now streaming down her cheeks.

Tudsdale and Jenkins stepped from the office.

"Where is he?" Jenkins asked.

Blue pointed as the crowd parted, giving Jenkins, Tudsdale, and her a clear view of the street and Anderson.

He lay on his stomach, just as Blue had imagined, his clothes thick with gray dust. She surveyed him for the briefest of seconds. A part of her hoped he still lived. But did it matter? Maybe to someone, but not to her. Not now. Not after what he'd done to her and to Isa. Isa? Was she alive? Oh, how Blue hoped she was. She needed to get back to her. How long had it been? Two days? A year? A lifetime?

Jenkins and Tudsdale kneeled beside Anderson.

"He's alive," Jenkins said.

The crowd made a collective gasp.

It surprised Blue that she felt genuine relief to hear the news.

"Send for the doctor," Tudsdale ordered.

A man in the crowd, with glasses and a large nose, waddled down the street to some unknown destination that housed the elusive doctor.

The marshal and the sheriff lifted Anderson to his feet.

He moaned and asked for water.

They untied him and walked him inside the building.

"Coward," someone yelled.

"You deserve everything you get, Anderson," cried another.

Jenkins turned to the crowd. "All right, folks. The show's over. Go on home."

The group slowly dispersed.

Blue followed the officers into the room.

They sat Anderson on a chair and offered him water. He gulped, letting it run from the corners of his mouth, down the front of his dust-caked shirt, leaving mud lines, like miniscule rivers. Blue thought of the dynamite and how she and Isa had blown the dam to hell and back. Isa?

Anderson handed the cup to Tudsdale and then moved his left arm to his chest and cradled it. "She tried to kill me. Arrest her," he said.

Tudsdale shook his head and looked at Jenkins. "I told you."

Jenkins lifted Anderson from the chair. "The only one who's going to jail is you."

Anderson tried to escape Jenkins's grasp. "No. You don't understand. She tried to kill me."

"And what were you doing at *her* ranch," Jenkins asked, "trying to play patty-cake?"

Anderson started to fight him.

Tudsdale stepped in and forced Anderson's arm behind him. "Get in the cell. I've been waiting a long time for this."

They ushered him into the end cell and locked the bars. "The doc will be along in a while," Tudsdale said.

"I'll be out of here in a couple of days," Anderson shouted. "You'll see. You'll all pay for this."

Blue removed her hat and held it in her hand.

The sheriff and the marshal came to the desk. "Can you give a statement, Blue?" Tudsdale asked.

Jeremiah arrived. "Blue? Are you all right?"

Blue felt as if she were sinking into quicksand. Her knees started to buckle. She couldn't get any air, and the room began to spin.

CHAPTER TWENTY-EIGHT

I've had enough of being in this bed," Isa said.

Martha patted her hand. "It's only been four days since you were shot."

Isa repositioned. It was hard to move with one hand while the other was securely wrapped against her chest. "Martha, please, help me up."

"I think you should wait."

"The fresh air and a short walk will do me good." Isa swung her legs over the edge of the mattress. Her shoulder and side throbbed, but it was good to be sitting at last.

Martha called Etta, and Etta came into the room. "Good morning. How's things in here?"

Isa scooted closer to the edge. "I'm going to get up." She caught the surprise on Etta's face.

"Already?" Etta asked.

"She's determined," Martha said. "Stand on her left, and very carefully hold her if she needs it."

Etta placed her hand on Isa's back. Martha tucked her arm around her and lifted her under her right side. Isa stood with little effort.

"Oh! It feels wonderful." She took two steps, sucked in a breath, and cringed. The pain shot through her shoulder and side and seemed to explode. "I believe I'll sit."

Martha grabbed the chair and set it behind her, then eased her down.

"You're right, Martha. A little at a time," Isa said.

She remained in the chair and gazed out the window, watching Gertie chop wood. The sharp pain lessened, then faded into a dull ache. She closed her eyes in relief.

"What day is it?"

"I believe it's Saturday," Martha said. "Though I can't be sure."

Etta excused herself and left.

Martha finished making Isa's bed and then helped her into it.

Isa eased in, and Martha propped the pillows around her.

"I can never tell you what your care has meant, Martha."

"You just heal and get better."

Rosemary knocked softly on the bedroom door. "May I come in?"

"Yes. But only for a little while. She's just getting settled," Martha said.

Rosemary brought the chair near Isa and sat.

"How's everyone?" Isa asked.

"Fine."

"Any sign of Blue?"

"No. Not yet. I expect she'll be back any time. I think we should go check on the herd. We've got the wood ready for winter, the outside repairs are done, and there's enough feed for the horses and the other animals to get us through until spring. The ranch is in good shape."

"You've all done well, and I know Blue will be pleased."

Rosemary stood. "Etta will be going with me to the herd. We'll stay the night and be back tomorrow."

Rosemary's voice seemed to echo. Isa nodded and closed her eyes. "Be safe." She drifted off before she could say good-bye.

By evening she felt stronger.

Gertie brought her meal. "Martha said for you to eat it all. And I'm to stay here until you finish."

Isa set the book she'd been reading on the stand. "Oh, you are, are you?"

"What's the name of your book?"

"*The Scarlet Letter*, by Nathaniel Hawthorne," Isa said.

"Isn't Miss Blue's lawyer named Hawthorne?"

"Yes. I believe he's Nathaniel Hawthorne's cousin."

"I never knew a famous person before," Gertie said.

"I doubt Jeremiah would feel he's famous, but his cousin certainly is."

"Is it a good story?"

"Yes. A woman makes some choices that get her into trouble, and then she suffers because the townspeople judge her and think they're better than her."

"I want to read it."

"I think other books are more important for you to read right now. Maybe when you're a little older."

To Isa's surprise, Gertie didn't protest but nodded and leaned back in the chair.

"We had a fine meal tonight," Gertie said. "I'm sure you'll like it. Potatoes and gravy, apple pie, green beans, and elk. But you can't have the meat. Martha said you aren't ready for it."

Isa smiled at Gertie's honest review. She lifted the cloth from the tray in anticipation. Then she sighed. Broth with a few vegetables and a slice of wheat bread. No potatoes. No gravy. No pie.

Gertie frowned. "Sorry. I thought you were going to eat what we had."

Isa patted her hand. "It's all right. Martha knows what's best for me right now." She dipped the spoon into the broth. "Tell me what's going on with everyone?"

"I've learned about politics and things."

"From who?"

"Rosemary. She's so smart."

Isa tore a piece of the bread and dipped it into the liquid.

"Last night Rosemary asked us what we would do if a colored gal showed up here for a job."

"Really?"

"Yes. And do you know what Etta said?"

"I have no idea."

"Etta said there won't be any colored gals coming here because the war liberated all of them and they went north, and even if they showed up, Miss Blue can't hire anyone else because she doesn't have any more money. Then Abigail got all mad and told Etta she didn't know what she was talking about. Laurel added her two cents. She said she knows plenty of colored folks, and they're just as fine as anyone else."

Gertie shifted in the chair. "Then Rosemary started talking about the Constitution and something called the Fifteenth Amendment, whatever that is. And then she got all fired up and said she thought Andrew Johnson, the President of the United States of America, should be impeached. I had to ask her what that meant. She said it meant fired from his job. Then she asked the rest of us what we thought."

"What did the others say?"

"Nobody had much to offer. But boy, Rosemary did. She started spouting about stuff I've never heard before."

"What kind of *stuff*?"

Gertie swallowed and her eyes grew wider. "None of us knew what she was talking about. She said, 'Andrew Johnson has done more to ruin this country than help it.' She said he allowed Southern leaders of the concession or sensation to be in Congress and the Senate. I don't even know what a senate is."

"What did the others say?" Isa asked.

"Nothing. We all just stared at her."

Isa laughed. "How's Adelita?"

Gertie waved her hand. "Oh, she's fine. She's eating a lot. I 'spect she's pregnant. Wouldn't it be grand if she had a colt for Miss Blue? He'd be mighty fine. Then she'd have the kind of stud she wanted. Of course, he wouldn't breed for three or four years, but he'd be something. Isa, do you think Miss Blue done right by making Anderson walk all the way to Carson City?"

Isa dropped her spoon. "What?"

"Um…Never mind."

"Tell me what happened."

"I didn't mean to upset you. I'm sorry."

"Gertie, tell me."

Gertie bit her lip. "I reckon you should ask Miss Blue when she gets back."

"No. I'm asking you." Isa had eaten all she could. She wiped her mouth with the napkin and laid it on the tray.

Gertie cringed. "Well, Miss Blue came out to the barn the morning they left and saddled Biscuit and told me she and Anderson were leaving. I asked her what horse she wanted to saddle for him, and she said none because he was walking." Gertie squirmed in her chair. She wasn't telling Isa everything. What had Blue done?

"And then what?" Isa asked.

"They left."

"She didn't just make him walk," Isa said.

"He…uh…He had his hands tied behind his back."

"Gertie, tell me everything."

"And he had a noose around his neck."

Isa gasped and held her arm. She peered out the window. What was Blue thinking?

"She was powerful mad, Isa. Powerful mad. And Anderson tried to catch me when I went to tie his hands."

"What did Blue do?"

"She damned near hung him on the fence. That sure straightened him out." Gertie smiled.

Isa covered her mouth. She took a breath and motioned for Gertie to take her tray. "I'm going to rest now."

Gertie picked up the setting. "I'm sorry, Isa. I didn't mean to cause you to fret."

"It's all right. I'm glad you told me."

Gertie left the room.

Isa wasn't glad. Her stomach churned. How could Blue have done that?

Martha came in a few minutes later. "I'm going to wallop that child. Are you all right?"

"Why would Blue do such a thing?"

Martha sat on the side of her bed and took Isa's hand. "She was beside herself with worry when you were shot. She couldn't sleep. She couldn't rest. She could only think about you and what Anderson had done. She tied him to the corral post and wouldn't allow anyone to go near him. I don't think she knew what to do with him at that point. You're the one who softened her heart."

"I did?"

"I think she was waiting to see what happened to you. She told Rosemary when they were leaving to take the bodies to Carson City that there might be one more. If you'd died, I'm sure she would have ended his life."

If Blue had been shot instead of her, what would Isa have done? She tried to give herself an honest answer, but the emotion of it carried her to exhaustion. Daylight faded and took her strength with it.

"You rest now and put this out of your mind," Martha said. "I'm sure she'll be back anytime, and you two can talk."

"If it's all right, I'd like a shot of whiskey."

Martha nodded. "I'll warm it with some cider and spice for you."

Isa woke the next morning with less pain and more energy. After breakfast, with Martha's help, she got all the way to the porch and sat in the rocker. The air was crisp, and the warmth of the sun radiated through her.

Laurel brought her a lap blanket and coffee.

"How's your hand?" Isa asked.

"It's sore, and sometimes I get a burning in my wrist, but I'm managing. I'm afraid I'm not much use to Martha. You've got some color back in you this morning."

"I feel much better today." For the first time since all of it had happened, Isa enjoyed being awake. But thoughts of what Blue had done still lingered, like the odor of fish on her hands. Would she have done it? Maybe.

She sipped her coffee and watched Adelita, Traveler, and the few other horses in the corral. Gertie sat on a bucket in front of the barn mending a bridle. Abigail was filling the trough with water.

Gertie dropped what she was working on and stood. She ran to Abigail and pointed north.

Abigail said something to her and then came to the house. "Rider. Coming fast."

"Just one?" Isa asked.

"Only one," Abigail said.

Martha came to the door. "Best get you inside, Isa."

"No. I'll be fine. Get my pistol and bring it to me. Abigail, get your gun and climb into the barn loft. Tell Gertie to get behind the wood pile. Where are the others?"

"Rosemary and Etta are still with the herd," Abigail said.

Martha brought Isa her weapon and stood beside her.

The rider slowed as he approached.

"It's all right," Martha said. "It's Thomas, from the dry goods store."

Isa slid her pistol under the blanket and waited.

His horse was covered in sweat and breathing hard. He dismounted and tipped his hat. "Morning. I hope I didn't give you a fright. I've been dispatched to give you a message from Miss Blue."

Isa leaned forward, anxious to hear.

He slapped his hat against the side of his pant leg.

"Well, out with it, son," Martha said.

He nodded and held his cover in front of him with both hands. He shifted and glanced skyward, then addressed them. "Anderson's trial is set for this Friday." He hesitated, inspecting his hand, his lips moving without words coming out. "That's five days from today. Miss Blue will be staying in town until then." He turned his attention to Isa. "If you're able, ma'am, you and the others are to come to testify. Miss Blue said to have Etta and Abigail remain here at the ranch."

"Anderson is alive?" Martha asked.

"Yes, ma'am."

Isa breathed a sigh of relief.

"Is that all?" Martha asked.

"Um, I believe so." He peered upward again. "No. You're to wear your finery to court, and I'm to wait for any messages you wish to convey."

"Laurel, take him in the house and get him something to eat," Martha said. "Gertie?"

Gertie came from behind the stacked wood.

"Walk his horse out and give him a good watering, then feed," Martha said. "And tell Abigail it's all right. She can come down."

Gertie nodded and went to the barn.

"Is Blue well?" Isa asked.

"Yes, ma'am." Thomas said. "She gave us a fright, though. Collapsed right there in the sheriff's office after she brought Anderson in."

Isa gasped and put her hand to her mouth.

"They took her to Mr. and Mrs. Hawthorne's house, and she rested for a day. But she's fit now. She said to tell you not to come if you're not up to it."

"We'll see about that," Martha said. "You clean up at the pump, and then go in and have something to eat."

Thomas nodded. "Thank you, Miss Martha."

Martha sat in the chair next to Isa.

"It's a relief to know she's well," Isa said. "And I'm glad nothing happened to her or Anderson. I'm anxious to get to her."

"I don't think it's a good idea for you to go," Martha said. "You can write your statement, and I'll hand it over to the sheriff. Blue will understand. I know she wouldn't want you to risk hurting yourself. It's a hard trip, even in the wagon."

"I'm going. And nothing you can tell me will change my mind. We'll take it slow and easy. We can put some bedding in the wagon, and I'll rest when I need to."

Martha shook her head.

"I'm going."

"Let's get you back to bed. You need to rest as much as you can. It's unwise to do this, but I've said my piece, and I'll say no more about it."

Isa was relieved Martha didn't press her, although she tried not to think about what'd been in the wagon. She called Gertie to the porch. "I want you and Abigail to give the wagon a good scrub and make sure it's dried in the sun."

"We scrubbed it when they got back," Gertie said, looking frustrated.

"Clean it again," Isa said. She shuddered. The thought of the bodies sent a sickening chill through her.

She had to focus now on taking care of herself so she could make the trip. They had two days before they needed to leave. Martha's concerns for her health might be justified, or was she just being overly protective? The trip wasn't all she'd need to deal with. Testifying and the long days of being up would take her energy.

Martha could be right. Maybe she shouldn't go. But Blue wouldn't have asked her to come if she didn't need her there. What if she didn't go? What would happen to Anderson? To Blue? The thoughts swirled through her mind. For now, she needed to take a nap.

CHAPTER TWENTY-NINE

B lue watched out the window as the people went by the dry goods store. Would Isa be able to make the trip? Could she endure it? Had it been too much to ask of her? What if she reinjured herself?

Nettie filled her cup with more coffee and placed a slice of peach pie in front of her.

"Eat that. It'll make your day go better," Nettie said. "Nothing like a piece of pie to brighten the morning." She refilled Jeremiah's cup, then went to another table and talked with the man and woman with three children.

"Blue, this is only a formality," Jeremiah said. "Anderson's trial is Friday. Your inquiry is not a trial. When you go before Judge Ruggles this morning, be straightforward and tell him the facts."

She watched his face for any hints of concern. What would happen?

"His Honor wants to make sure there's nothing suspicious about what you did. You're not charged with any crime. The best thing you could have done was bring Yates and Pup to the sheriff. Now, no one is going to hold it against you for going to Anderson's and warning him to stay off your property. Or for blowing up the dam. Anderson had no legal right to stop the water from going on its natural flow. And what you did is going to make the case against him even stronger."

"I did it because I was sick and tired of Anderson pushing me around and bullying me." She sipped her coffee. "If that was wrong, then I'll take my punishment."

Jeremiah shook his head. "Judge Ruggles is not going to fault you for it under the circumstances."

"Are Anderson and his lawyer allowed in the courtroom?"

"Not Anderson. Only his attorney, Higbee Alarid."

"What's he like?"

"To be honest, I think he's a crook," Jeremiah said. "He's had some questionable dealings in Virginia City, and he's a friend of Anderson's, so that right there tells you something. There's one more thing for you to consider."

Blue watched his eyes. Was he going to tell her that if the judge found any cause, she'd have to stand trial for murder of the men who were killed on her property?

"I'd like you to wear a dress."

Blue laughed.

"I'm serious. You need to appear as vulnerable as possible. And it will help. All of you need to wear them. Use every tactic you have."

"Why not? This whole thing is a sham anyway."

"It's not a sham. It's a formality."

"Why do I have to explain my actions to the judge? I only defended myself."

"Exactly. And I'm sure the court will come to that conclusion. We have four more days before Anderson's trial. It's good to get this out of the way now."

"Why did Judge Ruggles come early to Carson City? I thought he wasn't due here for weeks."

"He wasn't, but all this mess with Anderson convinced him to rearrange his schedule. He's up for reappointment soon and wants to make sure the people know he's doing his job."

This was all beyond anything Blue wanted to think about or even care about. Isa was who she wanted and who she thought about. "This needs to be over so I can go home."

Jeremiah touched her arm. "It will be soon."

Nettie came to the table. "Thomas is back." She pointed to the storeroom.

Blue almost bounded from her chair.

He stood at the entrance to the loading dock, talking with James.

"And you told them everything?" James asked.

Thomas nodded.

Blue stopped in front of him. "How is she?"

"I wasn't given a report on her condition."

"How did she seem? What was she doing?" Blue couldn't get the questions out fast enough.

"She was on the porch, sitting in a rocker when I arrived. She's pale. She and Miss Martha had words about making the trip, but I believe she's determined to come. They will wait two days before they travel to give Miss Isa more time to rest. Miss Martha told me to tell you they'll travel slow and not to worry."

"Thank you, Thomas. You've done us a great service," Blue said. She hugged him.

His face turned pink.

Blue returned to the Hawthorne house and borrowed a fine print dress from Elizabeth, Jeremiah's wife.

"I can't wear any of them, as big with child as I am," Elizabeth said. "I'm happy they get some use. I'll be praying for you, Blue." She hugged her. "Try not to worry."

Blue met Jeremiah at the courthouse, and they walked in together.

Sheriff Tudsdale and his deputy stood outside the courtroom doors near a small desk.

"No firearms are permitted inside," the deputy said. "Do you have any weapons to declare?"

Jeremiah opened his suitcoat. "No."

"And you, Miss Hutchings?"

"No."

He motioned them to go in.

Sheriff Tudsdale tipped his hat to Blue and smiled.

"Good afternoon," she said.

Blue saw two sections of four rows of benches as they entered through the double doors. The spacious courtroom smelled of tobacco smoke and men's sweat, mixed with the scent of wood. Just past the gallery, a railing the height of a man's waist extended the width of the room. In the aisle, they passed through an ornately carved swing gate. They stopped at two long tables separated by about six feet. Beyond that loomed an elevated desk and a grand-looking chair. A halfway-enclosed area with a plain wooden chair attached next to it. The room projected a sense of foreboding.

Jeremiah sat at the table on the right and motioned for Blue to join him. He placed his papers on the surface, and then they waited. And waited. Blue continued to survey the room. A smaller desk and chair occupied the space to the right of the judge's station. To the left, with a paneled wooden front, were two rows of eight chairs, the back row more elevated than the first. They were also enclosed by a rail. The jury area?

"Why sixteen chairs?" she asked. "Aren't there twelve people in a jury?"

"The extra chairs are for alternate jurors. In case someone can't continue."

Blue nodded.

A lone man carrying a worn, black leather case entered from the double doors behind them. He stood well over six feet, but he slouched as he walked. He strode through the swing gate and tossed his case onto the opposite table. It made a crackling sound as it slid across the slick wooden surface.

"I don't mind telling you, Lawyer Hawthorne, I intend to see to it that the truth comes out and justice is served at this inquiry."

"I'm quite sure it will be, Alarid," Jeremiah said. "Don't get your feathers ruffled already, or you'll be preening all afternoon."

He huffed and slumped into the chair.

A smaller, bald-headed man with glasses and carrying a ledger entered from the door near the judge's bench and sat at the small desk. "I'm Clerk Henry Dibbing," he said. "His Honor will be here shortly."

The room seemed to expand and fill with apprehension. Blue's heart pounded. What if the judge did feel she'd done something wrong?

About seven people entered through the courthouse doors and sat in the gallery behind Blue's table. Then three more. Then ten. Both sides of the aisle filled. Why were they here? Blue recognized the Morrises and Elizabeth. A thin, older man with a thick head of gray tousled hair entered and wormed his way in beside James Morris.

"Afternoon, Doc," James said.

There he was. The elusive doctor. He did exist!

The door by the large desk swung open.

Clerk Dibbing clambered to his feet. "All rise," he said loudly. "The Ninth District Court of Nevada is now in session. The Honorable Judge Clive Ruggles presiding."

The judge entered, a stout man with silver hair and glasses. He was dressed in a flowing black robe that covered his clothes to below midcalf. He appeared regal and authoritative. Would Blue get justice before a man like this? He ascended the two steps to his podium.

"All be seated," Clerk Dibbing announced. "This District Court inquiry is held in responsum to Caroline Bluebonnet Hutchings." He sat.

Judge Ruggles shuffled the papers in front of him, then cleared his throat. "This is an inquiry, not a trial, and I'll have silence from the gallery in my courtroom today. If you people can't control yourselves, you will be escorted out by Sheriff Tudsdale and his deputy."

"Mr. Hawthorne, are you ready?"

Jeremiah stood. "Yes, your Honor."

"Mr. Alarid?"

Alarid stood. "Yes, your Honor."

"Attorney Alarid, I'll have none of your shenanigans."

Some in the gallery laughed.

The judge banged his gavel. "Let's get to it." He lowered his glasses and peered over the top of them at Blue. "Are you the reason I'm here, young lady?"

Jeremiah motioned for Blue to stand. "Yes, Your Honor," he said.

"State your name for the record," Judge Ruggles said.

"Caroline…"

"Speak up," he said.

Blue's mouth was dry. She swallowed and forced her voice to emerge. "Caroline Bluebonnet Hutchings."

The judge smiled slightly. "I want you to come here and sit in this chair, Miss Hutchings." He pointed to his right.

"Yes, sir." Blue stood. She went weak in the knees and forced herself to keep walking to the area beside the judge's desk. She gripped the railing and sat, then glanced at Jeremiah.

He smiled and gave her a nod.

She took a deep breath, calming her racing heart that was about to explode in her chest.

"This is what's going to happen," Judge Ruggles said. "You're here today so I can get an accounting of your actions and to figure out if the state of Nevada should prosecute you for said actions. Do you understand?"

"Yes, sir."

"Very good. Swear her in, Henry, and let's begin."

For three hours Blue told the facts of what had happened on the ranch, how she'd taken Evans and Pup to the sheriff, and Anderson's attack. Jeremiah and Alarid peppered her with questions. Two times Judge Ruggles banged his gavel and told Alarid if he didn't stop, he'd be held in contempt of court. Blue managed to figure out that was a bad thing.

Alarid became belligerent and mean-spirited in his questioning, twisting and turning Blue's words so badly that even she began to feel like she'd committed a hideous crime. But each time she sank into despair, Jeremiah lifted her. Finally, the judge told her she could leave the witness stand.

Her palms were sweating, and her underarms were soaked.

She searched the crowd as she returned to the table, hoping to find an encouraging expression, but everyone was somber. She couldn't tell if they were sympathetic or outraged.

The judge placed his elbow on the desk and leaned his chin on his hand. He watched her for a moment. "Let's hear from you, Mr. Alarid."

Alarid began again to distort what Blue had said. By the time he'd finished, she didn't recognize the story.

The judge called on Jeremiah.

He rose and spoke the truth in a way Blue could admire.

"Your Honor, Miss Hutchings only protected herself, her property, and those she loves. I implore this court to administer reason and understanding. She acted within her God-given rights and the rights of the great state of Nevada." He sat.

Judge Ruggles positioned himself razor straight and studied them without speaking. He took a couple of deep breaths. He reviewed the papers in front of him as the minutes ticked by on the grandfather clock in the corner of the room. "I have some statements here from two women, a Rosemary Coghlan and Abigail Saunders. These are your hired hands who brought the bodies into town?"

"Yes, Your Honor," Blue said.

"You have all women working for you? Is that correct?"

"Yes, sir."

Jeremiah rose. "Mr. Anderson made it impossible for Miss Hutchings to hire men."

Alarid jumped to his feet. "Oh, I object, Your Honor. That is speculation and highly unlikely that Mr. Anderson had that much influence on the men in these parts."

"Shut it, Alarid. It's my turn now," Judge Ruggles said.

Some in the audience laughed.

The judge took another deep breath, fondled the papers, and then made eye contact with Blue. "Well, I've considered all the facts before me."

Blue held her breath.

"I find no fault in what you did, Miss Hutchings. This inquiry is adjourned." He banged his gavel.

A cheer erupted from the crowd.

Once again Clerk Dibbing jumped to his feet. "All rise."

Everyone stood.

Blue was so relieved she barely had the strength to get up. Jeremiah supported her elbow as the judge left the room.

Alarid glared at Jeremiah, grabbed his satchel, and stormed out.

Jeremiah grinned. "I told you it would be all right."

Blue didn't know if she should jump up and down or hug him. So she did both.

The following two days dragged on as she waited for Isa and the others to arrive. Townspeople invited her to eat in their homes from one end of Carson City to the other. Everywhere she went she was greeted and welcomed. Would they feel that way after Anderson's trial? She passed by the jail on more than one occasion and heard his shouted threats through the barred window. His anger had grown into a rage.

On Wednesday Blue decided to ride out to meet Isa and the others. They most likely would be camped along the river by sunset and start to town early Thursday. Isa would need to rest from the journey.

Blue saddled Biscuit and headed toward where she thought Isa, Martha, and the others would be. She timed it so she would be able to see the light from their campfire when she got close.

Three groups were camped along the river, and her party was the last one. Blue was so eager to see Isa, to touch her, she almost got tangled in the stirrup getting off Biscuit. But Isa wasn't at the campfire with the others.

Blue hugged Martha and greeted everyone. "Where is she? Did she make the trip?"

"She's in the wagon, resting," Martha said.

Blue's worry tumbled out of her like rocks down the mountainside. She climbed into the back as quietly as she could and scooted beside Isa.

Isa opened her eyes and smiled.

When their eyes met, all sound disappeared. All movement ceased. Only Isa existed in front of Blue.

"You're here," Isa said.

Blue maneuvered to Isa's right and slipped her hand under her. She lay as close as she could, careful not to hurt her. "I'm here. I've missed you so." She kissed her.

Isa pressed against her. "Caroline."

Her voice threaded into Blue's ear and trickled into her heart. "Isabel." Her name was all Blue could get out. She repeated it.

They laughed.

Blue stroked her hair and touched her face. She kissed her again. "How are you? Are you in a lot of pain?"

"Move to my left. I want to touch you."

Blue did as she asked.

Isa reached for her face and caressed it. "I can't believe you're here. It feels like a year since we've been together."

Blue took her hand and held it to her cheek. "Isa." She kissed Isa's hand. "I was so afraid I'd lost you."

Isa pulled her toward her and brushed her lips over Blue's. "Never. How I've missed you."

"I feel so full of you I can't speak," Blue said.

Isa touched her lips, then kissed her again. "My darling Blue."

"Isa, I love you. I love you." Blue nestled as close as she could.

"I wanted to be the first to say it," Isa said. Her smile was broad and full. "I love you, Caroline Bluebonnet Hutchings."

"You don't think I can say it, do you?"

Isa grinned.

"I love you, Isabel Juliana Segura Aguilar. It's the most beautiful name I've ever spoken."

Blue maneuvered to Isa's right again. She held her hand and lay next to her. Her senses were alive with Isa's scent, the feel of her skin, the color of her eyes. "I love you so much it hurts to think about it."

Isa tilted her head against Blue's shoulder. "Our love is here now, Blue. Let's never let it go."

They lay quiet in each other's embrace.

Blue held her until Isa's breathing was deep and even.

Once she knew Isa had slipped into a sound sleep, she climbed from the wagon and went to the campfire where the others were gathered. "How is she?"

"She's doing well," Martha said. "She's managing, as long as she can rest after being up for a while. What's the mood in town?"

"Like a circus. They're pouring in from all over. Virginia City. Silver Springs. You can't find a room to stay anywhere. There's even two gents from Santa Fe. The last stage that came in was so full they were packed in like bees in a honeycomb. Jeremiah and Elizabeth have arranged for us to place the wagon next to their house. Elizabeth has offered one of their rooms for Isa to stay in." Blue tossed a twig into the fire. "I can't wait for all of this to be over and get out of here."

Martha slipped her arm around her shoulder and drew her close.

"Miss Blue, do you reckon Anderson will put up a fight?" Gertie asked.

Blue told them about Alarid and what he'd done at her inquiry.

"Lord have mercy!" Laurel said. "What if he twists our stories like he did yours?"

"None of you have anything to worry about. Just tell the truth. Jeremiah Hawthorne will be the prosecutor, and he knows what he's doing."

"What's a prosecutor?" Gertie asked.

"He's the one that will present the case against Anderson."

"What did they decide to charge him with?" Rosemary asked.

"Attempted murder."

"What about robbery and destruction of property?" Rosemary asked.

"Jeremiah said the best case is the attempted-murder charge."

"Do you think he'll be found guilty?" Gertie asked.

"I hope so," Blue said.

"And what will happen to him if he is?" Laurel asked.

"He'll go to the Nevada state prison, just east of Carson City," Blue said.

Martha stood and warmed her hands over the fire. "And what will happen when he gets out?"

Blue stared into the flames. "I've asked myself that question many times."

How many years would he be in jail? What would happen when he was released? The thoughts kept clanging around in her head like a hammer striking an anvil. And what about Isa? Could she hold up under the questions and the ordeal? She'd been through so much, and she seemed so frail. But she was alive. That's all that mattered.

CHAPTER THIRTY

Isa walked to the district courthouse between Blue and Martha. Rosemary, Gertie, and Laurel were close behind. Gertie had thrown a fit bigger than a rabid racoon when Martha told her she had to wear a dress. The only thing that won her over was when Martha told her she'd go to jail for not complying with the court's wishes, and that Blue needed her to do it.

People were milling around outside. The crowd grew still when Blue and the others approached. Sheriff Tudsdale and Marshal Jenkins met them and led them to a smaller room outside the entrance to the courtroom.

"Someone will come and get you when it's time to testify," Tudsdale said, then shut the door.

"Can't you go with me, Martha?" Gertie asked. "Just being in here scares me to death."

Martha moved beside her and wrapped her arms around her. "We all feel that way."

Isa sat beside Blue in one of the sixteen chairs around a huge wooden table.

The door opened, and the marshal called Gertie.

One by one, hour after hour, they went into the courtroom. And one by one they returned pale and withdrawn.

Gertie had tears in her eyes when she came back. "It was just awful. Anderson sat there and eyeballed me like a cougar hunting his meal."

Martha hugged her. "You told the truth. And that's what's important."

"I didn't lie, but that other lawyer fella said I did."

Marshal Jenkins opened the door. "Miss Isa. They'll hear you now."

Blue stood and embraced her. "Take your time. Don't forget to breathe, and remember we're all with you."

Isa walked through the double doors. She'd never been in a courtroom before. And she'd never seen so many white, English-speaking Americans in all her life. Now she knew how Gertie had felt.

She swore to tell the truth on the Bible and then sat in the wooden box next to the judge.

He sat higher than she did, hovering above her.

She trembled but couldn't tell if it was from being scared or from a lack of strength.

Anderson discussed something with his lawyer.

Jeremiah Hawthorne asked her to recall the incidents.

Alarid immediately stood and spoke in a loud voice. "I object, Your Honor. This person is not even a citizen of the United States. How can we hear her testimony or believe anything she says? Why, she posed as a man when she first came here."

Jeremiah rose. "Your Honor, this is outrageous. What does it matter where she's from as long as she states the truth? The court has no reason to believe this witness would lie just because she's from another country."

Alarid countered. "She lied about who she is. And she was with Miss Hutchings when she threatened my client. How do we know she's not wanted for murder in her own country?"

Jeremiah waved his hand. "Your Honor?"

The judge banged his gavel. "That's enough, both of you." He looked at Isa. "You've been sworn to tell the truth. Do you know what that means?"

"Of course, Your Honor."

"All right. Here's what we're going to do. Mr. Alarid, you can voir dire the witness. You've got five minutes."

Alarid approached Isa. "Have you ever disguised yourself as a man?"

"Yes, sir."

Gasps resonated from the crowd.

He glared smugly. "Why?"

"To get to my uncle's in California without being attacked. When traveling alone, it's safer to appear as a man than a woman."

Women and a few of the men in the crowd nodded.

"And I needed work. No one will hire a woman for man-work, no matter how capable they are."

Several women applauded.

The judge banged his gavel. "Quiet. I'll have no social commentary from the gallery."

Alarid moved closer. "Are you saying the only reasons you dressed as a man, walked like a man, acted like a man, were to get to your uncle's safely and to get work?"

"Yes."

Alarid smirked. "If it was so important to get to your uncle's in California, why did you alter your plan?"

"Three of Anderson's men attacked me and left me for dead."

He threw his hands up and yelled, "I object, Your Honor."

The judge frowned. "To what? You're the one who's asking the questions. If you don't want to hear the answer, don't ask."

Members of the audience laughed.

"Were you at the Hutchings ranch on the day of the events in question?"

"Yes, sir."

"And why were you there?"

"I…"

The judge banged his gavel again. "You're stalling, Counselor. She can testify. Move on."

Alarid waved his hand. "I'm through anyway."

Both lawyers questioned her until her head spun. She grabbed the wooden rail, trying to keep herself from collapsing in a heap in the chair.

Jeremiah offered her a drink of water and asked for a recess.

It took all her strength to get back to Blue and the others.

Blue and Martha attended to her.

Jeremiah came into the room.

"How long is this going to continue?" Blue asked. "You can see she can't endure much more."

"We're almost finished. Isa, I'd like you to tell about the incident when you were attacked and how you knew it was Anderson's men, then describe the night they came after you, Martha, and Blue by the river. Then I think we'll be done."

Isa nodded.

Jeremiah helped her once more to the stand. "Your Honor, I'd like to express concern for this witness. She was badly wounded in the raid, and the court must consider her condition."

"Are you able to continue?" Judge Ruggles asked.

Isa nodded. "Yes, Your Honor. I believe it's my duty."

"Hear, hear," several men in the crowd yelled.

The judge banged his gavel. "Silence in this court or I'll clear the room."

Alarid objected.

"What for this time, Counselor?" Judge Ruggles asked.

"Your Honor, we don't know if this woman is even injured. And for all we know, she could be purposely misleading this court, or received that wound a different time other than the day of the alleged incident. We don't even know if it is from a gunshot."

Jeremiah rose. "Your Honor. I never said it was a gunshot wound."

"Well, whatever it is," Alarid said.

The judge sighed. "You have a point, Counselor."

Judge Ruggles surveyed the room. "Dr. Stevens."

The man called Dr. Stevens stood. "Yes, Judge?"

"Counselor, would you have any objections to Dr. Stevens giving his opinion as to the nature of the witness's wound?"

"No, Your Honor. That would be fine," Alarid said.

"Mr. Hawthorne?" the Judge asked.

Jeremiah stood. "Fine by me, Judge."

"Nettie Morris?"

Nettie stood. "Yes, sir."

"Would you accompany the doctor and testify as to what you see?"

"Yes, sir."

Isa was taken to the room Blue and the others were in.

Everyone was told to leave. Blue protested so loudly that she and Martha were permitted to stay.

When Isa, Dr. Stevens, and Nettie returned to court, the doctor attested that Isa's wounds were the result of a gunshot and approximately how old they were.

Isa retold the events as Jeremiah had instructed.

More questions.

More objections by both lawyers.

Finally, it was over.

The judge banged his gavel. "The Court is adjourned until tomorrow morning at nine a.m. And everyone better be on time."

Isa grabbed the railing and pulled herself up as relief washed over her.

Jeremiah assisted her to the adjoining room and then, with Blue and Martha, escorted them to his home, where Martha attended to Isa.

She lay on the bed in an upper room.

Blue came to her and held her hand.

"How do you think it went?" Isa asked.

"Jeremiah seems to think it went well. I'm testifying in the morning. You rest, and don't worry."

Isa drifted into a deep sleep. When she woke, the morning's sun shone brightly through the window. "Blue?"

Martha came into the room. "She's in court."

Martha attended Isa throughout the morning, but it didn't relieve Isa's anxiety for Blue.

In the early afternoon, after Martha had brought her lunch, there was a ruckus in the street. It sounded like someone banging pots and pans.

"What is that?" Isa asked.

Martha peered through the window. "I think the trial is over. The judge must have adjourned to make his decision."

"Why wasn't there a trial by jury?" Isa asked.

"Anderson wanted Judge Ruggles to hear the case instead of a jury. To be honest, not many in the entire area feel he isn't guilty. I guess he figured things were more likely to go his way if the judge heard his case, instead of all those he bullied and tried to destroy."

Isa forced herself to eat.

Finally Blue came into the room. She went to Isa and kissed her forehead and held her hand. "How are you feeling?"

"Better, now that you're here."

"Judge Ruggles said he'll announce his decision today at four o'clock. And Jeremiah wants me, you, and Laurel sitting at the table with him."

"Why?" Martha asked.

"I think he wants sympathy. He wants everyone to see what Anderson did."

The minutes ticked slowly by. Then an hour. Then three. Four. Finally it was time to go.

So many people filled the courthouse there wasn't any room, not even to stand. Marshal Jenkins opened the doors so people could linger outside and listen.

Sheriff Tudsdale escorted Martha and the others to the reserved seating behind Blue, Isa, and Laurel.

When the judge entered and all were seated, he banged his gavel and gravely surveyed the room.

"Before I announce my decision, I want everyone in this court to behave themselves." He continued to fix his gaze on the audience. "The crime of attempted murder is a serious offense and carries with it a serious sentence. No society can flourish without laws to prevent and deter violence and mayhem."

Marshal Jenkins and Sheriff Tudsdale moved next to Anderson.

"Franklin Bartholomew Anderson," Judge Ruggles said.

Alarid and Anderson stood.

"After consideration of all facts presented to this court, I hereby find the following. On the charge of attempted murder, namely Caroline Bluebonnet Hutchings and all persons present on her premises during the event, I find you guilty."

A thunderous cheer broke out.

Anderson stiffened. He slammed his fist on the table and violently shook his head.

The judge's face turned red, and he repeatedly banged his gavel. "Order…Order…in…this…court."

When the chaos subsided, he repositioned in his chair. "You are hereby sentenced to fifteen years in the Nevada State penitentiary and are immediately turned over to the marshal for custody and transport."

Anderson kicked his chair, sending it skittering to the side, then clenched his teeth.

Clerk Dibbing jumped to his feet. "All rise."

Everyone stood as the judge left the courtroom.

The officers fastened chains on Anderson and started to lead him from the courtroom.

He turned to Blue, his face contorted and dark. "This isn't over," he yelled.

Blue faced him.

Their gazes locked.

"I'll be right here," Blue said.

Isa moved closer to her.

Yes, they'd won. And Anderson was going to prison. But was it really over? His rage consumed everything around them. It sucked up all the goodness in the room.

And what about Blue?

Isa trembled with her own fury. Would Blue ever be able to let it go?

How could they put everything behind them and go on?

CHAPTER THIRTY-ONE

That night the day's events rattled in Blue's mind. Anderson's words—*this isn't over*—grated on her nerves. She tossed and turned. What would happen once he did his time and came back? Would he return to seek revenge? He acted like he would, but fifteen years was a long time.

She wanted to go to Isa, but Isa lay sleeping upstairs in the Hawthorne house. Blue remained wide awake in the wagon, unable to doze off. After a while, she heard someone knock on Jeremiah's front door. Muffled words were exchanged. The door closed, and then silence reigned once again.

Martha lay next to her. It should have been Isa.

"Blue?"

It took her a moment to recognize Jeremiah's hushed voice.

"Blue?" he repeated.

Martha sat. "Who is that?"

"It's Jeremiah," Blue said. "Just a moment."

She peeked out from behind the canvas. "What is it?"

"Come inside. There's news. And I'm afraid it isn't good."

Blue scurried from the wagon and accompanied him inside.

They sat at the kitchen table.

He grimaced. "Blue, Anderson has escaped."

"No!" Bile rose in her throat as she clenched her fists. "How?"

"He overpowered a deputy when they stopped for a break. He killed him and shot Marshal Jenkins."

"Will he live?"

"They don't know yet. Dr. Stevens is working on him now."

Her earlier concerns twisted into a tight knot of fear in her stomach. Where was Anderson? She had to know more. She had to know *everything*. "I need to talk with Marshal Jenkins."

"I'll walk you over to the doctor's office. It's not far from the hotel."

Blue told Martha and left with Jeremiah.

When they arrived, several lanterns were lit in the room. Sheriff Tudsdale and his wife, Melly, were on each side of the marshal, who lay sprawled out on a table.

Dr. Stevens hovered over him, working frantically. "Hold this tight against his stomach, Melly," he ordered her.

Marshal Jenkins moved his legs and moaned.

Blood ran from his stomach onto the table and dripped onto the floor. He lifted his head and glowered at the doctor. "Can't you get it? Hurry up!"

The doctor shook his head. "It's deep. I'm doing the best I can, Aaron. For God's sake, hold still."

"How can I? You've got your hand in my gut."

"Got it." The doctor pulled a long, metal instrument from the marshal's abdomen and held it up, revealing a bullet between the prongs. "You're tough as a hinge nail, Aaron. Any other man would have been dead two hours ago." Dr. Stevens dropped the lead into a metal pan and began stitching the wound.

"Thank God, Doc. I thought you'd never get it out. I need some whiskey."

The marshal glanced at Blue and Jeremiah. "We can talk as soon as Doc here fixes me up. Blue, you need to get home right away. Anderson was headed southeast."

Blue's heart sank.

"Wait in my parlor," Dr. Stevens said. "We'll be done in a few minutes."

Blue and Jeremiah moved to the anteroom and sat in the high-backed, cushioned chairs. Their silence seemed to expand the distance between them. Blue couldn't waste time sitting here when she needed to go home. Should she ride on by herself or leave in the morning with the others? What about Etta and Abigail? Would they be safe alone? Should she go search for Anderson or wait until he showed up at the ranch? Would he go home? Isa? She was vulnerable. Blue's head pounded.

Melly came in. "The marshal wants to see you, Miss Blue."

She led her to another room, where Marshal Aaron Jenkins lay on a bed.

Blue sat in a chair next to him.

"Melly, tell your husband to come in here, please. Hell, you may as well tell Jeremiah to come too," Marshal Jenkins said. "Blue, I'm going to do something I hope I don't regret."

Harmon Tudsdale and Jeremiah came into the room.

"You two are going to be my witnesses," the marshal said. "Blue, raise your right hand."

Blue did as instructed.

"Now say 'I' and state your full name."

"I, Caroline Bluebonnet Hutchings."

"Repeat after me. 'Do solemnly swear to uphold the laws of the state of Nevada.'"

Blue repeated his words.

"You can put your hand down. I'm authorizing you to act as my deputy for the sole purpose of capturing Frank Anderson. If you come upon him in any capacity, if possible, you are to bring him in and turn him over to Harmon or myself. Is that understood?"

"Yes."

"Now, you watch yourself. You get your people back home safely. Harman will form a posse to start tracking him from where he escaped. I want you to stay at your ranch. Try not to leave for any reason until he's captured or killed. We'll send word when that happens."

Blue stood. "If he comes after me, I won't hesitate to kill him."

"As long as it's in self-defense or to protect others, I don't have a problem with it. But don't you go looking for trouble. I have a feeling it'll find you soon enough. Would you like me to deputize a couple of men and send them to your ranch?"

She shook her head. "My girls are fair enough shots."

"I'm sure they are. They've already proved themselves. I'll send word to the surrounding ranches so they can also be on the lookout."

Blue and Jeremiah returned to his house. She went to the wagon but had little rest.

At daylight she climbed the stairs to Isa's room and lay beside her on the bed, watching her sleep. She had a peaceful expression. Blue didn't want to disturb her, but she reached over and brushed her cheek. "Isa," she whispered.

Isa's eyes fluttered open. A surprised expression crossed her face, then a smile. "Blue, you're here." She curled her hand under her chin.

"Something's happened," Blue said. "We need to leave as soon as possible."

Isa's eyes grew wide. "What? What is it?"

Blue told her everything, except that she'd been deputized. She didn't care about that. It wasn't important, because if Anderson came anywhere near her, Isa, or the others, she wouldn't hesitate to kill him.

Isa kissed her. "Would you send Gertie to help me? I won't be long."

They made the trip home without incident, but the hint of Anderson somewhere out there grew heavy and grated on Blue's nerves.

Each day that passed without word of his capture hung over her head like a funnel cloud, sucking out her energy and attention. She grew restless and unable to sleep. At night she'd wander the property, hoping to find him lurking in the shadows. On the fourth night, she walked past the barn and thought she heard a noise of movement. She turned and aimed the rifle but was startled to find Isa.

"Isa, what are you doing? I could have shot you."

"You've got to stop this," Isa said. "It's not good for you."

"How can I not do this? He's coming here. I feel it all around me."

"Then let me and the others help you."

"And what if he kills you or them? I could never forgive myself. He wants me, and I'd rather be the target out here than have him shoot you or the others to get to me."

"Is that what you're doing? Making yourself a human target? Giving him what he wants? You're becoming obsessed, walking around like you're already dead."

"What should I do? Allow him to come here and hurt you, or Martha, or the others?"

"No, but let us take some of this burden from you."

"I can't."

On the fifth day, Virgil Pettiman and his son Morgan arrived. Virgil came to tell Blue that Marshal Jenkins's deputies had searched everywhere for Anderson. "Seems they found a lone rider who'd been killed near Genoa, about fifteen miles from your property." His horse and rifle were missing. Anderson hadn't been spotted.

"The marshal thinks Anderson may have killed him, took his horse and weapon, and left the territory," Virgil said. "They lost his trail west of Genoa. He doesn't think they'll find him, but they aren't giving up yet."

Blue's hopes of his capture grew more distant. Maybe he did leave, for good.

Morgan had obviously accompanied his father to visit Laurel, and even Gertie teased her.

They immediately went for a walk, and when they returned, they announced their plan to marry in the spring.

After Virgil and Morgan left, Blue sat on the porch with Isa.

Rosemary and Etta approached them.

"Could we talk with you, Miss Blue?" Rosemary asked.

Isa started to get up from the rocking chair.

"No, Isa. Stay," Blue said. She placed her hand on top of hers.

"Would you be willing to stake us to work your silver mine if we give you seventy percent of what we find?" Rosemary asked.

"The silver mine? You do know it's been mined out?"

"We might be able to get something from it," Etta said. "It's worth a try."

"Do you know anything about mining, because I sure don't." Blue shrugged.

"People have struck veins long after a mine was supposedly dried up," Etta said. "And I know the basics."

"Have you two thought this through?" Blue asked.

Etta shifted back and forth. Rosemary folded her arms tightly against her chest.

"Seventy percent," Blue said. "And I supply the mine *and* the tools, *plus* your food and the wagon? What do you think, Isa?"

"It's their time and labor, and the mine's just sitting there. You never know."

Etta and Rosemary glanced at each other.

"I think my side of the up-front expenses is too steep," Blue said. "How about you two negotiate credit with Mr. Morris at the dry goods store and Luther Henderson at the livery, and bear the up-front expense yourselves, and we split sixty-forty because it's my mine?" Blue asked. "And we should put a time limit on how long you two dig." She imagined them coming out of the mine after a year with dark circles under their eyes, covered in dust, and emaciated from doing nothing but mining.

"How long will you give us?" Rosemary asked.

"Four months. If you don't find anything by then, we'll call it quits. By spring maybe we'll get some income from the roundup when we sell the horses. Then you'll be able to settle your debts for sure."

"We'll stay in the cave and come back every now and again," Etta said. "The weather will be tolerable in there. The snows won't come for a while yet. If we can't manage it, we'll give up."

"You two sure you want to do this?" Blue asked. "It seems like a hard idea, and it's bleak in there. I heard the coldest month is December. This is early October, and the rains will be here in February."

Etta glanced at Rosemary, and Blue glimpsed something in the way she looked at her. A hint of more than friendship. Was that why they'd been spending so much time together?

"We want to do this, Miss Blue," Rosemary said. "It's a desperate act, but it's worth it."

"We can't sit by and watch you struggle," Etta said. "We'd be pleased if you'd let us try. And the others want to join in when they can."

Blue took a deep breath. She studied Isa's expression for a moment. Then Isa smiled and shrugged.

"Are you absolutely sure you want to do this?" Blue asked.

"Yes, Miss Blue," Rosemary said. "Nothing ventured, nothing gained."

"All right. You've got four months. But promise if things get too hard, you'll return to the ranch."

Etta and Rosemary agreed and smiled, then left the porch.

Blue rubbed her chin. How long would they last in the mining business?

"They're right, Blue. It won't hurt anything," Isa said. "And it may be good for all of us." She massaged her shoulder.

"Is it bothering you?"

Isa shook her head. "It just aches every now and again. It gets better each day."

Four days later Blue, Isa, Martha, and the others gathered to say good-bye to Etta and Rosemary. Their spirits were high, but Gertie seemed anxious. She'd formed a close attachment to Rosemary.

"Keep studying, Gertie," Rosemary said. "We'll see what you've learned when Etta and I get back."

"I bet I'll be through most of your books by then," Gertie said.

Rosemary hugged her. "I'm sure you will."

They set off, Etta leading the packhorse.

That night dread overtook Blue. No matter how hard she tried, she couldn't shake it. She wandered the property. Maybe Isa was right. Maybe she was obsessed with Anderson.

She managed to get only two hours' sleep and woke suddenly at dawn. She sat straight up and drew up her knees, then wrapped her arms around them.

Isa turned toward her and touched her arm. "What is it?"

"Isa, I've thought about it all night. What if Anderson hasn't left the territory? What if he's still around here?"

"Why would he be? He knows he'll be caught. Why would he not leave? He's probably long gone by now and cheating and thieving his way through another area of the country."

"Genoa isn't that far from our property. There's plenty of places to hide."

"But why stay here, Blue? He knows he'll go to prison if he's caught. Why risk it?"

Why? That was the question Blue couldn't let go of. She remembered how he'd glared at her as they led him from the courtroom. "Hatred and revenge are powerful motivators. What if he's up in the mountains?" And then it hit her.

She bounded from the bed and started dressing.

"Where are you going?"

"I've got to check on Etta and Rosemary. I want to make sure they're all right. What if Anderson hid in the mine?"

"Would you like me to ride with you? I'm strong enough."

"No. I just need to make sure they're not in any danger."

"You shouldn't go alone."

Blue leaned in and kissed her. "I'll be fine. I'll be back later this afternoon."

She raced to the barn and saddled Traveler, then left.

It was quiet when she approached the mine. Too quiet. No voices. No sounds of digging or movement. And the animals were tied near the entrance, the packhorse still laden with some of the supplies.

She drew her rifle and dismounted, watching, trying to see inside. No light. The lanterns should have been lit.

The only way in or out was through that entrance. She stepped closer from the side, out of view of the opening. Should she go in? She decided to wait and settled herself slightly above the shaft and behind some boulders. She squatted, straining to hear or see anything. More silence. It alerted her senses even more.

If Anderson was in there, how could she flush him out? What had he done to Etta and Rosemary? Had he killed them? Or did he plan to use them as bait to get her inside to kill her?

The questions and uncertainty filled her mind so full it was hard to find room to reason.

She waited in silence and stillness a long time, trying to decide what to do, hoping she'd hear Etta's laugh or Rosemary's voice. Nothing.

Now, more certain than ever that Anderson was there, she pondered how to draw him out. Finally, she did the only thing she could.

"Anderson," she shouted. "I know you're in there. Get out here, now."

She heard scuffling.

"Drop your weapon, and I'll let you ride the horse you stole from the man you killed, and not make you walk to town this time."

More noises, then a muffled voice. A woman's voice.

Anderson appeared at the entrance of the mine with Etta in front of him, holding her close by the back of her hair. Her arms were tied behind her, a gag in her mouth. Her face was bloodied and bruised, and her shirt was torn.

Blue aimed, but from her angle and the way he held Etta, she couldn't get a shot at him.

"I knew you'd figure it out and be here sooner or later," he said. "Why don't you put *your* gun down and step out from behind the rocks?" He inched Etta farther out of the cave and edged around to face Blue. "I've got nothing to lose, and if you think I won't kill this whore to get to you, you're sadly mistaken."

Etta violently shook her head and tried to speak.

Anderson jerked her off the ground and then settled her back down. "I mean it. I'll shoot her."

Had he already killed Rosemary? "Where's the other one?"

"Don't you worry about her."

"Where's Rosemary?"

"She's tied up in the mine."

"Prove it," Blue yelled.

"Come see for yourself." He grinned.

"What do you want?" Blue asked.

"I'm going to take those horses there, and the pack animal. You'll give me your horse and your weapons."

"The hell I will."

He raised the pistol to Etta's head. "You'll do it. Right now." He turned more toward Blue.

A shot rang out.

Blue jumped and was ready to fire, prepared to see Etta slumped forward, her head red with blood. But what she saw shocked her.

Anderson had ducked, bending over her, and shifted to his right.

She spotted Isa as she stood at a vantage point farther up the mountainside, across from her.

Isa fired again, splintering rock and missing Anderson's head by inches.

Blue saw an opportunity. She aimed and fired.

Anderson fell onto the ground, motionless, blood oozing from the gunshot to the side of his head.

Blue signaled to Isa.

Etta ran to Blue, as Blue made her way toward her.

Isa slowly descended from her position.

Blue removed the gag from Etta's mouth and untied her hands. "Where's Rosemary?"

Etta grabbed Blue and held on to her. "She's all right. She's hog-tied in the mine."

Blue sighed in relief and waited for Isa to get to them.

Etta ran into the mine.

When Isa reached Blue, Blue wrapped her arms around her. "I can't believe you're here."

"I couldn't let you do this by yourself. I told you to let us help."

Blue continued to hold her. "You saved all of us."

"No. I missed. My shoulder's stiff. *You* saved us."

They stood in the sunshine, holding each other.

It was finally over. Hope flooded Blue's heart. She could see a future—with Isa.

Anderson's life had ended.

And hers and Isa's were just beginning.

Blue had a big dream, and Isa would be by her side to share it.

EPILOGUE

The barn smelled of hay and leather, and the fragrance of spring and the awakened earth lingered in the night air. The light from the lanterns flickered through the stall slats.

Isa's concern grew.

Adelita had struggled to give birth for too long. Something was wrong.

She knelt beside the horse's rump and immediately realized the problem. "The foal's out of position. I'll need to help her. Blue, come in here slowly and stroke her neck and talk to her. Try to get her to relax."

Blue unlatched the gate and slipped down beside Adelita. She rubbed her head and neck. "Easy, girl. You're doing good. It'll be over soon."

Gertie leaned on the upper boards. "Will the foal be okay, Miss Blue?"

"If Isa can get its legs into position, I think everything will be fine," Blue said.

Gertie slipped from the fence and paced, then sat on a bucket near Isa. "Can I help?" she whispered.

Gertie needed to be reassured and to feel a part of this, but Isa had her hands full. An agitated mare, an uncooperative foal, and an anxious partner were all she could deal with at the moment. She scooted closer to Adelita. "You've been a huge help, Gertie." She reached farther into the birth canal and gently manipulated the foal's forelegs. "You kept Adelita's stall clean and made sure she had fresh straw every day. You did your best, and now it's up to Adelita. I've got one leg into position. If I can just get the other straightened."

Adelita groaned.

"Easy." Blue soothed the horse and stroked her neck.

"Got it." Isa backed away as Adelita had another contraction. The foal began to slide out. "Let's leave her alone and let her get on with it."

She and Blue hurriedly left the stall.

Isa washed up as Gertie and Blue watched the delivery behind the fencing. When Isa finished cleaning her hands and arms, she joined them.

Gertie peered through the slats. "It's a boy. Look at him. Oh, Isa. He's going to be a fine stud."

Blue wrapped her arm around Isa's waist. "He's beautiful."

Isa hugged her. "He's magnificent. He's the spitting image of his sire."

He was a gift to them all, but especially to Blue, and Isa couldn't have asked for a better one.

Blue's remaining prized mare had delivered a fine filly two months before. But this colt was what they'd hoped for.

Blue lowered her head. "I can't believe it."

Isa pulled her closer. "He's the first of more good things to come."

"Let's call him Primus," Gertie said. "It means chief, head, or best in Latin."

Isa looked at Blue and smiled. "Primus it is, then."

They continued their vigil as Adelita and her new son made their way into the dawn.

❖

Four weeks later, Gertie led Isa, Blue, and the others through the pass to the wild herd, as she had assured them she could.

Biscuit shook his head and snorted. He obviously sensed the horses. Isa took a more secure seat in case he decided to react. "Stay ready," she said. "We're getting close."

"We need to climb that ridge to scout," Gertie said. "They should be over the next rise." She dismounted.

Isa and Blue did the same and handed their reins to Rosemary and Etta. They carefully traversed the steep grade and crouched.

"There they are," Gertie said. "Just waiting for us to gather them up like eggs in the henhouse."

Blue patted her shoulder. "Well done."

There were at least two hundred horses, and they seemed well nourished and fit.

They had started to descend the ridge to the others, when Isa spotted something farther down the pass. "What is that?"

Blue squinted. "I don't see anything."

Isa pointed. "There beyond that jagged outcropping. It's an animal of some type."

They mounted their horses and rode to the area.

"It's horse remains," Blue said.

"Only that horse had a saddle and bridle," Rosemary said.

They got off their mounts and scoured the area.

They found more evidence of another horse that most likely a wolf or cougar had half eaten.

"Over here," Abigail called. "It's a man. Or what's left of one." She gagged.

He was partially dressed. His gun belt and hat were near what had once been his right arm. The lower part of one leg had been torn off at the knee. What skin remained on his face and arm looked like tanned leather soaked in water. The tattered shirt and vest had a large, dark stain midway down the front.

Blue came closer. "I know who this is."

"Do you think it's him?" Isa asked.

"It has to be McCoy," Blue said. "Look at the size of his boot and the blood stain where he was gut shot."

"They must have made it this far but got trapped in the snow, and then the animals got to them," Gertie said.

"Where's the other one?" Rosemary asked.

"Maybe he got away, or maybe a cougar carried him off," Abigail said.

"Both the horses are here, so I don't see how he could have made it out on his own," Isa said.

"Should we bury this one?" Abigail asked.

"He's half buried now," Blue said. "I'd just as soon leave him here, but we should probably plant him in the ground. It's the decent thing to do."

They dug with whatever they could find and laid his remains in a shallow grave, then piled rocks on top of him.

Gertie took off her hat.

Isa couldn't bring herself to make the gesture but stood quietly.

"I won't take mine off for that no-good," Blue said.

Rosemary, Etta, and Abigail were silent and also didn't remove their coverings.

Gertie cleared her throat. "I'll say a word or two." She stepped forward and kicked a pebble, then glanced skyward. "Here lies McCoy. A sonofabitch if there ever was one. Lord, don't be too gentle with him. Amen." She put on her hat and mounted her horse. "We best get to the herd before they take off on us."

And that was the end of McCoy. Nobody expressed any remorse as they rode away.

They gathered a good distance from the horses to not spook them.

"We'll need to get downwind and come at them and drive them this way," Blue said. "Isa, you take the lead. Biscuit is the strongest. Rosemary, you take center right. Gertie, center left. Abigail, you, me, and Etta will handle the rear slack. Any questions?"

"Let's drive them fast so they won't have time to think," Isa said. "We can sort them after we get control. We'll save fifteen or so of the best mares for your herd, Blue."

Blue nodded.

"There's a box canyon about a mile and a half from here," Gertie said. "When we get there, we can separate the stallion and mares we want to leave, the ones we want to keep, and those for the contract."

"All right. Let's do it," Blue said. "Make sure we give Isa enough time to get to the front of the herd before we drive them full speed."

They mounted and swung around the edge of the horses.

Isa caught Blue's attention, waved, and went into a full gallop.

It was a beautiful sight to see.

The lead horses took off.

Isa bunched them immediately, guiding them through the pass.

Rosemary and Gertie were able to keep their sides tight.

The herd responded to each of the rider's directions.

Gertie moved toward Isa and helped her slow them, then took the lead and guided them to the box canyon.

They sorted the ones they wanted, released the stallion and mares to remain, and then drove the others to the agreed-upon spot for the cavalry.

After Blue received payment, they headed for Carson City.

Once in town, Blue paid their wages.

Nettie served them a fine dinner, with cherry pie for dessert.

When their meal ended, Etta and Rosemary stood.

"We best get in there and pay for our mining supplies," Rosemary said.

"Find out what the tally is," Blue said. "I'll cover your debt since you didn't find any silver."

They protested.

"We can't let you do that, Miss Blue," Rosemary said.

"It's all right," Blue said. "I'm sure you can use the money for other things."

"Yes," Etta said, and laughed. "Better picks and shovels."

"Don't tell me you want to continue mining that dried-out silver shaft?" Isa asked.

"We didn't get all of our agreed-upon time," Etta said. "I have a feeling about it."

"You'll probably come up empty-handed, but if you want to keep at it, go ahead," Blue said. "But you can't start until after summer."

Blue stood. "Isa, will you accompany me to Jeremiah's office? I have some legal business to attend to."

A man came into the dining area, his hat in his hand. He spoke to Nettie and then walked to their group. "Miss Blue?" he asked.

Blue smiled. "Yes. May I help you?"

"I'm Parker Jamison. I've come to ask if you're hiring. Some of the other cowboys in the territory have heard you're a fair and honest person, and we're looking for work."

Isa wondered how the others would react.

Gertie's face tightened. Etta took a step back. Rosemary stiffened.

What would Blue do? Let the women go now that men wanted to work for her? Isa was sure she wouldn't.

Blue's eyes twinkled. She winked at Isa. "I thank you for your interest, Mr. Jamison, but I have all the hands I need."

Disappointment crossed his face, and then he nodded and left.

Blue turned to the women around her and smiled.

Gertie tipped her new Stetson hat. Etta, Rosemary, and Abigail had tears in their eyes as they nodded and quietly left.

Isa and Blue exited the store and strolled the boardwalk.

Each person they passed greeted them warmly.

They entered Jeremiah's office.

He sat at his desk. Dressed smartly in a brown wool suit and vest, he stood and greeted them.

Isa and Blue took a seat in the two cushioned chairs across from him.

"Is it ready?" Blue asked.

Jeremiah nodded, sat, and offered papers. "It just needs your signature."

Blue silently reviewed the materials and then signed.

Jeremiah inspected the documents again. "Very good. Anderson had $41,287.00 in a bank in Santa Fe. Judge Ruggles made a decision last month. He determined it was income from your silver mine. It's all yours. The money has been deposited here at the Carson City bank in your name. He had no living relatives. With the judge's approval, the county took ownership of his land for payment of costs associated with his crimes and trial. They've had a buyer for it. Morgan and Laurel Pettiman."

Blue grinned. "That's good news."

Isa sat in disbelief. She had no idea Blue had been involved in this. She was overjoyed for her. Now she wouldn't worry about her and felt at peace knowing Blue had what she needed to continue to grow her ranch and live a good life.

"And the matter regarding my stepbrother," Blue asked.

"He filed to get your property, like we thought he would. The judge found in your favor. He has no legal leg to stand on." He handed her another document.

When she finished reading it, she turned to Isa. "Isa, this document puts your name on my deed and all other assets. In case anything ever happens to me, you will become the sole owner."

Isa lost her breath as a jolt shot through her. It took a moment to get her composure. "Me? Why not Martha?"

"You can give Martha anything you want. It's up to you," Blue said.

"But I…" She stammered. "I don't know what to say."

Blue smiled and took her hand. "You've always been a full partner. Now it's legal."

Isa wanted to kiss her, but she knew she couldn't. Not here. Not now. But later she would. They'd go to their favorite spot by the lake.

About the Author

Suzie Clarke is a native of Northeast Ohio and has a medical and business background. Before her life as a writer, she specialized in public health, working with women in all aspects of their lives. When not writing, she can be found spending time with her family, backpacking, or out on the golf course.

Books Available From Bold Strokes Books

Hands of the Morri by Heather K O'Malley. Discovering she is a Lost Sister and growing acquainted with her new body, Asche learns how to be a warrior and commune with the Goddess the Hands serve, the Morri. (978-1-63679-465-5)

I Know About You by Erin Kaste. With her stalker inching closer to the truth, Cary Smith is forced to face the past she's tried desperately to forget. (978-1-63679-513-3)

Mate of Her Own by Elena Abbott. When Heather McKenna finally confronts the family who cursed her, her werewolf is shocked to discover her one true mate, and that's only the beginning. (978-1-63679-481-5)

Pumpkin Spice by Tagan Shepard. For Nicki, new love is making this pumpkin spice season sweeter than expected. (978-1-63679-388-7)

Sweat Equity by Aurora Rey. When cheesemaker Sy Travino takes a job in rural Vermont and hires contractor Maddie Barrow to rehab a house she buys sight unseen, they both wind up with a lot more than they bargained for. (978-1-63679-487-7)

Taking the Plunge by Amanda Radley. When Regina Avery meets model Grace Holland—the most beautiful woman she's ever seen— she doesn't have a clue how to flirt, date, or hold on to a relationship. But Regina must take the plunge with Grace and hope she manages to swim. (978-1-63679-400-6)

We Met in a Bar by Claire Forsythe. Wealthy nightclub owner Erica turns undercover bartender on a mission to catch a thief where she meets no-strings, no-commitments Charlie, who couldn't be further from Erica's type. Right? (978-1-63679-521-8)

Western Blue by Suzie Clarke. Step back in time to this historic western filled with heroism, loyalty, friendship, and love. The odds are against this unlikely group—but never underestimate women who have nothing to lose. (978-1-63679-095-4)

Windswept by Patricia Evans. The windswept shores of the Scottish Highlands weave magic for two people convinced they'd never fall in love again. (978-1-63679-382-5)

A Calculated Risk by Cari Hunter. Detective Jo Shaw doesn't need complications, but the stabbing of a young woman brings plenty of those, and Jo will have to risk everything if she's going to make it through the case alive. (978-1-63679-477-8)

An Independent Woman by Kit Meredith. Alex and Rebecca's attraction won't stop smoldering, despite their reluctance to act on it and incompatible poly relationship styles. (978-1-63679-553-9)

Cherish by Kris Bryant. Josie and Olivia cherish the time spent together, but when the summer ends and their temporary romance melts into the real deal, reality gets complicated. (978-1-63679-567-6)

Cold Case Heat by Mary P. Burns. Sydney Hansen receives a threat in a very cold murder case that sends her to the police for help, where she finds more than justice with Detective Gale Sterling. (978-1-63679-374-0)

Proximity by Jordan Meadows. Joan really likes Ellie, but being alone with her could turn deadly unless she can keep her dangerous powers under control. (978-1-63679-476-1)

Sweet Spot by Kimberly Cooper Griffin. Pro surfer Shia Turning will have to take a chance if she wants to find the sweet spot. (978-1-63679-418-1)

The Haunting of Oak Springs by Crin Claxton. Ghosts and the past haunt the supernatural detective in a race to save the lesbians of Oak Springs farm. (978-1-63679-432-7)

Transitory by J.M. Redmann. The cops blow it off as a customer surprised by what was under the dress, but PI Micky Knight knows they're wrong—she either makes it her case or lets a murderer go free to kill again. (978-1-63679-251-4)

Unexpectedly Yours by Toni Logan. A private resort on a tropical island, a feisty old chief, and a kleptomaniac pet pig bring Suzanne and Allie together for unexpected love. (978-1-63679-160-9)